The Long Dream

The Long Dream

Richard Wright

PERENNIAL LIBRARY

Harper & Row, Publishers, New York
Cambridge, Philadelphia, San Francisco, Washington
London, Mexico City, São Paulo, Singapore, Sydney

To my friends
Edward C. Aswell and Paul R. Reynolds,
whose aid and counsel made this book possible

Appreciation is expressed to New Directions for permission to quote from Dylan Thomas's *When once the twilight locks no longer*. Frederick A. Praeger, Inc., was kind enough to allow me to quote from O. Mannoni's *Prospero and Caliban*.

A hardcover edition of this book was originally published by Doubleday & Company in 1958. It is here reprinted by arrangement with the Estate of Richard Wright.

First PERENNIAL LIBRARY edition published 1987.

Library of Congress Cataloging-in-Publication Data

Wright, Richard, 1908–1960.
  The long dream.

  I. Title.
PS3545.R815L6   1987   813'.52   86-46111
ISBN 0-06-080869-1 (pbk.)

87 88 89 90 91 OPM 10 9 8 7 6 5 4 3 2 1

Part One

Daydreams and Nightmares...

Sleep navigates the tides of time:
The dry Sargasso of the tomb
Gives up its dead to such a working sea;
And sleep rolls mute above the beds
Where fishes' food is fed the shades
Who periscope through flowers to the sky.

DYLAN THOMAS

1

He felt seized by a whirlpool of despair as his mother tucked the bedcovers about his shoulders, and his voice rose in a protesting wail:

"Leave the light on!"

"I'm turning the light out," she vetoed the plea, arranging his clothes upon a chair. "You can't sleep with the light burning." Her mood altered; she stooped and pecked his cheek with her lips. "Nighty night."

"Leave the door open," he begged.

"I'm shutting the door." She spoke firmly but kindly.

The light clicked out and he shut his eyes upon welling tears, hearing his mother's heels tapping across the floor.

"Mama!" he flung his ultimate appeal and checked her footsteps.

"Yeah, Rex."

"When Papa coming?"

"When he gits here, he'll be here. I'll wake you up."

"How can Papa see how to fish in the dark?"

"Papa has a flashlight and the moon's shining."

"And the fishes, can they see in the dark?"

"They see good enough."

"How Papa catch the fishes?"

"He puts a worm on a hook and puts the hook in the river, and when the fishes bite, he pulls 'em out and—"

"And when he bring 'em home, you going to cook 'em?"

"Yeah." She sighed. "Nighty night, Rex."

He heard the door closing and he stiffened.

"Mama, do fishes bite?"

"If you fool enough to put your finger in his mouth, he'll bite you."

3

"Mama, what do fishes do?"

"Fishes are busy being fishes. Now, go to sleep. Nighty night."

The door snapped to and he accepted the inevitable. He stared into the warm darkness, recalling that he had never seen a fish; the only image he could form of one came from his picture book, which depicted them as wild, ugly, six feet tall, and hankering to bite. He drifted toward sleep and dreamed that he saw a huge, angry fish waddling toward him with a gaping mouth. Yeah; he'd crack it over the head with a stick and make all the blood come out. . . .

. . . and he picked up a baseball bat and got ready to hit the fish but when he looked it was not the fish but Chris the big boy who lived down the street and who always played with him and Chris had a baseball in his hand and said: "Rex, you want to play ball?" and he said: "Yeah, Chris!" and Chris said: "Okay. Try and hit this one!" and Chris threw the ball and he swung his bat: CLACK!, the ball rose into the air and Chris said: "You only five years old, but you hit like a big-league player!" and he waited for Chris to pitch again only it was not Chris this time but a seven-foot fish who had the ball and he was scared to death but he could not run and then the fish threw the ball and it hit him in the mouth wedging itself between his teeth and he could not take it out and could not swallow it and he knew that the fish had done to him what his papa did to fishes catching him on a hook and the fish was coming at him with gleaming red eyes and he tried to scream but could not and he could see the fish's mouth opening to swallow him . . .

He stirred restlessly, swallowing the lump of terror in his throat.

"Rex!"

The sun was splashing his room and he saw his mother standing beside his bed.

"Git up! Papa's here! He's brought a lot of fishes!"

With pounding heart, he looked about warily, wondering if any fishes were lurking in his room.

"Put on your robe and slippers. . . . You hear?"

"Yessum," he whispered as his mother left.

He rolled from bed and his sleep-numbed fingers groped for

a slipper and fumblingly tried to push it upon a foot. Bending, he located the foot, then the slipper, resolving to bring the two together, but his foot missed the slipper. He sighed, gazing blankly, feeling slumber recapturing his limbs. His mother's voice boomed:

"Rex!"

He started nervously. "Yessum!"

"Come on and see the fishes!"

This time he was lucky; foot and slipper met. He began working on the right foot, but each time he sought to jam his foot into the slipper, he failed. Blinking slowly against sleep, he felt his foot accidentally sliding into the slipper. He picked up his robe and searched for the sleeves. But on which arm did a sleeve go? And, really, did it matter? Dozing, he eased himself upon the bed.

"Rex!"

He jerked awake; his mother stood in the doorway, holding a strange object in her hands.

"Don't you want to see the fishes Papa brought?"

Oh, she was holding a fish! With parted lips, he advanced and stared at a wriggling, gray shape. But *that* couldn't be a fish . . .

"He little," he said.

"He's big enough," she said.

"He alive?"

"Yeah. But he won't be for long. I'm going to kill 'im."

"How, Mama?"

"I cut 'im open with a knife. You'll see."

Wondering, full of doubt, he struggled into his robe and followed his mother into the kitchen, where his father was standing beside the stove drinking a cup of coffee.

"How's the boy?" his father hailed him. He put his cup aside and reached him in a giant step and lifted him toward the ceiling.

"Hi, Papa," he mumbled, looking apprehensively about. "Where the fishes?"

"There they is." His father inclined his head toward a full zinc pail upon the table.

He was lowered to the floor and he edged forward and saw a dark movement on the surface of the water in the pail, then he made out a mass of white-bellied objects.

"Go on and touch 'em," his father commanded.

He poked a tentative finger at an oblong shape; it moved and he leaped away.

"They bite!" he wailed.

"Aw naw," his father said, laughing.

"Scaredy cat," his mother said.

"Watch me," his father said, lifting a fish that flopped to and fro in his fist. "Here. Take it, Rex."

"Naw!" Then he sniffed distrustfully. "They *smell!*"

"Sure." His father chuckled. "All fish smell."

"But they smell like . . ." His voice trailed off.

His limpid brown eyes circled and rested wonderingly upon his mother, for that odd smell associated itself somehow with her body.

"Kill 'em, Mama," he urged her.

He watched her take up a knife, scrape scales, whack fins, then slit a fish down its side.

"But there ain't no blood."

"Not much blood in a fish," his mother mumbled preoccupiedly.

His mother's fingers groped inside the fish's white belly and drew forth a small batch of entrails.

"Rex, you don't seem to like my fishes." His father fumbled in the heap of entrails. "Watch me. I'll show you how to make a balloon."

"For real, Papa?"

His father unfolded a bit of sticky fish entrail and put it to his lips and puffed into it and, lo and behold!, a translucent, grayish ball swelled slowly, glistening in the morning's sun.

"Aw . . . Can I make one, Papa?" he asked breathlessly.

"Sure." His father handed him a fish entrail.

"What is it, Papa?"

"It's the fish's bladder," his father explained. "Go on. Blow into it. . . ."

He put the fish flesh to his mouth and paused, wrinkling his nostrils against the odor; he puffed and the fish flesh began to distend.

"Look!" he yelled. "I blew up the fish's belly!" He stood admiring the balloon. "I'm going to make a *big* belly this time," he vowed, taking a bladder and blowing eagerly into it. Tingling with excitement, he inflated the bladders as fast as his mother disemboweled the fishes. "Look!" he called, holding aloft an air-filled balloon.

"They ain't bellies; they bladders," his father told him.

"How come you call 'em bellies?" his mother asked him.

"Don't know," he mumbled and then puffed strongly at another one.

But in his mind there was floating a dim image of Mrs. Brown who had a baby and her belly had been big, big like these balloons.

"I like making fish bellies," he sang.

"They fish *bladders*," his father corrected him, laughing.

Later that morning, after his father had gone to his undertaking establishment, Rex took a handful of fish bladders and visited his playmates.

"Watch me blow up a fish belly!" he called.

Critically, Tony watched Rex's inflating a bladder, then he said scornfully:

"Aw, I know that. But they ain't *bellies;* they *bladders.*"

Zeke and Sam joined Tony in insisting that bladders were bladders, but Rex would have none of it.

"They *bellies*," he said obstinately.

"FISHBELLY!" Tony shouted, bending with laughter.

"FISHBELLY!" Sam screamed teasingly.

"FISHBELLY!" Zeke took up the scornful chorus.

Stricken, he looked at their laughing, derisive faces and turned and ran home, crying, stung with humiliation. And that was how he got his nickname that stuck to him all his life, following him to school, to church, tagging along, like a tin can tied to a dog's tail, across the wide oceans of the world. Soon he got used to it, and, in time, actually forgot the origin of it. He became simply *Fishbelly* and answered to that name without hesitation. Among his friends he finally became known as *Fish*.

2

It was Fishbelly's first downtown errand and he moved almost creepingly, walking close to the buildings, trying to make himself invisible. His right fist clutched a note that his mother had entrusted to him to take to his father in the undertaking establishment. Aw, wouldn't Papa be surprised to see him coming all alone through the office door. . . . He was passing an alleyway when he heard a shout:

"Hey, boy!"

He paused, lingering, looking at a white man who was standing and staring at him. Behind the man were three other men, kneeling upon the ground.

"Aw, leave that nigger boy alone," one white man said.

"Come here, boy!" the man who was standing called.

"Nawsir," he said, shaking his head.

His heart thumped. Ought he run? Or stand still? His father had always cautioned him to respect white folks, that is, if he ever had anything to do with them. And now, for the first time in his life, he was facing them all alone. The man who had called him was now advancing; he watched the man until he was some ten feet from him, then he whirled, running, yelling:

"Naw!"

In one stride the man had hold of him and lifted him into the air; he kicked wildly, feeling justified now in resisting.

"Naw! Naw!"

"Shut up, nigger! I ain't going to hurt you," the man said, putting him down, but keeping a tight grip upon his hand.

He attempted to twist away, but the man's fingers flexed and made pain flash through his palm.

"My mama told me—"

"Awright. It'll only take a minute," the man spoke in a brusque, impersonal tone devoid of threat.

That calmed him a bit. The man half led, half dragged him to the other three men who were kneeling about a pile of green paper money heaped upon the ground. Holding his breath, he stared at their dead-white *whiteness,* at their gray, blue, brown eyes, at their black, brown, and blond hair that capped their skulls. He had never been so close to white people before and they seemed like huge, mechanical dolls whose behavior he could not possibly predict.

"For Chrissakes, Ned, let that nigger go," a man drawled in disgust.

"This nigger's going to bring me luck," the man holding him said. "This nigger's young and ain't never shot no dice." The man bent low and asked: "You ever shoot dice, nigger?"

Fishbelly stared into blue eyes that baffled him. Not quite understanding what shooting dice meant, he felt it safer not to answer.

"Can't you talk, nigger?"

"D-don't know no dice; nawsir," he groped for words.

"Good! Then you'll roll these bones for me," the man said.

"Nawsir," he mumbled.

"Oh yes, you are," the man said.

"Yessir," Fishbelly reversed himself.

"Niggers are born with luck. You ain't shot no dice, so you got *all* your luck. I'm going to borrow some of it," the man holding him said.

"I want to go home," he sobbed.

"Here's a nickel, nigger," the man holding him said.

The proferred coin slackened his flow of tears. Men who gave you nickels never hurt you, because all of the men who had ever given him nickels had never hurt him.

"How old're you, nigger?" the man holding him asked.

"Six," he whispered.

"Then you got all your luck," the man pronounced.

He blinked; it sounded bad, that word "luck"; it rhymed with a word that he had heard a boy say at school and the teacher had washed out the boy's mouth with soap.

"Nawsir," he disavowed.

"You got luck, but you don't know it. Now, roll them dice."

In the back of the undertaking parlor he had seen dice in the hands of the men who worked for his father, but he had never understood the game. Nevertheless, he knelt in obedience.

"Take the dice, nigger," the man holding him said.

The dice dropped into his quivering right palm. The man who held him now threw a wad of green bills upon the ground and said:

"I'm betting a hundred. The nigger's shooting for me."

The other men threw money down.

"Okay, nigger. Rattle and roll them bones!"

Tears blinded him; he understood nothing; he shook his head.

"Ned, goddammit, I quit!" one exclaimed, rising.

"If you quit, I'll kill you," the man holding him said. "I want a chance to git my money back."

"But that damned nigger's crying . . ."

"When a nigger cries, that's proof he's got luck," the man holding him said. "Them tears of his is like virgin's blood. His luck ain't never been touched. Roll them dice, nigger."

Fishbelly's arm refused to move.

"Don't you know how to roll 'em, nigger?"

"Nawsir," he whimpered.

"Give me them dice. Now, watch me." The man took the dice and shook them and let them bounce off his palm to the hard clay. The dotted cubes spun and stopped. "Can't you do that?"

"Yessir," he whispered, feeling the dice being put into his hand.

"Nigger, you left-handed?"

"Nawsir."

" 'Cause if you was, you ain't got no luck. Now roll 'em."

Feebly, he agitated the dice and flung them, watching the blurred, spotted white facets twist and finally freeze on the clay.

"*Seven!* Goddamn!" the man holding him yelled, scooping up the money and jamming it into his pocket.

"I quit," a man said. "You either shoot your own dice or there's no game!"

"This nigger's going to roll my dice," the man holding him

said. "It's my money I'm betting, ain't it?"

"Awright," the protesting man relented. "What are you shooting?"

"Four hundred," the man holding him said.

Green money was piled again upon the earth.

"Okay, nigger. Roll 'em," the man holding him said.

Terrified, Fishbelly shut his eyes and rattled the dice and felt them tingling off his fingers to the ground.

"*Eleven!*" the man holding him cried. "Good God in heaven!"

He opened his eyes and saw the man grab all the money and cram it into his pocket. One white man's face grew red with anger.

"Git that nigger out of my sight 'fore I kill 'im!"

"Touch this nigger and I'll kill *you*," the man holding him said. "Shooting eight hundred. Who'll cover me?"

Green money floated to the ground.

"I'm in," one man sighed.

"I'll cover you," another said.

"I'm with you," the third muttered.

"Nigger, if you shoot another seven or eleven, you'd better not been born," one man said.

"Okay, nigger, roll 'em," the man holding him said.

He juggled the speckled cubes and let them fly off his palm; they whirled and halted.

"Eight," the men sang.

"That's your point, nigger!" the man holding him said.

Feeling that he had done something wrong, he began to weep.

"Roll 'em! What you waiting on, nigger?"

He mixed and threw the dice; they tumbled and stood still.

"Six," the men chorused with bated breath.

"Roll 'em, you black bastard!" one man called.

He jiggled the dice and flung them; black dots stared at him.

"Nine," the men chanted.

"I want to go home," he wept pleadingly.

"If you don't make your point, I'll break your neck," the man holding him said.

11

With blurred sight he clacked the cubes and tossed them out.

"Five," the man hummed.

"Roll 'em, nigger!"

He shook the dice and let them fall.

"Ten," the men called.

"Don't stop, nigger! Keep 'em rolling!"

When he dashed the dice this time, there was an explosion of sound as they stopped:

"EIGHT!"

He saw his captor scooping up the money. The four men now stood. Fishbelly heard: *"Pssstt!"* Hot spittle spattered against his cheek; he lifted his hand and dabbed at it, sobbing. A man tried to kick him, but his protector shoved the attacker away.

"Don't queer my luck, you bastard!" his defender growled.

"Git that nigger out of my sight!" one man yelled.

His benefactor put a dollar bill into his hand.

"Okay. Run, nigger!"

He stared, afraid to believe that he was being set free. Then he turned and ran, hearing a shout:

"Don't hit 'im!"

A brick crashed at his heels, spinning and sliding in the dust. Sprinting to a corner, he ducked around the edge of a building, stumbling, and the men were out of sight. But he kept running. He came to a curb and plunged headlong into the middle of the street. An auto horn blared and there was a screeching of tires on concrete and a black car loomed suddenly out of nowhere, blocking his path. He halted, panting, blinking. From out a car window a white face thrust and a man's voice yelled:

"What in hell you trying to do, nigger? Git killed?"

He swallowed, then ran again. A block from his father's undertaking establishment he slowed, sweating, trembling. Oh, Gawd, his father must not see him crying. . . . With doubled fists he dried his eyes, wondering how he could account for the dollar. If he told the truth, his father might well whip him. Oh, yes; he would say that he had found the dollar. He saw his father waiting for him on the steps.

"Fish, where in Gawd's name you been?" his father demanded worriedly. "Your mama said she was going to send you a hour ago."

"Just walking," he said evasively.

Feeling choked, he sat in the office while his father, who could not read, took the note into the back to have his embalmer decipher it. His father returned, folding the note, saying:

"So you came all the way by yourself, hunh?"

"Yessir," he said, looking off.

"You wasn't scared, was you?"

"Oh, nawsir," he lied.

"Son, here's a dollar for you. Give it to your mama and ask her to save it," his father said. "You growing up, now."

He took the dollar, thinking of the one in his pocket.

"What you say when somebody give you something?"

"Thank you, Papa." He stared at the floor, then called meekly: "Papa . . ."

"Yeah, Fish."

"What's 'dice'?"

"'Dice?' 'Dice' is gambling, Fish. And don't you ever do it. You'll lose all your money. Ha, ha! How come you ask?"

"Just wondering. But don't somebody win when somebody lose?"

His father gaped, then wagged his head.

"Sure . . . Fish, you the smartest nigger boy I ever saw!"

"Papa, what's 'luck'?" his voice came lonely and scared.

"'Luck?' 'Luck' is when you git something for nothing," his father said, laughing indulgently, absent-mindedly.

"Could somebody steal your 'luck,' Papa?"

"Well, if they did, you wouldn't never know it till it was too late."

There was a long silence.

"Suppose you found a dollar in the street, Papa?"

"Now, that'd be really luck, Fish."

"Then I'm lucky, 'cause I found a dollar," he lied softly, exhibiting the white man's dollar.

"You got *two* dollars now." Doubt showed on his father's face. "Where you git that other dollar?"

"Like I said, in the street. . . ."

His father stared, Fishbelly trembled, feeling that his lying thoughts were visible in his eyes.

"Son, you didn't take that dollar from your mama, did you?"

"Oh, nawsir," he protested, dismayed to be called a thief.

"Then where you git it?"

"Found it in an alley," he lied.

"Somebody dropped it," his father said in a faraway tone. "You ask if anybody lost it?"

"Nawsir. Nobody was there but some white men who—"

"*They* see you pick up the dollar?"

"Yessir," he lied stoutly.

"And they didn't say nothing?"

"T-they j-just said I was lucky," he stammered.

"Aw, that's how come you ask me what 'luck' was, hunh?" His father chuckled. "Fish, you a smart boy. Keep that dollar. A white man dropped it and you found it, so you got some of *his* luck, see? Mebbe you going to be one of them that's lucky in life." He frowned. "Nobody said nothing when you picked up that dollar?"

"Nawsir," he lied, his right arm trembling.

"Awright, son. Can you git back by yourself?"

"Yessir," he said, pocketing the money. He was afraid, but afraid to admit it.

His father led him to the sidewalk. As soon as he turned a corner, he began a quiet weeping, a sniffing with dry throat. He had had to lie to his father, both for his father's sake and his own; but he felt that his lying had been justified.

3

He stood awkwardly upon the front steps. His mother, clad in a gingham dress and wearing a kerchief, fussed with his tie, smoothed his shirt collar, and babbled cajolingly:

"Now, lissen good. . . . Go to the undertaking parlor and tell Papa that Mr. Cantley was by to see 'im. Mr. Cantley's coming back at six o'clock and Papa's got to be here."

"Yessum," he mumbled, resenting her treating him as though he were blind, deaf, and dumb.

"Now, what'd I tell you to tell Papa?"

He drew a deep breath, frowned to concentrate, and repeated her message.

"That's right," his mother approved. "And git a loaf of bread for supper from Mr. Jordan's. And when you cross Perkins Street, stop and—"

"—look both ways," he mocked slyly, repressing a tinge of scorn.

"You trying to sass me, boy?"

"No'm," he recanted. "I ain't sassing."

"I heard what you said and how you said it. . . . Now, go," she directed him, pecking his cheek and shoving him gently.

He descended the steps, sensing her eyes upon him, and it made him walk stiffly. But, turning the corner, he sighed, regained his self-possession feeling the road's powdery dust caressing his naked toes. His mother always inhibited him, but among his playmates he was free, lively. Though he had but seven short years behind him, his manner was winning, his melting brown eyes inspiring trust. He never attacked a hostile object frontally, but subdued it with smiles, guile, at last getting his way. He was habitually shy and the only time he ever got really angry was when he was made to feel inferior or embarrassed. In fact, he had a grudge right now against that loudmouthed, snotty-nosed Tony, who had, Zeke informed him, tricked him out of one of his best agates. "Just wait till I git my hands on that liver-lipped ape," he vowed.

Through a haze of heat loomed Mr. Jordan's store, whose front porch was crowded with loitering railroad workers. He readied himself to be laughed at, scorned. His parents had cautioned him against these roustabouts. "Son, they your *color,* but they ain't your *kind,"* his mother had told him. "I touch 'em only when they *dead,* Fish, and I wouldn't do that 'less I was paid," his father had drawn the line.

As he passed them he mumbled:

"Good afternoon."

There were a few grunts; but, after he had entered, there was a loud burst of laughter that made him wince. They were making fun of his white shirt, of the house in which he lived, of the fact that he was "Fish, old man Tyree's son . . . The undertaker, you know . . ." Golly! Why couldn't he wear overalls and be like the other boys? He was supposed to be better than these men, but they made him feel lower than a snake's belly. He moved to the counter, inhaling mackerel, coal oil, and overripe bananas.

"Hi, Fishy-O!" Bald, round-faced, potbellied Mr. Jordan hailed him, spewing a jet of tobacco juice into a sand-filled box.

"Hi, Mr. Jordan," he piped, placing a dime upon the greasy counter and smiling automatically. "I come for the bread."

"Here 'tis." The old man tossed a cellophaned loaf toward him.

He grabbed for the bread, but missed it. It thudded upon the flour.

"Look at 'im," Mr. Jordan jeered chucklingly. "Shame on you! You want to be a ballplayer and you can't catch a loaf of bread."

"I wasn't looking for you to pitch it," he muttered lamely, flushing hot from shyness.

"How's old Tyree?"

"Fine, I guess. I'm going to see 'im now."

"Well," drawled Mr. Jordan, "tell Tyree to take good care of them bodies."

"You mean the dead folks?"

"Ha, ha! Just you tell Tyree what I said; he'll know what I mean. . . ." Mr. Jordan's irony was joyous.

"Yessir," he mumbled.

The old man advanced with his right fist behind him.

"Guess what's in my right hand and it's yours," he teased the boy.

"A wineball?" he asked hesitatingly.

"Right!" Mr. Jordan said, laughing. "Now, catch it!"

Fishbelly's right hand speared the wineball in mid-air.

"That a boy!" Mr. Jordan approved. "Where your manners?"

"Oh, thank you, sir," he sang, the wineball in his cheek.

He ducked through the door, hearing Mr. Jordan's cackles. Mr. Jordan's playfulness had allayed his timidities and he ignored the loiterers. Sucking his wineball, he began tossing the bread aimlessly into the air and catching it. Why had he missed the loaf when Mr. Jordan had thrown it? Well, he'd practice some. . . . He flung the loaf a yard high and retrieved it. Absorbed, he flexed his muscles and let go with all his might and the loaf, its cellophane wrapping sparkling in the sun, rose majestically toward a vaulting sky and, as it crossed the face of the sun, he lost sight of it. A liquid splash reached his ears. "Where it go?" He poked about in tall grass. There it was. . . . But, oh Gawd . . . Through the smashed cellophane wrapping snow-white bread slices had burst and lay pell-mell in the center of a huge pancake of soupy, dark green cow manure. He gaped, stupefied. What Mama going to say? He bent over the scattered bread and extended a tentative finger at a slice soaked as though in a pureé of creamed spinach. "Naw!" Overcome, he stood. Self-defense made him imagine what should have happened: he had been sauntering along, peacefully and obediently, and had stumbled and the loaf had fallen into the circle of cow-mess. . . . Naw! There were gaping holes in that lie. The cow manure was some ten feet off the path and no loaf of bread could go that far in falling. But supposing he had tripped and spilled the bread? But that lie was no good either. He could already hear his mother saying: "Come on and show me what you tripped over. . . ."

His misty eyes fought back pending tears. Ah, yes; he could beg his father for a dime to buy an ice-cream cone and use that

17

dime to replace the bread. His shattered universe began reassembling itself. Upon reaching the undertaking parlor, he pocketed the wineball, for he had no taste for candy now. Entering, he smelled that eye-stinging, pungent odor of formaldehyde. He called in a lyrical tenor:

"Papa!"

A vague echo answered. Athwart the office's front window was a gray, satin-padded coffin into which he had an audacious impulse to climb and play dead, lying stiff, closing his eyes, holding his hands rigidly at his sides—a prank that had always angered his mother, but had made his father laughingly exclaim: "Ha, ha! I tell you that little devil ain't scared of nothing!" But, naw . . . He was in trouble, he had to find a dime.

"Papa!" he called louder.

He waited. Where was Papa? He peered at the hanging gravity bottles in the embalming room, at the long white table upon which bodies were drained of blood, hearing an odd, rhythmic: *bumpbump bumpbump bumpbump.* . . . What was that? He went down the hallway toward the storeroom and the strange sound became stronger, clearer.

"Papa!" he called once more, listening, wondering.

Some cloudy instinct checked his calling again. He found the waiting room empty, then headed toward the guest room, the door of which was slightly ajar; and that pounding sound, charged now with an urgent significance, beat out of the darkness upon his ears: *bumpbump, bumpbump, bumpbump.* . . . His lips parted and he stifled a prompting to flee; he pushed the door noiselessly in and his bare feet advanced him silently and catlike into the room. His pupils dilated and he saw upon a bed the shadowy outlines of his naked father: two staring red eyes, a strained, humped back; and he heard harsh breath whistling in an open throat. Stunned, he backed to a wall. Was his father ill? Aw, maybe his father was working upon a dead body? His clearing vision made out another body, but it was not a dead one. Terrified of betraying himself, he nestled into a corner. A slither of dim light from the edge of the window shade revealed sliding sweat on his father's concentrated face. He wanted to scream, but his locked throat could make no sound.

The pummeling in the shadows grew more frantic, faster; there followed an explosion of breath and a sudden stillness reigned in the room's fetid air. He managed to swallow, then his choking tension found release in tears.

"Who that?" his father demanded in brutal challenge.

"Oh, Lawd!" a woman's voice wailed.

Fishbelly saw a naked, black body leap from the bed.

"That you, Fish?" The dread in his father's voice was replaced by a scared hope.

His sobbing would not let him speak.

"What you doing here?" his father demanded accusingly.

He still could not reply.

"Your mama here?" his father asked in a clipped whisper.

"N-nawsir . . . S-she's at home," he gasped.

"Holy creeps!" the woman exclaimed, then broke into a laugh.

"Shut up," he heard his father tell the woman.

A quick, meaningful image of his mother, cool and brooding, hovered in his mind and he knew that this unknown, laughing woman was in his mother's place.

"What you doing in here, Fish?" His father's voice was softer, more thoughtful now.

And before he could reply, his father joined the woman's hysterical laughter.

"Git that child out of here," the woman said. "I got to git my clothes on."

He wanted to run, but dared not. How big was the wrong he had done? Would he be beaten for it? But it wasn't his fault; he had only been obeying Mama. . . .

"How long you been in here?" His father was nervously tender.

"Little while," he whimpered. "Mama sent me . . ."

His shadowy father was rushing into his clothes and he smelled an odd odor and was whisked back through time to that morning when his father had brought home a pail of fishes and he was in the kitchen seeing heaps of fish entrails that his mother had piled upon the table. Before his eyes floated a huge, glistening balloon.

"Papa," he begged, pleading guilty to a wrong whose name he did not know.

"Git into the office. And don't leave till I talk to you," his father ordered.

"Yessir," he promised.

He went down the hallway and into the office and sank into the big armchair, feeling his tiny legs dangling toward the floor. He had blundered into the mysterious world that grownups hid from children and now he was praying that that world would be forgiving, merciful. . . . On the wall a calendar that held the photo of a laughing white girl strolling along a sandy beach, her blond hair blown back, her lips holding a cigarette, her legs as white as bread, and her rounded breasts billowing under satin. . . . "But she's *black*," he whispered, recalling the patch of black woman skin illumined by the dim lance of light that came from the edge of the window shade. And he was black . . . And his father was black . . . He sensed a relation between the worlds of white skins and black skins, but he could not determine just what it was.

Footsteps in the hallway made him cock his head. He heard the woman's silvery laughter and his father's telling the woman good-by. . . . Would he be punished? And he had spoiled that loaf of bread. . . . He had offended Mama and now he had offended Papa. He needed solace. Suddenly he remembered the wineball in his pocket; he fished it out and slid it into his mouth and was comforted by the sweet-sour taste. The woman, dressed and wearing a hat, appeared in the doorway. She was brown, plump, smiling. She wrinkled her nose and shook a forefinger at him.

"Nasty boy," she said.

He flinched, feeling bleak. The woman left and he heard her heels cross the wooden porch outside. It wasn't his fault, going into that room. . . . His father entered briskly, chuckling, not glancing at him, knotting his tie.

"I didn't hear you come in, Fish," he said matter-of-factly. Then, with studied kindness: "But how come you went poking 'round all over the place? You could've called me and—"

"I did, Papa. But you didn't hear me."

"I was 'tending to a customer, Fish. But why you hide in that corner?"

"I was scared," he said.

"Scared? What made you scared?"

"Nothing," he mumbled, sensing that his father was worried.

"Then what was you scared for?"

"Dunno," he confessed in a barely heard mumble.

He was on secret ground. Self-defense prodded him to pretend innocence. He surmised that his father was groping for a way to evade acknowledging that had happened and it made a tiny spot of hope glow in him.

"Mama send you?" his father asked him finally.

"Yessir." He was now certain that his father was seeking a way out of a mysterious difficulty, for he was kind now, too suddenly kind. But he needed that kindness. "Mama sent me . . ." His voice died.

"Yeah? What Mama say?"

"I forgot," he whimpered. And his forgetting induced confusion and the sense of panic consequent upon that confusion washed his mind of memory.

"How come you always forgitting?" his father scolded indulgently.

"That noise scared me," he pleaded his cause. "And that woman . . ."

His voice trailed off as his father's eyes glared wrathfully, like the eyes of a cat in the dark.

"Fish, don't you remember I told you *never* to talk about what you see in this 'shop'?"

"Yessir, Papa."

"Now you just forgit what you *think* you saw or heard, see? That woman was here to see me about how she wanted her dead mama fixed."

"Yessir," he whispered, not believing.

Anxiety was urging him toward deception; and, at bottom, there was in him a profound admiration for his father's ability to lie with such indignant righteousness. He was convinced that he was witnessing a very important event.

"Now, just you learn to keep your mouth shut about this 'shop.' Don't you say nothing to nobody—at home, at school, or in the street. . . . If you go talking, you'll git us both into trouble. . . . Now, what Mama tell you to tell me?"

"I can't remember," he sighed.

His father circled him tenderly with an arm.

"Awright, Fish. We all forgit sometimes. But what you crying about?"

"Papa, I dropped a loaf of bread and Mama's going to whip me," he gulped. "Then I got scared when I saw you and the lady. . . . Papa, what was you doing to the lady? I thought you was acting like a train."

His father's eyes went blank; then he sucked in his breath, threw back his head, and bellowed a whinnying laugh.

"Ha, ha! Acting like a train? Fish, you real funny. . . ." He averted his face, muttering: "Mebbe I did look like a train . . ." He was suddenly serious. "Son, don't you cry about that old loaf of bread. Here . . ." He thrust two dimes into the boy's hand. "Git that loaf of bread and buy yourself a ice-cream cone. You and me's friends, see? You say nothing about what you see in this 'shop' and Papa'll say nothing about that bread."

"Yessir," he sighed, his sense of that wild scene in that dim room fading. What a kind, magical man his father was!

"And tell Mama I'll be along about eight—"

"Oh, Papa!" he exclaimed, smiling through tears.

"What, son?"

"I remember now . . . Mama said Mr. Cantley was by to see you. She said he's coming back at six tonight and you got to be there."

He saw the corners of his father's lips drop.

"I won't be no more train today," his father mumbled. He turned to the boy. "Tell Mama I'll be there. But keep your mouth shut about this 'shop,' hear?"

"Yessir, Papa."

"Now, git along."

He skipped happily out of the office and into streets gilded by the sun's last rays. Not only would he buy another loaf of bread, but he would have an ice-cream cone. And, what was most important, he shared a dark secret with his father; he did not grasp the nature of that secret, but he was confident that time would reveal it. Already that awful scene in that dim room was being replaced by a hunger to get home and play with his electric trains.

From that day on, thundering trains loomed in his dreams —hurtling, sleek, black monsters whose stack pipes belched gobs of serpentine smoke, whose seething fireboxes coughed out clouds of pink sparks, whose pushing pistons sprayed jets of hissing steam—panting trains that roared yammeringly over far-flung, gleaming rails only to come to limp and convulsive halts—long, fearful trains that were hauled brutally forward by red-eyed locomotives that you loved watching as they (and you trembling!) crashed past (and you longing to run but finding your feet strangely glued to the ground!), and that night his dreams were no exception . . .

. . . *he ambled barefooted and bareheaded under a molten sun and over hard red clay singing:*

> *When I'm a man*
> *I mean to buy*
> *A dozen barrels*
> *Of pumpkin pie . . .*

and he'd eat 'em all even if he got the bellyache yes there's that roundhouse Mama don't want me to go down there he shot a glance over his shoulder for she'd told him a thousand times to stay away from those trains for he'd get hurt but I'm a man he told himself as he rounded a bend in the road and saw the giant shed where black beautiful locomotives stood Lawd there was a big brand new one oh Jesus he'd like to drive it he looked around nobody was in sight he grasped hold of the steel bar and hoisted himself up into the cab gee whiz levers wheels handles he timidly caught hold of a jutting bar and pulled it and the locomotive began to throb and move slowly at first and then with increasing speed as it plunged forward bumpbump bumpbump bumpbump and he looked out the window seeing a solid wall of black telephone poles flying past and the sky had red sparks for stars and the locomotive rocked left right up down with mighty expulsions of breath and he was so scared that he shut his eyes and screamed: "Papa! Papa!" and he crouched in a corner of the cab nestling into a heap of glistening coal feeling that he had done something terribly wrong and was going to be whipped for it. . . .

4

One morning Fishbelly strolled down a narrow alley, slashing with a broomstick at tin cans, small stones, and shards of glass. He spied a hunk of brick, paused, assumed a batter's stance, then lammed the brick, feeling a sensation of power as it skimmed hummingly over the dust. "A triple into right field!" he sang in ecstasy. He ambled on, searching for a rock that could serve as a baseball. He slowed, staring at a four-inch white rubber tubing lying in a clump of weeds. One end of the tube had a tiny ridge about its top; the other end was closed, rounded. He picked it up and examined it. Was it a balloon? Naw. But it looked as though it would be a good sheath for the top of his bat. He drew the rubber tubing over the handle of the broomstick; it fitted perfectly. Gosh, he'd show this to the gang. . . . Using the translucent tubing as a protective glove for the stick's top, he swung along past a wooden fence and let the end of the stick slide against the pickets: *clackclackclack* . . .

"Fishy-O!" his name sang through the air.

Yeah; there they were on the steps of Mr. Jordan's store.

"Zeki-O! Sammy-O! Tony-O!" he answered them.

Zeke, fat, genial, was lolling upon the steps. Sam, short, nervous, aggressive, stood with his hands in his pockets. Tony, tall, lean, was bouncing a rubber ball off the side of the house.

"Look what I got!" Fishbelly exhibited his rubber-caparisoned stick.

"Gee, it's pretty," Tony said.

"Let me see it," Sam said, taking the stick.

"Where you git it?" Zeke asked enviously; he took the stick from Sam and, holding it by its rubber-covered handle, brandished it.

"I found it in the grass," Fishbelly informed them.

"Give you a nickel for it," Zeke offered.

"Don't want to sell it," Fishbelly rejected the offer.

"Hi, snots!" a bass voice greeted them.

They all ran toward a tall, brown-skinned young man of about eighteen. Chris wore a blue suit, a bow tie, a snap-brimmed hat, and dangled a cigarette from his lips.

"Hi, Chris!" they hailed Chris with a chorus.

"Give me a cigarette," Zeke begged.

"You snots too young to smoke," Chris said, smiling.

"I'm four years older'n Fish and Sam," Zeke boasted.

"You still too young to smoke," Chris told Zeke.

"Where you going, Chris?" Fishbelly asked hero-worshippingly.

"To work, like always," Chris answered.

"You still bellhopping at the West End Hotel?" Sam asked.

"Still there," Chris said.

"Chris, look what I found for my stick." Fishbelly extended the tip of his rubber-capped bludgeon.

Chris started at the glistening rubber, looked from one of them to the other, then burst into a loud, long laugh and stepped back.

"You damned fools!" Chris branded them with a shout.

"What's the matter?" Fishbelly asked, blinking.

"Don't touch that thing; it's *nasty!*" Chris exclaimed.

"It's clean; I just found it," Fishbelly said.

"You-all just nasty little stinking babies." Chris simpered.

"Why you don't like my stick?" Fishbelly asked.

"It ain't the stick, you fool. It's that rubber," Chris explained. "Your Papa see you with that, he'll beat hell out of you."

"Why?" four child voices asked wonderingly.

Chris hesitated.

"It's just nasty," he repeated emphatically.

"What it for?" Four pairs of eyes were wide with bewilderment.

"That the first time you-all ever seen one of them things?" Chris asked with a splutter.

"Yeah," the four of them breathed in answer with eyes dazed with lack of comprehension.

"Give me that damned thing!" Chris grabbed the stick by its bare tip and hurled it over a high fence and into a patch of weeds.

"My stick!" Fishbelly wailed tearfully.

"Lissen," Chris lectured them. "Don't play with that stick no more. It's *nasty,* I tell you."

"What you mean, Chris?" Zeke asked.

"When men make love and don't want to make babies or catch a disease, they wear rubbers like that," Chris explained.

Four pairs of eyes stared, trying to understand.

"What they do?" the boys chorused, singsonging.

"You monkeys don't understand nothing!" Chris became furious. *"That* rubber's been in a woman's 'bad' thing."

Four pairs of eyes began to clear. In rough terms they understood that men were different from women, and, if that rubber tubing had been in a woman's "bad" thing, then it was nasty *indeed*. . . .

"Fish, you fool!" Zeke yelled.

"I didn't *know,"* Fishbelly murmured, stunned. He felt that he had made a fool of himself and his eyes walled.

"He found a glove for his bat," Sam giggled.

"I'm going to wash my hands!" Zeke shouted, turning and running.

"Me too!" Sam and Tony yelled, following Zeke.

Chris looked compassionately at Fishbelly and laughed.

"You'd better wash your hands too," Chris suggested.

Fishbelly wanted to join his friends, but shame paralyzed him. Then he about-faced and ran, hearing Chris's dunning laughter. He reached home and barged into the bathroom and twisted the tap and seized a bar of soap and began lathering his palms, creating a cloud of foam. He rinsed his hands, seeing a monstrously distorted image of the woman's "bad" thing and he felt unclean again. For a second time he soaped his fingers, his cupped hands brimming with glittering suds.

"Fish!" his mother's voice called.

"Hunh?" he grunted, starting guiltily.

His mother peered around the jamb of the bathroom door.

"What you doing there, Fish?"

"Washing my hands," he muttered defensively.

"How come?" she asked, astonished.

"They dirty," he mumbled.

She stared and laughed.

"That's the first time you ever did that without me asking you to," she said and left.

Sulking, he dried his hands, still feeling unclean, then wandered out upon the front steps. He never wanted to see his pals again, for he was sure they were going to tease him. Why was he always doing something wrong?

"Fish!" his mother called.

"Hunh?"

"Now, you just stop that 'hunhing' me," she snapped.

"Yessum," he answered properly.

"What happened? Thought you was playing with the boys . . ."

"I was."

"You-all had a fight or something?"

"No'm," he hummed with averted face.

"Awright, little man," his mother said jovially. "You don't have to tell me."

She left shutting the door. He was full of fuming anger, but he did not know against whom.

5

Sunday evening in August. Fireflies made yellow streaks in the star-filled, velvet dark. In weedy ditches frogs belched and crickets sang. Tolling church bells rolled through the sultry night. Here and there gaslights created pools of haze.

Fishbelly waited upon the porch steps for his parents to leave; after they had seen a movie, they were stopping at Franklin's Chicken Shack for a "nip and a bite," and he would be free to join his gang upon the gaslit corner for a bull session. He inclined his head as the Dixie Special thundered past on the horizon, moaning three times in the humid darkness.

His mother and father appeared in the doorway.

"I want you in bed at ten, Fish," his father said. "Good night."

"And don't forgit to turn out the light," his mother said.

"No'm. Good night," he said.

The moment they had gone, he was scurrying down the block. Yeah; there were Zeke, Sam, and Tony outlined in the cone of sheen cast by the gas lamp.

"Here comes Fish. Ask 'im."

"Yeah. Ask Fish."

An argument was raging and the shouts were so raucously violent that Fishbelly could not understand his friends' words.

"Hush, everybody!" Zeke screamed.

"But don't tell 'im *nothing!* Just *ask* 'im, see," Sam advised angrily.

"Yeah, yeah," Tony agreed.

"What's happening?" Fishbelly asked, looking from one to the other.

"We talking about something and we wonder what *you* think," Zeke explained.

"Yeah? What?" Fishbelly asked, feeling flattered.

Zeke cleared his throat, repressed a laugh, then asked:

"Fish, you want to go to *Africa?*"

Fishbelly blinked, looking from black face to black face.

"Hunh? To *Africa?*" Fishbelly asked. *"What for?"*

Zeke and Tony stomped their feet with glee. Sam scowled.

"I *told* you!" Zeke screamed triumphantly.

"Fish, you sure looked funny when you heard that word 'Africa'!" Tony whooped.

"But who's going to Africa?" Fishbelly asked, seeking the point of the debate.

"Nobody but damn fools!" Zeke said emphatically.

"Nobody but fatheads!" Tony growled.

"You niggers don't know nothing!" Sam railed at Zeke and Tony.

"Who's a nigger?" Zeke asked, fists clenched.

Sam glared. Fishbelly wondered if Sam would hurl the supreme insult.

"A nigger's a black man who doesn't know who he is," Sam made his accusation general.

"You calling *me* a nigger?" Zeke pressed threateningly.

"You *know* what you is?" Sam countered without retracting.

"Sure, I know," Zeke said.

"Then why you asking me?" Sam questioned logically. "A nigger's a black man who don't know who he is, *'cause he's too damned dumb to know.*"

"Lissen to the professor," Tony sneered.

"When you know you a nigger, then you ain't no nigger no more," Sam reasoned. "You start being a *man!* A nigger's something white folks make a black man believe he is—"

"Your papa's done stuffed you with crazy ideas," Tony said.

"Your old man's got Africa on the brain and he's made you a copycat," Zeke pronounced.

"What you-all talking about?" Fishbelly asked, troubled, puzzled.

"Sam says we want to be *white*," Zeke bared the bone of contention.

"You *do!*" Sam repeated his indictment.

"Sam, why you say that?" Fishbelly asked. "We all black—"

"You straighten your hair, don't you?" asked Sam bitterly.

"Aw, that ain't trying to be white," Zeke contended.

"It is! Why you put lye and mashed potatoes on your hair?" Sam asked scornfully. "You kill your hair to make it straight like white folks' hair!"

"Naw! It's to make it look *nice*," Tony said.

"That's 'cause you think white folks' hair looks nice, and white folks' hair's *straight*," Sam stated.

"THAT'S A LIE!" Zeke shouted.

"I don't want my hair looking like no mattress," Tony said.

Fishbelly shifted uneasily from foot to foot. His hair, too, had been straightened and he liked it that way, but he did not want to think of why he had had it straightened.

"You-all just 'shamed of being *black*," Sam charged directly.

"Aw, Sam, stop that kind of talk," Fishbelly begged nervously.

"You just don't want to hear the truth," Sam judged.

"And Sam, whose papa's a janitor, knows the truth," Zeke resorted to personal insult.

"Now you talking just like a nigger," Sam branded Zeke.

"Stop, you-all!" Fishbelly screamed. "This is *crazy* talk!"

"Sam started it; he said we ought to all go back to Africa," Zeke mumbled.

"You lying! Don't put words in my mouth! I was only telling you what my papa said," Sam enlarged his theme. "Papa said we all fighting that Hitler and that's a white man's war and we black folks ought to be helping Africa—"

"Your papa's wild," Zeke flung at Sam.

"Let me talk and let Fish be the judge!" Sam yelled.

"That's fair," Fishbelly said.

"Okay. But I don't want to go to no Africa," Zeke muttered.

"Me neither," Tony hissed.

Sam now stared at Fishbelly and asked:

"Fish, what's your *color?*"

"M-my c-color?" Fishbelly asked stammeringly. "Hell, man, can't you s-see I'm *black?*"

"Yeah?" Sam asked ironically. "And *why* you black?"

"I was born that way," Fishbelly said resentfully.

"But there's a *reason* why you got a *black* color," Sam was implacable.

"My mama's black. My papa's black. And that makes me black," Fishbelly said.

"And your mama's mama and your papa's papa was black, wasn't they?" Sam asked softly.

"Sure," Fishbelly said with a resentful hum, afraid of the conclusions to which his answers were leading.

"And where did your mama's mama's *mama* and your papa's papa's *papa* come from?" Sam next wanted to know.

"F-from A-Africa, I reckon," Fishbelly stammered.

"You just reckon?" Sam was derisive. "You know damn well where—"

"Okay. They came from Africa." Fishbelly tried to cover up his hesitancy.

Sam now fired his climactic question:

"Now, just stand there and tell me what *is* you?"

Before Fishbelly could reply, Zeke and Tony set up a chant: "Fishbelly's a African! Fishbelly's a African!"

"Let Fish answer!" Sam tried to drown them out.

"I'm black and I live in America and my folks came from Africa," Fishbelly summed up his background. "That's all I know."

"Your folks was *brought* from Africa," Sam sneered.

"We just like everybody else in this country." Tony tried to make black life in America seem normal.

"Naw!" Sam rejected that interpretation. "Them Irish and them English is white folks. Fish is a African who's been taken out of Africa. Fish ain't no American. Ain't that right, Fish?"

"Y-Yeah, but that was a long time ago when I came from Africa—"

"But you still black, ain't you?" Sam taunted him.

"Sam, you jackass," Zeke said. "Now, Sam, tell me: What's *Roosevelt?*"

"Roosevelt's American," Sam replied calmly.

"And so's Fish," Zeke tried to clinch the argument.

"You *wrong!*" Sam shouted. "Roosevelt can do what he wants to, and Fish *can't!*" Fish thinks he's American, but he ain't. Now, my papa says all black folks ought to build up Africa, 'cause that's our true home—"

"*You* go to Africa!" Zeke hollered at Sam.

"Go *now!*" Tony screamed with rage.

"All I know about Africa's what I read in the geography book at school," Fishbelly mumbled, unwilling to commit himself.

"Sam wants us to git naked and run wild and eat with our hands and live in mud huts!" Zeke ridiculed Sam's thesis.

"I want to stay where I am," Fishbelly confessed finally.

"Okay," Sam agreed sarcastically. "Nobody wants to go to Africa. . . . Awright. Who wants to go to *America?*"

The three boys stared incredulously at Sam.

"Sam's done gone stone crazy," Tony moaned.

"We awready *in* America, you fool!" Zeke yelled.

"Aw, naw, you ain't!" Sam cried hotly. "You niggers ain't

31

nowhere. You ain't in Africa, 'cause the white man took you out. And you ain't in America, 'cause if you was, you'd act like *Americans—*"

"I'M AN AMERICAN!" Zeke thundered.

"Nigger, you dreaming!" Sam preached. "You ain't no American! You live Jim Crow. Don't you ride Jim Crow trains? Jim Crow busses? Don't you go to Jim Crow restaurants? Jim Crow schools? Jim Crow churches? Ain't your undertaking parlors and graveyards Jim Crow? Try and git a room in that West End Hotel where Chris is working and them white folks'll lynch your black ass to hell and gone! You can't live like no American, 'cause you ain't no American! And you ain't African neither! So what is you? Nothing! Just *nothing!*"

"We crazy to listen to you," Zeke said with weary disgust. "I'm going."

"Me too," Tony said. "Sam's papa's done *mixed* him all up."

"If I'm *mixed* up, then you *messed* up," Sam said.

Zeke and Tony walked off. Fishbelly had not known what side to take. He had sympathized with Sam, yet he valued Zeke's and Tony's esteem.

"Wait till they try to git a job, then they'll know they ain't nothing but niggers," Sam spoke with sadistic masochism.

"I ain't no nigger," Fishbelly's voice hummed sullenly.

"To the white folks, you a nigger," Sam said flatly.

"That only 'cause some of our folks act bad," Fishbelly said.

"Then you *agree* with the white folks?" Sam asked.

"Don't agree with acting bad," Fishbelly qualified himself.

"White folks say you bad 'cause you black," Sam analyzed. "And there ain't nothing you can do about being black."

Fishbelly suddenly hated Sam's fiercely angry face that shone like polished ebony in the dim glow of the gaslight.

"Stop talking *race!*" Fishbelly pleaded with burning throat.

"Man, there ain't nothing else to talk about," Sam crooned sadistically. "When you a nigger, you's *all* nigger and there ain't *nothing* left over."

"Your talk makes me mad," Fishbelly grumbled. "I'm going."

As he turned to leave, Sam's hand came upon his shoulder.

Fishbelly shied off, shoving Sam away.

"Don't push me, nigger!" Sam warned.

"Don't touch me!" Fishbelly hissed.

Before they realized it, they were breathlessly grappling with each other, their taut black faces inches apart. Fishbelly's right fist shot against Sam's head and his left fingers grabbed Sam's collar. Sam socked a left into Fishbelly's face. Fishbelly lowered his head and butted Sam's stomach. Sam retaliated by lifting his right leg and sending the toe of his shoe against Fishbelly's shin.

"Don't kick me, nigger!" Fishbelly sobbed.

"You hit me *first!*" Sam accused with a shout.

Their feet became entangled and they fell sideways over a curbstone. They rose, fists clenched, confronting each other, neither wanting to fight, but neither knowing how to leave the battle with pride intact.

"I knew you was just a nigger," Sam swore.

"You blacker'n me, so you more nigger'n me," Fishbelly branded Sam.

Stung, Sam lashed out with his right; Fishbelly ducked and Sam's swing carried him stumbling down the sidewalk. Ten feet apart, they glared at each other.

"If you'd hit me, I'd've cut your damned throat," Fishbelly panted.

"I hope them white folks *kill* you!" Sam burst out.

"I hope they kill you *first!*" Fishbelly topped Sam's bitter wish.

"I hope they kill your black mama!" Sam hurled.

"I hope they kill your mama *and* your papa!" Fishbelly surmounted Sam's dire hope.

Some twenty feet apart now, they glowered toward each other through a moist, hot darkness washed by the feeble gleam of the gas lamp.

"If I was white, I'd lynch you and your whole goddamned family," Sam reveled in vicarious revenge.

"But you *ain't* white; you *black,* black like me, and you going to *always* be black!" Fishbelly panted in triumph, turning and running.

He had had the last word and he quivered with hysteria. He slowed, glanced over his shoulder at Sam's lonely shadow slouching away in the gloom. When he reached home he sank upon the steps, emotionally exhausted.

"I didn't want to fight," he moaned.

He groped his way into his dark bedroom. Without turning on the light, he undressed with fumbling fingers, then stood breathing heavily in the warm darkness, snared by an anguish that he could not understand. He crossed to the dresser and snapped on the light and stared openmouthed at the reflection of his tear-stained black face in the mirror. He grimaced at that reflection, then sucked a volume of hot liquid from his saliva glands and spat, spattering the glass.

"Nigger," he whispered in a voice that was like an escaping valve.

Turning, he flung himself upon his bed and jerked the covers over him. He lay trembling for a long time and finally fell into a deep sleep, oblivious of the burning light.

Three days later he and Sam had forgotten that they had ever fought, and about what.

6

Clad in dungarees and T shirt, Fishbelly stood in a corner of a vacant lot with a baseball clutched in his left hand and a bat dangling from his right. Fanning out some forty yards from him and spaced at about thirty-degree angles apart, were Sam, Tony, and Zeke, each with a gloved left hand. Fishbelly coolly regarded Tony and called:

"Tony!"

"Ready!" Tony answered and shaded his eyes with his glove.

Fishbelly tossed the ball, and, as it fell, he swung his bat, *clack!*, banging the ball sharply, looping it toward Tony, who, face tilted sunward, ran joggingly to left and right as he judged the falling ball, whose course was being veered by a strong wind. He stopped and the descending ball thudded against his leather-covered palm.

"Good!" Zeke called commendingly.

"Perfect catch!" Sam approved.

Tony so calculated his throw back to Fishbelly that the ball landed about six feet from Fishbelly, who easily speared it with his bare left hand as it bounced.

"Zeke!" Fishbelly announced.

"Ready!" Zeke signaled.

Fishbelly was about to toss the ball preparatory to batting it when Sam's voice checked him:

"Hold it, Fish!"

Fishbelly froze, baffled. Tony motioned his thumb to the right and Fishbelly turned and saw plump, short, black Aggie West, a glove under his arm, coming mincingly toward him. Fishbelly frowned. Aggie West showed a wide, sweet smile.

"Hello, Rex," Aggie greeted Fishbelly by his Christian name.

Fishbelly scowled, for he despised anyone so pretentious as not to call him *Fish*. . . . Tony, Sam, and Zeke now advanced and, when all four of them were together, they glared at the smiling Aggie.

"Look, sissy! Beat it!" Zeke was harsh.

"I want to play ball," Aggie mumbled musically.

"Naw, you pansy," Fishbelly said. "Now, *go!*"

"Why can't I play?" Aggie seemed indifferent to his frigid reception.

"'Cause we don't want to play with fruits!" Sam snarled.

"Why don't you want to play with me?" Aggie enunciated correctly.

"Play the piano, you fairy," Tony said. "That's all you fit for!"

"I love to play the piano and I also love to play ball," Aggie explained.

"Homo, leave us alone!" Fishbelly's eyes were like brown granite.

"Don't yell like that," Aggie protested with pained eyes.

"'Don't yell like that,'" Zeke mocked Aggie's too feminine voice.

"Why are you boys so brutal?" Aggie asked wonderingly.

"Who in hell you calling 'brutal'?" Tony asked.

"You're brutal if you won't let me play with you," Aggie said.

Tony looked about distractedly. Near his feet lay a sharp, flat stone as large as a baseball; he stooped, picked it up, and faced Aggie.

"Spook, I'm counting to *three,* and when I git to three, you better be running," Tony gave notice.

"You wouldn't hit me with that stone, would you?" Aggie spoke with gentle reproof.

"The hell I won't!" Tony vowed with a snarl. *"One!"*

Silent, Aggie kept a fixed smile.

"Two!"

"Sonofabitch!" Fishbelly spat, averting his eyes.

"THREE!"

Tony hesitated, then drew back his arm and let fly the stone. Aggie ducked, twisting his body, and the stone landed squarely in back of his head, just above the ear, and at once a sheet of blood gushed, flooding the back of Aggie's shirt, forming a red collar about his neck. Aggie straightened with stricken eyes, his lips quivering.

"Scat, you sissy!" Fishbelly yelled.

Aggie blinked against tears gushing from his eyes.

"Move on, queer nigger!" Zeke screamed. "Shove off!"

Aggie's lips parted, but he did not move or speak. Nervous hysteria made Sam advance and snatch the baseball out of Fishbelly's hand. Lifting the bat, Sam lashed Aggie across the chest. Tony, Zeke, and Fishbelly kicked, slapped, and punched Aggie, who walked groggily, turning, stumbling toward a field, not protesting the raining blows. They followed Aggie to the edge of a stretch of young, waist-high corn where they paused and silently watched the retreating Aggie, staring at his sunlit, blood-drenched shirt gleaming amidst the sea of green corn.

"Goddamn," Zeke muttered.

"I tried to kill 'im," Tony spoke through clenched teeth.

"Why won't he leave us alone?" Fishbelly whined. "I hit 'im so hard I hurt my hand. . . ."

They stood awkwardly, unable to recapture the yen for play.

"Hell, mebbe we oughtn't've done that." Tony was regretful.

"But when we tell 'im to go 'way, he won't go," Fishbelly argued in self-justification.

"We treat 'im like the white folks treat us," Zeke mumbled with a self-accusative laugh.

"Never thought of that," Sam admitted, frowning.

"Why you reckon he acts like a girl?" Fishbelly asked.

"Beats me," Tony said. "They say he can't help it."

"He could if he really *tried*," Zeke said.

"Mebbe he can't. . . . Mebbe it's like being black," Sam said.

"Aw naw! It ain't the same thing," Zeke said.

"But he ought to stay 'way from us," Fishbelly said.

"That's just what the white folks say about us," Sam told him.

They were silent, avoiding each other's eyes. Suddenly Fishbelly yelled with simulated couldn't-care-lessness:

"What the hell! Let's play ball!"

"Sure," Zeke said, running out onto the field.

"Bat 'em out, Fish!" Tony called, trotting to his position.

"Let her rip!" Sam shouted to blot out self-doubt.

"Here's one, Sam!" Fishbelly called.

His bat hooked a falling ball, *clack!*, and sent it high into the air. Waltzing from left to right, Sam caught it with one hand.

"Good!" Zeke judged.

"That was a big-league catch!" Tony said enviously.

Fielding the incoming ball, Fishbelly lined it toward Zeke and watched it taper off over Zeke's head and fall into Zeke's hand. But deep in him was an irritation that he could not stifle though he played frantically till sundown.

7

One autumn afternoon Fishbelly raced home excitedly from school and was lucky and happy to find his father at home and not, as usual, in the undertaking establishment. Before he dropped his strapped bundle of schoolbooks, he blurted:

"Papa, that farm fair's open Thursday afternoon and them that want to go can git off from school . . ."

"Thursday?" his father echoed. "I got two burials Thursday."

"Aw, Papa!" Fishbelly wailed in disappointment.

"Sorry, Fish. I can take you Friday."

"But Thursday's the only day for colored folks, Papa."

"Can't help it, Fish,' his father spoke matter-of-factly.

"Let me go with Zeke, Sam, and Tony. They going by *themselves*—"

"Naw!" his mother put her foot down. "Them boys is older'n you."

"Zeke and Tony's only four years older'n me. But Sam's my age. . . . Shucks, I ain't no baby; I won't git hurt."

"Well, Emma," his father began reflectively. "Fish could go with the others. Folks think he's older'n he really is 'cause he's so tall."

"Please, Mama."

"Depends on your papa," his mother said.

"Okay," his father consented. "Go along with the boys." His father paused. "But don't you go gitting in no trouble. Keep shy of them white folks. You don't know 'em and you'll rub 'em the wrong way, not even meaning to."

"Yessir, Papa," he promised solemnly. Then hurriedly: "I want to tell the gang . . ."

And before anyone could object, he darted shadowlike out of the house.

Next two days the school grounds seethed with the wild tales of two-headed dogs, of the fattest lady in the world, of a cow with alligator's paws, of a man with three legs, of a boy with a calf's face, of a dumb girl who miaowed like a kitten. . . .

Thursday afternoon the four of them made their way across town, keeping silently reserved while traversing the white business section. They had bought their tickets at school and, upon reaching the entrance to the fairgrounds, they halted, looking about uncertainly.

"Let's follow the crowd," Tony said.

"Can't you see where *we* go in?" Zeke spoke irritably, pointing to a ticket window over which a painted sign announced:

COLORED TICKETS

"But my ticket ain't *colored*," Sam protested with a bitter snicker, exhibiting a slip of paper. "It's *white*."

"Aw, Sam, shut up," Zeke scolded. "Ain't no time for race talk."

Surrendering their tickets to a cold-eyed white woman, they entered and moved among babbling throngs, listening to piping calliopes, blaring brass bands, and the twanging lilts of hurdy-gurdies. Wooden stalls sold popcorn, cold drinks, hot dogs, dolls, walking sticks, and taffy. They gazed at grunting dogs, placid cows, huge bulls, and other prize farm produce.

"Shucks, we can see this stuff any time," Zeke said.

"Let's skip this," Fishbelly suggested.

They passed jugglers, fortunetellers, patent-medicine vendors guaranteeing to cure any illness.

"Look," Sam whispered. "There's white folks here too."

"And they said this was *Colored* Folks' Day," Tony said.

"It is," Fishbelly tried to reason. "But white folks can come too, if they want to."

"But we can't come on *their* days," Tony pointed out.

"Hell, it's a *white* folks' world," Sam said cynically.

"There you go, talking *race*," Zeke chastised Sam.

"Just telling the truth," Sam defended himself.

"If Sam starts arguing race, I'm going home," Zeke said.

"You can't git away from race," Sam said and fell silent.

They came upon a girl show where five half-nude young white women danced swayingly in the waning light of the afternoon sun; a jazz band, composed of black men partially hidden by a burlap curtain, made rhythm jump. The boys paused at the edge of the crowd and gaped at shimmying white skin. A white barker singsonged, hinting at smut to be seen inside:

"Only ten minutes 'fore the greatest sex show on earth starts! It's daring, forbidden; it'll make you feel like sixteen again! Git your tickets now so you won't have to stand up!" The barker pointed leeringly to a quivering blonde whose red lips smiled wetly above the upturned faces. "See this Eve in all her natural glory!"

"Let's go in," Fishbelly said with suppressed excitement.

"Sure, man," Zeke conceded, entranced by undulating hips.

"Yeah," Tony agreed. "Let's git tickets."

"Nigger, can't you see that *sign?*" Sam spat.

"*What* sign?" Fishbelly asked.

"There . . . Under the ticket window, fool!" Sam gestured.

They looked; the sign declared:

NO COLORED

"Goddamn," Zeke cursed in a whisper and turned away.

"Why they call this Colored Folks' Day?" Fishbelly asked.

"White man don't want you looking at their naked women," Sam snickered. "And I wouldn't give a dime to see one neither."

They wandered off sullenly. Later, fortified with bags of hot buttered popcorn, they strolled amidst crowds until they chanced upon a black minstrel show in front of which two black-faced comedians and a tall, brown girl swayed and sang upon a wooden platform. A gimlet-eyed, hawk-faced white man droned through a megaphone:

"Come in, folks! See Jack and Mack and this long, brown drink of water! A cigar's a cigar, but this gal's a good smoke.

She's a red-hot mama who'll make a preacher lay his Bible down, make a wildcat squall! Come in for the black-and-tan treat of a lifetime!"

"Let's see this colored show," Sam said.

"Okay," Zeke assented.

They paid and entered a tent where a mostly black audience was ranged along wooden benches. Partly nude black girls danced trancelike to the beat of a three-piece jazz orchestra. Finally, the two stars of the show, Jack and Mack, who had been enticing the crowds outside, rushed in and a general dance took place with singing. Afterwards, Jack and Mack lingered in front of the burlap curtain. Their white-painted mouths occupied one third of their gleaming, blackened faces and they moved listlessly as they spoke, their eyes wandering boredly, as though they had done the routine so long they could enact it in their sleep.

Jack, *rubbing his hands together:* Well, if it ain't my old friend, Mack! Hi, man! Where you been all my life?

Mack, *with gusto:* Hi, man! I been working my tail off on a farm, planting hogs and killing beans.

Jack, *frowning:* Hunh? Ohhh! You mean planting *beans* and killing *hogs,* hunh?

Mack, *surprised:* Yeah, man! That's what I *said!*

Jack, *smiling, nodding:* Guess so. Now, what you going to do?

Mack, *eyes shining:* I'm buying me a bobtailed buggy and a rubber-tired horse.

Jack, *blinking:* What? Ohhh! You mean you going to buy a bobtailed *horse* and a rubber-tired *buggy?*

Mack: Hell, yeah, man. That's what I said, didn't I?

Jack, *staring:* Hunh-huh. Reckon so. Now, what you going to do?

Mack, *with ecstasy:* I'm taking a long drive into a yellow gal to meet a country.

Jack, *scratching his head:* Hunh? Ohhh! You mean you going to take a long drive into the country to meet a yellow gal?

Mack, *indignantly:* That's what I said! Man, stop trying to mess me up!

The boys laughed delightedly, sensing that the jokes consisted of inversions of simple meaning; they waited tensely on the edge of their bench.

Jack, *nodding:* You got a bobtailed horse and a rubber-tired buggy. And you done met a yellow gal in the country. Now, what you going to do?

Mack: I'm marrying a diamond ring and I'm asking that yellow gal to give me quick.

Jack, *bewildered:* Oh, yeeah.... You mean you giving the yellow gal a diamond ring and asking her to marry you quick?

Mack, *stomping his feet in anger:* Hell, that's what I said! Stop repeating my words!

Enthralled, the boys sat through a second show. When they emerged, it was night.

"Man, that show was cool," Sam said, wagging his head.

"It was crazy," Zeke said.

"We better be gitting home," Tony advised.

"Naw, man. Not yit," Fishbelly begged.

They drifted a few hundred yards and came across another sideshow whose banner proclaimed:

HIT THE NIGGER HEAD
Three baseballs for 50¢

They pushed their way delicately into a packed, shouting mass of white men and saw, about fifty feet behind a wooden barrier, a black man's head protruding from a hole in the thick canvas. Trembling gas flares made the whites of the man's eyes gleam and gave his flashing white teeth a grisly grin. A barker shouted:

"Come on, folks, and hit the nigger! He's chained and can't run! His skull's iron and his head's solid rock! Here's a chance to hit a nigger like you really want to hit 'im! Buy a bargain:

42

three big-league baseballs, all genuine, for fifty cents! Who wants to hit the nigger!"

Fishbelly gaped at the "nigger" head nightmarishly spotlighted by gas flares. A tight-lipped white man handed up fifty cents, saying:

"I'm going to kill that nigger."

"Here you are, sir." The barker handed down three baseballs.

The white man approached the barrier, placed two of his balls upon it and, holding the third ball in his right hand, backed off, the crowd parting willingly to give him room.

"Knock that nigger's brains out!" An eager shout.

"I'll pay for his funeral!" Laughing philanthropy.

The white man wound up, ran forward, hurled the ball with all his strength, whizzing it toward the "nigger" head, which ducked easily to one side. The ball thumped whammingly against canvas.

A sighing laugh swept the watching crowd.

"Just wait; I'll kill that black sonofabitch," the white man resolved as he snatched his second ball.

"That's what I'm here for!" the "nigger" head, showing a wide, white grin, shouted from the canvas in a high-pitched, yet defiant voice. "Ha, ha! Hit me, white man!"

Fishbelly quivered. He had never heard a black man speak to a white man in so challenging a tone, yet that tone had a certain pathos, for the body belonging to it was chained to the hole in the canvas.

The white man stared malevolently at the grinning black face, devising means of attack. Fishbelly's stomach tautened as he watched the white man aim carefully and let go the ball; the black face edged sideways, letting the ball thud dully against canvas. The crowd crowed with throaty, sadistic laughter.

"Ha, ha! Hit me, white man!" the "nigger" head called invitingly.

"I'll kill you," the man swore, taking up his last ball. Fixedly, the man stared at the "nigger" head, then feinted, and the elusive "nigger" head bobbed in false response; next came a motion so swift that Fishbelly's eyes could scarcely follow it. The white man's right arm lashed forward, straight from the shoulder, without any wind-up, and the ball zipped away. The "nigger" head veered out of range and the ball landed against canvas, *plop!*

"Goddammit, how did I miss 'im?" the white man asked shame-facedly.

"Ha, ha! Oh, the white man, he miss!" the "nigger" head howled.

"Wouldn't let folks do that to me," Fishbelly muttered.

"Me neither," Sam said.

"Hell, that guy's making his living," Zeke said.

"I'd starve 'fore I'd make it that way," Tony said.

"White foks can't respect you when they can throw balls at you like that," Sam said.

"Awright, now. No goddamn *race* talk," Zeke ruled.

Another white man tossed three balls at the "nigger" head and missed. Fishbelly felt that he had either to turn away from that grinning black face, or, like the white man, throw something at it. That obscene black face was his own face and, to quell the war in his heart, he had either to reject it in hate or accept it in love. It was easier to hate that degraded black face than to love it.

"I'm going to try to hit 'im," Fishbelly said, suddenly finding release for his rising tension.

"Yeah, let's try," Tony dared to join him.

"I want to try too," Zeke said in a scared voice.

"Goddammit, I ain't in this," Sam said, turning away.

Fishbelly, Zeke, and Tony bought three baseballs each and waited patiently for their turn at the "nigger" head.

"Niggers want to hit the nigger!" Sadistic anticipation.

"Niggers ought to be able to hit niggers!" Snickered logic.

Embarrassed, Fishbelly wanted to surrender his balls and leave, but that would have made him even more ashamed. Zeke was the first to try, aiming carefully, but missing with his three pitches. He stepped aside, avoiding the watching, grinning white men. Fishbelly hurled his three balls nervously and all went wide of the ever-dodging "nigger" head target.

"Hit me, nigger!" the "nigger" head hollered, grinning.

"I'm going to kill that nigger," Tony pledged and faced the barrier.

A potbellied white man chanted in a lion tamer's voice:

"Hep, hep, hep, nigger!"

Tony flinched, then feinted at the "nigger" head, which bobbed. He threw.

"Hep, hep, hep, nigger!" the lion tamer sang.

Tony missed.

"Niggers can't hit the nigger!" Amused observation.

Hating the commenting voices, Tony threw his second ball without any wind-up.

"Hep, hep, hep, nigger!" the lion tamer sounded.

Tony's second ball was off the mark. Tony, without pausing, hating himself and the white men and the "nigger" head, let go with his last ball.

"Hep, hep, hep, nigger!" the lion tamer sped the ball on its way and it smacked, bip!, into the grinning mouth of the "nigger" head, bouncing high into the flaring gaslight.

The crowd went crazed with glee.

"HEP! HEP! HEP!" the lion tamer chortled.

"The nigger hit the nigger!" An orgiastic cheer.

"I hit you!" Tony sang in frenzy, glaring at the "nigger" head, whose mouth was bloody.

"You didn't hurt me, nigger!" the "nigger" head yelled defiantly through puffed lips.

"I'll hit you again!" Tony raged, searching his pockets for money.

"Naw," Zeke whispered. "Let's go!"

"As long as you can hit that nigger, I'll buy you all the balls you want, nigger," the lion tamer offered.

"Nawsir," Tony mumbled, suddenly abashed.

"Niggers don't want to 'hep' no more," the lion tamer said sadly.

"Come on, you-all," Sam begged.

They walked for ten minutes before anyone spoke.

"I hit that sonofabitch," Tony said tensely.

They continued without speaking for a long time.

"It's gitting late," Sam informed them.

"Yeah. We better go," Tony said.

They found a "FOR-COLORED" gate and struck out for the Black Belt.

"Look!" Fishbelly pointed toward cars parked in a dark field. "Circus folks live in them trailers."

45

"Let's see 'em," Zeke said.

"Be careful, man," Sam said. "Mebbe somebody's around."

"Naw. They all still at the shows," Zeke said.

They wove in and out among the darkened trailers and amidst clothes drying on improvised lines.

"Hello!" A feminine voice sounded softly in the gloam.

They halted. The white woman whom they had seen upon the platform of the girl show was smiling at them out of the shadows.

"Looking for something special?" the woman asked.

"No'm," Zeke breathed.

"You boys got any money?" the woman asked.

They did not reply.

"Come closer. Don't be afraid. I'll take you in for five dollars apiece," she said, unbuttoning her blouse and baring her big white breasts in the half-light.

"Naw!" Sam exploded and ran.

Zeke, Fishbelly, and Tony stood transfixed, then whirled and followed Sam. When they were far beyond the trailers, Zeke called out in panic:

"Hey, you-all, *stop!*"

"Hell, naw! Let's git out of here!" Fishbelly panted.

"STOP!" Zeke warned with a scream. "If a white man see us running like this, he's going to think something's wrong, sure as hell!"

"You so right," Tony sighed, slackening his pace to a walk.

"Okay," Fishbelly panted, slowing.

Sam's dark figure flitted ahead in the night.

"SAM!" Zeke yelled. "WAIT!"

Sam braked his speed and they overtook him.

"Goddamn, man! That sure was lynch-bait!" Sam burst out.

"Man, I can't dig these white folks," Zeke said, shaking his head.

"Never saw a white woman do that before," Fishbelly said.

"I couldn't hardly breathe when she opened her dress," Tony said.

"She wasn't no different from that nigger who let you throw balls at 'im," Sam said.

"Everybody, stop!" Fishbelly ordered. "Lissen: say nothing

about that white woman, see? Our folks'll never let us out again."

"You right," Zeke said. "My papa'd have a fit."

Pledging secrecy, they walked homeward. They paused at a crossroads where they had to separate.

"That woman scared the daylight out of me," Zeke confessed.

"And they kill us for sluts like that," Sam said.

"I'm sorry I went to that damned fair," Tony said.

"Me too," Fishbelly said. "But say *nothing*, hear?"

"Yeah, man. I dig you."

"Sure, man. Folks wouldn't understand."

"Both *colored* and *white'd* think we bothered the woman."

Fishbelly watched his friends leave, then he remembered too late that they had been too nervous to say good-by. A cold sweat covered his skin as he walked with downcast face through the hot dark.

8

"I wonder," Fishbelly's father said one evening as he rose from the dinner table, "just how much of a man Fish is. . . ."

Fishbelly lifted his head sharply, mopping his mouth with his napkin.

"What you mean, Papa?"

His father lit a cigar, puffed, looking pensively ahead. His mother sat with lowered eyes, trying to repress a smile.

"Tyree, Fish's too young for that," she said.

"Too young for *what?*" Fishbelly demanded. "What you-all talking about?"

"Dead folks," his father said brutally.

"I ain't scared of no dead folks or ghosts," Fishbelly said.

"You sure?" his father asked.

"You ever saw me scared?"

"Naw. For a fact, I never did," his father said.

"What you want me to do?" he asked, looking from father to mother.

"Well, mebbe I'll try you, son," his father said. "Me and Emma and Jim's going to Jackson for the Undertakers' Convention tomorrow. Jake's sick and Guke's off on vacation. Nobody's on duty tomorrow night. Now, I was wondering if you and Sam and Tony and Zeke'd like to stay up all night and look after things in the 'shop'?"

"Sure, Papa. What do we do?" He tingled with excitement.

"Just answer the phone and git in touch with Dr. Bruce; that's all."

"There going to be any bodies there, Papa?" Fishbelly asked.

"Not 'less somebody hauls off and dies and is brought in," his father said. "Would that scare you?"

"Nawsir, Papa. You want me to ask the boys?"

"Awright," his father said. "But you'll have to stay up all night and 'tend to the phone."

"Sure. That ain't nothing, Papa."

Elated, he sped through the streets, spreading the news of the adventure. Hot diggity dog . . . They'd stay up all night; they'd have Coca-Cola, ham sandwiches, candy bars, a thermos of hot coffee, a pack of playing cards, and a package of cigarettes. . . .

Next afternoon, directly after lunch, the boys were conveyed to the undertaking establishment.

"Anything you boys think you'll need?" Fishbelly's father asked.

"Nawsir, Mr. Tucker," Sam said.

"This is a picnic," Fishbelly gloated.

"Now, tell me, who's scared of ghosts?" Fishbelly's father asked.

"Not me!" they chorused.

"I say you boys ought to stay in the basement. It's cool and it's right under the office and you can hear the phone ringing," Fishbelly's father told them.

"Yessir, Mr. Tucker," Zeke said.

Alone, they fell upon the ham sandwiches, devoured the candy bars, and drank the Coca-Cola. They sat about the office desk, playing blackjack.

"Suppose a dead man was sent in?" Sam asked suddenly.

"That wouldn't be nothing," Fishbelly said, shrugging.

"I'd like to see one," Zeke mused. "I ain't never been close to no dead folks. You ever touch one, Fish?"

"Sure. Lots of times," Fishbelly said, flipping down a card.

"What it feel like?" Sam asked.

"Cold meat. Just cold meat, that's all. His hand was just like yours or mine, only cold . . ."

"Give me a cigarette," Tony said. He was nervous.

"Let's go down to the basement," Fishbelly suggested.

The basement was cooled by a draft blowing through an opened window high up in the front wall; it framed a slice of the night street and they could see passers-by floating along the sidewalk above. Beyond, and in the background, the faint sheen of a gaslight drenched the pavement. Along the rear wall was a long white table upon which blood was drained from dead bodies. Zeke gingerly inspected the sinks, rubber tubing, gravity bottles, and sniffed the stinging odor that seemed to cling to the very walls.

"Gee, my eyes burn," Zeke complained.

"Mine's watering," Sam said, wiping his eyes.

"That's that formaldehyde; it's strong," Fishbelly told them.

"Fish," Zeke began, "just what do Jim do to the dead folks?"

Fishbelly pursed his lips and looked solemn.

"Papa don't want me to talk about that stuff," he said. "It's secret."

"Aw hell, man. You can tell *us*," Tony said.

"Sure," Sam said. "We ain't going to tell nobody."

"Folks got crazy ideas about what happens in here," Fishbelly explained, laughing. "Hell, it's simple. Jim drains the blood out of 'em and puts formaldehyde in 'em; that's all. You can git a man ready to go into the ground in less'n an hour. But the hard part's something nobody thinks about. Jim's always cussing 'cause he can't make dead folks look like they *ought* to look and—"

"What you mean?" Tony asked.

"Man, when you take their blood out 'em and put formaldehyde in 'em, they just *won't* look right sometimes. Jim asks for the dead man's picture and he keeps patting and shaping the dead man's face, trying to make it look like that picture, and most times he just can't make that dead bastard like that picture. Then the dead man's wife'll come in and say: 'That ain't Bob. He didn't look like that. . . .' Then Jim has to work on 'im some more."

"But how come Jim can't make 'em look right?" Sam asked.

"'Cause the flesh gits soft," Fishbelly explained. "And sometimes that formaldehyde makes 'em look too *light*. Once Jim embalmed a real black nigger and he got waxy and rosy, like an Indian, and the family wouldn't have 'im. Said he was somebody else. Jim had to *paint* that nigger black 'fore the family'd take 'im." Fishbelly examined the faces around him. "Now, take Tony," Fishbelly pointed. "Tony's face's too thin. Tony'll *never* look right dead. He'll be either too thin or too fat. Tony's got the kind of face that'd make a undertaker drink a quart of whiskey—"

"Stop talking about my face!" Tony yelled, laughing with serious eyes.

"Tell us some more," Zeke begged.

"There's that stuff about gas in the stomach," Fishbelly said. "Sometimes so much gas gits in a dead man's belly that he sits up straight and hollers!"

"*Stop!* That's enough," Zeke said.

"Old Zeke's scared and I'm glad," Sam sang.

They were silent, their eyes wandering about the room. Sam walked over to the high window and looked out. The headlights of a passing car gleamed and vanished. Fishbelly joined Sam and said:

"We can see folks passing and they can't see us."

Tony and Zeke grouped themselves about Fishbelly and Sam, their black faces lifted upward.

"Look," Zeke called softly. "Here comes a gal."

"Lawd, she's got a pair of legs!"

"Her hips rock and roll like jelly!"

"Watch me," Zeke warned them.

Zeke opened his lips and sucked in a chestful of air, and,

when the girl's legs were about a foot from Zeke's head, Zeke screamed:

"BAAAAAAAAAAAAAAAAW!"

"Ouuuuuuuuunw!" the girl yelped, jumping as though she had been goosed. She stopped, twisted about and clapped both of her hands protectingly between her thighs. For a split second she was frozen, then she broke into a wild run.

Hilarity galvanized the boys: Fishbelly drummed his fists against the wall; Sam stomped in a frenzy of mirth; Zeke and Tony embraced each other and danced, howling.

"We made her jump out of her skin!"

"We scared that poor *black* gal *white!*"

"Lawd, I bet a million dollars her pants is wet!"

When their laughter had simmered down, Fishbelly said:

"Let's wait for another one."

"Yeah. Yeah."

They stared silently upward, their hearts thumping heavily, their senses enthralled by the fact that they could, with an expulsion of breath, catapult people out of stances of normality and into fearful frenzy.

"Lissen," Zeke said. "When we see another one, let's all holler at the same time, see? I'll count: one, two, *three. Then* we *go.*"

"Yeah. Yeah."

"Anybody coming?"

"Naw . . . The street's empty," Zeke said.

"How come folks so scared?" Sam asked.

"Beats me," Tony said.

"Say, turn out the light," Zeke suggested.

"Sure." Fishbelly complied by switching out the electric bulb, plunging the basement into darkness.

"What time is it?"

"Must be after one. . . . Most folks in bed now," Tony sighed.

"You-all sleepy?" Fishbelly asked.

"Hell, naw. Man, I could stay up all night scaring folks."

"Shh . . . somebody's coming!"

"It's a woman."

"Say, she *white*. What she doing out here amongst niggers?"

"Mebbe we oughtn't scare her, hunh?"

"How come? She just like the other one, ain't she?"

The woman came forward in the yellow mist of the gas lamp, her heels going *clackclackclack* on the sidewalk; finally she was so close that they could see her face.

"She young, about twenty. . ."

"I bet a fat man she's scared to death awready."

"One," Zeke whispered.

They began sucking air into their lungs.

"Two," Zeke intoned softly.

Their chests felt like taut balloons.

"Three!"

"BAAAAAAAAAAAAAAAW!"

The woman jerked stock-still, her hands fluttering; then she gave a piercing, frantic scream that was followed by a breathless, orgiastic whimpering that died to plaintive moaning. Her legs doubled, her body teetering and sinking slowly to the pavement. The boys stared hypnotically at the woman's face, which was like a white sheet of paper in the dark street. Zeke simpered and fell silent. The woman rolled over on her back and her body began to form an arc from head to heels, rigid, curved.

"What she doing?"

"Don't know."

"Damn . . . Hope she ain't dying or something."

The woman's arched buttocks jerked in thrusting, pelvic movements that began slowly and increased in momentum until they reached a climax. Then there was deep sighs and the convulsive movements gradually abated, tapering off. The woman's body now lay flat upon the pavement.

"She acting like she in bed with a man," Zeke said.

"Reckon we ought to call somebody?"

"Hell, naw! They'll say we raped her or something."

"Hope she ain't dead. . . ."

"I'm pulling down this window," Fishbelly whispered in terror, mounting a chair and lowering the window, leaving an inch of space through which he could peep at the woman.

"Suppose she tells the police and they come here?"

"Say, we ought to git out of here."

"Hell, naw! Running now's crazy! We stay and if anybody

asks us anything, we don't know *nothing,* see?"

The woman stirred, then lifted her head and looked about with a wan face, supporting her body upon an elbow. She rose unsteadily and began whimpering again, walking forward, looked apprehensively over her shoulder.

"Jeeeeesus," Zeke whispered.

"Let's don't scare no more folks," Sam said.

"Come on. Let's get upstairs," Fishbelly said.

He shut the window. They groped in the dark, filled with a sense of another world, an invisible, powerful world stretching out there in the silent night—a *white* world.

"Reckon she'll tell?" Tony asked in a scared voice.

"What could she say?"

"Hell, she can say she was raped."

They entered the office and stood in the dark.

Brriiiinnnnnnnnng!

The phone's metallic ringing shattered the dark and the boys' muscles grew stiff. They could hear one another's breathing.

Brrriiiinnnnnnnnnnng!

"Oh Lawd, I got to answer," Fishbelly whispered stickily.

"Naw, naw," Zeke objected with fury.

"Don't touch that phone," Tony commanded.

Brriiiiinnnnnng! Brrriiiiiiinnnnng!

"I got to answer," Fishbelly whined.

"Goddamn," Zeke cursed. "Mebbe it's the police."

"Mebbe somebody's dead," Fishbelly said, groping his way to the phone. His hand found the receiver and lifted it from the hook. "Hello," he spoke meekly.

"That you, Fish?" his father's voice hummed over the wire.

"Hi, Papa." He covered the transmitter with his palm and whispered to the boys: "It's Papa . . ."

"Everything awright, Fish?"

"Sure, Papa."

"Any phone calls?"

"Nawsir."

"You boys sleepy?"

"Nawsir, Papa. Everything's fine."

"Lissen, Fish. We starting out from Jackson right now. We ought to git in about eight, see?"

"Yessir."

"What's the matter, Fish? You sound kind of scared."

"Nawsir. We awright."

"Ha, ha! You-all see any ghosts around there?"

"Nawsir, Papa."

"Good-by, Fish."

"Good-by, Papa."

He hung up and turned to his friends in the dark.

"Papa asked if we saw any ghosts and I told 'im, 'Naw.'"

"But we *did* see ghosts," Zeke said with a protesting laugh.

"That white woman was one hell of a ghost," Tony mumbled.

They sat quietly until streaks of daylight began to filter through at the edges of the window shades.

"Wonder what happened to that woman?" Zeke asked.

"I don't want to know," Fishbelly said.

"Me neither," Sam said.

"I want to forget that woman," Fishbelly sighed.

"Me too," Tony said.

9

His first serious illness descended upon him without warning. One winter afternoon while he was lolling at his desk in school, an acute constriction lodged itself in his throat and rendered him almost speechless. He complained timidly to his teacher, old, fat, black Mrs. Morrison, and asked to go home. She sent him brusquely back to his seat, telling him that the class would soon be dismissed. Fuming, he fought against vertigo, feeling his body growing swiftly hot and damp. Then the barnlike classroom, heated by a potbellied, red-glowing stove, began to spin floatingly. He grasped the edge of his nicked desk, fearing that he was going out like a light. Mrs.

Morrison was conducting a geography lesson about Lapland, calling first upon one pupil and then another to read a passage. Blurred reindeer herds in bright, snowy forests swam before his aching eyes, then Mrs. Morrison's shrill soprano voice rasped at him as from out of a dream:

"Fish, take up where Ethel left off!"

"Yessum," he mumbled vaguely.

His effort to rise was too much and he slumped back into his seat and the room turned faster. His glazed eyes singled out the black stovepipe running along the ceiling above Mrs. Morrison's head and he had the illusion that she had risen, had seized that stovepipe and was swinging it at him. Hunching his shoulders, he leaped up, ducking to dodge the imaginary blow.

"Don't hit me, ma'am!" he exclaimed thickly.

A burst of laughter leaped about him, compounding his confusion. He glared dully, still watching Mrs. Morrison advancing and retreating, brandishing the stovepipe. The grinning teeth in the roomful of black faces bewildered him. Only partially conscious, he sensed that his classmates thought that he was clowning, sassing the teacher. He slid into his seat and a moment later Mrs. Morrison's two hundred, black-skinned pounds stood belligerently before him.

"Boy, what did you say?"

It was all so unreal that he grinned foolishly, petitioning absolution with a sickly smile, feeling sweat on his skin and an ache in the very marrow of his bones.

"I-I ain't d-done nothing. Don't hit me," he stammered.

Shrill laughter filled the classroom.

"I dare you to say that again," Mrs. Morrison said, leveling a forefinger at him.

Stupor robbed him of speech and his lolling posture made him appear so ludicrous that his classmates howled gleefully.

"Stand up, boy!" Mrs. Morrison barked, gesturing wildly.

He shrank, shielding his face with his hands. The bedlam in the room mounted.

"Boy, I said stand up!" Mrs. Morrison commanded.

He could not move. Mrs. Morrison grabbed him and yanked him to his feet and he swayed in her grip, wriggling like a rag doll. His classmates began to clamor.

"Watch for her right, Fish!"

"Put up your left, Fish!"

"Are you going to behave or must I whip you?" Mrs. Morrison asked.

He shook his head, trying to signal his helplessness.

"Answer me, boy!"

He sagged downward and half dragged fat Mrs. Morrison with him. Sweat popped on his pinched, black face.

"Miz Morrison, I think he sick," a black girl whispered.

The room fell silent. Fishbelly recalled only fragments of reality after that: strange hands helping him out into the fresh air; his stumbling homeward with Zeke at his side; his being put to bed; his mother's weeping; his father's frowning black face; the doctor's saying that he had pneumonia. . . . Then came a blackout from which he emerged to submit to injections of drugs and to taste acrid powders on his tongue which he washed down a parched throat with hot lemon tea.

He lay one midnight in a swamp of fever, staring vacantly, panting through cracked lips. He was suddenly rigid with terror, for in a corner of his room stood a giant, magically luminous spider whose thin, frizzly legs curved downward into blackness, its baglike body seemingly filled with a dangerous fluid held precariously in a delicate, transparent membrane. Stricken, he watched the spider's roving, glowing eyes and saw the long, fuzzy legs beginning to move and the trembling, sacklike body, weighted with liquid, inching implacably forward, heading for him.

"Naw," he moaned in despair.

On it came and its two eyes, pools of burning phosphorous, widened and glared directly into his own.

"NAW!" he screamed, hypnotized by his own projected horrors.

In a flicking movement the spider was suspended above him and he saw the quickness of its breathing in the pulsing of its fragile membrane. Through the spider's gaping mouth he glimpsed nauseous vistas of thin, red teeth. . . .

"NAW! NAW!" he screamed again and again.

Light blazed and his parents stood beside him. He rolled his eyes, seeking the vile projection, catching fading vestiges of an after-image. He felt his mother's cool, soft palm upon his damp forehead.

"Go to sleep, son," she said.

"Poor tyke," his father mumbled. "He really sick."

"You out of your head with fever," his mother sighed.

She laved his hot limbs in alcohol diluted with tepid water and drying him with a fuzzy towel, tucked him securely in bed.

"That spider," he breathed.

"Shh . . . Try to sleep," she whispered.

Next morning he awakened listlessly. His parents were still asleep. Some unconscious impulse made him lift his head sharply and look at the window, through which streamed a gray dawn. Then Tony was there, hoisting himself onto the sill and into the room. His lips parted in anger as Tony grimaced at him and opened a drawer of his dresser and began pulling out his nylon shirts—shirts so white that Tony had teasingly called him "white boy" . . .

"I'm taking these," Tony said, his mouth twisting scornfully, tauntingly. "Black sissy boy wearing white shirts . . ."

"Don't you touch 'em!" he shouted. "Put 'em back!"

He rolled from bed and stumbled weakly across the room, flaying his arms clumsily, trying to clout a shadowy Tony. His mother was suddenly beside him and he looked at her anxious face, then at a strangely dissolving Tony whose ghostly arms overflowed with heaps of diaphanous nylon.

"Tyree!" his mother called. "Come and help me with Fish!"

They pulled his resisting body back to bed.

"Don't let Tony take my shirts!" he wailed heartbrokenly.

"Tony ain't here, Fish," his father soothed him. "Be quiet. You going to be awright." He turned to his wife. "Better call Doc again."

"Doc said the fever'd last for a spell," she sighed.

His parents' solidity anchored him again in reality; he closed his eyes and turned his face to the wall, unmindful of his shirts.

That afternoon he still thrashed in fever. Feeling a crawling sensation on the back of his left hand, he rubbed it idly against the bedcovers. An itching of the back of that hand set in and he lifted it and was startled to see a huge fly poised on the skin. He brushed at it, but it clung strangely. With the fingers of his right hand, he scratched to dislodge it, but, in doing so, he discovered that there were now *two* flies. . . . He clawed at them only to find that the back of his left hand was studded with black flies adhering tenaciously, their tiny feet sunk into his flesh. His right hand, too, swarmed with clusters of them. He shuddered, nervously scraping his fingers first down the length of one arm and then the other, but failing to remove them. He sat up in bed, whimpering, tugging at his hot flesh; then to his dismay the skin of his hands and arms began to peel, shredding off in long, shriveled strips like black rubber, leaving his flesh a gleaming, raw red. The dreadful illusion extended itself and there appeared on the raw red flesh clouds of flies that could not be budged. Panting, he slapped his hands frenziedly against his arms, legs, and chest; the flies remained glued to his bloody, vulnerable flesh and he closed his eyes and did not stop shouting until he felt his mother's arms about him. Quietened, he lay trembling. Furtively, he glanced at his hands: the skin was black, smooth, intact, free of flies. . . . He sighed and closed his eyes in sleep.

His fever abated slowly and within a week his room had shed its alien aspect; and the sun now sparkled upon the windowpanes with no overtones of the sinister. Slumbering infantile traits were reawakened in him when his mother spoke to him in low tones, beseeching him to eat, even feeding him brimming spoonfuls of chicken broth and anxiously watching him swallow. Gradually he began to relish his food and a returning tingle in his muscles made him want to run in the sun and feel wind stinging his cheeks. He convalesced propped against pillows, reading, or staring at daydreams in which he was always the dominant actor. Now that he was better, not only did his mother stop her doting, but she absented herself for hours to do work for the Mount Olivet Baptist Church.

"Don't leave me," he wheedled. "I want you here."

"Lots of folks is much sicker'n you, son," she explained. "Me working for the church is how I thank Jesus for healing you."

He sulked, silent, jealous of Jesus. . . .

During his mother's absence one afternoon a gnawing rumble was in his stomach—an aching hunger that only a boy could have who had been on a diet for ten days. Mama or no Mama, he was going to eat. He slid from bed and walked into the kitchen on wobbly legs, feeling a bit dizzy. On the stove an iron pot of beef soup simmered, emitting odors of onions, tomatoes, and celery, fogging the kitchen windows with moisture. He yearned for soup, but preparing a plateful was too troublesome. He searched for bread or fruit. The coal stove throbbed and the eyes set in the lid glimmered red. In the top warmer he saw the jutting end of a tin pan. Ah, corn bread ... He'd get a hunk of that bread and eat it in bed. His pajamas bagged about his gaunt twelve-year-old body as he dragged a chair to the stove, climbed weakly upon it, and reached for the tip of the pan. It was beyond his fingers. Stretching, he leaned farther forward, his face feeling waves of quivering heat waft up from the glowing lid. Prompted by an intuition of danger, he hesitated. Though the tip of the tin pan was an inch beyond his finger tips, it was a mile away. His knees felt weak and he began to sweat. Tiptoeing on the sheerest edge of the chair, he spanned his body up and across the sizzling stove; and, just as his fingers touched the tip of the pan, he felt the chair sliding from under him and he crashed upon the seething lid, the right side of his neck falling squarely upon sweltering metal, and he could hear, as the chair smashed against the floor, a frying crackle as his neck, like a pork chop in a red-hot, ungreased skillet, stuck itself to the sizzling iron. The shock paralyzed him, rendered him mute. Then his body winced against a surging ocean of searing fire and he gulped air into his lungs and screamed. He had the sensation that someone had pinned him onto the blazing lid; prodded by reflex, he rolled from the stove to the floor, engulfed by a tide of agony. He leaped up in a galvanic posture of protest and screamed so continuously that it was one uninterrupted expulsion of breath. Maddened by stabbing bolts of pain, he ran, barefooted and in his pajamas, out into the sleet-covered street, his hands wildly beating the wintry air, his lungs emptying in shrill cries.

Neighbors led him back into the house and put him to bed, where he lay moaning and walling his eyes, unable to speak, choked with a gag of solid, radiating hurt. It was not until two hours later that he could tell them that he was not delirious, that he had fallen upon the stove and burned himself. The family doctor entered the house a moment after Fishbelly's mother, who had been hastily called, returned. The burn was serious and the doctor silently despaired. Two days later the doctor told Tyree and Emma that had the burns gone a quarter of an inch deeper, he could not have saved the boy.

Fishbelly now felt justified in burrowing himself into his mother; and she, wallowing in guilt, let him. The comfort he drew from her was sensual in its intensity, and it formed the pattern of what he was to demand later in life from women. When he was a man and in distress, he would have to have them, but his need of them would be limited, localized, focused toward obtaining release, solace; and then he would be gone to seek his peculiar, singular destiny, lonely but affable, cold but smiling, and strongly insulated against abiding relationships.

10

Recess. The schoolyard rang with shouts. Black boys swarmed over dusty ground. Zeke had snatched a little boy's cap and was running with it, waving it teasingly aloft to provoke laughter at its checkered pattern of yellow and black. The six-year-old owner of the cap was weeping and there were protests rising from some of the boys.

"Aw, Zeke, give 'im back his cap!" Fishbelly called.

"Leave that little snot alone, Zeke!" Sam chided.

"Come and git it!" Zeke yelled, sprinting across the yard, slipping past grasping fingers.

Fishbelly joined the chase. As he ran he glimpsed, at the far end of the schoolyard, Mr. Davis, Sam's father—a short, thin, dour man who lived a few doors from his house. He watched Mr. Davis take Sam and lead him hurriedly away. Puzzled, Fishbelly stared. Mebbe somebody's sick, he thought. He followed Zeke's trailing pursuers, then slowed, seeing Zeke's father, Mr. Jordan, yell and beckon to his son. Zeke ran toward his father and Fishbelly saw Mr. Jordan seize Zeke's hand and shove him into a car whose door was open. "What's wrong?" he asked himself aloud, watching Mr. Jordan's car speed forward. He heard a boy shout:

"Zeke's done took the cap!"

"Naw! There 'tis!"

Zeke tossed the cap out of the car as the car turned a corner.

"Bet Zeke's old man's going to beat 'im about something," a boy observed.

Fishbelly solemnly retrieved the cap from the dust and flung it to its owner. He had just seen two of his friends taken from the schoolyard by their parents. "What's happened?" he asked himself again. Chatting and winded, the boys moved toward the school entrance. Then Fishbelly was startled to see his father rushing toward him and behind his father was the family car parked at the curb, the door open, the motor running. . . .

"Hi, Papa! What's the matter?"

Wordlessly, his father grasped his arm and jerked him forward. "Come on!"

"But what's the *matter,* Papa?"

"Shut up and come on!"

His father pushed him ahead, but he twisted around.

"What's happening?"

"GAWDDAMMIT, GIT INSIDE, WILL YOU?" his father shouted hysterically, ramming him brutally through the car door.

Too stunned to protest, he saw his classmates looking at him in astonishment. His father, face sweaty, eyes bloodshot, leaped behind the steering wheel, flung the gear into first as his foot stomped upon the clutch and the car lurched forward, throwing Fishbelly against the back seat so hard that his breath was knocked out of him. Then he saw his father's right hand dart like a snake runing for its life and lift a gun from the seat and lay it across his lap; he put the car into second, shooting past red lights. Fishbelly could taste the brass savor of danger upon his dry tongue, and, because he did not know what that danger was, it became all-embracing. He stifled an impulse to weep and was surprised that he could master his emotions.

"Papa, what—?"

"When I ask you to do something," his father rasped, "do it! And don't stand like a fool asking, 'Why?' Hear?"

"Yessir. B-but what's w-wrong?"

The car sped for minutes in silence.

"There's trouble." His father was terse. "I'll tell you about it."

Distant pistol shots cracked dryly through the summer air.

"Git on the *floor,* son!" his father ordered.

"But, Papa—"

His father's right hand snatched him and jammed his head against the floor. He lay there, hearing more shots. He lifted his head.

"Tell me, Papa . . . What's happening?" he whimpered.

"It's a race fight and I'm trying to git you home, son."

"Race?"

"Yeah. A riot, son. It's the *white* folks . . ."

The speeding car tires whirred over asphalt and goosepimples prickled on his skin. *The white folks . . .* The phrase rang in his mind like a black bell sounding. He had long heard of the terror that white people meted out to black people, but this was the first time in his life that he was fleeing before that terror.

"Some of our folks done something wrong, Papa?" he asked, accepting guilt before he knew the facts.

"Looks like it," his father mumbled.

Well, whatever happened, he would stick by his father and die at his side, if necessary. The thought made a sense of bitter exultation rise in him as he strained his ears for the sound of more shots. Then he was asking himself why were they running instead of fighting? Pity for his father dawned in him. One either fought or one surrendered. But he and his father were running. . . . He swallowed a lump of shame in his throat.

"I got to git you home," his father said huskily, turning the steering wheel sharply and cementing Fishbelly against the side of the car.

"Where Mama?"

"She home," his father breathed.

He felt that his guts wanted to heave themselves up as there flashed in him a picture of thousands of black people running. The car tires crunched gravel, then a sharp bump told him that they had entered the driveway of his home.

"We made it," his father sighed. "We together, no matter what happens."

Yeah, one ran and was glad to be safe! More shots sounded and he had a yearning to be where those shots were. . . . The car stopped and his father opened the door.

"Git into the house, son."

He tumbled out, expecting to see white faces peering over the top of the fence; but the yard was quiet, empty.

"Fish, come on!" his mother was calling.

She stood on the back steps, her face bloated with fear. And, as he neared her, he rejected her. Were these scared and trembling people his parents? He was more afraid of them than he was of the white people. Suddenly he saw his parents as he felt and thought that the white people saw them and he felt toward them some of the contempt that the white people felt for them. When he reached his mother, she folded him in her arms and he suffered it, but he wanted to shrink from her as though from something unclean. Yet he knew that he could never put what he was feeling into words.

"Thank Gawd," his mother sobbed.

"Git inside," his father hissed, running forward, gun in hand.

Wordlessly, they entered the kitchen. His father shut and locked the door while his mother lowered the window shades. Fishbelly could hear his father's heavy breathing. His mother sat at the table, dabbing her eyes with a handkerchief. More shots rang out and there was the sound of cars roaring past in the street.

"They want blood," his father muttered, gripping his gun.

"Papa, what happened?" he asked for the third time.

"Keep quiet and let Papa handle things," his mother cautioned.

"I'll tell you later, son," his father said. Then he whirled and stared at his son, blurting: "You twelve years old and it's time you know! Lissen, Fish: NEVER LOOK AT A WHITE WOMAN! YOU HEAR?"

"A *white* woman?" he asked softly, wonderingly.

"Tyree, don't talk to 'im like that," his mother protested.

"He's old enough to *die,* so he's old enough to *know!*" his father whispered fiercely. "I should've talked to 'im about this a long time ago. Sooner he knows, the better."

"Tyree, *later,*" his mother wailed. "He's just a *child*—"

"In white folks' eyes he's a *man!*" his father thundered, then paused, swallowing. "Emma, you got to let me do this *my* way. I'm responsible for Fish. He's got to *know!*"

Fishbelly felt a creepy sensation grip his skull. This was a ceremony. He did not think it; he felt it, knew it. He was being baptized, initiated; he was moving along the steep, dangerous precipice leading from childhood to manhood. He waited, tense. Shots exploded in the street before the house and his father ran to the window and peered out.

"Git on the floor!" his father ordered.

Fishbelly lay on the floor beside his mother and he could hear sobs in her throat.

"They gone," his father sighed after a silence.

Fishbelly stood, fighting against shame. His father paced the kitchen; in the dimness Fishbelly could see his shadowy face looking now and then at him. His father paused and fronted him.

"Son," he said slowly, "soon sap's going to rise in your bones and you going to be looking at women. . . . Look, son, BUT DON'T LOOK WHITE! YOU HEAR?" His voice grew bitter. "Son, there ain't nothing a white woman's got that a black woman ain't got. Ain't nothing but a white-woman tramp's going to have anything to do with you nohow, so don't git killed 'cause of a tramp. Keep away from 'em, son. When you in the presence of a white woman, remember she means *death!* The white folks hate us, fight us, kill us, make laws against us; but they use this damned business about white women to make what they do sound right. So don't give 'em no excuse, son. They hate you the moment you's born and all your life they going to be looking for something to kill you for. But don't let 'em kill you for *that*. There ain't no bigger shame for a black man than to die fooling with a no-good white gal. You hear what I'm saying, Fish?"

"Yessir, Papa," he breathed.

His mother's head was bowed upon the kitchen table.

"The white folks in this town hate me," his father continued in a bitter whisper. "They hate me 'cause I'm independent. I bury the black dead. They wouldn't touch a black man's dead body even to make money, so they let me bury 'em. . . ."

Fishbelly stared, trying to understand. But too much had been hurled at him too quickly. The notion of "looking" at a white woman seemed so farfetched as to be funny, but he feared the fear that was now showing on his father's shadowy face. He also feared white people, but he did not know them; he feared them because he had been told that it was the safe thing to do. He had spoken to perhaps six white people in all his life: Larry Heith, who was his father's lawyer; the mailman; the white clerks in the downtown stores.

His mother rose and embraced him, taking leave of his childhood, of his innocence.

"It's awright, Mama," he mumbled, struggling for self-possession.

Then they froze. A volley of shots echoed from the center of town.

"Something's *happened*," his father murmured.

"How long it's going to last, Papa?"

"Gawd knows, Fish. We just have to wait," his father explained. "There ain't nothing we can do. They outnumber us ten to one!" His father's voice rose in a hoarse scream. "TEN TO ONE! YOU HEAR?"

"Yessir, Papa. What started the fight?"

"They caught one of our boys who wasn't doing right . . ."

"Always be careful, son," his mother pleaded.

"Yessum, Mama," Fishbelly said. He spoke to his father: "Who was the boy, Papa?"

"Hush," his mother said, tugging at him.

"You know 'im," his father said accusingly.

"Who?" he asked, startled.

"It was Chris, son," his mother whimpered. "They caught 'im in the hotel with a white gal."

Fishbelly's lips parted. *Chris?* Naw! Chris, who worked in the West End Hotel, who was his friend, who was twenty-four years old, who was the hero of all the boys in the neighborhood . . . !

"I-is h-he d-d-dead, Papa?"

"He might as well be," his father was bitterly laconic.

"But, Papa, I just saw Chris last night in—"

"Shut your mouth, boy!" his father shouted. "Never let me hear you say something like that again! When a man's being hunted down, don't you be a fool and go saying you *know* 'im, see? If you do, the white folk'll kill you *too*." He lowered his head. "Son, this is race war, life and death." His voice grew husky. "They fight us in the street, in the church, in the school, in the home, in business—they fight us *everywhere*."

Again he was ashamed of his father's fear. If his father could not defend him, then who could? He was lost, and so were all black people. The sense of it hit him and his knees felt weak.

"But what can we do, Papa?" he asked, his eyes roving.

"We can *run*," his father said with twisted lips.

They were silent. Fishbelly could see at the window edge that night had fallen outside. He rose and groped unconsciously for the electric switch. His father slapped his hand.

"Goddamn, Fish! Ain't you got *no* sense?" His father was furious. "I'm talking to you and you don't learn *nothing!* Now, don't you know why we ain't turning the light on?"

"Sorry, Papa," he mumbled, hating himself.

Humbled, he sat and stared into darkness.

"That's awright, Fish" his father said soothingly. "This ain't your fault. I been keeping this terrible stuff from you. But I got to tell you what life is for black folks. Tonight you git your first lesson and you got to remember it all your life. Keep your eyes open and learn. This is what you got to live with each day. But I don't want it to keep you from being a man, see? Be a man, son, no matter what happens."

His father was saying one thing, but acting another. He suddenly wanted to get out of his presence. He rose and moved gropingly toward the door leading to the hallway.

"Where you going?" his mother demanded.

"To the bathroom," he spat defiantly.

"Leave 'im alone, Emma," his father said. "This ain't nothing easy he's learning tonight."

Sensing the route by touch, he made his way to the door of the bathroom and went in. The shock of his reaction to his terror-stricken family had flooded him with anxiety and he could hear blood pounding in his temples. Why had his family never mentioned honestly this business of white people before? Why had none of his teachers ever spoken of it in school? Why had Reverend Ragland always avoided preaching about it in church? More amazed than ever, he now recalled that both his mother and father had always used an unnaturally mannered tone when speaking of white people, and he knew that it had been to hide feelings of which they were ashamed. To Fishbelly it was clear that those powerful, invisible white faces ruled the lives of black people to a degree that but few black people could allow themselves to acknowledge. He felt confused, for his feelings were sweeping him in a direction for which he had no preparation. From that night on, he was intuitively certain that he had a winking glimpse of how black people looked to white people; he was beginning to look at his people through alien eyes and what he saw evoked in him a sense of distance between him and his people that baffled and worried him.

One thing he now knew: the real reality of the lives of his people was negated; the *real* world lay over *there* somewhere—in a place where white people lived, people who had the power to say who could or could not live and on what terms; and the world in which he and his family lived was a kind of shadow world. But how had it gotten like that? Fishbelly did not know if his feelings were right or wrong, but he knew better than to seek enlightenment from his parents.

Sitting tensed, he stared in the dark and tried to imagine how he would talk to a white boy or girl and his mind went blank. He mused upon how close they were, the blacks and the whites, and yet how far apart. Each morning and each afternoon, on his way to and from school, he passed white people and it was as though they did not exist for him and as though they did not see him! How could they exist right *there*

in front of his eyes without his thinking of them constantly?—
especially when they were so powerful? Was it some defect in
him? No; that could not be, for Tony, Zeke, and all his other
classmates hardly ever mentioned white people. Only Sam
did, but Sam's wild ideas did not make sense. Were his parents hiding something from him? Like they hid how babies
were born? Like how they never mentioned how women were
made? There must be something truly terrible about white
people, or they would be more talked about among his own
people.

And he could not recall ever having seen his father talking
normally to a white man. True, his father did not work for
whites like Sam's and Tony's fathers worked; his father never
rode streetcars, trains, busses; his father never ate in any but
black-owned restaurants. Hence he and his family had never
experienced obvious Jim Crow. He'd heard about Jim Crow,
of course, but whenever he had thought about it, which was
seldom, it had always been in terms of black people not having enough money to avoid such experiences.

He had gone with his father one Saturday morning into the
bank and they had waited in a line in which white people were
standing. He had heard white people talking to the white teller
clerking behind the window, but when his father had gotten to
the window he had not said anything; he had just simply
handed in his bankbook, and then had picked up the bankbook
and left. But, as they were leaving, the white man behind his
father had spoken cheerfully to the bank teller. "Good morning, Kim." And his mother had also practiced that same silence when he had accompanied her to the post office. Why
were black people so silent all the time in the presence of
white people?

His fingers groped vainly for the roll of toilet paper. Hell
. . . He had a daring idea to switch on the light; but, no; his
father would tan his hide good for that. He had already begun
sneaking smokes and had taken to carrying matches; he felt
his pockets. Yes; he had some. . . . He struck a match and
cupped its flaring flame between his palms. He lowered his
head, his eyes becoming riveted upon a stack of old, yellow-
ing newspapers piled in a corner behind the bathroom door.

On the front page of the dusty top sheet was a photograph of a white woman clad only in panties and a brassière; she was smiling under a cluster of tumbling curls, looking straight at him, her hands on her hips, her lips pouting, ripe, sensual. A woman like that had caused Chris to die. . . . But what had Chris done to the woman? Given her a baby? Raped her? Beat her? Or had Chris been doing to the woman what the boys talked nervously about upon the street corner under the gas lamp? He admired Chris and was sorry that he had to die, but to risk your life for *that* was something. . . . The woman in the photograph was pretty; there was no hint of evil or death about her. How had Chris met the white woman who had caused his death? He knew that if he asked his father that question, his father would shout and storm in a frenzy of fear and say that he was crazy. No; he would ask the boys; maybe they would know.

His match flame dwindled flickeringly and, at once, he scratched another to life, stood, snatched the newspaper from the top of the pile, ripped the face from it, then folded that paper face and jammed it into his pocket. He didn't know why he had done that; he had acted before he had been aware of it. But he knew that he wanted to look at that face again and he would never be able to stop thinking of what had happened to poor Chris until he had solved the mystery of why that laughing white face was so radiantly happy and at the same time charged with dark horror. The match flame turned blue, dying; the blackened matchstick guttered out; but the luminous image of that laughing white girl's face lingered on in his mind, glowing and drawing heat from a magnetic source deeper and brighter than the fire of the blazing match. Why had black men to die because of white women? The mere fact that Chris had been or would be killed (and that was the most awful part of it; his father had assumed that Chris *had* to die!) fastened his imagination upon that seductive white face in a way that it had never been concentrated upon any face in all his life. He rose abruptly, seized the roll of toilet paper, tore off a length, mumbling:

"Papa's scared. Mama's scared. They *all* scared."

Hearing water tumbling, he went out and, just as he was

about to enter the kitchen, he heard the phone in the parlor ringing shrilly. His father opened the door, caught hold of his arm, and asked:

"You awright, son?"

"Sure, Papa," he tried to purge his voice of resentment.

His father pushed him inside the kitchen.

"Stay with your mama," his father ordered.

All the reverent awe he had once felt for his father had gone. Sitting in the dark by the side of his mother, he heard his father talking over the phone. Shortly, footsteps sounded in the hallway and his father entered the kitchen with firm tread and switched on the light. Dazed by the sudden glare, Fishbelly sat bolt upright, his mouth open. His father's face was haggard, washed-out, and the tic in his right eye was so sharply pronounced now that he seemed engaged in a continuous, vulgar winking. He sat waiting for an explanation of this return to unexpected normalcy.

"It's over," his father announced simply, harshly.

"What happened?" his mother asked.

"Chris's body was found in a ditch just outside the school-yard," his father said. "Old Gus White found 'im and told his mother. She got Dr. Bruce and rushed out there. The body's at my place now."

"Gawd, naw!" his mother moaned and closed her eyes. "Poor Mrs. Sims . . ."

"They kill 'im, Papa?" he asked.

"Who *else* could've killed 'im?" his father countered with ironic agony. Then soberly: "Yeah. They killed 'im." He tossed his gun nervously in his palm. "And I'm *glad!"*

"Don't say that," Emma reproved him.

"Papa!" Fishbelly sang out his astonishment.

"Yeah. I know. You think I'm hard to say anything like that." The tired black face was loose, twitching. "But I know what I'm saying. It's a good thing he's dead. . . . Sure, I'm sorry for that poor little damn fool Chris. . . . But this is something much bigger'n Chris, Emma. You a woman and you don't know what life is in the South for black folks. Lissen: when them white folks get all roused, when they start thinking of us like black devils, when they start being scared of their own shadows, and when they git all mixed up in their minds about their women—when that happens they want *blood!* And won't nothing on this earth satisfy 'em but some *blood!* And there can't be no peace in this town 'less they git their *blood!* When white folks feel like that, *somebody's* got to die! Emma, it was either you, me, or Fish—"

"Naw," Emma breathed in horror.

"—or *some*body! This time it was poor Chris. And I'm glad it was Chris." He swallowed. "We weak and we got to be honest. . . . We can live only if we give a little of our lives to the white folks. That's all and it's the truth. Chris was just twenty-four. But he should've known better than to touch a white woman."

"But mebbe he wasn't *guilty!*" Emma wailed.

"He was *guilty,*" his father ruled. "That boy was tempted by that white gal and he had no more sense'n to bite, like a damn fool!" His rage was so furious that he was speechless.

Fishbelly felt that his father hated the black people now.

"But how they know he's guilty?" his mother argued. "He didn't git no trial—"

"They found 'im in the gal's *room!*" his father thundered.

"Chris was working at that hotel for his living, Tyree," his mother pleaded.

"There's other ways to make a living," his father declared.

"You lucky, Tyree," his mother sighed. "You don't work for white folks. . . ."

"I'd die 'fore I work for 'em!" his father screamed.

Fishbelly now felt that his father hated the white people too.

"Poor Chris," his mother sobbed into her hands.

His father's sudden changes of attitude had filled Fishbelly with wonder; there had been in those changes a bitter pride, but also a black defeat. He knew intuitively that his father, hating the demands of the white folks, had made a bargain with himself to supply the blood that he felt that the white folks wanted in order to buy a little security for himself, but, since his security could be had only by making victims of black men, he hated the black men too. All of which meant that he was consumed by self-hatred.

"Chris died for us," his father muttered. He pocketed his

gun, picked up his hat, crossed to the sink and drew a glass of water and lifted it to his lips and drained it in one gulp.

Fishbelly felt his father's eyes searching his face.

"Git your hat, Fish."

"Where you taking 'im, Tyree?"

"He's going with me," his father said.

"Naw! It's too dangerous!" his mother cried. "It's night now—"

"Ha, ha!" His father's hollow laugh made a shiver go down Fishbelly's spine. "There ain't no danger now, Emma. Them white folks is quiet now. Most of that mob's home in bed or dead drunk. They had their blood-fun. . . . You know, after killing a black man, they git nice and quiet and kind for a little while."

"Fish's just a child still," she protested.

"He's going to be with me. Nobody's going to hurt 'im 'less they hurt *me* first. Tonight I'm showing Fish what life is—"

"But there might be shooting—"

"Emma, Fish's my responsibility. If something happens to 'im later, it's my fault. Come on, son."

His mother stuffed her clenched fists between her teeth and gave vent to muffled sobs.

His father caught his arm and led him down the hallway, switching on lights as he went. They crossed the front porch, went into the yard, then around to the car and got in. Slowly, silently, they rolled out of the driveway and into the street. Gas lamps gleamed like strings of pearls through the quiet, hazy summer night. Fishbelly felt small and alone and afraid, even though his father, buoyed by feelings of blood sacrifice and armed with a gun, was at his side.

"Fish, from now on you and me's got to be together," his father began in a low, rumbling tone. "There's a lot you got to know and you starting in tonight." He nodded gravely. "To live in this world's to be in danger."

"Yessir. But, Papa, why you say *we* always got to pay?" he asked.

"'Cause we ain't strong enough to fight back, son."

"But don't we ever fight, Papa?"

"Sure! Now, don't you go thinking we black folks is cowards. Black men fight every day—"

72

"You say the white folks won't kill nobody else now. How you know, Papa?"

"I feel it, son. You'll understand this when you git older."

"But do *we* ever kill any white folks?"

"Don't talk foolish," his father scolded irritably. "I told you we was *outnumbered*. If we try to kill them, they'll kill us *all*. . . . Listen, Fish: I'm in business. We own our home. I got about forty thousand dollars' worth of property rented out. How come? 'Cause I 'tend to my business and leave white folks alone. If I didn't, I wouldn't be where I am. You got to learn to be *smart*, son."

Fishbelly was baffled about the power of dollars to wipe out shame and he was silent. They rolled through dim, empty streets and slowed at an intersection and pulled abreast of a white policeman directing traffic.

"Good evening, Mr. Officer. Everything awright?" The voice was high-pitched, unnatural.

The officer stonily eyed the black face behind the steering wheel and spat.

"Yeah. Everything's quiet, Tyree."

"Ha, ha! That's just *fine!*"

They rolled ahead and Fishbelly wanted to shut his eyes and stop up his ears. Was this what his father wished to teach him? The car halted in front of the undertaking establishment where several black people stood in a dark, mute knot. Spiderlike, a black hunchback rushed up.

"It was *me*, Tyree," the man purred eagerly. "I got it for you."

"Yeah?" Tyree was offhand.

"And I want *ten* dollars this time," the hunchback maintained.

"I'm giving you *five*, like always," Tyree said.

"But this was *dangerous*, Tyree," the hunchback whined. "You said when it was dangerous, it'd be *ten*—"

"Awright, ten," Tyree relented.

"Can I git it now?" the hunchback asked. "I need it, man."

Fishbelly saw Tyree take out a ten-dollar bill and fling it to the hunchback, who scuttled off.

"Who was that, Papa?" Fishbelly asked as Tyree strode toward the door, jangling keys.

"Old man White," his father explained. "He finds me bodies 'fore Curley Meeks gits 'em. Competition, son. Understand?"

"You mean he *looks* for dead folks for us?" Fishbelly asked.

"Sure, Fish. Some folks sell sugar. I'm selling coffins. But I can't sell a coffin till I git a body. I got five fellows out scouting for me. We call 'em body snatchers."

A tall, well-dressed brown man stood before the locked door.

"Hi, Doc," Tyree mumbled. "Where's the body?"

"Inside," the doctor said softly, without emotion. "It was in my car, but it was messy. I had your man put it inside. . . ."

"What they do to 'im, Doc?" Tyree asked in a whisper.

"Wait till you see what the white folks did to *him,*" Dr. Bruce answered in a wry singsong.

"They had a picnic, hunh?" Tyree asked.

"Picnic, hell. They had a circus," Dr. Bruce said.

Fishbelly followed Tyree, who, when across the threshold, turned and yelled brutally over his shoulder to the silent crowd:

"Now, you folks break it up! Nobody can come in here 'cept Chris's relatives. All the rest of you go 'way. Standing there'll only make the cops show up. Now, *git!*"

A short, plump, brown woman with a deadpan face stepped forward, her body tense, her hands clasped before her.

"I'm his mother," she whispered.

"Come on in." Tyree waved her forward.

When Chris's mother, Fishbelly, and Dr. Bruce were inside, Tyree slammed the door and locked it.

"Jim!" Tyree yelled.

"Yeah, Tyree, I'm here."

A gaunt, black man with a bony face and red eyes entered.

"Where you put 'im?"

"In the back room, Tyree," Jim mumbled.

"Awright. Let's see 'im," Tyree said, darting a worried glance at the locked door. "Wish them goddamn niggers'd go home," he grumbled. "They'll rouse them white folks standing 'round like that."

Chris's mother sobbed as they filed slowly down the hallway and into a rear room. Fishbelly crowded close to watch.

A dirty, bloody, tattered human form lay face down upon a table.

"Mrs. Sims," Dr. Bruce said, circling the woman with his arm, "I'm afraid you won't know your son now. . . ."

"Lawd, help me," she prayed, leaning forward with shut eyes, too terrified to look.

"Tyree, you want Fish to see this?" Dr. Bruce asked.

"Yeah," Tyree answered roughly. "I want 'im to see what happens."

"I get you," Dr. Bruce said.

Mrs. Sims opened her eyes and saw her son's broken body and screamed and lunged forward, flinging herself upon the corpse.

"Chris, baby, this ain't *you!* Naw, naw, Gawd! This *can't* be! It ain't *true!* It ain't *right!*" Mrs. Sims cried, clinging hysterically to the dead body. Then she keened with shut eyes: "Gawd didn't do this to me! He *couldn't.* No matter what you did, son, Gawd didn't want you to die like this! I carried you in my body; I felt you growing; I birthed you in pain; I gave you life with my blood! Now, *this* . . . Naw, naw, Gawd! Somebody somewhere's got to tell me why you died like this. . . ." She lifted her loose, wet face to the glaring, naked electric bulb. "Gawd, *You* didn't do this! You *couldn't!* And You got to do something to stop this from happening to black women's children! If I had to do it over again, I wouldn't have no child! I'd tear it out of my womb! Women don't bring children into the world to die like this! Gawd, take Your sun out of the sky! Take Your stars away! I don't want Your trees, Your flowers no more! I don't want Your wind to blow on me when my son can die like this. . . . I'm standing 'fore Your throne asking You to tell me: What did I ever do wrong? Where's my sin? If my only son was to be killed, then tell me and I'd kill 'im. Not them white folks. . . . Lawd, we ain't scared to die. BUT NOT LIKE THIS! Gawd, talk to me. As long's I live, I'll be asking You to tell me why my son died like this. . . ."

The doctor pulled the stooped, weeping woman from the room. Jim shut the door, his red eyes glittering with rage. They stood gazing bleak-eyed at the body of Chris in a silence so agonizing that Fishbelly wanted to scream. The opening door made them start; the doctor came forward.

"I put her to sleep in the guest room," Dr. Bruce said.

Fishbelly trembled as he recalled that room and the time when he had stood terrified in the darkness while a thundering locomotive with two red eyes gleaming had trampled amid harsh breathing the body of a black woman and now he realized that that must have been what Chris had been doing when the white folks had surprised him with the white woman. His father's clipped voice cut his train of associative memory:

"Jim, take off his clothes!"

"Okay, Tyree." Jim advanced with a pair of scissors.

Six-footed Jim grasped Chris's right shoulder and, with deft movement, twisted the body over. Chris's bloated head and torso turned first, then the legs followed, violently, shaking rigidly for a few seconds, as though the body still lived. Tension gripped Fishbelly; the conflict in his mind between the lifeless, torn form before his eyes and the quick, laughing image of the Chris he had known was too much. He swallowed, ran his dry tongue over his lips, shifting his weight from his left to his right foot, staring disbelievingly at the blood-clotted, bruised face showing distinctly in the unshaded bulb's blatant glare.

"They must've killed him right after lunch," Dr. Bruce observed. *"Rigor mortis* has set in."

Dr. Bruce's fingers probed delicately into the mass of puffed flesh that had once been Chris's cheeks; there was no expression on those misshapen features now; not only had the whites taken Chris's life, but they had robbed him of the semblance of the human. The mouth, lined with stumps of broken teeth, yawned gapingly, an irregular, black cavity bordered by shredded tissue that had once been lips. The swollen eyes permitted slits of irises to show through distended lids.

"Extensive lacerations," the doctor commented in a undertone. He bent over Chris's head with a tiny medical flashlight. "The right ear's missing," Dr. Bruce pointed out calmly, indicating a dark blot of blood on the side of the head. "Seems like it was scraped, sheered off. Could have been eaten away by the friction of asphalt against the side of the head. No doubt they tied him to the back of a car and dragged him through the streets. Could've been damned painful, that. . . ."

Dr. Bruce beckoned to Jim. "Cut off his shirt, Jim."

"Okay, Doc."

Jim inserted the tip of the scissors randomly into the shirt and, snipping, soon had the mangled neck bare.

"They lynched 'im," Tyree breathed indignantly.

"No," Dr. Bruce coolly overrode that definition. "Lynching's illegal. They claimed that the boy resisted arrest and they deputized three thousand men to catch him—"

"That's *still* lynching," Tyree insisted.

"Well, we won't quibble," Dr. Bruce said. "They intended killing this boy and the form of the killing didn't matter." The doctor scrutinized the neck, arms, and chest. "No gunshot wounds," he commented. "Guess they thought shooting was too good for him." The doctor paused, then resumed: "While killing this boy, the white folks' actions were saying: 'If any of you do what this nigger did, you'll end up like this!'" Dr. Bruce's fingers explored the neck. "The neck might've been broken in *two* places or more...Can't tell without a postmortem."

"Was his neck broken right away, Doc?" Tyree asked.

"Can't say, Tyree," the doctor said. "In cases like this, *who* knows? I doubt even if Chris knew what was happening to 'im, so much was happening and so quick. Maybe the neck was broken at once and he didn't suffer, then it might've been broken at the end, after he'd lingered—"

"If that happened, he suffered a *lot*." Tyree sighed.

Dr. Bruce stared thoughtfully at the electric bulb, then said:

"Tyree, we've been tortured by whites for three hundred years, and nobody has learned anything from it. If they'd tortured us as a scientific experiment, maybe we'd know more about human reactions under pressure. But they tortured us for their own special, morbid reasons. I'm not advocating human torture for the sake of scientific experiments." The doctor laughed ruefully. "But, Tyree, you just suggested something that, as a doctor, I ought to know, and I don't. My guess is that when three thousand screaming white men trap you and you know you're going to die, you're not worried about a little pain....If I'd been Chris, I'd've been praying that I wouldn't be scared, that I'd die like a man. Now, Tyree, I'm going to say something that'll make you think I'm balmy.

Those *whites* suffered more than this boy. Only folks who *suffer* can kill like this. . . ."

"But what they suffering *from*, Doc?" Tyree asked.

"I don't know," the doctor confessed. "I'm not white. If I were, I'd devote my life finding out why my kind kills like this." Dr. Bruce turned to Jim, commanding: "Strip 'im, Jim."

"Okay, Doc."

Jim snipped the ragged trousers and underwear from the body; then, with an incongruous delicacy, untied Chris's shoe-laces, pulled off the shoes, and peeled down the socks.

"The nose is almost gone," Dr. Bruce pointed. "Because of the rope knot against the neck, the head was flung about when they turned corners and the resulting abrasion destroyed the nose." Taking Chris's head between thumb and forefinger, the doctor twisted it around. "The left cheek has been split by a gun butt." Lifting Chris's clawlike hands, he studied the blackened wrists. "His hands were tied; in fact, I wouldn't be surprised if they hit 'im *after* they'd tied his hands." The doctor now turned the body on its side and, holding it in position, indicated a rupture through which a blob of pearly intestine gleamed. "I'd guess," Dr. Bruce spoke haltingly, impersonally, "that a kick did that, and it must've been delivered when he was already dead. In most cases of strangulation the stomach muscles grip the protruding intestine. But in this instance there seems to have been no muscular reaction." Dr. Bruce frowned, then resumed: "I'd say the toe of a shoe did that." He rolled the corpse upon its back and carefully parted the thighs. "The *genitalia* are gone," the doctor intoned.

Fishbelly saw a dark, coagulated blot in a gaping hole between the thighs and, with defensive reflex, he lowered his hands nervously to his groin.

"I'd say that the genitals were pulled out by a pair of pliers or some like instrument," the doctor inferred. "Killing him wasn't enough. They had to *mutilate* 'im. You'd think that disgust would've made them leave *that* part of the boy alone. . . . No! To get a chance to *mutilate* 'im was part of why they killed 'im. And you can bet a lot of white women were watching eagerly when they did it. Perhaps they knew that that was the only opportunity they'd ever get to see a Negro's genitals—"

"But why they want to *see* 'em?" Tyree asked, astounded.

"Oh, they want to see 'em all right," Dr. Bruce said. "You have to be terribly attracted toward a person, almost in love with 'im, to mangle 'im in this manner. They hate us, Tyree, but they love us too; in a perverted sort of way, they love us—"

"You crazy, Doc!" Tyree exploded. "That's no way to *love* folks!"

"It's crazy, but it's true," the doctor said. "Their love for us is full of fear. Tyree, I knew Chris. He told me about that white girl making advances to 'im. I warned 'im not to touch her. But, because she was white and different, he was tempted. But after two years she turned 'im in. Why? She felt guilty. She wanted 'im and yet she was scared. . . . So, when she had 'im killed, she solved both problems at once. She had 'im and paid for it, that is, *he* paid." The doctor laughed in his throat. "I'm sure she feels fine tonight." He closed Chris's thighs. "Well, there he is," the doctor finished and backed away from the table.

"Yeah," Tyree intoned dryly, a hunted look in his eyes. "He's my job now."

At the end Fishbelly was surprised he was still standing; the doctor's descriptions had so engrossed him that he had temporarily forgotten his initial shock.

"I've got to wash up," the doctor said, looking around the room. "Take care of Mrs. Sims, hunh, Tyree?"

"Sure," Tyree mumbled absent-mindedly. "Okay, Doc."

"Good night," Dr. Bruce said.

"Good night, Doc," Tyree, Fishbelly, and Jim called.

The doctor closed the door silently. The three of them remained staring at Chris's body. Tyree suddenly clapped his hands to his eyes.

"Goddamn!" he whispered fiercely.

"It happens every day," Jim said in a faraway voice.

"But I can't git used to it!" Tyree shouted.

"Yeah. I know," Jim mumbled.

"The inquest'll say he was killed 'resisting arrest,'" Tyree sighed. "Well, notify the police, Jim."

"Right," Jim answered, staring into space.

"Come on, son," Tyree said, holding the door open. After

Fishbelly had gone out, he banged it shut.

He followed his father down the hallway and into the office. He was tired and wanted to go home. His father went to a desk drawer, took out a bottle of whiskey, opened it, and tilted it to his lips.

"I wish to Gawd you was old enough to help me with this bottle, son," he said, dropping into the leather chair, holding the bottle by its neck, leaning back in the chair and closing his eyes. "But you don't need this stuff yit. When you git a little further along the road, you'll find it helps, son. When you got to look at Chris lying on that table, it *helps*." He was silent for a long moment. "Fish, you know how I make my living?" Then, without waiting for an answer: "I make money by gitting *black* dreams ready for burial." He looked at his son, then at the bottle. "Mebbe you don't know what I mean, hunh? A black man's a dream, son, a dream that can't come true. Dream, Fish. But be careful what you dream. Dream only what can happen. . . . If you ever find yourself dreaming something that can't happen, then choke it back, 'cause there's too many dreams of a black man that can't come true. Don't force your dreams, son; if you do, you'll die; you'll be just one more black man gone, one more black dream dead. . . . Fish, the main thing for a black man is to live and not end up like Chris. Most folks on this earth don't even have to think about dying like that. But *we* do. For most folks to die like that'd be a accident. For us, that accident comes too damned often to be called a accident. When it happens every day, it ain't no accident no more. It's a law, a law of life. Fish, to outwit that law's your main business in life. Some folks have to go into business. The black man's born in business. Fish, we all got to die sometime. But not like *that*. I'm too proud to die like that. I'd do anything on this earth to keep from dying like that. I'd kill myself first. Son, I ain't talking like no preacher. I'm just talking like a man. All men want women. But don't you ever want 'em so much that *that* can happen. . . . If there's any religion for you, son, Gawd knows, it's that. I feel that if that happened to me, I'd be 'shamed, even if I was dead. Son, even death couldn't stop me from hating myself if that ever happened to me."

Fishbelly was too full to speak. Of all the emotions churning in him, he was sure of only one: he held toward his father a nameless hatred; yet, at the same time, he felt more dependent upon him. He looked at the body slumped in the chair, at the black hand gripping the bottle, and he sensed that that deceptively lolling posture was hiding fear, restless scheming. A heavy sigh reached his ears; yes, Mrs. Sims was waking up in the guest room and he knew with swift instinct that his father was brooding rapaciously over the body of the mother of dead Chris. He's waiting for her, he told himself with dismay.

An uncertain footstep sounded in the hallway. Mrs. Sims, haggard and red-eyed, stood in the room.

"Mr. Tyree," she called in a whisper.

Tyree remained still, with eyes closed.

"He sleeping?" Mrs. Sims asked Fishbelly.

"Yessum," he lied.

Mrs. Sims took timid hold of Tyree and shook him.

"Mr. Tyree," she called humbly.

"Hunh," Tyree grunted, opening his eyes and blinking.

"Take me home," Mrs. Sims begged. "I'm scared. . . ."

"Sure, honey," Tyree said with abrupt heartiness, rising, still holding the bottle. "Don't want these damned white folks bothering you. . . . Say, how about a little drink, honey?" He proffered the bottle.

Mrs. Sims took the bottle and sank dazedly into a chair.

"They killed my only baby," she whimpered.

"Go on and take a nip. Do you good," he urged her.

She inclined the bottle to her lips. Fishbelly saw her shapely, big breasts and he felt suddenly lost, alone.

"Come on, son. I'm dropping you off, then taking Mrs. Sims to her place. Poor woman's all tuckered out." He bent to Mrs. Sims. "Come on, honey. Bring the bottle."

Fishbelly went out first and stood upon the front porch in the moist darkness. He had no anchor in this restless sea. He peered through the edge of the window curtain and saw his father's arms about Mrs. Sims and he turned away, growling through clenched teeth: "I *hate* 'im! I hate everything!"

Mrs. Sims came out on Tyree's arm.

"Git in the back seat, Fish," Tyree ordered.

"Yessir," he whispered.

From the back seat he saw his father take his right hand from the steering wheel and slip it about Mrs. Sims's shoulders. He shut his eyes. The car rolled slowly through the night and finally stopped in front of his home.

"Okay, son. Tell Mama I'll be in later."

"Yessir."

The car roared off and he felt hot tears wetting his cheeks. He had the sensation of being poised on the brink of a vast void and he had either to leap across and join his father or remain where he was. But his father had gone.

"I hope they kill you *too!*" he hissed with rage. Then stunned at what he had said, he wailed, "Naw!" He fought off guilt, choked back jealousy. His flooding emotions ebbed and he stood alone, dry-eyed, struggling toward independence.

"That you, son?" his mother called. "So glad you home. . . . Where Tyree?"

"He working," he lied with stiff lips.

"Son," his mother sobbed, circling him with her arms.

He shrank.

"What's the matter, son? Just want to kiss you—"

"Lemme alone," he growled.

"That ain't no way to talk to your mama," she reproved him.

"I'm tired. I want to go to bed," he said.

There was a tense silence.

"Awright," she sighed.

He had fled her for all the days of his life; he had shed his emotional swaddling clothes.

Half an hour later he was in bed, tossing open-eyed in the dark upon his pillow, trying to make meaning out of the haunting images thronging his mind. Then he was dreaming. . . .

. . . he was in Mama's and Papa's bedroom and there was a big white clock with a white face and two white hands flung wide as in warning and the white face was like God's face that Reverend Ragland said would burn you forever in a lake of fire if you didn't behave and he tiptoed to the door to see if anybody was watching and went to Mama's dressing table to look at bottles of perfume rouge lipstick and under the little bench that Mama sat upon was a strange little thing he

stooped yes it was a fish belly wet stinking crumbled with fuzzy hair and he laughed nervously and suddenly he started for the clock began a loud striking like somebody beating a drum TICK TOCK and the clock began striking thunderingly DONG DONG and he was amazed when the clock spoke DON'T DON'T and he heard a puffing like a train HMPFF HUMPFF and he saw a locomotive with coaches like he got at Christmas and the locomotive's stack pipe touched the fish belly HUMPFF HUMPFF and the fish belly began swelling pumped up by the stack pipe and getting like a balloon like Mrs. Brown's stomach before she had her baby and glowing yellow HUMPFF HUMPFF and the clock said DON'T DON'T and then the fish belly was so large he had to step back and make room for it to swell it grew so big that it began filling the room blocking the doors windows he could not get out he was trapped and the belly got bigger pushing him against the wall and he heard the locomotive HUMPFF HUMPFF and the clock warned DON'T DON'T and the fish belly pressed hard against his face and he felt he was smothering and he shouted: "NAW! NAW!" and the fish belly was so big and tight the thin skin stretching and he knew something was about to happen "NAW! NAW!" and the belly burst PUFF! and out of the collapsing balloon ran a flood of blood and he saw the naked bloody body of Chris with blood running to all sides of the room round his feet at his ankles at his knees rising higher higher he had to tiptoe to keep blood from reaching his mouth and it was too late it was engulfing his head and when he opened his mouth to scream he was drowning in blood. . . .

Panting, he awakened in the dark and switched on the light. So vivid had his nightmare been that it seemed impossible that no vestiges of its horror remained. He was prompted to rush into his mother's and father's bedroom, but instinct checked him; that was no good. . . . He had to learn how to live alone with these images of horror. He sighed and closed his eyes in sleep.

Next morning he was tired, listless, but unable to recall a single item of that nightmare.

11

In Fishbelly's Black-Belt living the echoes of Chris's death died slowly away. From pulpits, sweating black preachers thundered cryptic sermons describing all death as the work of God's Mysterious Hand meting out divine justice to the earth's sinful inhabitants. Tyree deplored Chris's death, but declared that it had come at a moment to have good effect upon Fishbelly. Emma exhorted her son to distrust the lure of the world, to turn his back upon the snares of the flesh, and seek the Kingdom of Heaven. If, during the next three years, Black-Belt flowed smoothly, it was due more to mental paralysis than fear of physical danger. Though Chris had been popular and well loved, the barbarous manner of his death constituted a challenge that could not be met without a total disruption of daily life, and, in the end, nothing happened save bitter cursing among Clintonville's black minority. The Clintonville *Times,* the two-sheeted, Negro weekly published by the high-school principal, devoted a black-bordered column to Chris's funeral, but refrained mentioning the cause of his death.

September of Fishbelly's fifteenth year found him not far short of his physical growth, five feet ten in height, lanky, with flesh covering his bones with little or no fat to spare. He walked with a hint of gliding and his arms were longer than average, swinging in wide arcs as he moved. His artificially straightened hair went back from his forehead over his skull like a solid black cap. His skin was black like Tyree's, but with a touch of Emma's brown lurking in its depths. His tenor voice matched his large, limpid brown eyes, eyes that rested softly, almost lingerly upon their object and dominated his flattened nostrils and irregular lips. He had a habit of lowering his head before speaking, a characteristic that stemmed from an innate modesty, but which served to make him appear more considerate or thoughtful than he really was. Almost invariably a fleeting smile preceded any remark he made, a smile that hid tremendous reserves of self-confidence which he had as yet felt no need to display.

Conditioned to dependence, he took it for granted that Tyree would launch him into the stream of life when the time came. He never pushed his advantages at home, in the street, or at school, not because he was afraid, but because he simply felt no need for contentiousness. For the present he had what he wanted most: home, friends, and quiet kinds of fun. Strife and tension might well loom ahead, but he did not anticipate them. He sensed his future in terms of two dubious, troubled perspectives: the beckoning shape of female bodies and the dark doubtfulness of being black, but his lack of experience kept him from reducing these pending problems to concrete worries. His environment was replete with laughter, easy talk, singing, eating, and he knew that his people had learned to cloak with jovial casualness their most important emotions and he liked it that way.

He lived in a world in which nothing was permitted and everything done, in which denunciation accompanied practice. Hence he knew well the meaning of those vague rumors and alarms sweeping his blood and glands. Black girls, with their giggling and talking, were no longer negative creatures who did not "understand," but a substratum of life whose chief traits were marking time until he and his black brothers were old enough to go to them and give them their duties and destinies. And, to Fishbelly, this interpretation of woman was as it should have been; it was in this fashion that his environment had presented woman to him. Indeed, the pending gift of woman was something delightful, a gratuitous pleasure that nature had somehow showered down upon the male section of life alone, and he waited for that gift as one would wait for a new and different kind of Christmas with Santa Clauses going up instead of coming down chimneys. He and his gang joked loud and long about the physical pleasures they would inherit, but as yet their knowledge was hearsay. Each waited patiently for someone else to announce that he had unlocked the physical individualities of his manhood. But there was no rivalry.

Neither were there any romantic overtones in their waiting. The moon, the stars, the sign language of the bursting buds of spring, the coded messages of autumn with its harvests of fruit and grain—none of this related to women and their role, and had anybody tried to make a connection between women and the vast processes of growth and decay in the world, they would have stared blankly, then laughed with hearty condescension, exclaiming:

"That guy's *nuts!*"

Arriving upon the high-school grounds one morning, Fishbelly saw Tony coming toward him with wide, shining eyes.

"Man, I been waiting for you," Tony said mysteriously.

"Yeah? What's cooking?" Fishbelly asked.

"Man, you'll die," Tony teased him.

Fishbelly caught Tony's shoulder, spinning him around so that he could look directly into his face. A cryptic smile screened Tony's secret.

"Come on, man! Spill it!" Fishbelly exploded impatiently.

"Play it cool," Tony advised. "I'll tell you. Old Zeke's gone and done it."

"What?"

"You know what I mean," Tony chastised him.

"I don't," Fishbelly said, thinking of women, but afraid to commit himself for fear of being wrong.

"Zeke had a gal. . . ."

Fishbelly gaped, then both of them bent over with laughter.
"Who?"

"Man, I can't tell you—"

"Then to *hell* with you," Fishbelly snapped, turning to leave.

"W-w-wait, man," Tony's lips bubbled with laughter.

"First, swear you won't tell a *living* soul!"

"Cross my heart."

"It was Laura Green."

"Naw!" Fishbelly was thunderstruck. "But she's in the church choir—"

"Hell, that ain't nothing. Women in the choir do it too."

"But she's older'n Zeke."

"Eight years older."

"Where her husband?"

"Working nights in the post office."

Again they bent double with laughter.

"Damn . . . Tony, how it happened?" Fishbelly demanded.

"Well"—Tony imitated an adult as he basked in Zeke's exploit. "Zeke said she called 'im and told 'im she wanted to talk to 'im about church work She took 'im into her bedroom and started talking serious-like, you know. Zeke said he guessed what was coming, but he wasn't too sure. She knows his ma and pa and her house is just four doors from his. Well, all of a sudden, she hauled off and started kissing 'im—"

"Christ!" Fishbelly yelled.

"—and 'fore he knew it," Tony related, "she had her clothes off and had turned out the light. Zeke said it all happened so fast it made 'im dizzy. And I believe it, 'cause Zeke came straight to me and, Fish, that guy was trembling. . . ."

"What he pay her?"

"Pay *her?* Nothing. She paid *him!*"

"Holy Moses!" Fishbelly said. "Was Zeke scared?"

"Don't know. But when I saw 'im, he was one *gone* man!"

"How Zeke say he felt?"

"Zeke said it'd make a jackass bray his head off!"

Laughter bent their knees almost to the ground.

"Goddamn," Fishbelly breathed, staring gravely.

The school bell rang.

"Them women's ringing their bells for us, man," Fishbelly said meaningfully.

Tony's eyes widened as he saw the point.

"You damn tooting," he said.

During his classes Fishbelly brooded upon Laura Green, mulled over the physical sensations that Zeke had gotten from her and the risks that Zeke had run to get them. And upon the street corner that evening, under the cone of yellow haze cast by the gas lamp, the gang met Zeke, who held the center of the stage. Intimidated by Zeke's having touched the quick of life, they were reluctant, at first, to ask him too many questions.

"Zeke, this lie about Laura Green," Fishbelly began with a nonchalant, twisted smile, "is that a *true* lie or just a *plain* old lie?"

Chuckles rumbled in throats. Zeke looked pityingly at Tony,

Fishbelly, and Sam, then his eyes grew ironical, quizzical, and he burst into a loud, mirthless laugh.

"Hell," Zeke drawled. "You dumb niggers sleeping and letting all the good stuff in town go begging."

"Zeke," Sam spoke shrewdly, "you *know* you lying about Laura Green—"

"I think he's telling the truth," Tony defended Zeke.

"What you think, Fish?" Zeke asked with an aloof smile.

"Zeke, you a dog and I kind of believe you," Fishbelly said.

Zeke kept a deadpan face. Tony waited. Sam shrugged, then blurted:

"Zeke's *lying!*"

"You niggers just a bunch of crazy babies," Zeke spat scornfully. "The women waiting for you and you here *talking*. Hell, yes. I cut Laura Green! And since then, I done cut *two* more, dammit!"

Zeke's three friends blinked, too astonished to speak. Zeke saw their opened lips and he fell into a spasm of hilarity.

"Now, I know you *lying!*" Sam was emphatic.

"You lying as fast as a dog can trot," Fishbelly said.

"You trying to pull wool over our eyes," Tony accused.

"Have it your way." Zeke shrugged. "I just come from the woods where I had little Betty Roxy. I *got* something from her, so help me Gawd."

"Lying's going to make Zeke's tongue rot off," Sam said.

"Betty Roxy?" Tony exclaimed.

"For *real*, Zeke?" Fishbelly asked, trying to grasp it all.

Zeke had never before made so tall a claim and they did not know if they should believe him or not. They were wishing that his tale were true, for, what Zeke could do, they could do; but had he told them the truth?

"And who was the *other* one?" Sam asked, trying to trap Zeke.

"Tillie Adams," Zeke rattled with aplomb.

"Aaaaaaaw," Fishbelly sang, his tone wavering between sneering and laughing.

"Now, mebbe you had Laura," Sam reasoned. "But them *other* two—Zeke, you *lying!*"

"If you ain't lying, then I ain't born," Tony said.

"Listen," Fishbelly argued. "Betty wouldn't touch you, Zeke. She's too damned scared of gitting a baby. She *told* me so. She ain't giving out *nothing*."

"I know," Zeke drawled with tolerant superiority. "But I cured her of that."

"How?" Tony asked.

"You niggers lissen and let me tell you something." Zeke repressed his laughter, looking from face to face. "It ain't hard to talk 'em into it. You just got to know how to jive 'em, see? Now, look.... About four hours ago I propositioned Betty down at Franklin's Chicken Shack and, sure enough, she gave me that song and dance about not wanting no babies. She said: 'Zeke, don't take me for a crazy fool. You insult me. I'm going to handle you with kid gloves from now on. I ain't aiming to take my mama no baby.'"

"I *told* you!" Sam shouted joyfully. "Betty ain't—"

"Wait," Zeke cut Sam off. "Let me finish. Man, I got 'round that. I told Betty that she didn't have to have no babies. I told her: 'Betty, you dead right not to want to git no baby and you with the right guy not to have nothing like that happening.' I told her: 'Betty, remember that time I got hurt playing football?' She said: 'Yes. You was in the hospital, wasn't you?' I said: 'Yes. Well, you know I was hurt down *there*. A muscle was cut and when the doctor operated on me, he saw it and told me I couldn't *never* make any babies. So, Betty, baby, don't be scared—'"

"That's a lie if I ever heard one!" Fishbelly yelled.

"Zeke, you crazy!" Tony roared.

"Zeke's dreaming," Sam said, shaking his head.

"I swear it's true," Zeke said soberly.

"You say you can't make no babies?" Fishbelly asked.

"Sure. I can make babies," Zeke said.

"Then why you lie to Betty?" Sam asked.

"Hell, I was softening her up, gitting her wet," Zeke said.

Zeke's friends ran four feet away and bent over, laughing. They came back shaking their heads, gasping.

"And what she say?" Fishbelly asked.

"Well, she was kind of thoughtful-like when I told her that," Zeke related. "By that time we was walking out by Doc Bruce's Grove, you know, the dance hall.... I told her:

'Betty, you foolish to pass up all this good loving when nothing can happen to you.' Then she asked me: 'Zeke, you telling me the truth?' And I said: 'Swear to Gawd, Betty; it's the truth. But don't you go 'round telling other folks what I said.' Well, she let me kiss her then and started crying, you know, soft-like. Man, when they cry, you *got* it. It's a funny thing. . . . I took her off into the woods and started in real serious. But she asked me four or five times: 'Zeke, you sure you can't make no babies?' And I said: 'Honey, I can't make no babies, for real.' Then she just melted. Man, I *cut* her and was she *glad!*"

"Zeke, you *never* said you couldn't make no babies," Sam charged.

"Goddamn, Sam, you acting as dumb as Betty," Zeke sputtered.

"Baby Jesus." Fishbelly sighed with jealousy.

"She really let you?" Tony asked, astonished.

"I swear to Gawd and cross my heart," Zeke swore.

"But suppose she gits a baby on 'count of that?" Fishbelly asked.

"Hell, Betty's no virgin," Zeke defended himself with moral indignation. "She can't prove any baby she gits is mine. Man, them women's easy. Make 'em feel safe and you *got* it."

Zeke's pals stood looking off silently, their faces stamped with envy.

"Hell, I wouldn't do *that,*" Sam mumbled, troubled.

"Me neither," Tony said.

"You tricked her," Fishbelly murmured.

"I-I didn't really mean to," Zeke stammered, laughing. "But. . . . Hell, when you soft, you hard; and when you hard, you soft."

Mirth came to their lips and died away. Then suddenly they screamed with delight. They had not believed Zeke, but now that his technique had been revealed, they saw that it was possible.

"And Tillie Adams?" Tony asked. "You git her too? Come clean, Zeke."

Zeke shook his head at their bewilderment.

"Hell," he said. "She was easier'n Betty; she was a pushover. I asked her: 'Tillie, how about it?' She acted like she didn't know what I meant. 'I'll wrassle you' I told her. She knew what that meant and she said: 'You'll never wade in this muddy water 'less you got rubbers on. And you ain't got no money to buy none.'"

"Zeke's the biggest liar in the world," Fishbelly moaned.

"He's blowing his top," Sam declared.

Zeke pulled from his pocket a flat package and opened it.

"I had *three* of 'em," he said, exhibiting the contents. "Now, I ain't got but *two*. I used one on Tillie."

"Zeke, you gone woman crazy," Fishbelly pronounced.

"I'd make love to a snake if somebody'd hold it so it wouldn't bite me," Zeke stated brutally.

Fishbelly reached out and caught hold of Zeke's collar and threatened him:

"Man, if you lying, I'll shoot you! You really cut Tillie?"

"It's the truth, man," Zeke vowed. "The *whole* truth, nothing *but* the truth, so help me Gawd."

"Okay. I believe you," Fishbelly said, releasing him.

"I'm buying some rubbers!" Sam shouted.

"We got to catch up!" Fishbelly said.

"Hell, yes," Tony seconded.

"But let me tell you what happened with Tillie," Zeke continued, laughing. "Man, I had to pay two dollars for them damned rubbers and I was mad, 'cause that was all my money. I wanted to git even with Tillie, so, just 'fore I went to work on her, I turned my back and tore a little *hole* in that rubber—"

"Naw!"

"Good *Gawd*, Zeke!"

"I swear I *did!*" Zeke yelled, laughing defensively.

"She was giving," Fishbelly said. "Why did you trick her?"

"That was dirty, Zeke," Sam said.

"Zeke, you fooled that gal," Tony said in a hardly audible voice.

"Damn right," Zeke admitted, looking off and smiling. "I didn't want to lose my good stuff like that. . . ." A sadistic self-love glowed in his eyes.

They stared openmouthed at Zeke, then howled with laughter until they were breathless.

"Zeke, you a hundred and ten per cent pure sonofabitch,"

Sam gasped, wiping spittle from his lips with the back of his hand.

"Gaaaaaaawd daaaaamn," Fishbelly sang, his eyes shining with enlightened respect for Zeke.

"Zeke, you a red-hot killer out of this world," Tony sighed.

"Hell, I wanted that gal and I took her," Zeke growled.

Awe held them silent.

"How was it, Zeke?" Fishbelly asked softly.

Zeke laughed and did not reply.

"Well, talk, man," Tony insisted.

"I can't tell you," Zeke said patronizingly. "You just got to go through with it yourself." He assumed a wistful air. "Laura asked me to drop in tonight, if I had time." He looked at his watch. "Well, kiddies, I'm blowing. See you tomorrow at school."

They watched him leave without opening their mouths. They could think of nothing to say. And Zeke's going left an awful emptiness in them. Now and then one of them laughed uneasily.

"Zeke's got guts," Fishbelly said, wagging his head.

"Right," Tony assented.

"Goddamn," Sam breathed reverently.

"Well, Fish, what you waiting on?" Tony asked. "Bertha Lewis lives right back of you. Go to work, man."

Fishbelly smiled but did not answer.

"I'm turning in," Tony said suddenly.

"So long."

Fishbelly and Sam stood in a mutually embarrassed silence. They were getting to be men, but they did not know what to do or say about it.

"I got to be gitting in." Fishbelly yawned.

"Me too. Be seeing you."

"Okay."

Well, what Zeke could do, he could do. But Fishbelly did not realize that he was destined to follow Zeke's road in a more telling manner; he could not even guess that he stood on the verge of a baptism of emotional fire that had a stronger character, a deeper meaning, a more abiding import than that which Zeke had had.

12

At noon one day, after he had gobbled his pork-chop sandwich and gulped his pint of milk, Fishbelly paced alone at the far end of the schoolyard, his black fingers gripping his algebra book. He was trying to memorize a set of rules relating to binomial theorems. On edge, worried, he had a lengthy examination due in an hour and each time he thought that he had the rules firmly in mind he could not apply them to the equations. He wanted to shut the book and hurl it out of sight.

"Fish!"

He glanced around, frowning. Tony's lean form loped forward and halted in front of him. Tony's chest heaved and his eyes shone.

"Come on, man! Quick!"

"Don't bother me, Tony!" Fishbelly growled.

"You missing something *great*." Tony implied that Fishbelly ignored him at his own risk.

Fishbelly lowered the volume and stared in exasperation.

"Can't you see me studying, man?"

"Don't you want to see the Garden of Eden?" Tony asked.

"What?" Fishbelly had been seduced by Tony's tone.

"Zeke's got them pictures, man! They about *white* folks!"

Fishbelly shut his book with reflex action.

"Where's Zeke?" he asked, roused.

"In the boy's john."

"You playing at rick?" A hinted threat was in his voice.

"Hell, naw!"

Fishbelly snorted and, with Tony at his heels, broke into a wild sprint, weaving between the milling boys, and plowed into the entrance of the lavatory and elbowed a path for himself.

"Zeke! Zeke!" he called.

"You run like a bat out of hell," Tony panted, pleased.

Amid sounds of running water and babbling voices, Fishbelly pushed through a dense crowd, breathing ammonia fumes of urine and the reek of emptying bowels.

"Zeke, where are you?" he screamed.

Collective laughter greeted his question.

"Come on, Fish!" Zeke called. "That bell'll ring soon!"

Fishbelly butted through a mass of boys and found Zeke.

"Git away you-all and let Fish in," Zeke urged.

When Fishbelly confronted Zeke he saw an extended pack of post cards.

"Here's what makes the world go 'round," Zeke murmured.

Fishbelly took the pack and a dozen black faces thrust themselves over his shoulders and elbows.

"Hold 'em up, man!"

"I want to see 'em!"

Kinky heads blocked Fishbelly's vision and he ducked away and protected himself by standing face to a wall. Feeling the pressure of surging bodies, he looked down and a sensation of unreality seized him; he was staring with parted lips at the naked, tensed bodies of white men and women in various stances of sexual exercises.

"Goddam," Fishbelly sang in a tone of awe.

"Stop pushing!"

"I can't see 'em!"

"They white folks?"

"Sure, nigger! Can't you *see?*"

Fishbelly slid the top photo under the stack and another fleshy vision of physiological contortions confronted him.

"Jesus Christ! Look at her face!" Surprise.

"Her eyes is closed!" Astonishment.

"She likes it!" Amazement.

"Nobody could take my picture doing *that!*" Moral disgust.

"Them goddamn white folks!" Fascinated fear.

Fishbelly withdrew a photo and stared at another forbidden vision.

"Them white folks ain't no good," a tall boy said and moved away, spitting.

Howling laughter went up.

"Percy's spitting like it was *his* mouth!" a boy crowed.

Fishbelly's heart trip-hammered. How daring were white folks? Then another vision replaced the photos and he saw the naked, bloody, dead body of Chris prone upon the table under the yellow glaring electric bulb. A flash of heat covered his skin, then he grew cold. He was looking at the naked white world that had killed Chris, and the world that had killed Chris could also kill him. He stared at the last photo and returned the stack to Zeke.

"That's a bitch," Fishbelly sighed; his palms were sweaty.

"Goddamn right," Zeke said.

"Where you git 'em from?"

"Old man Fairish. Got to take 'em back right away."

"THE MAN'S COMING!" A sadistic hoot.

Black faces jerked in expressions of panic.

"IT'S PROFESSOR BUTLER!" An insistent yell.

Zeke palmed the photos and tiptoed to stare over the heads of boys screaming and scrambling for the door. Fishbelly's heart skipped a beat; to be caught with "dirty" pictures meant expulsion from school. He sucked in his breath as he saw Professor Butler's black face pushing its way into the lavatory.

"Take 'em, Fish!" Zeke extended the photos in nervous frenzy.

"Naw," Fishbelly whispered. *"Drop* 'em and *run,* man!"

"WHAT'S GOING ON IN HERE?" Professor Butler called.

Zeke lowered his right hand and let the photos fall from his shaking fingers, then he joined the crowd surging past the angry face of Professor Butler who was still yelling and forcing his way forward.

"What's happening in here?" Professor Butler called again.

Fishbelly and his pals crashed through the door and into the yard.

"You got 'em?" Fishbelly asked Zeke.

"Naw. I dropped 'em," Zeke confessed in shame.

"Goddamn," Tony muttered.

"I could kill the bastard who told," Zeke cursed.

"Let's git away from here," Tony urged.

They walked hurriedly to the front of the schoolyard and stared back at the boys' lavatory. Professor Butler suddenly filled the doorway and his hands held the photos.

"Oh Lawd," Zeke breathed. "Them things cost twenty dollars."

"Poor Zeke." Fishbelly was dumbfounded.

Professor Butler's tight, black face stared at the boys and the schoolyard was quiet, too quiet. Professor Butler shoved the photos into his pocket and walked to the school building and went in.

"What you reckon he's going to do?" Zeke asked with dry throat.

"What fool told on us?" Fishbelly asked in fury.

Minutes later the school bell rang and the boys and girls lined up, side by side. Professor Butler mounted the stone porch and announced:

"Girls, enter your classes. Boys will remain standing."

Murmurs rolled through the student ranks. Black faces looked about bewilderedly. In Professor Butler's left hand was a bell and, with his right, he took hold of the rounded tip of the bell's tongue and tapped it against the bell's metal side, sending a hollow ring out over a sea of kinky heads.

DANG!

"Silence!" Professor Butler called.

The murmurs faded.

"We can git expelled for this," Tony moaned.

"If he asks us anything, we say *nothing,*" Zeke instructed.

"Right."

Again Professor Butler tapped the tongue against the bell.

DANG!

"Attention, girls!"

Girls stood still and straight in black-skinned rows.

Once more Professor Butler tapped.

DANG!

"Right face!" Professor Butler ordered.

Three hundred ebony faces whirled to the right. Professor Butler rhythmically tapped the bell tongue against metal.

DANG—DANG-DANG-DANG . . .

"Forward march!" Professor Butler commanded.

Girls tramped forward, right feet hitting the dusty ground with each bell tap; they advanced to the concrete walk and then wheeled and marched toward the school door. With breasts and buttocks shaking, with black eyes snapping in amazement at sullen and silent boys, the girls swung past. A black-faced girl poked out her red-tipped tongue and made a face of derision at Zeke.

"He's going to beat you," the sassy girl taunted.

"Go to hell," Zeke whispered.

"I'll meet you there," the girl rejoined.

Soon only rows of silent boys stood. Professor Butler lowered the bell and asked:

"What boy brought those filthy pictures to this school?"

Silence.

"I'm asking again: Who brought those pictures here?"

Not a boy moved or spoke.

"Looks like I'll have to punish every boy here," he said.

"What pictures?" Zeke asked boldly.

"Zeke Jordan, go to my office and wait there for me," Professor Butler decreed.

"Jesus," Zeke breathed. He quit the line and walked self-consciously into the school entrance.

"We don't know nothing about no pictures," a small boy said.

"Joe Sneed, go to my office and wait for me," Professor Butler dictated.

Joe Sneed walked through the school door.

"Now, who'll confess about those pictures?"

Fear of getting into trouble rendered three hundred black boys tensely mute.

"The following boys," Professor Butler intoned, "will go to my office and wait for me: Raymond White, Jack Hilton, Charles Hutton, and Ricky Page . . ."

Fishbelly relaxed, knowing that the principal was guessing. The boys whose names had been called were the trouble-makers of the school and Fishbelly watched them walk to the door and enter sullenly.

"He's going to sweat 'em," Fishbelly told Tony.

"But why he pick on Zeke first?" Tony wanted to know.

"Beats me," Fishbelly said.

"Attention!" Professor Butler called.

Boys stood straight and solemn.

"Forward march!" Professor Butler ordered.

DANG—DANG-DANG-DANG . . .

They filed to their classes to the beat of the bell. Fishbelly was disturbed, his mind swarming with contraband. He felt keenly alive, but split into spheres of fear and wonder. But, strangely, when he sat down to solve his algebraic equations, he found himself working them with ease. Between problems, he stared dreamily through the window, sensing a teeming, brightly spangled world that he had to explore, yet that world was somehow menacing. Would he be expelled? Would Zeke break down and confess?

The moment school was out, he and Tony rushed to meet a grinning Zeke.

"What happened?" Fishbelly asked.

"I got my damned pictures back," Zeke announced triumphantly.

"Naw!" Tony gasped.

"How?" Fishbelly demanded.

"Man, them pictures was lying right on his desk under a book," Zeke explained, enjoying their bafflement. "Soon's I got into that office, I started looking for 'em and found 'em. Professor was too scared to keep them pictures in his pocket. . . . I hid 'em in my shoe, under the sole of my foot . . ."

"But didn't he ask who had 'em?" Tony asked.

"Sure. And he searched us all, but he forgot to look in our shoes," Zeke related. "Man, I had some fun with that black, scared fool of a professor! I kept asking 'im: 'What kind of pictures?' And that fool was too *scared* to tell me."

"He's more scared of naked white folks than white folks wearing clothes," Fishbelly said, laughing.

"Man, git away from here with them pictures," Tony warned.

"Yeah," Zeke said. "I got to take 'em back."

Zeke ran off.

"Zeke's bold," Tony said.

"That ain't no lie," Fishbelly agreed.

They walked silently to the crossroads where they parted. Fishbelly strolled homeward thoughtfully. The honking of an auto horn made him look around and he saw a blue convertible car rolling down a dusty street and in it was a young white woman, black-haired, rouged. He stopped and stared at her until her car turned a corner.

"Jesus Christ," he breathed.

13

Long after the terror induced by the lynching of Chris had died down, a series of natural disasters fell upon Clintonville and kept alive a sense of dread in the minds of the Black-Belt people. First, a drought parched the fields, blanketing the streets and houses with a fine layer of dust, coating the vegetation a dull yellow, cracking the clay along the riverbanks, drying up the beds of creeks and ponds, and veiling the town in a hazy pall. Next came a season of abnormally heavy rains that washed out roads and bridges, causing creeks and rivers to overflow, and undermining the foundations of many of the houses.

"I know it's hard on some folks," Tyree declared in a tone of solemn satisfaction, "but it ain't hurting me none. If they burn or drown, I bury 'em in the end. Business is damn good, I done bought six new flats to rent out and I'm gitting a brand new Buick."

Emma, however, was of another mood. As the rain continued, she hinted ominously to Fishbelly:

"When the weather's like this, it means Gawd's talking to man."

"He's talking about what, Mama?" Fishbelly asked, amused.

"He's warning us about our evil ways; that's what," she said.

"You mean about how the white folks killed Chris?" he asked.

"That's only *part* of it," she spoke mysteriously.

He pretended engrossment in his studies, knowing that it was pointless to debate his mother's queer notions. As she rattled on, he inclined his head, as though weighing her irrational prophecies, but he was asking himself why God sent torrents of water upon white people *and* black people when His aim was only to warn the whites.

"But, Mama, we ain't done nothing," he reminded her.

"Gawd sends His rain upon the just and the unjust," she said.

"Then why be just, Mama?" he asked, then bit his lip.

"Now, you just shut your foolish mouth," she scolded him. "'Cause you studying schoolbooks don't mean you know about Gawd."

He held his tongue, realizing that the world his mother saw eluded him. (One day Tyree, when speaking of Emma, had said complainingly: "Son, your mama's awright, but she's gitting a little odd. It just happens like that with women. Don't know why. She's starting to gabble in a funny way. . . .")

Fishbelly hugged with fierce jealousy that emotional posture of independence that had been so accidently conferred upon him on the night of Chris's death. Always somewhat embarrassed in his mother's presence, he sought the outdoors: playing ball, fishing, hunting, roaming the woods, and, when he could sneak the opportunity, loitering in poolrooms. But that rainy season increased his mother's peevishness toward him.

"I know," she declared on one occasion, apropos of nothing in particular, "you starting to think of gals. But you be careful, boy."

It was as true as if she had spied on his daydreams. Goddamn! A guy couldn't think without somebody knowing it.

His mother's bossing of the house annoyed him; he fumed when she asked him what he thought of the lace curtains that she had hung; he refused point blank to comment upon whether her new dress was pretty or not; and he evaded her request to search the catalogue for the kinds of flowers she wanted to plant.

"What's gitting into you, Fish?" she demanded.

"Nothing," he said sullenly. "Why you picking on me?"

"Now, lissen to 'im!" his mother exclaimed, shaking her

head knowingly. "I know. You think I don't, but I *do!*"

"What you accusing me of?" he asked her.

"Gawd's making you into a man, but *watch* out," she cautioned.

He glanced up from the kitchen table where he was studying and gazed pityingly at her, smiling.

"Don't you go a-scoffing at Gawd, boy," she chided him.

"No'm" he said, wishing she would shut her mouth.

"I see you grinning when I give you advice," she charged.

"Mama, what do you want me to do?" he demanded angrily.

"Don't let your manhood turn you into a devil," she warned.

One day the washerwoman discovered a half-smoked cigarette that he had left thoughtlessly in the pocket of a dirty shirt. He had just come in from school and his mother met him in the hallway.

"Go in the parlor and set down, son," she ordered him.

Her tone told him he was in for a scolding. But what had he done? He followed her into the parlor and she stood sternly straight before him.

"Son, you done taken to smoking, ain't you?" she asked. His eyes widened. Had she seen him smoking somewhere?

"No'm," he lied.

"Don't stand there and lie in my face, boy!" she flared.

Her moral rage startled him. How had she found out? He had been ever so careful, had chewed gum to annul tobacco on his breath.

"Aw, I did smoke *one* one time," he confessed partially.

"Son, Gawd don't want you to smoke," she said flatly.

He blinked. She was so positive about God's desires that he felt that she had come fresh from a conference with Him.

"Yessum," he whispered placatingly, to avoid further scolding.

"Gawd don't want you breathing smoke into your lungs," she declared.

"Yessum. Our teacher told us it wasn't no good for—"

"It's worse'n that," his mother informed him. "Smoking's *sin,* son. Lissen, Gawd made your eyes to *see.* He made your stomach for *food.* He made your throat for *water.* If Gawd had wanted you to smoke, He'd made you a chimney on the side of your head—"

He crumpled with laughter at the image of a bit of round, pointing flesh beside his ear; and he was stunned when the flat of his mother's palm smacked stingingly across his face. He leaped to his feet in hot anger, but controlled himself.

"Don't you laugh at Gawd in my presence!" she blazed.

It was the first slap he had had in years. He turned on his heel and walked from the room.

"Fish, you come back here!" she clamored.

He went through the front door and down the steps toward the gate.

"Rex!"

She was sorry now, for she had called him "Rex"; he kept on down the wet sidewalk under a wan sun and breathed air that was like heavy steam. Yes, she wanted to talk to him and, in the end, she would apologize, but he wanted none of it. Her slap had stung his vanity. His quick steps soon took him beyond reach of her strident voice.

"She slapped me for *nothing,*" he told himself furiously.

A moment later his name was shouted through the sultry air.

"Fish-O!"

Zeke was coming toward him. They met and spoke with subdued shyness, each afraid of making a sentimental fool of himself.

"It stopped raining," Zeke announced the obvious.

"Yeah, man. About time," Fishbelly mumbled.

He knew that Zeke's mentioning the end of the rain prefaced a subject that Zeke was obliquely approaching. They traversed a street intersection before speaking.

"Wilson Creek's 'way down and the mud's wonderful," Zeke said significantly, looking off. "Come on and help us in a mud fight."

Fishbelly paused and laughed, bending and resting his palms upon his knees, squinting at the puddles of water on the pavement.

"You sure love them mud fights," Fishbelly teased him.

"Huh." Zeke rejected that superior attitude. He defended the sport: "They lot of fun and—"

"—and you git all plastered with mud," Fishbelly said. "Naw, man. Count me out."

"Water washes off mud." Zeke was rational. Then he sneered: "I know . . . You think you too good for a mud fight!"

"Naw, man. That ain't it," Fishbelly said.

"Then come on. What you got to lose?" Zeke said urgingly.

His mother had exacted from him a most solemn promise that he would "never, *never* fight with mud balls like them other boys," and his engaging in one would be a good reprisal for that unfair slap that she had administered. He had long wanted to participate in a mud fight, but his parents' injunctions had always stopped him. But suppose he did? His worst punishment would be a whipping, and maybe his father would now think that he was too old to be chastised like that. . . .

"Man, Teddy and his four fighters asked us to a war down at Wilson Creek," Zeke told him. "But we ain't got but *three* fighters. We told Teddy you wouldn't fight and he said you was scared of *him*—"

"That sonofabitch Teddy ain't got *nothing* to do with me not fighting," Fishbelly said tensely.

"Then come on," Zeke begged.

Yeah, it was time to put that Teddy in his place once and for all, for Teddy, of all the Black-Belt boys, was the only one who had not let off teasing him about his nickname. Other boys called him "Fishbelly" with no overtones of scorn or laughter or snickering; they did it respectfully, affectionately even, with full honor. Only Teddy had smirkingly dubbed him "sardine," "mackerel," "eel," "whale," and had had the audacity to add an insult that had baffled him as much as it had delighted his pals. Teddy had said: "How come they call you 'Fishbelly'? You don't know, but *I* do. Fishes is to the sea what buzzards is to the air; they scavengers! Now, a fish's belly's *white* and Fishbelly *feels* he's white. But his white is on the bottom, on the belly, where you can't see it. That's how come Fishbelly puts on airs, lives in a big house, primps. Old Fishbelly's white 'cause his papa's a great big whale eating *dead folks!*"

And he had listened while his pals had melted with laughter. He had wanted to paste Teddy, but had sought emotional compensation in muttering:

"One of these days I'm going through Teddy like a dose of castor oil!"

"There he goes!" Teddy had yelled triumphantly. "He's like white folks! He can't *take* it!"

"Stop playing with my name," Fishbelly had warned Teddy.

"Aw, Fish, Teddy's only teasing," Zeke had told him.

Well, the day had come to get even with that goddamn grinning black sonofabitch, Teddy. . . .

"Let's go!" Fishbelly shouted his resolve.

"WAR'S DECLARED!" Zeke yelled gleefully.

They reached the steps of Zeke's father's store where Teddy's and Tony's armies of mud fighters, black soldiers who used mud balls for bullets, awaited them. They met quietly, their repressed aggressions rendering them cautious toward one another. After evasive greetings, Teddy asked Fishbelly:

"You want a war?"

"Suits me," Fishbelly replied nonchalantly.

"Then it's on," Teddy said, grinning.

"Look," Tony admonished, "no rocks, no iron in them balls, see?"

"Okay," Teddy agreed.

"Keep quiet," Sam advised. "Don't let nobody know where we going."

"Right," Zeke said, glancing uneasily over his shoulder into his father's store.

"We go first; you guys come later." Sam organized the expedition.

"Okay."

Tony and his army set out, whistling, looking as innocent as possible. A mile farther they halted and glanced about. No one was in sight. They slithered through a barbed-wire fence, entered a thick wood and went forward over soggy earth.

"Look," Zeke commenced. "To beat 'em, we ought to have a plan. Let's all go for *Teddy*, 'cause he leads the enemy. If we make *'im* run, the others'll run, see?"

"I'll buy that," Tony said.

"Good idea," Sam agreed.

"And let's make big mud balls," Fishbelly counseled.

Having mapped out the war, they brimmed with confidence, for they felt that their plan was foolproof. Excess of energy made Zeke lift his voice in song:

> Old man Bud
>> Was a man like this;
> He saved his money
>> By loving his fis'

Laughter fluttered up out of their stomachs and into their nostrils and echoed over the fields.

"Where you git that song?" Tony asked of Zeke.

"I heard your papa singing it," Zeke said mischievously. Sam yodeled:

> Adam and Eve
>> Was setting on a rock;
> Adam said to Eve:
>> "Lemme see your bock."
> Eve said to Adam:
>> "Now ain't you 'shame'
> To call my sock
>> Such a dirty name . . ."

Fishbelly embraced a tree and howled, spittle drooling from a corner of his lip. The others slapped their thighs and guffawed.

"Nigger, where you git that song?" Zeke asked of Sam.

"I found it in the Bible," Sam said.

"Sam," Fishbelly called affectionately.

"What?" Sam answered.

"I ought to shoot you," Fishbelly said giggling.

Tony lifted a soft baritone:

> When your spirit rises up stiff
>> Looking for angel's hair
> Git down on your knees for a gift
>> And work your back in prayer . . .

"Man, that's cool and crazy!"

"It's way out of this world!"

"You can kill yourself praying like that," Zeke said.

Laughing, they advanced across a stretch of plowed land and walked over a grassy field in which their feet sank into spongy earth. Now and then scudding clouds effaced the overhead sun, making shadows flicker over glittering green grass. Blue and yellow butterflies swung over mounds of tufted earth. From behind towering trees came the cheeping of birds and from far off floated the faint lowing of a cow.

Fishbelly bellowed a lyric in which they all joined:

> *There was a man*
> > *By the name of Rosenthal*
> *Who had a goat*
> > *Tied in a stall.*
> *One night that goat,*
> > *Feeling mighty fine,*
> *Ate three red shirts*
> > *Right off the line . . .*
>
> *Mister Rosenthal said:*
> > *"That goat must die!"*
> *So he tied him to*
> > *A railroad tie.*
> *That train did blow:*
> > *"Toot toot toot!"*
> *But it blew in vain.*
> > *That goat coughed up them shirts*
> > *And flagged that train . . .*

The strains of the melody died away amid the trees and there was silence.

"I love harmony," Sam said wistfully.

"Me too," Zeke concurred.

"Man, music's wonderful," Fishbelly declared.

"We black folks sing better'n anybody in the whole world," Tony boasted.

They came to a creek in which sunlight flashed on the surface of yellow-brown water.

"There's Old Man River," Tony sang laughingly.

"It ain't no river, but it'll do till the real thing comes along," Fishbelly said.

Stretching away for ten yards or more on both sides of the

creek lay flat sheets of yellow-brown clay mud, virginal and smooth.

"Wow!" Sam said, rubbing his palms together.

They rushed forward and tested the consistency of the mud by plunging their fingers deep into the wet, cushy earth, scooping up fistfuls of sticky clay and kneading them into round balls. Their black hands turned yellow-brown.

"I could kill a bastard with this," Zeke vowed, weighing a solid, heavy mud ball in his right palm. "I'm exploding a Mississippi atom bomb," he told them, rearing back, raising his arm and letting go his mud ball, whizzing it against a tree trunk: *bleeeeeeek!* Tiny mud particles spattered high into the sunlit air. "Goddamn!" Zeke congratulated himself.

"Here's a Dixie hydrogen bomb," Fishbelly announced as he wound up and tossed his mound of mud, splashing it against another tree trunk: *bliiiiiik!* It spread out round with jagged edges radiating, excess mud spewing in yellow streams, drenching the vegetation. "A bull's-eye!" Fishbelly sang.

"Superman couldn't dodge this one!" Tony called his turn, hurling a hunk of mud that sailed through the air and veered downward with a sliding motion toward the surface of the creek water and skidded straight across and buried itself in mud on the other bank.

"Now me!" Sam chanted, flinging his mass of mud at a tree not more than four feet away. It landed: *spleeeeesha!* Mud showered over them, coating their black faces with yellow streaks of silt. "That's my Molotov cocktail!" Sam yelled, scraping mud from his mouth.

"Goddamn," Zeke protested splutteringly, wiping mud from his eyes. "You going to cripple us 'fore we start."

"No more practicing," Fishbelly ruled. "Let's wait for the enemy."

They lolled upon the grass, their eyes shuttered against sun dazzle. A bumblebee droned past. A grasshopper jumped, vanishing behind a leaf. Sam plucked a weed stalk from the ground and began nibbling thoughtfully at it.

"Zeke," Sam called in a soft, appealing drawl.

"Hunh?" Zeke grunted.

"I want to ask you something *real* serious," Sam said slowly.

"What?" Zeke asked, his eyes half closed.

"What would you do with niggers if you was a white man?" Sam posed his problem.

"I knew it!" Tony shouted accusingly. "Sam's got a *racial* boil on the brain!"

Fishbelly moved nervously and said nothing.

"Sam, you talk like the white folks *own* you," Zeke spoke with disgust. "If I was a white man, I'd ask you why you ask me that. . . ."

"But we live with white folks," Sam argued. "You can't move without 'em."

Zeke affectionately circled Sam's neck with his forearm and said with a laughing growl:

"I'd burn all you bastards up with an atom bomb!"

The idea struck them so forcibly that they leaped to their feet and laughed. But Sam's eyes, though full of mirth, were bewildered.

"But why you want to burn up niggers?" Sam asked. "Niggers ain't done nothing to you."

"I'd burn niggers 'cause they scared," Zeke spat.

"Aw naw," Tony wailed in opposition.

"That ain't true." Fishbelly's voice shot out in self-defense.

"Anybody here who ever fought a white man, raise his hand," Zeke challenged.

"That ain't fair," Fishbelly protested. "Why we want to fight white folks? They ain't done nothing to us—"

"They just made you slaves one time," Sam blocked him.

"Aw, that was long time ago," Tony said.

"I don't like this *race* talk!" Fishbelly was vehement. "Sam would think of something like that."

"I want to know," Sam said, turning to Zeke to pursue his quest. "Suppose you was a white man, what would you do with us?"

Fishbelly and Tony stared at Zeke's face, which became relaxed, dreamy. Sam waited.

"If I was a white man," Zeke drawled in a distant voice, "I'd be rich. . . ."

"And you'd have a lot of servants and you'd be living in a great big house," Tony said.

"Awright," Sam said, participating in the fantasy. "You'd be a-sitting in your parlor with paintings and books all 'round you—"

"And you'd have a pretty blond wife nestling up to you," Fishbelly added to the picture.

"Awright," Zeke smilingly assented to the fantasy. "There I am . . . I'm smoking my pipe . . . Nigger jazz is coming over the radio . . . Bottles of scotch on the table . . ."

Zeke, imitating a rich white man: Sam, you said you wanted to see me? What you want, nigger?

Sam, acting with dignity: I want to talk to you about justice for black folks—

Zeke, amazed: Nigger, what you mean talking to me like that? What do you want with justice? You gitting along awright, ain't you?

Sam, indignantly: I'm talking about us gitting good jobs, Mr. Zeke. We black folks—

Zeke, haughtily: What you niggers always whining about? I ain't your master! Go git you a job! Goddammit, *make* a job! We white folks made ours, didn't we? When you ask me for justice, you make yourself a slave. Nigger, git away from here and stop bothering me. Git to hell out of my house, or I'll shoot you—!

Sam, enraged, draws a gun and shoots Zeke: There! You goddam white bastard! I shot you first!

Zeke clasps his hands over his heart, walls his eyes, and sinks to the grass.

Zeke, in a hoarse whisper: Nigger, you done shot me. . . . Why you do that?

Sam, yelling angrily: 'Cause you *mean*, that's why!

Zeke, dying: Nigger, you done beat me . . . You the best man . . . Here, take my house, my money, and my wife . . .

Repressing their giggles, Fishbelly and Tony watch Zeke die. Tony suddenly smiles and then comes forward, imitating a woman's walk and voice, his right hand on his hip.

Tony, *simpering:* Sam, darling . . . What a big, strong man!
You done killed my husband . . . Winner take all . . . Kiss me
. . . All I have is yours!

Sam, *confused, blinking:* That ain't what I meant . . .

Unable to play-act any more, Fishbelly, Tony, and Zeke fell
upon Sam, laughing at him.

"You *see:*" Zeke yelled. *"You scared!"*

"Sam, you said you wanted some justice," Fishbelly argued. "I'm talking about equal chance—"

"The trouble with us," Tony railed angrily, "is we don't
know what we want. The only thing wrong with niggers is
that they scared to *death!*"

"They so scared they scared to say they scared," Zeke
summed it up in a singsong voice.

"You-all talking about black folks like white folks talk
about 'em," Sam pointed out.

"HEEY!" A voice floated over the fields.

"Here they come," Zeke said. "Let's git ready."

Teddy and his black soldiers were crossing the marshy land.

"The first one to run's a granny-dodger!" Teddy taunted.

"I'll bet a million dollars we'll make you cry for your ma's
tits!" Fishbelly predicted.

"Put your money where your mouth is!" Teddy countered.

Tony confronted Teddy and began defining the rules of the
pending mud war.

"Your army's on that side of the creek and we over here,"
Tony indicated, gesturing toward the front lines.

"Okay with me." Teddy was crisp.

"And the first one hollering: 'Stop!' is *out,*" Tony drafted
another article of war.

"Right," Teddy accepted.

"Let's go! *Action!*" Tony issued the order of the day and
assembled his black troops.

Teddy led his infantry to a tree that had fallen athwart the
creek and his men scampered precariously across.

"Git your shirt off!" Tony yelled.

"Check!" Teddy echoed.

Eight black bodies flashed in the sun against the yellow-brown mud.

"Make bullets!" Tony signaled.

"Right!" Teddy acknowledged the signal.

Eight pair of hands began a frantic scooping up of mud, which was rounded into balls and stacked behind trees selected as fortresses. They labored silently, breathing heavily, now and then cocking their heads to make sure that the enemy was observing the conventions of mud war and to determine the amount of ammunition amassed by the adversary.

"Lissen," Sam said, pausing. "I got a idea. . . . "

"What?" Tony asked.

"I'll be a decoy, see? I'll run out and when they chunk at me, you-all single out Teddy and git 'im—"

"Sam, you got something there," Fishbelly agreed.

"Okay, I'll tell you when to run, Sam," Tony said, smiling grimly, pleased.

"All set?" Teddy shouted.

"Hell, yeah!" Tony's voice cast echoes far into the tall trees.

Glistening black bodies leaped behind tree trunks. Hands gripped mud balls and heads peered cautiously, searching for targets. The only sounds were the soughing of wind in trees and the chirping of birds. From Teddy's army across the creek a mud ball hurtled through the sunshine, swishing past tree leaves, crashing into an oak behind which Fishbelly crouched: *plooooop!*—flinging mud pellets far and wide. Fishbelly's muscles tautened to return the fire, but Tony's fierce whisper checked him:

"Hold it, Fish! Sam, git ready to run out, hunh?"

"Right," Sam concurred.

Another sizzling shot from Teddy's forces landed just above Zeke's head: *fliiiiik!*—exploding drops of mud everywhere, dappling the surrounding tree trunks. Zeke moved to retaliate, but Tony grabbed his elbow.

"Easy, Zeke."

More mud balls fell, but there were no direct hits.

"What you white-livered niggers waiting on?" Teddy tried to provoke them.

"We attack when we ready," Tony replied.

"They all out in the open now," Zeke analyzed the situation. "Now's the time to go."

Ducking, weaving, Sam scuttled out over stretches of mud, halting for a second to make himself a target, then bobbing away. Mud balls choked the air and Sam dodged among them. A murderous yell went up across the creek and Teddy and his blackly gleaming army rushed pell-mell down to the water's edge to take better aim at Sam. Deployed far from their fortresses, Teddy's army madly bombarded Sam, who flitted like a black ghost among the trees. Teddy reached the end of the log lying athwart the creek and his infantry, cannonading a furious barrage, pressed close behind him.

"Attack!" Tony screamed the command for action.

Tony and his men glided from behind their fortresses and scattered over the oozy silt and let go with showers of mud balls, one handful after another, all straight at Teddy. Aw, a hit! A solid, doughy blow pelted plunkingly into the center of Teddy's face, *cluuuush!*—covering his features with a liquid mask, turning his ebony skin a yellow-brown. Teddy's arms flew out jerkily, like the extremities of a doll manipulated by wires. Teddy stood stock-still, wiped the mud from his eyes, and stared; then he turned, snatched up his shirt, and flew wildly off among the trees.

"We GOT 'IM!" Fishbelly screamed in joy.

Teddy's three soldiers also retrieved their shirts and high-tailed it after their leader.

"WE DONE BEAT 'EM!" Tony shouted.

Reveling in victory, Fishbelly turned to share the fruits of the rout with his pals. But only Tony was near him; Zeke and Sam, too, were running wildly through the woods. Baffled, Fishbelly frowned and looked at Tony, whose face was filled with terror.

"Lawd," Tony whimpered, looking over Fishbelly's shoulder.

Fishbelly spun about and saw two white policemen bearing down upon him with drawn guns.

"Stop right where you are, niggers!" a policeman commanded. "And put your hands up!"

Fishbelly's first impulse was to run, but those pointing guns made him know that that was foolish. He held his breath and slowly lifted his muddy hands above his head. Tony stood close to him, his hands also raised.

"Please, sir," Tony moaned.

Fishbelly glanced around; all had escaped except him and Tony. A lump of dread clogged his throat. He ought not to have come here. He was in trouble because he had disobeyed his mother and father. . . .

"Both of you, turn 'round and march ahead," a policeman snapped.

"Please, sir. Our shirts," Fishbelly begged in a whisper.

"Git into 'em quick and no monkey business!"

Fishbelly scrambled into his shirt, his eyes blurred by tears. Then, before he realized it, links of steel clamped hard on his wrists.

"We warned you niggers against trespassing," the tall policeman said.

"But we ain't done nothing," Fishbelly whimpered. "Please, let us go home."

"You going to jail, then to a reformatory," the fat policeman said. "Now, walk straight to the highway."

As in a dream, with temples throbbing, Fishbelly marched beside Tony, stumbling over wet, plowed earth, crying, shivering, ashamed of the mud caking his face and hands. They halted before a police car whose rear door was open.

"Git in," one of the policemen ordered.

Fishbelly climbed in and sank down, his body leaning stiffly forward, his eyes staring blankly. The door was slammed shut and he sighed and slumped in his seat, his head lolling against the cushion. A clap of white thunder had split his world in two; he was being snatched from his childhood. The white folks were now treating him like a man, but inside he was crying and quaking like a child. Lawd, don't let 'em hurt me, he prayed.

His roused senses registered the ride into town in a distorted manner: he stared at the black mole on the back of the tall white man's freckled, leathery neck; a fly buzzed persistently about his eyes and no amount of brushing at it with his cuffed hands could make it leave; a streak of yellow matter oozed from Tony's flaring nostrils to his upper lip. Minutes later the police car swerved and stopped alongside a curb flanking an outdoor soft-drink bazaar. One of the policemen signaled a white waitress wearing a pair of tight-fitting shorts, a brassière, and a tiny white lace apron that jiggled suggestively about her hips as she walked.

"Two ice-cold Cokes, tootsie, and make it snappy," the tall policeman ordered.

"Right. Coming up," the girl sang flatly, waddling off, darting an impersonal glance at the two, silent, handcuffed shadows in the back seat.

Fishbelly stared at the girl's white face, her pink cheeks, her ruby-red lips, and her sky-blue eyes—and he remembered Chris. . . . The world he saw was alluring but menacing. To be anywhere but here, to see any world but this . . . He longed hotly for the sanctuary of his Black Belt, for the protection of familiar black faces; but, while yearning for his absent world, he knew that that world had lost its status and importance in his life. The world he now saw was the real one; that other world in which he had been born and in which he had lived was a listless shadow and already he was ashamed of its feebleness, of the bane of fear under which it lived, labored, hungered, and died.

Involuntarily and wonderingly, he stared at the girl's blue eyes as she floated sensually toward the car, her hips swaying. She carried a dainty tray upon which stood two sweating bottles of Coca-Cola from whose necks jutted two translucent straws. As though hypnotized, he gazed at the girl while she served the policemen, collected her money, and walked mincingly from the car.

"Hot stuff, eh, Clem?" the fat one said.

"A dime a dozen," the tall one grunted.

"Ain't no difference in the dark." The fat one snickered.

"Always another one just like the other one," the tall one said, sipping his Coke.

Fishbelly heard them, but he was staring at the girl. Then he was startled to see that the tall man had turned and had been watching him while he had been watching the girl.

"Something on your mind, nigger?" the tall one rasped.

"*Sir?*" Fishbelly's heart leaped into his throat.

"You staring at the gal, *nigger?*" he demanded.

114

"Nawsir," Fishbelly protested in a tense whisper.

"Then take your goddam eyes *off* her!" he ordered.

"Yessir," he breathed.

With an abject desire for obedience in his heart, he looked at the policeman's weather-beaten face and then felt his eyes straying magnetically toward the girl. . . .

"Goddammit, nigger! Stop *looking* at that gal!" the tall one shouted.

Fishbelly opened his mouth to say, "Yessir," but his dry tongue could not move.

"Ain't you going to answer when a white man speaks to you, nigger?" the man asked, tossing the empty Coca-Cola bottle out of the car.

Fishbelly felt as though he were whirling floating like a scrap of paper swept by wind currents. He was losing awareness of his legs, his arms, and his head felt light, giddy.

"You ain't going to answer me, hunh, nigger?" the tall man growled, flinging open the door of the car and leaping out.

With unblinking eyes, Fishbelly watched the white man take a knife from his pocket and flick open a long, gleaming blade and extend its pointed tip toward him.

"I'm going to fix you so you won't *never* look at another white gal," the white man vowed through bared, shut teeth and moved to the rear door of the car and flung it open. "Nigger, I'm going to *castrate* you!"

An enormous curtain of black appeared and dashed itself against Fishbelly's eyes. He had fainted, had passed out cold. When he revived he saw the two policemen standing before the open door of the car and staring at him. Fishbelly parted his lips to scream, but his constricted throat could make no sound. He grew conscious of Tony's elbow nudging his ribs.

"Fish, wake up. The gentlemen's talking to you," Tony whispered pleadingly.

Fishbelly stared dully at the men, at Tony, and felt a queasy sensation in his stomach that made him fight against losing consciousness again.

"Well, I'll be a jack rabbit's papa!" the tall man exclaimed, amused, amazed. "That nigger sure to hell *really* fainted!"

"He went out like a light," the fat one said in a tone of wonder.

"Seeing's believing. . . . Whoever heard of niggers *fainting?*" the tall one asked. Then in a voice of rough amiability: "Where you learn to faint like that, nigger?"

Fishbelly swallowed, unable to take his eyes off the man's face.

"Aw, come on. Let's take 'em in," the fat one said.

"Goddamn, you live and learn," the tall one said, chuckling absent-mindedly. "Niggers *fainting*. That's one for the books. Wait till I tell the boys about this."

The car rolled again. Fishbelly was now fully awake and a terror that he had been too preoccupied to feel seized him; his heart roared, seemingly about to hammer its way out of his chest; beads of sweat popped on his wrinkled brow. An urgent anxiety gripped him; there was something he had to do . . . But what? The car pulled to another stop alongside a stretch of country road and Fishbelly's hysterical imagination pictured the two policemen dragging him from the car and lynching him as Chris had been lynched. But the tall policeman turned to him and asked in an indulgent tone:

"Nigger, you want me to unlock them bracelets? Hold up your hands."

Expecting a trick, Fishbelly lifted his arms; then fear made him jerk out of reach.

"Goddammit, nigger! Don't you want your hands free?"

Hesitantly, he raised his linked wrists again. The handcuffs were unlocked.

"That better, nigger?" the policeman asked.

"Yessir," he sighed.

The policeman roared, brushed his cap back on his forehead, and erupted with laughter.

"A nigger fainting! Now I've seen everything," he spluttered.

The white men joked in low tones as the car got under way. Fishbelly stared unseeingly, once more a prey to anxiety. He held himself stiffly, on the verge of hysteria. The fingers of his freed right hand lifted and hovered indecisively in air, moved tremblingly to his lips, then descended to his groin, fumbling. Yes; he was intact; he had not been castrated while he had been unconscious. . . . He sighed, looking about like a sleepwalker, licking his lips with a dry tongue, seeing again the vision of Chris's bloody, broken body inert upon the table under the glaring electric bulb. The car was now purring through the paved streets of town, and, for a moment, he was three blocks from his father's undertaking establishment! Oh Gawd, if he could find a way to let his father know! Then his imagination was suddenly filled with an image so compellingly terrible that he gave a violent start.

"What's the matter with you, nigger?" the tall man asked. "You got the jumps or something?"

"Nawsir," he answered in a low whine.

"Don't pull another fainting fit," the fat one said. "You'll kill me."

Fishbelly was now one bundle of guilt that oozed from the pores of his skin. He had a terrifying sensation that the white men could see through him, could detect a haunting image that he could not get rid of, a plaguing image that ought not to have been in his mind. In his rear right trouser pocket was his billfold and where it pressed against his upper back hip his skin raged with a circle of sizzling fire that seared his flesh like that time when he had fallen upon the stove and burned himself. Creased and tucked into his tattered billfold was the frayed photograph of that laughing white woman wearing only panties and a brassière—that photograph that he had impulsively torn out of the newspaper in the toilet on the night that Chris had been killed! Ah, Gawd . . . What could he do? He was convinced that if the policemen found that picture of the white woman in his pocket, they would kill him. Somehow he had to get rid of it before they reached the police station. (He did not realize that the opposite side of the newspaper carrying the white woman's photograph contained a crossword puzzle, and that, if questioned, he could say that he had torn out the bit of paper for the sake of that puzzle!) With a sly movement, he eased his right hand back of him and slipped the billfold out of his pocket, hoping that if the policemen saw him they would not think that he was reaching for a knife or a gun. He fished the scrap of paper out of the billfold and let the billfold drop to the floor of the car. Now . . . He crumpled the paper hard in his palm, balling it. But what could he do with it? Throw it out of the car window? No. The policemen would surely see it flashing away in the sunshine. And if he tucked it

117

into the crevice in the back of the car seat, they would find it later and would certainly know who had left it there. Aw yes; he knew. He would chew it and swallow it; he would *eat* it. That was it!

The car was now cruising through the sunlit streets of the downtown section and he knew that he had but a few moments. He lifted his right hand to his mouth and coughed to cover his guilty action, then slipped the crushed paper between his teeth. Gawd . . . It seemed as big as a baseball! He held it for a few seconds on his tongue, then began trying to grind it to softness. But his saliva would not flow. Desperately, he ground the paper between his back molars, hoping to reduce it to pulp. The car slowed in front of the police station; he stiffened, feeling that he had to swallow that half-wet wad or be lynched. He centered the lump on his tongue and threw back his head and tightened his lips to swallow; the mass of the paper stuck in his throat and he gagged. Again he attempted to swallow it, to choke it down, but he gagged once more, leaning forward involuntarily, feeling on the verge of vomiting. But, no . . . He had to get that damned thing down into his stomach. He shut his eyes, stretched his neck, clamped his throat tight, and held his breath; the lump moved a fraction of an inch.

"You sick, nigger?" the tall policeman asked.

The car stopped. Fishbelly lifted tear-filled eyes of terror to the white man's face, negatively shaking his head.

"Dammit, nigger, don't you throw up in this car," the tall man warned.

That did it; that reproving voice choked the chunk of balled paper down his throat. He held still, unable to breath as he felt it sinking slowly; then he had it down, had swallowed it. He straightened, gulping air into his gasping lungs through gaping lips as his eyes walled. His intestines heaved in protest and he swallowed again and again. Yes; he had eaten it; it was inside of him now, a part of him, invisible. He could feel it moving vaguely in his stomach. So taken up had he been with eating the telltale picture of the white woman's face that he did not know that not only had the car stopped, but that both policemen had gotten out and were staring at him. Even Tony was gaping at him.

"Kind of delicate nigger," the tall man mumbled wonderingly.

"You sick, Fish?" Tony asked him in a scared voice.

He did not answer; he leaned back in the seat and groaned.

"You ever been arrested before, nigger?" the fat man asked.

"Nawsir," he breathed through chattering teeth.

"You acting mighty guilty about something," the fat man observed thoughtfully.

"Nawsir," he repeated.

"I better check and see if you got a record," the fat one said. "Awright, niggers. Pile out and walk ahead."

Surrounded by blue-coated policemen, Fishbelly stumbled out of the car and moved dazedly forward, approaching a soaring white building whose top he could not see. But he was a little more at ease now; the white men would never find that contaminating picture of the woman's face that was still burning with a terrible luminosity in the black depths of him. They could never prove him guilty, but he felt guilty in a way that they could never imagine or grasp.

"This way!" a man called when they reached the door.

A few moments later Fishbelly and Tony were seated in the cleanest, quietest room they had ever been in in their lives, and they felt cold, lost, and alone. Dire possibilities thronged Fishbelly's mind: Would they beat him? Why had he fainted when he had been threatened with castration? When confronted with white people, he had been weaker than he thought and he hated himself for it. He was irrationally convinced that he had to undergo some pain, or shame, and he hoped that it would come quickly and let him be. The guilt that possessed him made him not only resigned to make atonements, but he anticipated them. But what he dreaded most was the taunting threat of that knife pointed at the quiveringly secret parts of him.

Through the steel bars of the door he saw the dim face of a big clock whose hour hand pointed toward seven and he knew that his mother and father were at supper. . . . Or were they waiting for him? Had Zeke or Teddy or Sam spread the news of their being arrested? Or had they been too afraid to tell anyone?

"You reckon the others told our folks?" he asked Tony.

"Don't know," Tony grunted dispiritedly.

"How we going to let 'em know?"

"My papa's going to kill me," Tony wailed, giving vent to what mattered most to him.

"Hell, man, we better be thinking about what we going to tell these white folks," Fishbelly reminded him.

"You reckon they going to let us go after while?" Tony asked, wishing that the police would treat him with the indulgence that his family did.

"Sh." Fishbelly signaled for silence.

From far down the corridor came the hollow echoes of footfalls and bursts of masculine laughter that increased in volume as they neared the barred door.

"Aw, Clem, you *fooling!*" A shouted, chesty laugh.

"The *hell* I am! You'll see!" A high-pitched, snorted retort.

"There ain't no niggers like that!" A protest couched in tones of compassion.

"I got to *see* this! No nigger living can trick me!" A crooned declaration.

"I'll swear to Gawd he did!" Lyrical, hilarious insistence.

"What did you do to 'im?" A prompting, drawling question.

"I'll show you. Wait." A song of anticipatory sadism.

"I'd rather believe in a nigger virgin than believe what Clem's saying!" A sensual voice full of lilting contentiousness.

Four uniformed men appeared in front of the barred door. Fishbelly and Tony, whose heads had been resting against the wall, jerked forward and stared.

"Which one plays possum?"

"That black one with the long straight hair," the tall man who had arrested them pointed to Fishbelly.

"That cute-looking nigger with the big eyes?"

"That's him."

"Clem, that nigger was leading you up the garden path," a stout blond young man chided.

"I'll be damned if he was," Clem countered with rolling confidence as he unlocked the door and entered. "He went out like a light. . . ." He directed his words now to Fishbelly. "Didn't you faint for me, nigger?"

Fishbelly's nails bit into his palms and he did not answer.

120

"Goddamn, ain't you got pretty hair, nigger. What you put on it? Ham fat?"

Hoarse chortles sounded in the men's throats.

"Both niggers got straight hair. White folks' niggers, hunh?" Clem asked.

Fishbelly let his eyes glance at their faces, then fall.

"You say that nigger fainted?" a policeman asked sarcastically. "Not *him*. He's a sassy nigger if I ever seen one."

"Naw. He's just a little scared," Clem explained in a purring voice. "Watch me soften 'im up a bit."

The policemen advanced and Fishbelly watched them with hate in his eyes. He felt that they lived in another world and no gesture or word of his could ever reach them. The only thing that he could do to them that would ever really matter would be to kill them. But his hate melted into fear as Clem bent over him and made mock movement with his arm, as though to strike him, but the gesture terminated by Clem's lifting his hand to his head, scratching the back of his neck while he screwed up his nose. Fishbelly shrank with swimming eyes, his tongue half lolling out.

"He ducked like Joe Louis!" A singing statement.

"That nigger's got some rabbit in his blood!" A bubbling comment.

"Come on, nigger. Open up. How you feeling?" Clem asked.

The impulse to reply rose in him, but the constriction in his throat permitted no words.

"Don't you hear me talking to you, nigger?" Clem growled. "How you feeling?"

"Awright," Fishbelly heard himself answering, but was immediately angry with himself for having done so.

"You mad at me, nigger?" Clem asked in a low, teasing voice.

"Nawsir," Fishbelly whispered. He was in despair at not being able to remain silent.

"And how you doing there, old lover man?" Clem asked Tony.

"Awright," Tony breathed.

Clem made a quick movement as though to pat the top of Tony's straight hair, a gesture that galvanized the boy into a stance of hysterically defensive action; he leaped away, tumbling over backward from the bench, his head striking an iron pipe that ran along the base of the wall.

"What you doing somersaults for, nigger?" Clem demanded, inflecting his voice to simulate surprise.

Resonant chuckles filled the room. Tony lay on the stone floor, his body doubled up tightly like a fetus in the womb, the flaring black fingers of his hands spreading and shuttling over the black of his head while he keened:

"I ain't done nothing! Please, sir!"

"Git up from there, nigger!" A clipped tone of command. "I didn't touch you."

Tony wept, not moving. Clem reached down and grabbed a fistful of Tony's muddy shirt and yanked the boy to his feet. Tony's legs sagged and his head tucked turtlelike into his hunched shoulders as his extended fingers shot frantically over his mussed hair to shield his head from a possible blow.

"You stop that crying, nigger, 'fore I give you something to cry about!" A sarcastic command couched in terms of intimacy.

"Aw, put that weeping nigger in another room," one suggested. "We want to see this other nigger do his act."

"Yeah," Clem agreed, shoving Tony into the arms of another policeman. "Take this nigger out."

"But wait for me, hunh?" the policeman who was taking Tony out called impatiently.

"Okay," Clem consented.

Fishbelly stared ahead, as though unaware of their presence, feeling sweat trickling down from his armpits. The policeman who had escorted Tony out came rushing back, eyes shining, panting:

"Okay. Let her rip!"

"Nigger," Clem began pleasantly, "I want you to do me a little favor. I told my friends here that you was a real passing-out artist. Now, you just take it easy and pull a little faint for me, see?"

Fishbelly looked stonily into space and did not reply.

"Don't you want to co-operate none with me, nigger?" Clem asked softly.

Fishbelly sat like a slab of black granite.

"Ain't you talking none this afternoon, nigger?" There was an edge of rising anger in the voice now.

Fishbelly felt the muscles of his stomach tightening; he refused to look at the man or speak. Clem took a quick step backward, whisked out his knife, flicked open the long, gleaming blade and approached Fishbelly, poking the tip of the gleaming blade at his groin.

"This time I'm going to cut 'em off and hang 'em up in the sun to dry!"

The man crouched and lunged at Fishbelly and, in spite of himself, he felt the return of that sensation that had claimed him in the police car: his feet, his legs, and his arms faded from him and his head swam. . . .

"Nigger, you ain't going to faint, hunh? Well, here goes!"

Clem caught hold of Fishbelly's thigh and again that gigantic black curtain hurtled toward his eyes and he was gone, falling into a black pit. He came to a moment later, lying prone on the stone floor with laughter ringing in his ears and feeling cold water drenching his face and chest. Clem towered over him with an empty tumbler in his hand.

"Okay, nigger." The voice was soft, sensual. "I think you can still go and see your gal; you can even git married."

Fishbelly lay with dull eyes, the room and the men in it fading and focusing about him.

"You see how his arms flipped?"

"Goddamn, that nigger's eyes turned into his head like a window shade going up!"

Almost without breathing, he stared at the laughing faces.

"Okay, nigger. That's all. Git up now. . . . Hep!"

He could not obey; his limbs felt like water. He lifted his head in time to see a huge man with white hair come striding into the room and join the crowd.

"He did it, Lieutenant!" a voice called out.

"I thought Clem was lying," the white-haired lieutenant said. "Is it a trick, or does he really faint?"

"Naw, Lieutenant. It's the real thing," Clem said. He swung back to Fishbelly. "Hey, nigger! Git on your feet!"

Clem pulled at Fishbelly's arm and Fishbelly stood on wobbly legs; they eased him upon the bench and he sagged against the wall, staring sightlessly.

"That nigger's fooling you-all," the lieutenant said, his gray eyes appraising Fishbelly.

"Clem, show the lieutenant how you did it."

The white-haired lieutenant laughed rumblingly, chewing a long black cigar, his face amused, tolerant. Clem again whipped out his knife, flicked open the long, gleaming blade and edged forward.

"Naw!" Fishbelly whispered, swamped again by that sinking feeling of his body slipping toward oblivion.

When he was revived this time, he felt their hands propping him into a sitting position on the floor. The room rocked with laughter. Another man, wearing a gold star on his chest, entered.

"Hi, Captain."

"Hi, boys. Is this the fading nigger, Clem?" the captain asked.

"That's him in person, Captain," Clem said.

"You boys are pulling my leg," the captain said, laughing.

"Hell, naw!" the lieutenant said. He snapped his fingers. "He goes out like *that*."

"I don't believe it," the captain said.

"Okay. Watch this," Clem said.

The knife was again in Clem's hand and the blade pointed toward Fishbelly's groin. Fishbelly's eyes were riveted upon the tip of that knife blade and his lips hung open as he breathed, panting through his mouth.

"Awright, nigger! This time I'm really going to cut 'em off and sew 'em in your goddamn mouth!" Clem growled and leaped at Fishbelly.

Fishbelly felt all the sensations that he had felt before, but, this time, he was already advancing beyond the repeated experience. There was in him a deep, small hard core of detached hate; he felt that black curtain swooping toward him and he could sense his legs, his feet, and his arms beginning to fade. He blinked his eyes and continued staring at the tip of the knife blade pointing at his groin. He was ravaged by fear, but coldly conscious.

"What in hell you waiting on, old artist? Ain't you going to faint for me?" Clem demanded fiercely.

Slowly Fishbelly lifted his tired eyes and stared straight into the white man's face.

"Huh! The nigger ain't scared of me no more," Clem said.

Fishbelly stared wordlessly.

"I'm going to cut off what you love most, nigger!" Clem thundered.

Fishbelly did not bat an eyelid. Clem withdrew the knife blade and stepped back.

"Goddammit, he won't do it," he spat in disgust.

Relaxed laughter filled the room.

"He's used to you now, Clem," the lieutenant said.

"That goddamn nigger was fooling all along," the captain muttered, laughing.

Bleakly, Fishbelly stared at them. He was willing to die, but he would never faint again, not as long as he lived. They could not violate him that way anymore. He watched Clem's fingers snap the blade shut and slip the knife into his pocket. Clem then came to him and stared down into his eyes.

"Mad at me, nigger?" he asked softly.

Fishbelly's eyes were twin pools of blankness.

"Just playing with you, nigger. You know I wouldn't hurt a hair of your goddamn black nigger head, don't you?" Clem teased him.

Fishbelly tried to make his ears stop listening to the hateful voice.

"Awright, let's let this nigger rest a little," the captain said.

"Yeah. He's had enough," the lieutenant said.

Fishbelly watched them file out of the room as they laughed and talked among themselves. One policeman lingered behind at the barred door and looked at Fishbelly for a long moment. Then he smiled bitterly and murmured:

"They made a man out you today, didn't they, boy?"

He clanged the door shut and was gone.

14

Twilight stood behind the panes of the barred window and Fishbelly sat brooding, recalling that he had eaten nothing since noon. His nerves were strained, jumpy; he had been roused to so high a pitch of terror that he could not relax; he felt that all around him lurked hidden menaces waiting to leap. How long would they keep him in jail? What had happened to Tony? Had they beat him? Or had they let him go? And why had the white men ignored Tony and centered their attentions upon him? Then, just as he was dozing, the barred door opened and a policeman shoved a stumbling, sleepy Tony into the room.

"Here's your side-kick, old pass-out artist!" the policeman shouted and vanished, banging shut the door.

Awkward and tongue-tied, the two boys regarded each other warily. Fishbelly yearned to talk, but he did not know what to say, for his feelings baffled him. The emotionally devastating experiences he had undergone during the past six hours eluded his grasp and hung suspended in his psychological digestion like stubborn, cold lumps. And his quick, raw pride was wincing because he thought that Tony was thinking contemptuously of him for his having fainted when the policeman had threatened to castrate him. "But I didn't want to pass out," he wailed bitterly to himself. "I couldn't help it. . . ." And he was glad that they had taken Tony out of the room before they had recommenced their teasing torture. What made white people act like that?

"They beat you?" Tony asked, in a tone that betrayed ignorance of how to express compassion.

"Naw." Fishbelly play-acted nonchalance. "You?"

"Naw."

126

"They just kept trying to scare me . . . with that knife," Fishbelly confessed haltingly.

"But how come they do that to *you?*" Tony asked, frowning.

In an intuitive, confused way Fishbelly knew why they had selected him for torture; they had not so much selected him as he had presented himself as a victim. The guilt in him stemming from the photograph of that white woman that he had had in his pocket had thrust him compellingly toward them. But he did not understand all this well enough to explain it. His growing sense of manliness made him say to Tony:

"I don't know."

"Shucks, mebbe they just teasing us," Tony muttered with a forced laugh, trying to redeem their shame.

"Hunh? Yeah. Mebbe." Fishbelly assented to that odd interpretation, though he knew that that "teasing" had been the deadliest he had ever known.

Toward nine o'clock a white-jacketed, bald-headed black man unlocked the barred door and shuffled in with sandwiches and two paper containers of milk.

"You work here?" Fishbelly asked respectfully.

"Me?" asked the waiter in a sticky, cracking voice and laughed. "Naw, man. I'm just a trusty, that's all."

"You in jail just like us?" Tony asked.

"That's right, sonny," the trusty said.

"What they going to do with us?" Fishbelly implored naïvely.

The bald-headed trusty eyed them skeptically, then said in a tentatively cynical cry:

"That all depends on what you-all done done. . . ."

"We ain't done nothing," Fishbelly and Tony sang.

The trusty stared at them for a moment, his eyes growing ludicrously wide; then he burst into a long, too-violent laugh that terminated in a physical contortion that was just short of a cute dance step.

"Yeah?" the trusty asked with compassionate sarcasm. He nodded his head and wiped his mouth with the back of his hand and crooned: "That's that same old lie that everybody tells that comes to this jail. Let them tell it, ain't nobody in this whole jailhouse ever did a goddamn thing! They *all* innocent as newborn babes!"

"But we was just *playing!*" Tony whined.

"That's *all*, just playing!" Fishbelly insisted.

"Oh yeah?" the trusty's tone was singingly suspicious. "But just what *kind* of playing was you-all a-doing? Plenty people in this world's been *hanged* just for playing. They had that poor Chris Sims in this jailhouse and I heard 'im crying and moaning back there in his cell 'fore they let that mob in to take 'im out. He told them white folks that he was just *playing* with that white gal, that he didn't do nothing wrong, that he didn't mean nobody no harm. But they *killed* 'im just the same."

"Naw!" Fishbelly stood and his voice rose in shrill insistence. "There ain't no white gal in this," he cried, seeing Chris's bloated body lying under the glaring electric bulb. "We was just playing on a white man's property, that's all. They call it trespassing. . . ."

The trusty took a quick, backward step and stared wide-eyed at Fishbelly; he shook his head and turned away, mumbling warningly:

"Goddamn, nigger, don't you go gitting all excited and worked up in this jailhouse." The trusty turned and advised wryly: "White man see you gitting all steamed up like that and he's *sure* to think you done done something dead wrong."

"There ain't no white gal in this," Fishbelly felt impelled to deny the accusation a second time. He sat, staring in agitation.

The trusty studied them, dislodging his false teeth with his tongue and then settling them again upon his gums with a clicking sound.

"How old is you-all?" he asked them.

"Me? I'm nineteen," Tony said.

"I'm fifteen," Fishbelly said.

"You-all just boys," the trusty observed slowly. "Now, if you-all telling the truth, then you ain't got much to worry about. They going to come to you and ask you some questions in a little while and then mebbe you'll git out soon. You got folks?"

"Yeah," Tony said. "My papa's Silas Jenkins. He runs a woodyard . . ."

"Tyree Tucker's my papa," Fishbelly said. "The undertaker on Douglass Street—"

"Naw? You kidding?" the trusty asked, blinking.

"I swear," Fishbelly said.

"Goddamn! Then why didn't you tell them white folks?" the trusty asked. "Them white men *know* your papa—"

"They didn't give me time; they didn't ask me!" Fishbelly wailed.

The trusty weighed Fishbelly with his eyes and rubbed his gnarled fingers over his bald skull.

"I know old Tyree," he said slowly. "I'll git word to 'im, if you want me to . . . I can go out, you know." He paused, fear gleaming dully in his sunken eyes. "But if you niggers lying to me, I'll git you if it's the last thing I ever do on this earth, see? Don't want to git in no trouble on 'count of no no-good niggers—"

"Just phone my papa and tell 'im I'm in jail," Fishbelly begged. "He home now."

"I'll see." The trusty screwed up his eyes and took a backward step, then asked drawlingly: "What's your nickname?"

"Fish. They call me Fishbelly."

"Awright. I'll see," the old trusty said and left.

An hour later a young man entered carrying a notebook. Both boys sat with their eyes nervously following the man's fountain pen as it raced over sheets of paper. It was the white man's eyes, mouth, his facial expression in general that they were really longing to study in order to snatch some fleeting clue of their fate, but they knew better than stare at him directly lest they create the impression of "sassiness"; instead, their eyes concentrated upon the gold band girting one of the white man's fingers, upon the creamy whiteness of his nylon shirt, and the finicky manner in which he took pulls from his cigarette, exhaled smoke through his nostrils, then balanced the cigarette delicately upon the edge of the wooden bench. The man's yellow-gray eyes had vouchsafed them only a casual glance that ascertained that they were human beings of a sort. They waited, trying to muster enough courageous wisdom to permit their refuting any serious accusation and yet be respectful of white authority. These contradictory impulses made them fidget, for they had not only to defend themselves, but, at the same time, try not to offend—try to please. After offhandedly asking their ages, addresses, names, and where they had been apprehended, the man, to their amazement, rose to leave.

"But, mister, we wasn't doing nothing!" Fishbelly's tone was pitched between a timid statement and a meek plea.

"You're booked for trespassing," the man said, grinding out his cigarette with his heel.

"We was just playing," Tony moaned.

"When can we go home?" Fishbelly asked with averted eyes.

"When they're through with you, you'll know," the man said. "They'll take you to juvenile court in the morning—"

"We sleep in jail?" Tony asked in a whisper.

"That's right. You won't be the first nigger that ever slept in here," the man said and strode out, clanging the door shut.

"They won't even lissen to us," Tony sobbed.

A few moments later Fishbelly saw beyond the bars of the door the dim shapes of a white man and a black man approaching. The black man looked familiar; his shirt collar was open and he walked with a too-careless stride. Good Gawd! *It's Papa*. . . . Fishbelly leaped to his feet and rushed to the bars of the door, trembling with excitement.

"Tony, Papa's here," he called whisperingly over his shoulder.

Then, as Tyree neared him, Fishbelly called out boldly: "Papa!"

But Tyree gave no sign of having heard. When Tyree was directly opposite the door, Fishbelly reached impulsively out to touch him and he was stunned when Tyree bellowed:

"Git on back there and sit down, Fish!"

Rebuffed, he backed away from his father. Did Tyree think he had committed a serious crime? Then he became aware that Tyree was stiff, unnatural in his manner. The white man unlocked the door and said:

"There they are, Tyree. You can talk to 'em for a few minutes."

"Oh, thank you, sir, Chief," Tyree chanted humbly, bowing.

Fishbelly understood now; his father was paying humble deference to the white man and his "acting" was so flawless, so seemingly effortless that Fishbelly was stupefied. This was a father whom he had never known, a father whom he loathed and did not want to know. Tyree entered the room and looked at him with the eyes of a stranger, then turned to watch the retreating white man. When the white man had turned a corner in the corridor, Fishbelly saw a change engulf his father's face and body: Tyree's knees lost their bent posture, his back straightened, his arms fell normally to his sides, and that distracted, foolish, noncommittal expression vanished and he reached out and crushed Fishbelly to him.

"My son," Tyree mumbled in a choked voice.

"Papa!" Fishbelly cried.

Tyree suddenly pushed the boy away from him and looked at his face, his arms, his legs.

"You awright, Fish?"

"Er . . ." Fishbelly recalled that rasping voice threatening to castrate him, thought of that shining knife-blade tip pointing at his groin, remembered his fainting, heard again those derisive laughs ringing in his ears—but he knew that this was not the time to talk of all that. And he wondered, with a flash of intuition, if he could ever talk of it; there was too much shame that he had to overcome before he could speak of that. "Yessir," he lied softly.

Tyree walked to the door, then turned and faced them, trying desperately to control himself.

"Everything's going to be awright," he said in a sad, husky voice. He turned to Tony. "Hi, Tony."

"Hi, Mr. Tucker," Tony piped with suppressed glee.

"I saw your papa," Tyree told Tony. "Now, I want you boys to set down and lissen to me."

The boys sat and stared reverently at Tyree's face.

"*Obey 'em!*" Tyree shouted in a thunderous whisper, clapping his hands to emphasize each word. "Don't dispute 'em! Don't talk back to 'em! Don't give 'em no excuse for *nothing!* Hear?"

"Yessir, Papa. But they—"

"Shut up and lissen to me, Fish!" Tyree drowned out his

son. "I ain't got long to talk to you, so lissen! Say 'yessir' and 'nawsir' to 'em. And when they talking, keep your mouth *shut!*"

"But Papa—"

Tyree leaped forward and grabbed his son roughly about the shoulders and shook him till his teeth rattled.

"SHUT UP, FISH, AND LISSEN!" Tyree croaked, his eyes glistening with a mingling of love and fear and hate. "You now in the hands of *white* folks, boy! Git that through your damned *head!*"

Fishbelly stared mutely at his father, then his eyes fell in surrender. His father was scared for him and was imploring him with a frightening passion to knuckle under.

"You-all'll git out in the morning," Tyree said, sighing. "The chief of police is my friend and he told me so. . . . Now, Fish, you come straight to me at the office, see?"

"Yessir, Papa. How's Mama?"

"She awright," Tyree said. "But that judge is going to parole you to me, see?"

"They paroling me, Papa?"

"Yeah. From now on you do what I say." Tyree laid down the new law. "It ain't going to be your mama no more. You obey *me,* see. The chief of police said that."

"Yessir," he whispered, nodding gravely.

His heart was troubled by clashing currents of gratitude and degradation. He was ashamed of this scared man who was his father, but this frightened man was protecting and defending him.

"Time's up, Tyree," the white man called from the door.

"'By, son," Tyree said, rising and leaving quickly. He bowed as he went out of the door. "Thanks a million, Chief."

After the door had been shut, Tony whispered joyfully:

"We gitting out, man!"

"Yeah," Fishbelly said lamely.

"Ain't you glad, Fish?" Tony asked, staring at him.

"Hunh? Oh yeah, man," Fishbelly mumbled.

He was all alone; that was it. He did not really have a father!

"No more mud fights for me, man," Tony swore, shaking his head.

Fishbelly knew that someday his father would die and that he would be left alone to grapple with white people and the idea filled him with dread. What would he do then? Naw, naw . . . He could not think of that now, for he could not imagine any way of meeting them other than of violence, and he hated that. . . .

A distant gong clanged metallically through the jail. A policeman unlocked the door, calling:

"Awright, you niggers. Git to your bunks!"

They filed out and half an hour later they were stretched upon hard bunks in the dark, their tired bodies relaxing. Tony was soon snoring in sleep, but Fishbelly was wide-eyed, pondering. What could make white people leave you alone? Money? That was what Tyree had always said. And Tyree's having money was why Tyree had been able to come so quickly to see him in jail. Tyree's having money was why the trusty had telephoned as he had promised. And if those police had known that he was Tyree's son, they surely would not have tauntingly teased him with those threats of castration. And if Tyree could command a little respect like that with a little money, ought not one be able to command a great deal of respect with much money? But how big a sum of money did one need? He drifted into an uneasy sleep filled with vivid but shifting dreams.

Next morning the bald-headed trusty hustled them through tepid cups of unsweetened black coffee, bowls of soupy oatmeal, and plates of stewed prunes.

"I knowed Tyree had a son called 'Fish,'" the trusty told Fishbelly with slow satisfaction. "That's how come I asked you your nickname. You seen your papa yit?"

"Yeah. He was here."

"Aw, I knowed it. Tyree's done put in the 'fix' for you-all," the trusty said with a grin.

The trusty led them down a corridor to a big, gaping door over which was a gilt sign proclaiming:

CHILDREN'S COURT

Flanked by Tony, Fishbelly entered a packed throng of intently watching white faces; the air about him was full of buzzing conversation. He shrank, not knowing from what di-

133

rection danger would strike. Before him, at an uplifted pulpit-like table, and behind a curving railing, sat a tall, black-haired white man wearing horn-rimmed glasses—and Fishbelly knew that that black-circled-eyed man was the judge. He and Tony stood at the back of the room, guarded by the trusty and a white policeman. The judge pounded a gavel and said:

"Silence!"

Then he heard his name being mentioned in a loud voice:

". . . Rex Tucker vs. Robert Vinson and Anthony Jenkins vs. Robert Vinson . . . Charge: Trespassing . . . Apprehended by Officers Clem Johnson and Vernon Hale . . ."

"The judge's calling you," the trusty whispered. "Git on up there."

Fishbelly moved beside Tony toward the railing behind which sat the tall white judge wearing horn-rimmed glasses. To left and right of the judge stood other white men consulting together in low tones.

"Are these the boys?" the judge asked.

"Yes, Your Honor," a white man answered.

Behind the judge Fishbelly saw a tall pole from which draped a huge American flag, and from a partly opened window wafted a slow breeze that stirred the flag's falling folds and he remembered that vast black curtain that swept before his eyes each time he had fainted. . . . No, no; he must not pass out now. Above the gently billowing flag was a golden, long-beaked eagle whose wings were spread and whose claws clutched shafts of jagged lightning. Fishbelly felt that that glittering eagle was about to swoop down upon him and peck out his eyes with its sharp bill. He was claimed by so deep a fear that he had the sensation of being enclosed in a dream.

"I'm letting you boys off this time, but next time you come before me it'll be the reformatory for you. I'm paroling you into the custody of your parents," the judge pronounced.

Fishbelly stared, wondering if it were true. A policeman leaned to them and said:

"Okay. Beat it."

"He's done let you off," the grinning trusty said, taking the boys by their shoulders and shepherding them through the door and down a big corridor. "Keep right on till you git to the street," the trusty said, pointing. "And tell Tyree I said to spank you good and hard."

"Yeah," Fishbelly mumbled, trying to grin.

Plagued by a sense of guilt, he walked with Tony down a hall whose imposing grandeur made him feel guiltier than ever. A moment later they stood uncertainly upon the sidewalk in the morning sunshine. Fishbelly had spent less than twenty-four hours in jail, but it seemed a million years. In a way that he could not explain, the look of the world had altered; he was aware now of an aspect of that world that he could never quite trust again. And then he realized what was bothering him: there were too many white faces about him and their presence seemed to be prompting him to perform and act whose name he did not know. Should he bow down, run, curse, or just try to act natural? And because he did not know what to do, he felt anxious, ill at ease. He longed for the haven of his Black Belt. Aw yeah; there was a road that skirted the outer edges of town, a road that avoided the white faces in the center of the city.

"Say," he suggested to Tony, "let's go by Bullocks's road."

Tony stared, his face twitching.

Yeah," Tony agreed in an understanding drawl. "I know what you mean. I don't like it *here* neither. . . ."

They walked briskly, wordlessly, yet not so fast as to attract attention; but when the sidewalks were empty they almost ran; yet each time they saw white faces they automatically slackened to a kind of shuffling gait. Though Fishbelly was unaware of it, he, too, like his father, was rapidly learning to act an "act."

They reached a highway bordering a thick wood and their pace slowed, their muscles relaxing. The blue sky grew real again, and the overhead, flaming disk of light became the familiar sun that they had seen all their lives.

"Them white folks is *mean!*" Tony wailed suddenly.

"I *hate* 'em," Fishbelly mumbled. "They ain't no good. They act like they done bought this goddamn world."

"But Papa says it's Gawd's world," Tony said.

"Yeah, but the white folks *own* it." Fishbelly was bitter.

Having exhausted their invective, they walked in silence

until they came to a fork in the road and paused. They were reluctant to part; separated, they had no way to share what had befallen them. They lingered, looking about in embarrassment.

"Well, I reckon I'll be seeing you," Tony mumbled casually.

"Yeah, man. So long." Fishbelly spoke absent-mindedly.

Yet they did not move, and neither did they look at each other. Tony picked up a stone from the roadside and flung it aimlessly into a patch of grass.

"Say?" Tony began in a whisper.

"Hunh?"

"I don't want nobody to know how I cried in that jail," Tony said at last, turning his back and kicking viciously at the curb.

And that was what Fishbelly had been waiting to talk about; they now proceeded to make a pact of secrecy about experiences they had shared but did not understand. Their anger against the white faces converted itself, like scudding mercury, into a possible anger against themselves. To feel shame before white faces was bad, but to feel shame before their own people was worse.

"If our folks ever know what happened to us, they'll *laugh*," Fishbelly said in fierce agreement.

"That's right. But they don't *have* to know," Tony decreed.

Tony stared at the distant horizon and Fishbelly looked gloomily toward the woods. There was more to be decided, but how was it to be done? Tony turned suddenly to Fishbelly and touched his shoulder, with a gentle plea in his eyes.

"Promise you won't talk about how I cried," he begged.

"Then you won't tell about me fainting, hunh?" Fishbelly asked with moist eyes.

"Hell, naw, man!" Tony swore fervently.

"Then it's all just between *us*, hunh?" Fishbelly asked.

"*You* say nothing and *I* say nothing," Tony outlined the pact, yet hinting at implied reprisals in case of its violation.

"Yeah, yeah . . . I ain't going to say a word," Fishbelly pledged. "I'm too *'shamed!*"

"Me too," Tony muttered.

But they still did not look at each other. They were deeply relieved, but somehow still uneasy.

"So long," Tony said suddenly.

"So long," Fishbelly sighed.

Tony headed down the road, reached a bend, turned, and waved. Fishbelly flashed a wry smile and waved back.

"Hope that bastard don't talk none," Fishbelly growled; he plunged amidst trees and was at once comforted by their quiet, shady gloom.

He advanced over snapping twigs, sensing the possibility of even more shame lying ahead of him, flinching at the idea of meeting his mother, his father, and his friends. Oh, if only he could flee to some place where he was not known, where people would accept him as a boy who was not scared, a boy who had not spent a night in jail! It was the first time that such a thought had entered his head and it frightened him.

Suddenly he was stiff, immobile, hearing a strange sound. "What's that?" he wondered aloud. A lonely yelping reached his ears from the center of the woods. "That's a dog!" he exclaimed as he identified the sound. "Must be sick or something. . . ." He pushed in the direction of the yelping, then paused. Aw, it seemed to be coming from behind a clump of thick bushes. He parted tall grass and plunged forward. Good Gawd. . . . he was staring at a large brown dog that lay squirming and gasping at the foot of a tree, giving out alternating yelps and whimpers.

"Puppy," Fishbelly called tenderly, involuntarily.

The dog, whose eyes had been closed, raised its head and stared at Fishbelly, yelping joyfully now, its tail wagging. Cautiously Fishbelly approached the animal, fearing that it was perhaps mad. But, no; the dog was wounded. "I bet a car hit it," he mumbled. The beast's head showed a hugh bruise and its back looked bent, twisted. Fishbelly stooped; yes, the dog's back was broken. It had no doubt been hit and had crawled here and could go no farther. He extended his hand and the dog licked it greedily, beseeching comfort, whimpering.

"Puppy, you in a fix," he breathed compassionately.

What could he do? Whose dog was it? Then he started,

recalling that he had just left jail, where he had been branded as a trespasser, and he rose to leave. The dog yelped, wagging its tail. He lingered. Naw, he couldn't leave a wounded animal like that. He stooped again to the dog; there was no doubt about it; its back was broken. Fishbelly's voice burst out in a throaty whine of resolution: "I got to do something. . . . Got to kill 'im so he won't suffer." He looked about for a stick big and heavy enough with which to beat the dog to death, but he found none. He walked distractedly into the woods, searching the ground. He saw a piece of brick, but it was not large enough. Next he came across an empty whiskey bottle. Aw yes; if he could smash this bottle with that brick, then maybe he could kill the dog with a sharp edge of glass. . . . He picked up the brick and shattered the bottle with it, then examined the jagged sweep of shard remaining attached to the neck; it had a flat edge as good and sharp as a knife blade.

He returned to the whimpering dog and watched its eyes walling in throes of distress. He bent to it once more and it licked his hand. "Gawd, can I do it?" The only sure way to kill it was to cut its throat, but the dog might bite him if he tried that. Yes, he could hold the dog's mouth with his left hand and then slash the throat with the glass that he held in his right. He hesitated. The dog writhed in bodily torment, its tongue licking caressingly at his fingers. He had to kill it or leave it here to wallow in endless pain. . . . Sweat filmed his brow. He glanced guiltily over his shoulder and then back at the quivering animal. Yes; he had to do it.

The fingers of his right hand gripped the neck of the shattered bottle and he watched sunrays glittering in myriad tiny, spectrumlike lances on the ragged, scalloped surfaces of the edge. A distant factory whistle emitted a long, melancholy hoot and he lifted his head; it was noon. High above him a plaintive birdcall drenched the sunshine with liquid melody. He brooded pityingly over the dog, whose pink, fuzzy tongue licked beggingly at his black skin. All he had to do was seize firm hold of that pointed mouth, clamp his fingers tight so that that mouth would not open and those fangs would not snag or snap him, then crash down with that sharp, flat edge into that breathing, hairy throat. The dog ceased whimpering; its mouth opened and the glistening tongue drooled limply out as the animal panted in the heat. No; he couldn't kill it; he hadn't the nerve. . . . He rose and stood, shuddering.

Pain prodded the dog to whimpering again and Fishbelly bit his lips. "I ought to call somebody. . ." No; he could not risk being arrested again for trespassing. Yet if he did not kill the dog, it would lie here and suffer for hours in this brutal sun, dying of slow torture. And there was not a drop of water that he could give the dog. He patted the animal's head, realizing that he had either to kill it or leave at once, for he could not endure that piteous yelping. A yellow butterfly flitted slowly before his eyes and he absent-mindedly watched it whirl veeringly over a wild hedge, out of sight. A bumblebee drove buzzingly past in a straight line. A big bluebottle fly whirred circlingly and then settled at a corner of the dog's eye; the dog shook its head, feebly trying to move a front paw. "He's paralyzed," Fishbelly whispered to himself, brushing the fly away.

The dog's brambled tongue licked again at his skin; the animal seemed to suffer less when it was in physical contact with him; it even managed to wag its tail a bit. "Somebody sure loved this dog." Then, with gentle determination, he closed the palm of his left hand over the dog's eyes and mouth and the dog let him and he knew that that dog had trusted its master or mistress. The dog was still for several seconds, then tried ever so softly to ease its head free. Fishbelly knew that he had to act at once or give up. Convulsively, he tightened his fingers about the dog's mouth and eyes and bent its head backward so that the throbbing neck lay vulnerable, exposed with its glistening brown hair. He flexed the muscles in his right arm, lifted it high into the air and then, gritting his teeth, brought down the razor-sharp edge of glass pointed at the animal's throat; his arm was as stiff as steel and the flecked edge of shard struck the throat and his arm felt the impact of the glass's edge upon the dog's flesh. The blade sank in easier than he had thought; the dog's body gave a slight heave and a tiny red jet of blood jumped bright and restless in the sunshine, splashing and covering his left hand with its running hot wetness and he heard the dog making muffled whines deep in its throat. He rammed the shard deeper, driving it home and

the dog's breathing became a series of grunts that slowly pe-
tered out. The dog's neck stiffened and he withdrew his hand.
The dog's brown eyes grew round, big, gleaming for a split
second, then turned glazed, remaining wide open, and then
slowly, partially closing and becoming dull, lusterless.

Fishbelly emptied his lungs in a sigh and sat back upon his
haunches and watched the shining blood gushing up from the
red well in the dog's throat—a flowing stream that issued in
nervous pulses and spread, running to the dry earth and soak-
ing the roots of the grass. "I must've cut a vein," he murmured. He hovered sorrowfully over the dog, hoping that it
would soon die. He saw the four paws come strangely, suddenly to life and wave involuntarily, indecisively, then grow
slowly still, limp, bending at the joints, the hairy paws dropping. The dog rolled over on its back and a lake of liquid
scarlet formed just to one side of and beneath it and blanketed
the earth, hiding the roots of grass whose green blades thrust
up and through it—a thick, red pool fed from the dog's
gashed throat.

From the asphalt of the invisible highway Fishbelly could
hear an occasional car swishing past and he inclined his head
slightly, still watching the drama of the dog's dying, still
clutching the neck of the bottle, his fingers seemingly unable
to let it go. The dog's dying gradually undid his tension and he
loosened his grip upon the neck of the bottle and found himself longing for a cigarette for the first time that day. The
dog's chest swelled, the hair bristling; then a heaving tremor
ran from the dog's head to its tail; its pink tongue hung life-
lessly out from between curving white teeth; the body gave a
long, violent twitch and Fishbelly knew that its passion of
pain was over.

As he knelt, the dog's dying associatively linked itself with
another vivid dying and another far-off death: the lynched
body of Chris that had lain that awful night upon the wooden
table in his father's undertaking establishment under the yellow sheen of an unshaded electric bulb. He was kneeling before the fact and reality of death, trying to come to terms with
them, seeking for a way to accept them. His father had buried
Chris's broken black body and had called it "a black dream

dead, a black dream that could not come true." Fishbelly had no dread or horror in him now; there was just an acute, detached, and sober wonder.

He contemplated the dog's corpse as though trying to detect some secret that it harbored. Then he bent forward and, before he realized it, he was acting out the role that Dr. Bruce had played that night in the undertaking establishment over the dead body of Chris. . . . Anchoring the dog's head firmly with his left hand to the grassy earth, he hacked the shard into the top of the dog's stomach, making down its middle an unwavering line of incision, slicing through hair and skin and into the white layer of fat and muscle of the dog's abdomen. Patiently he lifted the scalpel and retraced the glass edge over the bloody incision, and, this time, as the jagged end bit deeper, the muscular wall of the stomach opened and the inner organs, now drenched in blood, came to view.

He leaned forward, gazing at the heart, the lungs, the stomach, the liver, and the winding, ivory-white intestines, feeling neither compassion nor dread. Switching the scalpel from his right to his left hand, he reached tenderly into the gory cavity and cut loose all the vital organs and lifted them out, one by one, and laid them carefully upon the grass. When he had emptied the dog's torso, he rose and looked vaguely about, tossed the dripping scalpel casually into a clump of dusty weeds and stooped beside the dog and meticulously dried his sticky hands upon tufts of grass, rubbing his fingers and palms hard, until they were dry and free of blood.

"That's what they did to Chris," he spoke aloud, announcing an emotional discovery.

He had realized it all, had enthroned it in himself in the same manner in which he had swallowed the white woman's picture. When the whites came at him now, he would know what death was, just as he had anticipated death by fainting when the white men had threatened to castrate him. A need of his had been met and he was full of a meek and mute awe. He could live somewhat at peace now with himself; the world of white faces no longer had the power to surprise him.

Then, without a backward glance, he turned and walked through the woods, leaving the disemboweled dog strewn in the pitiless sun. There was in him no pride or arrogance; he had seen the worst and felt that he could take it if he had to; he could go ahead willingly resigned to meet whatever he had to face.

He neared a high, vaulting overpass spanning the highway and climbed a steep, twisting dirt path and he saw the gleaming tops of cars whizzing by in the sun. Then he halted, looking about in bewilderment. Was he dreaming? For the second time he heard odd sounds in the woods, but this time he knew at once that he was hearing a human being. A man's voice was calling out desperately:

"Heeey, boooy . . . Boooooy!"

He stopped and peered down into a welter of tree trunks and foliage, but could see nothing.

"Boy! Boy, come here! C-come h-here!" The voice was gasping, panting.

Hesitantly, he descended the path a few steps, going in the direction of the crying pleas. Yeah . . . Good Gawd! He crept further and saw a wrecked car lying on its side; the hood was smashed, the windshield shattered. He ran on down the path and stopped, gaped at an overturned Oldsmobile. From out under a crushed door the white, bloody face of a man protruded.

"Booy, help m-me . . ." A twisted mouth was calling.

Tingling with anxiety, he ran to within ten feet of the man and paused.

"S-see if y-you can g-get this thing off m-my shoulders. C-come closer," the man begged.

That pain-distorted face wrenched his heart. He ran to within a yard of the car and examined the wreckage. It was a bad job. Blood streamed from the man's right arm, as though an artery had been severed.

"Q-quick, b-boy . . . I'm weak . . . Lost a l-lot of blood . . . Get this d-damned door off m-me." The man seemed at the end of his strength.

"Yessir," he answered mechanically.

The hinge of the door was deeply embedded in the man's shoulder blades, and above the door was the weight of the car. Yeah, he had to try to lift that door and relieve the man's pain, then he would run to the highway and stop a car and ask for help . . . He bent and tugged at the edge of the twisted door.

"G-goddammit, q-quick, nigger!"

Fishbelly sucked in his breath; he froze, his eyes narrowing.

"Nawsir," he breathed, taking a backward step.

"C-come on!" the white face commanded. "You c-can lift it . . . My back's k-killing me. . . ."

Fishbelly was poised, collected now. The suffering *white* man had called him *nigger!* He had an impulse to turn and run, but pity and guilt held him still.

"Y-you hurt bad?" he asked the man softly.

"G-Goddammit, nigger! S-stop talking and h-help me . . ." The voice faded and the man's head sagged.

He stood undecided. Stifling panic, he approached the man again, his arm lifting slowly. The man's head lolled weakly to one side and, for a long moment, his eyes were closed. Fishbelly watched the gray eyes open and stare at him; then, impulsively, the man's right arm flung out and white fingers tried to seize hold of Fishbelly's right leg.

"Naw!" Fishbelly spat, leaping away, trembling.

White fingers clawed frantically in the blood-soaked grass and grasped a clod of earth and hurled it feebly. It fell short of Fishbelly's right foot.

"Naw, naw," Fishbelly protested.

The man glared with frustrated eyes.

"S-sorry, boy . . . I w-wouldn't hurt y-you . . . I'm crazy with pain . . ." The panting voice turned into a long sigh. "G-g-go and get s-somebody to h-help me. . . ." The man breathed heavily, then lifted his voice with sudden strength. "I-I was d-driving and tried not to r-run over a d-dog . . . Maybe I hit the d-dog . . . I don't know. M-my car went out of c-control . . . I smashed into the b-bridge, t-turned over, and rolled d-down here . . . All 'cause of that goddamned d-dog . . ." His voice became lost in his throat.

Looking steadily at the white man over his shoulder, Fishbelly climbed the sloping path a few yards and stopped.

"D-don't l-leave me, b-boy . . . I-I d-didn't mean to scare you . . ."

He kept on up the path until the white man's voice became a

distant echo. He understood now why the man had not been able to get help; no one could hear him. Then the whole picture became clear: That dog that he had so mercifully killed had been hit by that man's car; and, after hitting the dog, the man's car had plunged off the highway and tumbled down the steep embankment and had pinned him beneath it. From where he stood he could see the tops of cars speeding past and, by moving his eyes a fraction of an inch, he could also see the wounded white man. Yes; he would flag a car and tell the white people in it that a white man was hurt and bleeding to death down there. . . . He would have done what was required of him and he would go home. He gained the road and stood. Cars streamed past on the opposite side, but he was too frightened to yell or wave at them. Aw, here came a car, bearing swiftly down upon him. The car slowed of its own accord and then Fishbelly's reactions became so compounded that he scarcely realized what was happening. *It was the police car!* Its tires screeched and it halted at his elbow and Clem, who had held the knife at his groin, was glaring at him.

"Well, I'll be goddamned! It's our old fainting-artist nigger!" Clem fished his knife quickly from his pocket, flicked open the blade, and waved the gleaming tip threateningly. "Goddamn, if you wasn't old Tyree's son, I swear I'd operate on you right now! What in hell you doing here? Thought the judge told you to git home!"

Reality was dissolving before Fishbelly's eyes; before him lay a multiplicity of worlds and he could not believe in any of them.

"Yessir," he breathed.

"Awright, git *started!* Hotfoot it out of my sight, nigger, or I'll use this knife on you!"

"Yessir!"

His world was a flat stretch of vision that only his eyes could see; all the rest was blotted out. He walked hard on the hot macadam, fast, not daring to glance around. The police car rolled abreast of him for a few seconds and, from the corners of his eyes, he saw Clem's blunt face. There was a burst of laughter and the motor roared and the car shot forward, disappearing from view in a shimmer of heat, dipping over a rising lift in the highway. There was in Fishbelly's mind a melting image of a white man dying beneath a wrecked car, but it was neither compelling nor important. He had to get home, home to safety. He found himself running and he did not stop until he had reached the streets of the Black Belt. By the time he had forgotten that he had left a white man dying under a smashed car, and he did not ever afterward believe that he had seen it. Fear drove the sense of that reality completely out of his consciousness and he could never speak of it. Terror transmuted the image of that dying man into a flimsy figment of a fevered dream, buried it out of reach of memory.

He walked again, the tears in his eyes blurring the world. A voice sounded in him: *Papa! Papa!* Then he spoke aloud: "I ain't done nothing. . . . Why they act like that? I can't help it if I'm black . . ." He began to sob. "If I'm *wrong* 'cause I'm black, then I don't *want* to be black. . . ."

He came upon an old log lying beside the road and sank upon it. He heard someone coming; he turned; it was a black man. Ashamed of his tears, he averted his face. He sat until his world grew hard, real once more, until the storm in him was dead, until his tears were dry. He rose and walked; ahead was a grocery store and he realized that his stomach was churning with hunger. He found a dime in his pocket and he bought a loaf of bread and walked along in the sun, nibbling at the crust, savoring the taste, reconciled to the sky, the trees, the dusty road, and sensing his body as once more belonging to him.

15

In Douglass Street he spotted Tyree awaiting him upon the steps of the undertaking establishment. He tossed away the unfinished loaf as Tyree bounded forward, a white grin lighting up his face. Fishbelly grew tense, fighting against a scowl pulling at his lips. All the wisdom he knew counseled him to love and honor his father, yet his father was something that mocked everything that he thought a father should be. "He's grinning now like a rooster crowing, but he was meek as a lamb when he saw me in that jailhouse."

"Fish!" his father exclaimed, embracing him. "I was gitting worried. . . ."

"Hi, Papa," he tried to sound joyful.

"You awright, son?" Tyree asked, holding him close. "They let you out more'n a hour ago—"

"I was just walking," Fishbelly said lamely, seeing an airy image of the dying dog and the wounded man in the woods.

"I told that chief not to send you out in the police car," Tyree explained. "Didn't want these crazy niggers out here to see you with no police. They'd never stop talking."

"Oh," Fishbelly said. He kept his face averted, wanting to ask about the parole. "What—?"

"Goddammit, I knew you'd be out today." Tyree drowned him out, nodding exaggeratedly. "Didn't I tell you?"

"Yessir," he mumbled, suppressing resentment. "What—?"

"Ye see, Fish, these goddamned crazy white folks *respect* me," Tyree cut him off again in a high-pitched voice, throwing an arm over his son's shoulder. "I know how to handle these white folks." Tyree's cracked tenor rose in feigned lyricism. "Fish, I know these goddamn white folks better'n they know themselves. There ain't *nothing* I couldn't git from 'em if I tried. Son, you just lissen to your papa who brought you into the world and you'll never go wrong. I *know* and I *know* I *know!*" He broke off, his voice leaping in a joyless laugh.

Dismayed, Fishbelly felt that Tyree was shamelessly crawling before white people and would keep on crawling as long as it paid off.

"I'll show you how to twist these no-good white folks 'round your little finger," Tyree rattled on as they mounted the steps. "And don't you go gitting bitter about being in jail for one night. It ain't *nothing;* it's done happened to a lot of folks and ain't *touched* 'em." Tyree gargled a gratuitous laughter that died away. "You eat yit, son?"

"I ain't hungry," Fishbelly mumbled sullenly.

"Son, don't let these white folks git you down," Tyree counseled knowingly.

Fishbelly was speechless; he had been prepared for a scolding lecture about mud fights; instead, he was being greeted with counterfeit laughter and bogus bragging. He sensed that it was not about what had happened to him that Tyree was concerned; Tyree was hiding his own self-abasement. Fishbelly felt guilty before white folks and he knew that Tyree felt guilty before him.

"Me and you's got a lot to talk about and understand, son." Tyree's confidence sang as he led him across the porch.

The office was dimmed and cooled by drawn shades and Fishbelly stared intently at the silver-gray model casket standing before the window. "All black dreams ain't dead," he mused bitterly. "Some of 'em live and walk around, but they dead just the same." What stunned him was that Tyree had no inkling of how grotesquely obscene he was and he had a perverse impulse to make Tyree see himself as he saw him. But, naw . . . That was wrong.

"Sit down, Fish," Tyree said, taking a bottle from a drawer and tilting it to his lips. He cleared his throat and launched out with strong intent: "No real harm's been done. You safe here with me now and that's what counts. Your mama was having a fit, but I told her you was old enough to take care of yourself, no matter what happened. Shucks, you a chip off the old block; you Tyree's son and Tyree's got good sense." Self-indulgent laughter. "That trusty, Old Mose, phoned me you was in jail and I went to work quick. Ten minutes after he called, I was downtown in the city hall talking to the chief of police. Now, son, just relax and tell me slow and straight what you-all boys was doing. I ain't your mama or your teacher; I'm your father, son, a man like you going to be, the only man in the world you can trust. Now, what was you-all doing?"

With downcast eyes, Fishbelly told of the slap his mother had given him, of the mud fight, of the arrest, but when he came to his fainting in the police car, he groped for words, hesitated, and omitted it; and he also did not mention the policemen's threatening to castrate him in the jail and his fainting twice, to their general delight. And he failed to tell of his slaying and disemboweling the wounded dog; he knew instinctively that Tyree would never have understood it, for he did not understand it himself. And of course, he could never tell anybody why he had carried the photograph of that smiling white woman in his billfold and why he had felt compelled to destroy it by eating it in the car. And, while talking, there was in him no memory at all of the white man dying under the wrecked car. . . .

"That's all, Papa," he lied with a sense of bleak loneliness.

Tyree sat the whiskey bottle upon the desk and threw back his head and laughed.

"Goddamn, son, this is the most wonderful thing I ever heard! I wish to Gawd I was young and could run 'round with you and your friends. When I was a kid, I did the same damnfool things. Mud fights." He rolled the words nostalgically. "Son, I'm kind of glad this happened to you. You *learned* something. . . . I could've explained it till Kingdom Come and you wouldn't't've got it. But now you *know*. Now, from here out, you with *me*. You come straight from school to this office—"

"*Here*, Papa?" he asked, astonished.

"Yeah, *here*," Tyree was emphatic. "You study your lessons here. I'm taking charge of you. Now, go easy on your mama. Just say 'yes' and humor her along, see? That's the way to deal with women, Fish. Arguing with 'em is a waste of time. They just don't understand these things. I know; you at the age when too much sap's rising up in you and you don't know how to git rid of it. I'll show you what to do and the *right* way to do it. It ain't hard, Fish." He chuckled. "And we can handle these old dumb white folks, son. White folks see eleven inches on a foot rule; we black folks see the whole damn rule. Fish, the only way to git along with white folks is to grin in their goddamn faces and make 'em feel good and then do what the hell you want to behind their goddamn backs! And I'm going to show you how to do it. I'll show you everything. It's time you knowed about my business and a lot of other things. There's a heap of stuff about me you don't know, son."

Fascinated as much as repelled by Tyree's code of living,

convinced that Tyree was foully wrong, Fishbelly wanted to argue, challenge him, but he had no experience to pit against his father's cynical sagacity.

"Papa, how come they let you in jail to see me so quick?" he asked plaintively, bracing himself to feel contempt for Tyree's revelation.

"Now, you gitting *real* smart, son." Tyree chortled approvingly. "You starting to ask questions and that's a good sign. Son, Chief of Police Cantley knows me for twenty years. Friend of mine . . . By Gawd, I done buried many a black man he done shot to death. I did 'im favors, fixed up dead black folks he beat up, fixed 'em so you couldn't tell from looking at 'em that they'd been beat to death. I told 'im nice and sweet-like that you was in jail and that if he'd let you go, I'd take care of you. He knows I ain't never made 'im no trouble and that no boy of mine would never make 'im no trouble. It was easy, Fish. Son, I could almost git away with murder in this town. But you got to know *how!* Let me tell you the secret, Fish. A white man always wants to see a black man either crying or grinning. I can't cry, ain't the crying type. So I grin and git anything I want."

"But why they always want to see us crying or grinning, Papa?" Fishbelly asked with quivering lips.

Tyree stared solemnly at his son.

"I'll tell you," Tyree said rising. He clapped his palms to underscore each word: "Fish, white folks is scared to death of us!"

"But why, Papa?"

"White folks know damn well that if they give us *half* a equal chance, we'd beat 'em, come out on top—"

"But I *want* a equal chance!" Fishbelly bawled at his father.

Tyree sat, lifted the bottle and took a long pull, then placed it upon the desk and stared at his son.

"Fish, there's *ten* white men in this country for *every* black man," Tyree stated.

"Then there ain't nothing for me but to grin or cry?" he demanded. "I don't want *that!*"

"Be quiet, son," Tyree said. "You gitting excited 'cause you don't understand." Tyree sighed. "Lissen, my business is burying folks and half the black folks I bury was crazy enough to try to win against odds. Now don't you go and be a fool like that."

"But, Papa, ain't there no way except crying and grinning?"

A haunted look came into Tyree's eyes. He rose and bit his lips.

"Fish, just *you* tell me what you know about this problem." He grew sarcastic. "How *you* going to win?"

"But, Papa, crying and grinning ain't winning," Fishbelly argued, his face burning with shame.

Tyree crossed to his son and spoke in a soft, deadly tone:

"You going to be a problem to me, Fish?"

"What you mean, Papa? A problem? I just want to know—"

"Fish, take your choice: lissen to me or go it by yourself." Tyree put it to him straight. "I ain't going to stop you. . . ."

Fishbelly's mouth hung open. Tyree had implied that he would, if faced by white danger, abandon him! Tyree had pointed out the limits of his protection and the boundaries of his power as a black father.

"You mean the white folks'll kill us *all* 'less we cry and grin?"

"There you go!" Tyree spluttered disdainfully, throwing up his arms. "You know what you saying? Boy, you talking *race* war! Where you git them wild ideas? Lissen: if you git into trouble like that Chris, then I *can't* help you. Git that through your head. I could try, but I wouldn't be *able* to help you. And if I couldn't help you, it wouldn't be no use in *trying;* I'd only git killed too."

Fishbelly saw again that room in the jailhouse, that knife blade pointed at his groin, that black curtain dashing toward his eyes, those laughing white faces that had kindled terror in him, and he realized that there was nothing that Tyree could do to prevent its ever happening again. He bent forward and burst into tears.

"What you crying about, son?" Tyree demanded. Comprehension lit up his face. "Aw, yeah . . . Them white folks scared you in that jail, didn't they?" Tyree embraced his son, mumbling compassionately: "That's *nothing*. Don't go crying all your life about little things like that—"

"But you *said* to cry—!"

"I didn't mean that and you *know* I didn't!" Tyree was stung to anger.

On the day that Fishbelly had discovered how brutal the white world could be, he had also discovered that he had no father. And, as he wept, he realized that he had not wanted to weep, and it made him weep the more, weep for his father's fear and weakness, for the trembling he hid behind false laughter, for the self-abrogation of his manhood. He knew in a confused way that no white man would ever need to threaten Tyree with castration; Tyree was already castrated.

"Yeah, I know," Tyree murmured, patting his son's head. "They scared you and it was the first time. But it ain't *nothing*. You'll git used to it and think nothing of it . . ."

Fishbelly lifted his wet eyes to Tyree's face.

"You mean if the white folks hang me often enough, I'll git so I won't mind no more?" he asked with soft irony.

Tyree blinked and stepped back.

"What in hell you saying, Fish? Stop talking like that. . . . You trying to make fun of me or something?"

"Nawsir. But you said—"

"Shut up, Fish!" Tyree shouted.

The gap between them was complete. They could no longer talk, for their words no longer had any common meaning. Tyree stared at his son's sob-racked body and his eyes grew misty.

"I wanted to keep all this from you, Fish," he mumbled. "But how could I? It's life, son. We all have to face it. No use crying about it. We have to be men and take it."

Fishbelly wept afresh, taking leave of his father; and his father thought that he was weeping because of what he had suffered in the jailhouse! He was weeping for his self-delusion, for a father he did not have.

"Goddamn these white folks!" Tyree shouted suddenly. "They did this to you, a *child!*" He grabbed Fishbelly's shoulders and squeezed them. "I could kill 'em *all!*"

Fishbelly jerked his head up and cried out, trembling at the audacity of his words:

"Naw! You wouldn't! You too *scared!*"

Tyree stood stock-still, then leaped back, staring in disbelief at his son.

"What you say, Fish? *Goddamn!*"

"You scared, Papa! You scared *too!* Just like *me!*"

Tyree's body slumped. He turned and walked aimlessly about the room, then came and stared into his son's face, his eyes dull and stricken.

"You say that . . . to *me,* son?"

The enormity of Fishbelly's accusation filled Fishbelly with contrition and he yeared hotly to annul what he had said. He had only the semblance of a father and he was mocking even that semblance.

"Papa, please! I'm sorry," he gasped.

Tyree turned his back and walked to the desk and stood, his right arm shaking as with palsy.

"I'll be goddamned," he pronounced in gutteral tones of deep hurt. "My own flesh and blood calls me a *coward*—"

"Naw, Papa!" Fishbelly wailed with shut eyes. He rose, determined to beg his father's pardon, and ran to Tyree. Tyree pushed him roughly away.

"Git the hell out of my sight!"

"Papa, I'm sorry!"

"Shut your goddamned mouth!"

Fishbelly leaned against a wall while Tyree ranged to and fro, walking like a blind man.

"I see," he growled. "I got to break your goddamn spirit or you'll git killed, sure as hell! Where you git such crazy notions? Boy, look at what I done with my life! I'm black, but do you hear me whining about it? Hell, naw! I'm a *man!* I got a business, a home, property, money in the bank. . . . Is my life bad?"

"Nawsir. It ain't bad; it's just *hopeless,* Papa," Fishbelly was fighting his father again.

"Lawd have mercy," Tyree sighed. "Fish, what's got into you? You ain't thinking straight, boy. I done made something out of my life and I didn't go to school like you. I hire people with brains to do my embalming. . . . Don't git mixed up by what you read in books, boy. You tell me I'm scared, hunh? But do you know what I suffered? How I struggled to git what

I got? Goddamn, if you know so much, then go it alone, Fish! Git on your own. I won't stop you. Go!" Tyree became hysterical. "Git out! *Now! Go!*"

"Naw, Papa," he relented again.

"Naw! GO!"

"Please, Papa!"

"Shut up! You crazy, calling your papa scared!"

"I didn't *mean* it! I—!"

"I'm feeding, clothing you, sending you to school, and all the time you thinking I'm a fool. . . . Fish, mebbe I oughtn't take charge of you. I ought to let your mama handle you and see what'd happen." His voice rose in a shrill scream. *"You'll git killed, boy!"*

Fishbelly was crushed. Why had he taunted his father like that? He ran to Tyree, but was stopped when Tyree's right palm smacked into his face; stars danced before his eyes and his teeth ached.

"I'm scared, hunh?" Tyree asked with taut lips. "Say it again!"

Fishbelly's temper flared, then he sank to his knees.

"Naw, Papa! Please," he wept.

"Then take it back," Tyree demanded.

"Yessir. I'm sorry!"

"Snotty little whippersnapper!" Tyree was over his shock and felt that he had the situation in hand. "I was fighting white folks 'fore you was born." Now that he had the advantage, he was determined to conquer his son. "You just a calf still wet behind the ears, and you tell me I'm scared."

"I told you I'm sorry, Papa!"

"Being sorry don't mean nothing." Tyree was scornful. "Can you be sorry after you *dead?*"

Fishbelly had no more words; he could not be a man before the white folks and he could not be a man before his father.

"I'm responsible for you," Tyree intoned. "And, by Gawd, I'm going to do my duty. Till you old enough to take care of yourself, you going to walk a chalk line. Hunh! You know so much, yit you sit there crying!"

"Don't holler at me like that, Papa! *Please!*"

"Shut your mouth!"

"Yessir," he gulped.

"Now, stand up!"

"Yessir," he mumbled, rising on wobbly legs, his eyes blinded with tears.

"We got to understand each other tonight or else . . . Now, tell me: You going to obey me or not?"

"I swear I'll obey you, Papa. I'll do what you say." Fishbelly surrendered completely, abjectly.

"Who been talking to you?"

"Nobody, Papa. What you mean?"

"Tell me the truth or I'll *kill* you!"

"Nobody, Papa. I swear 'fore Gawd!"

"Anybody been talking commonism to you?"

"Naw, Papa."

"Then why you say I'm scared?"

"I don't know. I didn't know what I was saying."

"Fish, you going to obey me even when you don't understand what I'm asking you to do?"

"Yessir."

"And no back talk?"

"Nawsir, Papa. No back talk."

"Awright, son. Mebbe we can git along." Tyree sighed. "Now, git in there and wash that mud and dirt off your hands and face. You coming along with me. I'm going to see that you a man from this night on. But, first, we going to eat. . . ."

"Yessir."

16

Sullen, defeated, he dallied as he washed. He had tendered his future into his father's hands and he felt a snarling self-hate. His having branded Tyree as a coward had been an attempt to recover the self-esteem he had lost in the jailhouse, and now that accusation had rebounded in a manner that left him emotionally naked and numb. Oh, if only he could run off and never look at his father again! But where would he go? How would he live?

"Ready, Fish?"

"Yessir," he answered and re-entered the office.

"Come on," Tyree said, leading him out.

A blood-red sun was sinking behind dusty trees.

"We going home, Papa?"

"Naw. We eating out."

"But, Mama—"

"She knows. I phoned her." Tyree was laconic.

Sitting across from Tyree in Franklin's Chicken Shack, he ate smoked ribs and turnip greens and corn bread, washing them down with cold buttermilk; then came peach cobbler and coffee.

"Feel better?" Tyree asked with downcast eyes.

"Yessir."

Night had fallen when they emerged. Fishbelly followed Tyree silently, yearning to tell him that he was tired and wanted to go home.

"Where we going, Papa?"

"Just follow me," Tyree muttered as they mounted a steep street to the top of Ford's Ridge.

Ten minutes later they stood atop a hill in the dark. Below, the town of Clintonville lay spread with yellow lights twinkling far and wide.

"Son, see that long line of lights? That's King Street and it divides the white folks from the black folks. All the town to the left of King Street's *our* town. The rest is white. Now, Clintonville's got about 25,000 folks. 15,000 of 'em's white, and 10,000 of 'em's black. That black part's your kingdom, son. We got everything there and you can have all the fun you want. Someday I hope you going to be the richest nigger down there and I want you to lead our folks. When white folks want to know something about us they'll come to you. But I want you to be a educated leader, son. Not like me. . . . I'll help you, I'll back you to go to school and learn. From now on, I want to trust you. I ain't going to spy on you. Anything you want to know, come to me, Someday I want these white folks to lissen to you. Fish, that's the *key*. How the white folks

155

look at you's everything. Make 'em mad, and you licked 'fore you start. Make 'em feel safe, and the place is yours. Git what I mean, son?" Tyree's voice was sad, but urgent.

"I understand, Papa," he said meekly, not daring to look at Tyree.

"Fish, I'm taking you to a woman tonight. I want you to git some sense into your head and know what life is."

He turned and gaped at Tyree. A woman? Just like *that*? But *what* woman? A feeling of unreality engulfed him and he restrained a desire to laugh. What did having a woman have to do with courage, cowardice, and shame? Well, he could not argue; he had to obey.

"This running around creeks and sneaking smokes and talking big—all that's got to stop," Tyree mumbled to himself. Then he launched into an analysis: "You just gitting all choked up from too much ashes in your blood, that's all; you letting your manhood run up to your brains and that's dangerous. I'm going to show you what to do." He began to descend the hill. "Come on. We won't take the car. I want to walk a little. . . ."

Overawed, trying to link disparate facts, he could scarcely realize that the *moment* had come, had come directly after he had been slapped! He was mute with regret. He had a good father. How had he ever thought otherwise? He walked at Tyree's side, marveling at his wisdom, his generosity. His father was introducing him to the secret intimacies of life, opening all the dark, wonderful doors. He saw shadowy streets, heard sounds of traffic, but he was bent, with fear and gladness, upon an inward goal. He had often fantasied himself storming a dark, shy girl, overpowering her with his need, and making her like it; and now he was being taken to a girl whom, perhaps, he had never seen. "If she's old and ugly, I won't touch her," he told himself.

They turned, as he expected, into Bowman Street, where most of the bars, dance halls, and red-light houses were located. The boys of Bowman Street were tough; they fought, cursed, and knew a lot about life. Yet he was wishing that the experience he was going to meet was more like his dreams. . . .

Now and then some passer-by nodded and mumbled:

"Good evening, Mr. Tyree."

And Tyree, a big black man among little black people whose dead bodies he cleaned, embalmed, and dressed for burial, returned the greeting in a fashion suited to the financial or social standing of the person involved.

"Fish," Tyree spoke slowly, intimately, "what I'm showing you tonight is just something between *us*—what a father tells his son."

"Yessir," he whispered his agreement, humble in mien and mood.

"Now, I own the house where I'm taking you," Tyree explained, pausing in the middle of the sidewalk, holding a blazing match to his cigar, and eying the passers-by as he puffed. "I ain't in this business, son. But I'm broad-minded. You got to be broad-minded in this life. . . . The woman running this flat rents it from me and she's a straight sport. You can trust her. Now, Fish, nobody, not even your mama, knows I own this place; nobody knows but them that need to know. So don't go around mentioning my name about this place. The chief of police lets this house run and he gits a cut of what this house makes; I give it to 'im every Sat'day night. That's how come he let me in that jail to see you; that's how come you got out so quick."

Fishbelly breathed through lips parted in surprise. How stupid he was! Tyree did not quite own whore houses, but he had a lot to say about them! This man whom he saw every day and upon whom he depended for bread—this man knew the top and bottom of life, and he, his son, had called him a coward! Tyree not only violated the law, but violated that law with the law's *permission*. . . . His father was not what he hoped he was, but something utterly different. No wonder he had been slapped! Why, one day, as Tyree's only son, he would own these houses!

"Papa, I'm sorry about what I said—"

"Forget it, Fish." Tyree said tolerantly. "You didn't know any better. Lissen to me and you won't go wrong. Now, tonight, just be easy and natural and don't git excited and all tied up in yourself. It's the simplest thing in the world. Just remember that these women want to serve you, give you pleasure . . ."

"I never did before, Papa."

"That's why I'm taking you, son. After this, come here for your needs. Every Sat'day I'm giving you ten dollars for spending money. If you run short, I'll see what I can do. I want you to be careful, that's all. Ain't no sense in you gitting a lot of fancy notions about this thing. A woman's just a woman and the dumbest thing on earth for a man to do is to git into trouble about one. When you had one, you done had 'em all. And don't git no screwy ideas about their color. I had 'em white as snow and black as tar and they all the same. The white ones feel just like the black ones. There ain't a bit of difference, 'less you make one, and that's crazy. Fish, take these gals and leave 'em. Don't git moon-eyed about 'em; go from one to the other. That way you git to know 'em. Then when you ready to marry and settle down you know what you doing."

They stopped before a towering, wooden tenement which was known as the Bowman Flats.

"This is the place, Fish," Tyree told him.

"But Teddy lives here," Fishbelly said in wonder.

"Yeah," Tyree said. "Teddy's mama's in business too."

Life was disrobing itself. He was entering the orbit of Teddy's existence from outside and above. Teddy was anchored in this sordid tenement, but he, Fishbelly, could come and go when he liked, could take his pleasure and then turn his back. There was rising in him a sense of power and importance. They mounted the steps and the street lamps flashed on just as Tyree rang the bell.

"Don't let this stuff throw you at school, son," Tyree advised.

"I understand, Papa," Fishbelly said, trying to repress his excitement.

A looming black woman in a tight-fitting black dress flung open the door.

"Lawd, it's Tyree!" she exclaimed with a white grin. "And you with your son, Fish?"

"That's right, Maud," Tyree said.

"You men come right in," Maud urged them.

They followed Maud down a hallway and into a large parlor. Fishbelly had heard dark tales about the nature of Maud

Williams's biological commodities. Maud had a daughter, Vera, a high-school girl; she was tall, shapely, and the boys spoke of her in tense whispers.

"Make yourselves at home," Maud chanted in a throaty voice. "I'll git some drinks, hunh, Tyree?"

"That's a good gal," Tyree grunted, plopping himself upon the sofa and extending his legs. "Sit down, Fish."

Fishbelly sat warily upon the edge of a chair and looked about. How quiet and orderly and normal a whore house was! He saw Maud gazing lingeringly at him with a sly smirk; she ducked her head and grinned, shuffling her feet to indicate pleasure.

"Lawd, Tyree, I was wondering when you was going to bring 'im to let me break 'im in," she hummed and waddled out.

"See?" Tyree was offhanded. "She's ticked to death to help you."

Fishbelly managed a sickly smile.

"Her?" he asked dubiously. "Papa, I don't want *her.*"

Laughter poured out of Tyree.

"You got taste, hunh? Naw, son. Not 'less you want her. She'll git you gals your own age."

"Can I see 'em first?"

"Sure. Talk to 'em. Take your time, son."

"What's it going to cost, Papa?"

"Don't you worry about that. Maud'll put whatever you do on the cuff."

Fishbelly swallowed. Tyree was offering him the world.

Maud hustled in with a tray holding whiskey, Coca-Cola, and glasses. She allowed Tyree to serve himself, then she came smilingly toward Fishbelly.

"I brought you a Coke," she whispered sweetly.

"Thank you," he mumbled.

"Anybody special you want to see?" she asked.

"D-don't know," he stammered.

"Vera'll talk to you. She'll fix you up. Just feel free, son. We all here to serve you. . . ."

"Okay," Fishbelly said, taking a drink from the bottle.

As Maud left, Vera entered, bringing a scent of perfume.

"Hi, Fish," she greeted him.

"Hi," he said, more at ease now.

"It's good seeing you," she purred, laying a warm, moist hand upon his. "Heard about that trouble you had with them white folks. They bad, ain't they?"

"Naw!" Fishbelly waved his hand deprecatingly. "Wasn't nothing." His eyes strayed to see how Tyree was taking his first essay into manhood and he was grateful to find him gone from the room. "They didn't scare me none," he intoned boastfully. "White folks' bark is worse'n their bite—"

"You said a mouthful!" Vera's teeth flashed as she leaned forward.

Her reactions fired his confidence and he felt a growing hunger to capture her attention, to dominate her wholly. Never before had he spoken to anybody so eager to believe his every word, and he was finding it delightful.

"Them big-assed white folks is dumb!" Emphatic judgment.

"Dumb ain't no word for 'em! They just like us, but they too damned mean to admit it!" Hilarious agreement.

"They scared to death of us. They know if they give us half a chance, we'd beat 'em!" Uttered with sage confidence.

"Right!" Vera cried. She grabbed his thigh and squeezed it.

"I was going to knock one of them white bastards cold," Fishbelly let his fantasy run wild. "But I didn't want no trouble with the odds ten to one. I got better sense than that," he declared, relishing her pliable personality, intent upon evoking more assent from her, and glorying in how easy it was.

"Fish, you so quiet and wise." A memorized smile.

"I didn't want to mess up my plans with no trouble with white folks." A spontaneous lie.

"You Tyree's son and you even talk like 'im." Vera's eyes hung upon his face.

"Aw, I know how to handle these white folks." he stepped into his father's shoes.

"Gee, Fish, you lucky." Crooned admiration.

"Aw, that's nothing." Hinting at undisclosed marvels.

She was silent, assuming a posture that invited observation and Fishbelly drank her in, seeking more fantasies with which to beguile her.

"Fish, you want to hear some records?" she asked, gripping his fingers gently but purposefully.

"Sure," he said, rising.

"Then, come on, honey." she said.

He followed her, inhaling her perfume, looking as in a trance at her suggestively swaying hips. Yeah, the boys at school had whispered that she was "hot stuff," that she knew more about a man "than a monkey knew about coconuts"; but there had been no details, for Vera was "managed," was even the kind of girl that white men sought—a girl who was not perhaps the kind "that your mama'd want you to meet," but a "real fast gal" and, to boot, a first-class baby who knew her way around.

He entered her bedroom and stood at her side while she wound up the Victrola and put on a record. The blues jumped and Vera patted her foot.

"Come on, baby; let's dance." She slipped her arm about his waist.

"Ain't much good at it," he said and swung onto the floor.

"Let me lead you," she commanded gently.

"Okay," he assented.

He moved to the sensual despair of the beating music and his muscles stiffened as he felt her body weaving and twisting against his. When the record ended he followed her to the Victrola and watched her lift the arm holding the needle, then they were still. Vera pressed close to him, and, before he knew it, he found himself cupping her left breast with his palm and emitting a spontaneous smooth lie:

"Honey, I been wanting you for a long time."

"For real, Fish!" She pressed closer against him, so expertly timing her movements that Fishbelly was deluded into feeling that he was the aggressor.

She drew him upon the bed and all the raging tension, the burning shame, the fear, and the hate left him and he felt more concretely and deeply anchored in reality and he thirsted for more of this solace raining upon his senses. Her clinging lips blended with his and he kissed her greedily, drunk with the ardency of her responses, being swept and involved with her body. Her arm reached up and the light clicked out, leaving them in darkness upon the bed. Still kissing him, she undid her dress and he was mutely astonished at the passion that her naked breasts made leap into him. He was here with the sanction of his father and was accountable to no one but himself and the hot vibrancy of the answering body under his hands; and there was in him a foamy crest of surging desire, a pulsing of stars in his blood, an eager straining that unlocked tides bearing him toward shores of emotion better than he had hoped for and different from what he had thought.

When he emerged from the professionally voluptuous ministrations of Vera, he walked down the hallway toward the front door, feeling that he had been absent from the workaday world for a million years, and yearning for solitude in which to mull over the upheaval that Vera had caused in him. He was resolved to see her again and re-experience that sensually narcotic storm. Aw, there was Tyree. . . . They met wordlessly and he noticed that Tyree's eyes avoided his and he too shunned looking directly at him.

"Ready?" Tyree asked offhandedly.

"Yeah," Fishbelly said.

They were about ready to leave when Maud came running with a grin.

"This was a surprise, Tyree," she sang. "Come again, hunh?"

"Okay, Maud," Tyree mumbled, puffing at his cigar.

Maud's beaming face turned upon Fishbelly.

"Fish, you welcome here day and night," she assured him with a wet smile. "Hope you had a good time."

"Okay." His eyes sought refuge in the wallpaper patterns before him.

"'By, now," Maud spoke deep in her throat.

"'By," Fishbelly mumbled.

"Be seeing you," Tyree said.

They descended the steps and strolled down the street. Tyree paused occasionally, glancing into store windows. Fishbelly hankered to be alone, but knew of no way to hint it. Suddenly Tyree turned to him and asked matter-of-factly:

"Anything you want, son?"

He did not know. He blinked, thinking; then he seized upon his new status of freedom.

"Some cigarettes."

"Le's git some," Tyree said. Then, soberly: "You smoking much?"

"Naw. Just now and then—"

"But don't overdo it." Tyree entered a drugstore.

As he walked again, exhaling smoke, he became bewildered when Tyree gave a low chuckle and averted his face. Was Tyree laughing at him? He stiffened as Tyree stopped and grabbed him roughly but affectionately by the shoulders and rolled out a long, loud laugh of pure joy.

"Fish, *goddamn!*" Tyree's words crooned and died away deep in his diaphragm.

"What, Papa?"

"Damn, boy! Ha! ha! You can *go!* You took to it like a duck takes to water! You better'n I was at your age. Hunh! No fussing, no questions; the gate was open and you *leaped* through without looking back *once!* Ha, ha!"

"I do something wrong, Papa?"

"You did what you wanted, didn't you?"

"Yeah, but—"

"Then you did *right*." Tyree was positive. He hugged his son consolingly and burst into another loud, long laugh. "Goddamn! You was *fast!* No hemming, no hawing ... Fish?"

"Yeah, Papa."

"That wasn't your first time, hunh?"

"Yeah, Papa."

"Naw!"

"Yeah, really. I swear."

"Then you been practicing somewhere.... Nature's sure wonderful," Tyree declared, shaking his head soberly: "It was awright, son. But, next time, look 'em *all* over."

Fishbelly gaped.

"Was there others there, Papa?"

"Son, there was about twenty other gals waiting in the back," Tyree explained, his lips spluttering laughter. "You just hauled off and grabbed the *first* one that showed!" He cleared his throat. "That Vera took you like Grant took Richmond; Ha, ha! Vera ain't bad...." He sniffled, keeping his arm about his son's shoulder. "Maud said you sure needed it. Fish, when you git older, you going to look back on this night and laugh your damn head off!"

"I thought she was sending Vera to me—"

"That's what's so funny. She was coming to talk to you and

163

you grabbed her." Tyree simpered. Then he stopped and asked seriously: "How was it?"

Fishbelly mastered his inhibitions, then stammered:

"Awright, I-I guess. . . . I-I'm seeing Vera Saturday—"

"Naw!" Tyree exploded. "Son, you starting all *wrong*. Try the others. They all the same. Take it easy; you got all your life to fool with that stuff. . . . For Gawd's sake, don't go gitting crazy about the first girl you took."

"Okay, Papa," he agreed, more from respect than conviction.

"How many your pals got any experience?" Tyree asked.

"Just Zeke, that's all."

They were facing each other in the middle of the dark sidewalk. Tyree seized Fishbelly's arm in a hard grip.

"Tell me: you done forgot 'em, ain't you?" Tyree asked with deep-chested dogmatism.

"Well, I'm still thinking about 'em—"

"You don't know what I mean, Fish. Think *hard*. Ain't you done completely *forgot* 'em?"

"Who, Papa?"

"Them goddamn *white* folks?" Tyree's voice was savage.

Fishbelly was thunderstruck. Tyree had been hoping that a baptism of his senses would wash away any appeal that a white world had made to him. But had he been purged of those impressions of terror and promise?

"Ain't you done forgot 'em?" Tyree demanded insistently.

"Yeah, Papa." He was affirmative because it was expected of him.

"Didn't I *tell* you!" Tyree was triumphant. "That's why I took you there. It was *time*. . . . Didn't want you gitting all mixed up, Fish. Lissen, them white gals just like the black ones, and only a damn fool'd git killed 'cause of one. Hell, fact is, white gals ain't no good, nohow."

"You done had 'em, Papa?" he asked with rounded eyes.

"Sure, Fish. But them white women ain't *nothing*." Tyree's confessional intimacy was urgent. "I was fool enough once to risk my life to see what it was like and when I think about the chance I took, I sweat. I'd rather cut my throat than do anything wild like that again."

"But why you say they ain't no good, Papa?"

"Son, for one thing, they *lazy*. I like my women *frisky!*" Tyree melted with mirth at his own observation. He steered Fishbelly on down the sidewalk. "You okay, son. I knowed what I was doing. You and me's two men now. We more'n father and son; we *friends*. We can say anything to each other, hunh?"

Fishbelly's mind had been wandering.

"Hunh? Oh, yeah, Papa," he mumbled.

Until Tyree had mentioned the world of white women he had not thought of them in relation to the soaring experience he had had with Vera. But now there bloomed in his mind a memory of that ride in the police car: he was seeing that white waitress at the roadside soft-drink bazaar, seeing her red lips, the shimmying motion of her hips as she walked forward carrying a tray of Coca-Cola bottles; and, despite his having fainted when the police had "played" at castrating him, despite the cruel crucifixion of Chris, he knew deep in his heart that there would be no peace in his blood until he had defiantly violated the line that the white world had dared him to cross under the threat of death. He walked beside Tyree, verbally agreeing with him, but he was being magnetically pulled toward another and a more dangerous goal. A mandate more powerful than his conscious will was luring him on, subsuming the deepest layers of his being. The threats designed to create fear in him had fostered a secret surging of hot desire. A harsh challenge: *You are nothing because you are black, and proof of your being nothing is that if you touch a white woman, you'll be killed!*

And, curiously, he felt that he was something, somebody, precisely and simply because of that cold threat of death. The terror of the white world had left no doubt in him about his worth; in fact, that white world had guaranteed his worth in the most brutal and dramatic manner. Most surely he was something, somebody in the eyes of that white world, or it would not have threatened him as it had. That white world, then, threatened as much as it beckoned. Though he did not know it, he was fatally in love with that white world, in love in a way that could never be cured. That white world's attempt to curb him had dangerously and irresponsibly claimed him for its own.

"It's going to be awright, son," Tyree sang blithely as they strode down early morning Black-Belt streets, streets in which no lights shone. "Everything's all straightened out, hunh?"

"Yeah, Papa," he lied preoccupiedly, but a cold awe had lodged itself at the core of him.

He tossed for a long time in bed, resolving that he would return to Maud's and ransack that vein of experience. Yes . . .

. . . *he was shoveling coal into a roaring firebox and feeling the runaway locomotive rocking careening down steel rails and each time he scooped up a shovelful of coal he saw the countryside trees telephone poles houses lakes and then he glanced at the white engineer who was looking out of the window at the steel rails with his hand upon the throttle calling: "MORE COAL!" and he shoveled the shining lumps flinging them onto the glowing seething bed and the white engineer called again: "MORE COAL!" and when he scooped up coal the lumps rolled away and he saw the legs body face of a naked white woman smiling demurely at him and the engineer bellowed: "MORE COAL!" and he looked to see if the engineer saw the naked white woman but his eyes were looking at the steel rails and he scooped coal being careful not to touch the naked white woman then he was terrified as she seized hold of his shovel and smiled at him and the engineer bawled: "MORE COAL!" and he was standing between the two of them sweating fearing the woman would speak or the engineer would see the woman he had to do something either hit the woman with the shovel or hit the engineer yes he could escape from both by leaping from the speeding locomotive the woman now pulled teasingly at his shovel and her lips opened to speak and he said: "Sh!" and the engineer yelled: "MORE COAL!" he dropped the shovel and leaped from the door of the cab into the whirling passing woods and he heard the white engineer and the naked white woman laughing as the train roared out of sight and he was tumbling over cinders finally hitting a wall and he was lying on his back looking up into the laughing face of Maud Williams who was saying: "Honey, you know better'n to try to hide a white woman in a coal pile like that! They was sure to find her. . . ."*

He awakened in the dark, sweating, sensing the dream images fleeing. He slept again; but when he rose next morning there was in him no memory of that dream.

Part Two

Days and Nights...

Naturally, the place they make for themselves . . . is very often of an inferior moral order and cannot fully compensate for their feelings of inferiority. They may run after this compensation by multiplying their "conquests," but they will never wholly attain it. The men are less fortunate . . . it is they who display the celebrated racial inferiority complex in its purest form, with its fantastic compensations in the form of vanity.

O. MANNONI

17

Next day Fishbelly met his pals with studied nonchalance and told of his debut into the realms of the flesh; but, to his chagrin, his announcement was dimmed when both Sam and Tony proclaimed that they had also, on the same night, treaded in the bay of woman. The four boys clung together for mutual moral buttressing, exchanging confessions, and swapping counsels; and, while pretending to discount the importance of their exploits, struck poses whose exaggerated naïveté betrayed their excitement.

Fishbelly's new status induced in him a great aplomb: ready pocket money, the termination of his mother's heckling, and deference from Tyree. The only protest Emma allowed herself was "All I can do is pray for you, son." Fishbelly never knew what Tyree, breadwinner and unchallenged dictator of his bailiwick, told her; but, whatever it was, it worked.

Fundamentally more intelligent that Tyree, he quickly found that he could manipulate Tyree's motives for ends beyond Tyree's ken. His respect for Tyree's money checked his tendency toward overt hostility and shunted his behavior into postures of pretended respect. He was more afraid of the white world than he was of Tyree, who had, in a measure, conquered that world. He unconsciously reasoned in this manner: "Papa, you are black and you brought me into a world of hostile whites with whom you have made a shamefully dishonorable peace. I shall use you, therefore, as a protective shield to fend off that world, and I'm *right* in doing so."

He was so determined not only to possess girls with his father's permission, he was also resolved to establish his right to come and go as he pleased. An ingenious tactic sprang full blown in his timid but turbulent heart, guiding with subtle niceties his raids upon Tyree's purse, his abuses of Tyree's fears, his prying as much as possible out of Tyree short of making him angry and shutting off the flow of funds. And he knew the split second in which to halt his smiling depredations, when to hang his head wistfully and mumble that he was sorry, when and how to seize upon one new liberty after another, but always withdrawing circumspectly if Tyree bristled, yet advancing boldly when Tyree's back was turned, counting heavily upon Tyree's entrenched sense of guilt to mitigate punitive sanctions.

Instead of Tyree's efforts divesting the white world of its allure, rendering that world paltry, those efforts lent that world more seductive power than ever in Fishbelly's mind; for upon what kind of model could Fishbelly elect to build his life if not upon the negative image of a father whom he loved but loathed, and upon vague, distorted conceptions of a surrealistic white world drifting to him through racial walls? To Fishbelly the Black Belt was a kind of purgatory, a pit of shame in which he had been unjustifiably consigned. But how could he ever climb out of that purgatory, escape that pit? He did not know.

The chief trait that his new role disclosed in him was something that neither he nor Tyree had foreseen. He had never been a brilliant student, and, in his second year of high school, he was managing with little better than average grades. And Vera's sensual baptism of his senses removed the contents of his textbooks even further from his mind. He knew that the world with which he would have to grapple was not hinted at in school, and Tyree's egotistical boasting had not helped matters when, on his first afternoon in the office, he had declared:

"Fish, there's more to be learned in this office than in all the high schools in this country."

Fishbelly's silent but hearty agreement would have dismayed Tyree.

Hitherto he had gone to school on his own, but now Tyree offered to drop him off each morning in the car on his way to his office.

"Look here, Fish"—Tyree was intimately confidential that first morning—"I got to pick up somebody. Friend of

170

mine . . ." He cleared his throat. "A young lady . . . Now, you don't need to mention you ever saw her, see."

"Sure, Papa. I understand," he said quickly.

"Do you?" Tyree asked and laughed.

"That's your business, Papa."

"Good boy," Tyree mumbled, pleased. "Anybody asks you about me, you don't know nothing."

So that was why Tyree had never dropped him off at school before! He was picking up a young woman about whom he had to keep his mouth shut. Okay. Every hour was disclosing the secret workings of the adult world. The car stopped in front of a frame house set back from the street.

"Don't think you know this gal," Tyree said, signaling three times with his horn. "She's Mrs. Gloria Mason."

A moment later a young mulatto woman hurried forward, heels clicking and hips swaying. Cosmetics defined her eyes and her lips.

"Let her in, Fish," Tyree ordered.

Fishbelly sprang out and held the door open. The woman, in her late twenties, dazzled Fishbelly by her yellow skin, her ample bosom, her easy laugh, and her smiling brown eyes. She was the best-dressed woman he had ever seen at close quarters.

"Fish, this is Gloria." Tyree introduced them.

"Hi," Fishbelly said.

"It's wonderful meeting you, Fish," Gloria said, shaking his hand and getting into the car. She glanced at his schoolbooks. "On your way to school? Studying hard?"

"Kind of," Fishbelly drawled. He sat next to her beside the door.

As the car moved off, he marveled at how lucky Tyree was because Tyree could do as he wanted, and he vowed that someday he would do the same. Gloria filled him with wonder because she did not speak in that whiny way so characteristic of the black people he knew. She held her head high, enunciated her words clearly, her attitude brimming with confidence. Vera flashed through his mind and he recalled Tyree's saying that he would look back upon that night at Maud Williams's and laugh his damn head off! He had treated that slut of a Vera like a princess, but he needed no further proof that he should not see her again; he could do *much* better than that.

Gloria confounded him not only because she had the air of a white woman, but because she *acted* white. What, then, did acting *white* mean? She acted correctly. But what did acting *correctly* mean? She did not act like a black woman. And how did *black* women act? He recalled that fight he had had with Sam that evening under the gas lamp on the street corner and he remembered Sam's saying that black people were *niggers*. . . . Well, Gloria was certainly not a nigger. Indeed, she behaved like those white girls in the downtown department stores where he bought neckties.

Fishbelly had only Black-Belt standards by which he could judge Gloria, and she transcended those standards. He was forced, therefore, to account for her in terms of furtive glimpses of the white world. Vera was an ignorant bitch compared to this Gloria whose face could have been an advertisement in a newspaper. He saw again the police car and the white girl serving drinks to the policemen who had threatened to castrate him and he remembered how he had chewed and choked down that photograph of the smiling white woman, and, for a moment, he was confused.

"Okay, Fish. Here's your stop," Tyree told him.

He climbed out of the car and shut the door.

"So long, Papa." He looked at Gloria. " 'By."

"Good-by, Fish," Gloria smiled at him.

"Say, Fish?" Tyree's eyes were twinkling.

"Yeah, Papa."

"What you think of Gloria?"

He started. Had Tyree been reading his mind? A mood of daring seized him.

"She's so cool it's crazy," he said and left, hearing Gloria's and Tyree's laughter echoing behind him. He turned and wistfully watched the car vanish around a corner. What a gal!

"Fish!"

He whirled. Zeke came forward with an armful of books, grinning.

"Hi," Fishbelly said.

"Who was that dish with your papa?" Zeke asked, wide-eyed.

"Wasn't she a doll?" Fishbelly demanded admiringly.

"Where he find her?" Zeke wanted to know.

"Wonder if she got a sister?" Fishbelly asked, his eyes lifted.

"Man, I could *use* her," Zeke declared.

The school bell rang.

"Come on. We going to be late," Fishbelly called, laughing.

"Hell, let's cut school today," Zeke said suddenly.

"And do what?" Fishbelly asked, willing but puzzled.

"I know where we can go for a hot time," Zeke said, taking Fishbelly's arm and pulling him along. "That face on your papa's gal done spoiled school for me today."

They strolled under spreading, leaf-heavy chinaberry trees. Fishbelly had played hooky before, but never for the purpose that Zeke had in mind.

"Where we going?" he demanded.

"To the Grove, man," Zeke said.

"But the Grove ain't open, you fool!"

"Yeah, it is," Zeke was emphatic. "It runs twenty-four hours a day. All you got to do is knock on the back door."

"I want to see this," Fishbelly said.

The sunny morning streets made him glad to be free of those dogging, depressing classrooms; and it was good seeing black girls hurrying to cook in white families, black mailmen trudging under loaded bags, and black street sweepers pushing big brooms against mounds of dead leaves. The fine dust sifting through the air carried the scent of clay.

"Who owns this Grove?" Fishbelly asked.

"Dr. Bruce," Zeke told him. "But most folks don't know it. It'd hurt Doc's reputation if folks knew he was making money out of hot meat. The Grove's full of gals. . . . A tough nigger called Fats runs the joint and he'll be glad to fix you up."

Zeke's words evoked in Fishbelly a vision of the dead body of Chris under the unshaded electric bulb and he heard Dr. Bruce's telling how Chris had died. So Doc had the same pattern of making extra money that Tyree used with Maud Williams!

"You been to the Grove much?" Fishbelly asked.

"Just once," Zeke said. "And that was enough to make me want to go again."

On the outskirts of town they took a gravel road bisecting a dense wood, and, a mile farther, rounded a sharp bend and saw a huge, barnlike structure, to which a dirt track led. The building was dwarfed by surrounding oaks and elms from whose extending branches gray moss staggled groundward. About the structure was a growth of stubby wild grass, and, here and there, their dark green leaves glittering balefully, were magnolia trees whose dead-white, ghostly blossoms gave off a too-sweet perfume that cloyed the air. Other than a back and front door, and a tiny ventilating hole high up in the rear wall, the edifice had no openings or windows; wooden beams and rafters formed and supported the building and were spaced some five inches apart and were covered with weatherboarding of an unusually original design and substance. The Grove operated only in summer, and suspended from its high, shiny tin roof were cascading layers of thickly braided gray moss that formed a border about the roof's edge and took the place of clapboard for the building's four sides—a gay festooning that lent an air of the savagely rural to the bar–dance hall.

"Doc making a lot of money out of this?" Fishbelly asked.

"Man, the Grove's a gold mine," Zeke said, wagging his head.

"Well, Doc sells meat; your papa sells groceries; my papa sells coffins. . . . We won't go broke. Folks sure need them things," Fishbelly philosophized.

"That's right. Nobody can do without 'em," Zeke agreed.

Zeke mounted the back steps and Fishbelly caught muffled sounds of a rampaging boogie-woogie being beaten upon a piano.

"Listen to that salty dog," Fishbelly hummed, falling into a blue mood.

"I want to git high's a Georgia pine!" Zeke crooned, swaying to the music's beat and rapping three times with his knuckles upon the door.

"These gals . . . they gut-bucket or clean?" Fishbelly asked.

"Man, Doc guarantees these gals," Zeke sang.

"What you mean?"

"You catch something here, like clap or syph, and Doc treats you for nothing," Zeke explained.

"No kidding!"

"It's the truth. And he's got cheap rates for students."

"I'm a pimple on the pole of progress!" Fishbelly exclaimed, laughing. "Doc's sure up-to-date."

A tall, fat, red-eyed man in a dirty white apron opened the door.

"Hi, Zeke," the fat man said.

"Hi, Fats."

"Who's your side-kick?" Fats asked, eying Fishbelly suspiciously.

"Tyree's son, Fish." Zeke introduced Fishbelly.

Fats's eyes widened and his face brightened.

"Great day in the morning! The sun do move! Come on in, man," Fats welcomed Fishbelly. "You *way* overdue."

Fats led them to a tiny hallway that had a steep stair leading upward. Under the stairway Fishbelly could see a sweep of beer cases and barrels.

"Folks been asking about you," Fats told Fishbelly.

"How come?" Fishbelly wanted to know.

"'Cause you Tyree's son," Fats explained. "Plenty gals here waiting to meet you."

"Tell 'em to git ready, 'cause here I come," Fishbelly sang.

They laughed. Zeke and Fishbelly followed Fats up the main floor and entered a vast, high interior that was thick with the scent of beer and blue with tobacco smoke. Clamped bands of moss criss-crossed the tin ceiling. Three couples pranced lazily on the floor while a skinny, shirt-sleeved black man, with a glass of whiskey at his elbow and a cigarette slanting from his mouth, hammered the piano keys. About twenty girls sat at tables.

"See 'em?" Zeke inclined his head toward the girls.

"Yeah, man." Fishbelly offered Zeke a cigarette. "Smoke?"

"What you-all drinking?" Fats asked.

"Two beers," Zeke ordered. He struck a match, held the flame for his and Fishbelly's cigarettes, then flipped the still-burning match over his shoulder.

"Hey, goddam!" Fats yelled, stomping the smoldering match. "That moss's dry as hell. We don't want no fire in here."

Fats waddled off and they sat looking at the girls. Chairs

scraped on the wooden floor and three girls whose breasts were emphasized by thin, tight sweaters rose and sauntered toward them. Boogie-woogie walked on the piano keys.

"Dance?" a tall, near-white girl asked with a wan smile.

"We want to drink some first," Fishbelly told her. "Want some beer?"

"Sure," the girls chorused.

"Have a seat," Zeke invited, grinning, looking them over.

They sat. One was short, fat, jet black. One was yellow and plump. The third one, who had spoken first, was willowy and almost white in color.

"You-all sure is sports," the black girl commended smilingly.

"Playing hooky?" the yellow girl asked, fingering their schoolbooks.

"We studying anatomy," Fishbelly said.

The girls guffawed, expecting business.

"You dog," the black girl said, fawning upon Zeke with large eyes and wet lips.

Fishbelly distributed cigarettes while Fats served beer and scuttled back for three more bottles.

"I'm Gladys," the near-white girl said.

"I'm Fishbelly," he told her.

Fishbelly had settled upon Gladys the moment he had seen her. She was so white that he felt that he ought to be afraid of her, but he knew that he had no cause to be and she was available and it excited him.

"I'm Beth," the yellow one said.

"I'm Maybelle," the black girl said.

"Douglass High?" Gladys asked Fishbelly.

"Yeah, but not for long," Fishbelly told her.

"Graduating?" Gladys asked. "I did, four years ago . . ."

"Naw. Keep it quiet, but I'm 'quituating,'" Fishbelly said.

"I know what you mean," Gladys said, laughing. "I was glad to git away from those goddamm teachers."

"What they do to you?"

"If I ever know you better, I'll tell you," she said bitterly.

"Tell me now," he urged her, leaning toward her.

She looked at him, hesitated, then whispered in his ear:

"My English teacher gave me a baby. That's how he taught me verbs—"

"Old Professor Jefferson?"

"That's the bastard," she said, her sad eyes looking off.

Fishbelly liked her; she was not as pretty as Gloria, but she reminded him of her. She had defeated-looking, moist, hurt, brown eyes that were almost always downcast in gaze, and she had an air of sophisticated fatigue. She slipped her right hand possessively into the crook of Fishbelly's elbow and whispered:

"Let's dance."

"Right," Fishbelly said, and led her to the floor.

More intrigued with the feel of her body than with keeping time to the music, he was unaware that Zeke was dancing with Beth until he glanced around. Maybelle sat alone at the table and he saw her take a cigarette from his pack. When the music stopped, he led Gladys back to the table and called:

"Fats, four more beers!"

"Coming up!" Fats echoed from behind the bar.

"And what about *me?*" Maybelle asked challengingly, looking straight into Fishbelly's eyes.

The table was tensely quiet. Maybelle had been shunted out of the party and the cause was clear. Fishbelly looked pleadingly into Maybelle's bulbous, bloodshot eyes and felt guilty.

"Make it five beers, Fats!" Fishbelly called, relenting.

"Naw! Keep your lousy beer!" Maybelle's thick lips twisted scornfully.

"Maybelle," Gladys scolded her. "The boys made their choice—"

"Go to hell, you white-looking bitch!" Maybelle screamed in a sudden rage, leaping to her feet and sweeping the beer bottles clattering to the floor. "I ain't blind! I know they made their goddam choice! They want *white* meat! But you sluts ain't *white!* You *niggers* like me! But you the nearest thing that they can git that *looks* white!" She whirled upon Zeke and Fishbelly. "If you-all just dying for white meat, why don't you go 'cross town where there ain't *nothing* but white meat? You won't tell me? Well, I'll tell *you!* You scared of being killed like a dog! Ever since I been at this table, you goddam black sonsofbitching niggers ain't got eyes for nothing but *yellow* and *white* meat!"

"But you *black*, Maybelle," Beth said, smiling tightly.

"And I'm goddamn proud of it!" Maybelle flared.

"You *got* to be proud of it," Gladys said softly.

"Hey! What's going on here?" Fats called, coming and handing Maybelle her bottle of beer and lumbering off.

Maybelle tilted the bottle, sending a foamy stream to the floor.

"Lick it up," Maybelle sneered at Fishbelly.

"Shame on you, Maybelle," Beth said. "Pouring out the boy's beer—"

"You just drunk and jealous," Gladys said.

"Not till the day I die will I ever be jealous of you, you half-white bitch!" Maybelle snarled.

The boogie-woogie stopped. Fishbelly felt as though steel springs had entered his arms and he yearned to rise and smash his fist into Maybelle's sweating, black face. He knew that everybody knew what was happening, but he did not want to hear anybody saying it. To speak it aloud made one ashamed.

"Let folks be with who they like," Fishbelly growled.

"Sure," Maybelle took him up quickly, leaning forward, her drunken spittle flying. "White folks Jim Crow your black ass and you do the same damn *thing!*"

"Maybelle, go 'way!" Beth said. "I'm sick of your *race* talk!"

"I got as much right to be here as you, you yellow whore!" Maybelle screamed.

"Don't call me no whore," Beth said, rising.

"I didn't call you no whore," Maybelle corrected Beth. "I called you a *yellow* whore!"

Zeke pulled Beth back to her chair.

"Git out of my sight, you black bitch!" Beth shouted.

"Sure! I'm *black!*" Maybelle shrieked. "And this is a black man's bar! If you don't like it here, go to the white folks' bars. . . . Why don't you? 'Cause you can't! You love 'em, but you can't git near 'em!"

"Aw, hell," Fishbelly mumbled. "I don't like this."

"You want to do something about it, big boy?" Maybelle

challenged him. "I'm a woman, but I could goddamn well tangle with you!"

"Fats!" Fishbelly called.

"Why you call Fats?" Maybelle railed. "Do it yourself!"

"Yeah!" Fats waddled again to the table with a look of evil in his eyes. He too was black. "What's the trouble here?"

"Take this gal away 'fore I hit her," Fishbelly said.

"Hit me! Just you try—"

"You don't want her at your table?" Fats asked rhetorically.

"We got two girls with us already," Zeke explained lamely.

"Girls?" Maybelle's voice floated deridingly throughout the bar. "Ha, ha! Whores, you mean?" She spoke to Beth: "You a whore just like me!" She turned to Zeke. "What she's got smells just like mine! It feels the same. Even if you eat it, it tastes the same. You think it's better'n mine just 'cause it looks *white,* but it ain't white. You 'shamed of your color! You goddamn *white-struck* black fools just hungry for the meat the white man's done made in nigger town! Go on, you cheap niggers, and lap the white man's crumbs!"

"That's enough, Maybelle," Fats said quietly.

"Don't speak to me, you black baboon!" Maybelle flung at him.

Fats threw down his tray and sprang forward and grabbed Maybelle by the nape of her neck and one leg and, with a heaving motion, lifted her high into the air above his head.

"Put me down!" Maybelle screamed, squirming and flailing her arms.

"Throw that bitch out!" a man yelled.

"Throw her out!" a chorus rose.

Holding Maybelle aloft, Fats walked as though he were carrying a pillowcase stuffed with feathers. Maybelle kicked, sobbed, and drummed her fists into Fats's back. The piano began talking boogie-woogie. Another waiter ran forward and opened the door and Fats went down the steps.

"Stay out and don't come back till you sober!" Fats's voice shouted. He turned and slammed the door. "She's just drunk, that's all."

"Her mouth's too big," Gladys said.

"Let's have another beer," Zeke said.

"Right," Fishbelly agreed.

Fats tumbled forward with four more bottles.

"Everything awright?"

"Fine," Fishbelly said.

But it took all of three more bottles of beer to wash Maybelle's racist words out of Fishbelly's mouth. By that time he was too tipsy to care any more, and he was ready when Gladys held him tightly on the dance floor and asked in a whisper:

"You want to come with me?"

"I ain't got much money, baby," he told her.

"I ain't said nothing about money," she said. "All I want is that you come to see me often. I'm alone . . ."

"Let's go, baby. It's a deal. I like you."

"I like you too."

"You live near here?"

"Two minutes away."

Fishbelly turned to Zeke and called:

"We going!"

"We going too," Zeke said.

Fishbelly paid for the beer and the four of them went out into the sunshine. They paused, gaping. Black Maybelle lay prone upon the grass where Fats had tossed her; one naked shapely black leg and thigh sprawled akimbo; one plump forearm cradled her head; her thick lips were open; her cheeks were wet with sweat; and she was snoring with the sun beating full into her face.

"Good Gawd!" Beth exclaimed.

"Fats!" Gladys called.

Fats came to the door.

"Take that bitch out of the sun," Gladys ordered.

Fats stared, then scratched his head, declaring:

"Goddamn, I thought that gal was gone! And there she is sleeping right were I throwed her. . . ." He turned to Zeke and Fishbelly. "Ain't she like a baby, laying there sleeping it off? When she wakes up, she'll be sweet as pie."

He lifted Maybelle in his arms and lugged her into the dance hall.

"Poor thing," Gladys said, leading the way down a dirt path, and slipping her arm about Fishbelly's waist.

"Our books!" Zeke exclaimed, stopping.

"Oh, Fats'll keep 'em for you," Gladys said. "Don't worry. Nobody'll steal them books, 'cause nobody around here reads. . . ."

18

Fishbelly awakened in the dim and silent room, breathing warm, moist air, hearing rain drumming upon the shingled roof. For a moment vague panic made him lift himself upon an elbow and stare about.

"Fish," came the familiar whisper.

"Gladys," he sighed. "I didn't know where I was."

"Have a good nap?"

"Yeah." He yawned.

His eyes rested upon her white face in the warm gloom and he saw a faint smile on her lips, a sad smile that he had often to coax from her, a smile that seemed to stem more from an excess of sorrow than joy. She wore only a pair of nylon panties and the feeble electric bulb glowed on the red nipples of her firm breasts. Never had he known so much peace as with her, yet that peace was tinged with anxiety.

"You slept like a log," she said.

"I was tired," he mumbled.

"I love to watch you when you sleep," she said in a low voice.

"Hunh? Yeah." He stared at her. "Why?"

"Don't know. You seem like a baby when you sleeping."

He chuckled and stretched his limbs catlike in the semidark.

"Nobody ever watched me sleep before."

"You sure?" she asked teasingly.

"Gladys, I made love to other women 'fore I met you, but I never *slept* with 'em." He smiled ruefully. "It was always:

181

> "Vip
> *Vam*
> *Thank you*
> *Ma'am . . ."*

As was her habit, she laughed with her mouth closed.

"Some woman's watched every man while he slept," she said, staring off.

"Mebbe my mama did when I was a kid," he mumbled. "Say, any beer left? I'm thirsty."

"I saved a cold one for you," she said, taking a bottle of beer from an ice-filled zinc pail.

"Sweet gal," he said gratefully. He downed half of it and sat the bottle on the table next to the bed.

Gladys was mending a skirt, her head bent, the curls of her silky, glistening hair and her tawny skin gleaming in the beams of a tiny lamp at her elbow. He leaned forward and lifted his trousers from the back of a chair.,

"Going awready?" she asked.

He did not answer. He pulled four green bills from a pocket and handed them to her.

"Baby, here's thirteen dollars. . . . I got ten from Papa and begged three from Mama."

She rose and took the bills and pushed them under the dresser scarf.

"Thanks, Fish. I can pay the rent now," she mumbled.

"I know I don't give you enough," he said contritely.

"I ain't complaining," she said sweetly.

The times when he gave her money were the worst. He wanted to ask if she had enough for meals, clothes, rent, to give her mother, who took care of her bastard child; but, since he could not give her more, why ask? He knew what she did to make money and he did not want to think of it, for it only made him want to curse her. It had to be enough that she had told him that he was her favorite. Hunched on the edge of the bed, he fought feelings of guilt that he could not afford. How had so beautiful a girl gotten into such a mess?

"Gladys, your papa living?" he asked her suddenly, lighting a cigarette.

"Hunh?" She looked up sharply from her sewing and stared

182

at him with dark pools of eyes. "Yeah." She bent again to her needle and thread.

"What he do?"

"Sells lumber."

"He white?"

"Yeah," she said softly.

"He wouldn't marry your mama?"

"Why you asking me all this?" She sounded irritable.

"I don't know you, Gladys," he said with a cryptic plea in his voice. "I see you and don't know you . . ."

"A *white* man marrying a *black* woman in the South?" She spoke in the form of an ironic question.

"They could've gone North," he said, trying to keep overtones of argumentativeness out of his voice.

"He had a family," she said.

"Did he love your mama?"

She was silent for a long time.

"What's *love?*" she asked in a low hum, not looking up.

"Your papa in town?"

"Yeah."

"Ever see 'im?"

"Naw."

"Ever meet his family?"

"Hell, naw, Fish. They *white*. I'm *black—*"

"You ain't black," he said almost accusingly.

Rain pelted the roof. Gladys lifted her cloth and bit the thread with her teeth, took up her spool, held the needle close, and slid a sliver through its eye.

"I'm glad Mama's here to take care of my baby," she said, knotting the end of the thread.

"I'd have gone North, if I was you."

"For what?"

"Then you could live like you want to."

She looked at him, her lips parting in surprise.

"But I *do,*" she said.

That jolted him. She had accepted what had happened! She was indifferent to the white world, felt no resentment for what it had done to her. He had never had any intimate contact with that world, yet he hated it. Or did he? When he thought of that white world he hated it; but when he daydreamed of it he loved it. He would not now be asking her these questions if he did not revere that white world and hold toward it an attitude of mute awe.

"Know where your papa live?"

She clutched her sewing and laughed with pursed, closed lips.

"I had lunch with 'im last Saturday."

He joined in her bitter laughter, then broke off sharply.

"Say, did Professor Jefferson know your papa was white?"

"That my papa was white?" she repeated. "Yeah . . . But why you asking me all these questions? You don't want me no more?"

"You know it ain't that." He spoke testily.

Aw, she was fearing that he did not want her because she was a bastard, because her being a bastard had killed in her her quality of *whiteness*. He snuffed out his cigarette and lay flat on the bed. He knew that she hardly ever thought of the white world, yet he thought of it all the time. He had asked Gladys those questions because she, her mother, and that mythical white man who was her father were vague images in his mind and he was trying to trace the connection between those images and himself, his life. That day when Maybelle had been drunk she had said that niggers lapped up the crumbs left by white men who had had black women. In color Gladys was as white as the whites, and yet she was farther away from them than he was, so far away that she never thought of them. Yeah, Professor Jefferson had had her because she was a near-white bastard with no one to defend her. A white man had a black woman; that black woman gave birth to a near-white bastard girl child; and, because it was known that that near-white bastard girl child had had a white father, black men ran after her. And that near-white bastard girl child, in turn, would have a bastard baby that could ask protection of neither whites nor blacks. Such a girl could find men, but rarely a husband.

"You should've put the law on Jefferson and made him take care of your baby," he told her.

"Fish, I was running around," she said frankly, sighing. "It's his baby, but could I *prove* it? It's the living image of 'im; even his wife knows that. . . ."

184

He lit another cigarette, wondering: What'll happen to Gladys's little girl? Yeah, Professor Jefferson was light-skinned too. That little girl, like Gladys, would be a near-white child lost in a black world.

"You want me to put the big light on, honey?" she asked.

"Naw," he breathed.

She rose and went into a far corner of the room; there, in the shadows, she looked *completely* white. And it had been for a woman who had had the color of Gladys that Chris had been killed.

"What you thinking about, honey?" she asked him.

"Hunh? Nothing," he said.

The face of the woman he had choked down his throat that day in the police car had been smiling, but Gladys seldom smiled.

"Gladys, you ever hear of a guy called Chris Sims?"

"Chris Sims?" she repeated slowly. "Naaaw . . . Why?"

"They killed 'im."

"Who?"

"The *white* folks."

"Oh, *that* boy!" Gladys exclaimed. "I didn't know 'im, but I heard of 'im. I even saw 'im once. But, baby, you know one thing? I was a maid once for that woman he was mixed up with—"

"What?" Fishbelly stared with open mouth.

"Sure. That was when she was first married. Later she went into trade. . . ."

He hated that word "trade." He had told her once never to say it; he could never understand how she could speak of it so calmly.

"What was she like?" he asked.

"Like? Why you ask that?"

"Was she your size?"

"Naw. Stouter, shorter . . . Very blond. She hit the bottle too much. That's why her husband left her."

"She had a lot of men?"

Gladys's lips smiled twistedly.

"You always have a lot of men in the trade. . . ." She stared at him. "But why you asking—?"

"She ever have anything to do with us?"

185

"What 'us'?"

"Niggers," he said meaningfully.

"Not that I know of till this Chris mess broke," she said. "But why you asking—?"

"You mean she had Chris for money?"

"You have anybody for money in the trade," she told him.

He drained the beer bottle and lay back on the bed.

"How come you want to know about that woman?" she demanded. "She ain't nothing but a tramp."

"Don't know. It just came into my head like that," he said with soft abruptness.

They were silent. The yeasty room droned with the sound of rain.

"Gladys?"

"Hunh?"

"Come here."

She laid aside her sewing and went to him.

"Kiss me," he said.

When she bent to him, he seized her and tried hard, fiercely, as he kissed her, to drown out the vague, smoldering fear. If fire would burn him, then, maybe, by poking his finger into it, little by little, he would get used to it. But when he had tried, he was as far as ever from stilling that slow, raging fear that burned like a fever in his blood. He was still attracted to and yet afraid of that white fire.

19

After school, or, more often, after all-day sessions with Gladys, Fishbelly answered the phone in Tyree's office, took down addresses where corpses were to be picked up, and passed on the information to Jim, who, in turn, gave it to Jake and Guke, the two men who drove the combination hearse-and-ambulance. Fishbelly learned to receive weeping customers, to smile sadly when the occasion required it, to fake a lofty sympathy for his grieving clientele; and, at the same time, to say: "Well, we have to think of the bed, you know. . . ." And he would bring out the brightly colored catalogue containing photographs of coffins and their prices. "Anything you pick out, we got it in stock and I'll show it to you," he would say. The role gave him an exhilarating sense of power. He was Tyree's deputy and he loved it. Tyree commissioned him to order the gravity bottles, vats of embalming fluid, artificial grass for graves, the many varieties of caskets, cosmetics for corpses, women's dresses and men's suits, etc. And it was his duty to see that Jake and Guke did not get too drunk to execute their errands.

During winter and spring Fishbelly, neglecting his studies, saw Gladys regularly. He knew that he would fail his examinations and would have to repeat. One morning, while sitting in the Grove guzzling beer with Gladys, he heard the back door open and some wayward instinct made him turn his head. Tyree entered with Gloria and Fishbelly's fingers flexed about his beer bottle. Fearing a scene of public humiliation, he feigned nonchalance, looking straight ahead. Tyree passed him with a frown and stood beside Gloria at the bar. Fishbelly breathed easier. He had long dreaded this moment of discovery; well, his cutting school was now in the open. He was grateful that Gladys, who did not know Tyree, had not noticed anything.

Fats sidled to his table with a deadpan face.

"Somebody at the bar wants to see you," Fats said.

Fishbelly strode to the bar. Tyree was staring into his glass of beer.

"Hi," Fishbelly greeted Gloria. "Hi, Papa."

"Hello, Fish," Gloria smiled.

"Where you going when you leave here?" Tyree asked him coldly.

"To the 'shop,' Papa. Like always," he said, smiling.

"I want to see you there at five," Tyree said.

"Sure thing, Papa," he tried to sound normal. "Anything else?"

Tyree did not answer. Fishbelly knew that he was in for it. He rejoined Gladys.

"Your friend wasn't too glad to see you," she observed.

"Just some business," he lied, smiling. He always smiled, especially when he lied; it was reflex.

Tyree, steering Gloria before him, left a little later.

"Gawd, I wish I could really dress like that," Gladys said.

"She's cool, hunh?"

"Who's her sugar daddy?"

"A friend of my papa's," he lied compulsively.

"Didn't know there was any niggers that rich in town."

"Niggers got money," he mumbled.

Would Tyree cut off his allowance? Would he ask Doc to bar him from the Grove?

"What you smiling about, honey?" Gladys asked him.

"Nothing," he lied, still smiling.

"I know you, Fish. You *smile* when something's wrong."

"Nothing's wrong," he said, continuing to smile.

He lingered at the Grove until after four o'clock, then walked slowly toward the undertaking establishment. When he entered, he found Tyree and Jim seated at the desk, poring over books.

"Okay, Jim," Tyree said. "We'll finish this in the morning. I got to talk to Fish now."

"Okay, Tyree," Jim said. Jim rose. "Hi, Fish."

"Hi, Jim."

"How's school?"

"Oh, awright," Fishbelly lied, laughing softly.

"Study hard, Fish," Jim said. "We need you."

Goddamn, even Jim knew. . . . Jim left. He sat, smiling in spite of himself. He was afraid and he knew that his best tactic would be to pretend to agree with whatever Tyree demanded. Tyree sat at his desk with bowed head. Finally, in one movement, he whirled and asked:

"You heard what Jim just said?"

Not knowing how angry Tyree was, he decided to act dumb.

"What, Papa?"

"And I thought I could trust you," Tyree growled.

"What you talking about, Papa?" he continued evading.

"Didn't you see Jim helping me with the books?" Tyree asked whiningly, spreading his hand helplessly.

188

"Yeah, Papa. I saw 'im. He works for you—"

"You know goddamn well I ain't talking about *that!*"

"Oh!" Fishbelly pretended that he had just understood. "He's *helping* you—"

"WHY?" Tyree asked thunderingly.

He knew why, but he did not want to say it aloud.

"'Cause I'm *ignorant!*" Tyree confessed with rage. "I'm hiring 'im to read for me—"

"I'll read for you, Papa."

"Shut your goddamn mouth!" Tyree shouted. "You know what I'm talking about! I'm hoping you can soon take over here, but you chasing *meat!* What's the matter with you, Fish?" Tyree thrust his face near Fishbelly's. "You meat *crazy?*"

Dread made Fishbelly meek and mute.

"Naw, Papa."

"How long you been going to that Grove?"

"Fats done told you everything, Papa, and I ain't going to lie," he said contritely.

"How deep you in with that Gladys?"

"She just my gal, that's all, Papa."

"You ain't got her in no family way or nothing?"

"Naw, Papa. She a good gal, clean and—"

"She's meat, and that's all!" Tyree bellowed. "I don't care about *her!* I care about you, my *son!*" Tyree rose and towered over Fishbelly. "How much school you done cut?"

That got him, for he had lost track of the days.

"Few times," he mumbled vaguely. Then added quickly: "But I'm going to make it up, Papa."

"Hell, Fish," Tyree spat. He went to the window and stared out with his back turned. He spun. "I wanted you to git a education—"

"I am, Papa," Fishbelly insisted.

"You gitting a education at the Grove?"

"Naw," he answered frankly. His defense was so lame that he smiled. "Just relaxing a little." He laughed shame-facedly, looking off.

"If you laugh about this, I'll break your damned neck!"

"I ain't laughing, Papa," he said. "I'm *wrong,* Papa." He smiled sweetly, then grew serious. "I'm going to do better."

"Fish, for Gawd's sake, don't cut class for gals," Tyree begged. "I'm trying to git you somewhere, and you standing still. The white folks ain't doing this to you; you doing it to yourself. I'm hiring men to do my thinking and you chasing meat. I thought you was smarter'n that. . . . Fish, ain't you got no ambition?"

"Sure, Papa."

"To chase meat?" Tyree asked scornfully. "You don't need to know how to read to do that. . . . Fish, you done let me down." His voice broke.

Tyree verged on tears and it touched him as nothing else had.

"I won't let you down, Papa. I swear," he spoke fervently.

"What you going to do?" Tyree asked with a note of help-lessness that was new to Fishbelly.

"I'll *change*, Papa!" Fishbelly declaimed. "I'll start *now!*"

"I talked to your principal," Tyree told him. "He said you flunking this year. He thought I was taking you out of school to work in the office. Fish, you can take a horse to water, but you can't make 'im drink. If you just want to be a no-good nigger tramp, then I can't stop you."

"Papa, I'm starting to study this minute," he swore. "All I needed was for you to say what you said."

"It's up to you, son," Tyree said, picking up his hat. "Don't think you making a fool out of me; it's yourself you fool-ing. . . ." He swallowed and shook his head. "I'm off. . . . See you tonight."

"Okay, Papa. I'll study."

Tyree left. He sat at the desk and stared. Yeah, he'd study. . . . Footsteps sounded in the corridor. He turned. Jim stood in the doorway.

"Fish," Jim called.

"Yeah," Fishbelly answered offhandedly.

"Kid, I'm not meddling," Jim began. "But go to school and—"

"I'm going to school, Jim," he snapped.

"You can't run Tyree's business unless you finish school and get a license—"

"I know," Fishbelly spoke resentfully.

"You got a good father—"

"Look!" Fishbelly blurted. The anger that he had repressed before Tyree flared at Jim. "You work for Papa and you *educated!* I'll hire folks like you to run the business!"

Jim's mouth tightened.

"I can't tell you anything," he said and left.

To hell with Jim . . . He opened his textbook on civics and stared at print that refused to make meaning. He sighed, seeing Gladys as he had seen her that morning. He hesitated, then picked up the phone and dialed. He heard the phone ringing.

"This is the Grove. Fats speaking."

"Fats, this is Fish. Gladys there?"

"Naw. She just left. You know . . . She'll be back soon."

He flinched, burning with jealousy, knowing what that meant.

"When she comes in, tell her to meet me at Bowman and Rose in an hour. Hear?"

"Bowman and Rose. Okay. That all?"

"That's all."

He hung up, got his hat, and paused.

"Jim!" he called.

Jim came to the door of the office.

"Yeah, Fish?"

"I'm off."

"Okay, Fish." Jim looked at him soberly and shook his head.

"Hell," Fish whispered to himself and went out.

20

Gangly, deceptively aggressive, Fishbelly attained his sixteenth birthday by reacting sharply to his failure to pass his examinations. He had known it was coming, but when it actually happened he realized that he had not considered all of its many implications. For the first time in his life he admitted that he hated school. He was not in any way mentally deficient; he easily absorbed classroom facts; he was simply convinced that what classrooms told him had no vital relevance to his life. He now embarked upon the boldest decision he had ever made; he was going to quit school and get on with the business of living. He knew, intuitively, that the influence of his environment superseded in importance what the professors said. All his life he had been at school, but in a more drastic way than the educational authorities had devised.

After receiving his reports, he avoided Zeke, Tony, and Sam and made his way to the Grove; but, to his chagrin, he found them there.

"Come on, Fish, and have a beer," Zeke invited.

Fishbelly was morose, awkward; their avoiding mentioning his failure was worse than if they had flung it into his face.

"Man, we got news for you," Tony said.

"Yeah, I know. You and Zeke's going to college."

"And we got news for you too," Tony told Sam.

"But Sam's passed his exams," Fishbelly said.

"We ain't talking about *school*," Zeke said softly.

Fishbelly felt rejected; his future differed from that of his friends. If he went back to school, he would have to repeat, and he would rather die than do that. He sulked while Tony and Zeke and Sam vied with one another in juggling future plans.

"Man, law's for me," Sam declared.

"I'm going to study business administration," Zeke said.

"I ain't made up my mind yit," Tony said. "Anyhow, all that'll have to wait. . . ." He turned to Zeke. "Where you think they going to send us for basic training?"

"Don't know. Hope it ain't in the South," Zeke mumbled.

Fishbelly felt a shock.

"What you-all talking about?" he asked, fearing he had not understood.

"Man, we trying to tell you," Tony said. "We going to the Army."

"What? When this happen?" Fishbelly asked.

"We got notices this morning," Zeke said.

"You going, Sam?" Fishbelly asked. "You my age . . ."

"Naw. I ain't old enough," Sam moaned.

Fishbelly's loneliness deepened. Not only had he failed in school, but his closest friends were abandoning him. Gawd, the Army would have solved everything, but he was too young, and so was Sam . . . He ordered another beer, mulling over the nervous job of telling Tyree of his failure. Zeke's voice finally broke through to him.

"We having a farewell party here at the Grove on the Fourth of July," Zeke said. "Man, you got to come."

"Hunh? Sure. I'll be here," Fishbelly mumbled.

"Don't be a drip," Zeke chided him. "This dance's going to be *something!*"

"Okay," Fishbelly growled.

"Study this summer and you'll pass that exam this fall," Tony said.

"I'm quitting school," Fishbelly told them.

His three friends shifted uneasily on their chairs.

"My papa wouldn't let me do that," Zeke said.

"Mine neither," Tony said.

"I'm working, but I ain't going to quit," Sam declared.

"Don't care what Papa say, I'm quitting," Fishbelly vowed. His decision had rendered his friends speechless and he stared at them in open-eyed defiance. "Fats, a whiskey," he ordered.

"You going to be drunk," Zeke warned.

"I want to be drunk," Fishbelly said.

He had no more to lose. He downed his whiskey and asked Fats for another. He had failed, his friends were going into the Army, and he would strike for his freedom tonight. The hell with it all . . .

"Tyree ain't going to like it," Sam told him.

"I'm going to make 'im like it," Fishbelly muttered into his glass.

Yeah, he'd be adamant, absolutely defiant with Tyree. He downed his second whiskey and proclaimed:

"Tomorrow I'll be *free!*"

"Goddamn. You going to be a *man,*" Zeke said enviously.

"Your papa's got dough," Sam said wistfully.

"And I'm going to help 'im make and spend it," Fishbelly said; he was tipsy.

"Hell, let's git high then," Tony said.

Fishbelly was drunkenly pleased; he had swung them from their world to his.

"Fats, a bottle of whiskey here!" he bawled.

"Coming up, Fish!"

"Yeah," he said to his pals, looking sullenly about the table. "Let's git drunk!"

21

He wove through night streets marshaling arguments to tempt Tyree. He expected Tyree to storm, curse, and denounce him, but he was almost certain that, if he stood firm, Tyree would, in the end, acquiesce to the termination of his schooling.

He entered the office and found Tyree delicately "selling" Mrs. Felton, a tearful, black widow whose son, Dave, had just died of pneumonia. Fishbelly had known little Dave and he nodded sympathetically to the dead boy's mother. Two coffins were displayed: a gray one with bronze handles that had knocked about the "shop" for years; it was selling for $300; and there was a plain pine one being offered for $150. Fishbelly knew, of course, that Tyree was aiming to sell the $300 one. . . .

"It's a wonderful bed for Dave, Mrs. Felton," Tyree purred, patting the coffin's satin padding with his palm.

"But it costs too *much!*" Mrs. Felton protested, her wet eyes staring guiltily.

Fishbelly watched her like a cat about to leap. Mrs. Felton had obviously been "sold" on the $300 coffin; that is, she felt that she was committing a social wrong by refusing it.

"You gitting your money's worth with the gray one." Tyree implied that unless Mrs. Felton heeded his advice, she was throwing her money away.

"But I'm too poor for the gray one!" Mrs. Felton wailed.

Fishbelly went forward.

"Papa, Dave was a sweet kid, a friend of mine. Let's *help* Mrs. Felton. Why can't we lend her $150? She can pay $150 now and the other $150's a loan. She can pay us $5 a week—"

"If I could do that, I'd buy it!" Mrs. Felton cried.

Tyree clamped his teeth on his cigar. It was the first time Fishbelly had ever intervened in a sales talk and he had clinched it.

"Jim'll draw up the papers," Fishbelly explained. "Six per cent interest."

"Just like I pay for my television set," Mrs. Felton concurred.

"Sure," Tyree assented, trying not to look astonished.

"Take a seat, Mrs. Felton," Fishbelly said, pushing her a chair.

"Thank you, son. You so sweet," she sighed, sitting.

Jim drew up the papers, collected the $150, and showed Mrs. Felton where to sign the agreement.

"And if you got any problems, just git in touch with us," Fishbelly counseled her.

"You so kind," the black mother sobbed.

When Mrs. Felton, smiling through her tears, had gone, Tyree clapped Fishbelly on the back.

"Goddamn, Fish! How'd you do that? I been trying to unload that lousy box for years, and you sold it in less'n a minute!" Tyree exclaimed.

"It was easy," Fishbelly said matter-of-factly. "A coffin's like anything else—coal, sugar, potatoes. . . ."

"Sure," Tyree agreed, chewing his cigar. He sank into a chair and broke into a compliment: "Boy, that head ain't on your shoulders for nothing."

Luck had buttressed his bid to convince Tyree that he could be tactful, could handle people, could manage situations— that, though he was young, he was ripe for business. As soon as Jim had gone into the rear of the "shop," Fishbelly opened up.

"Got something to tell you, Papa, and it ain't so good."

"You ain't made some gal big, hunh?" Tyree demanded. "I

don't want to be no grandpa till you git married. Don't believe in that kind of looseness."

"It ain't nothing like that, Papa. I got my marks today." He looked Tyree straight in the eyes. "I failed."

"Hell, Fish," Tyree said in disgust.

"Goddammit, I just couldn't help it, Papa."

"After me taking all that trouble to break you in with women, I didn't think you'd go *meat* crazy!"

"It ain't that, Papa. I *failed,* that's all."

Tyree slapped his thigh and studied the floor.

"Fish, you can't be a funeral director if you can't finish high school. In the old days you could embalm with no schooling. But not now. Is my business going to stop when I'm dead. Boy, you act weak-minded. You got to repeat and lose a whole year—"

"*Naw,* Papa!" He swallowed, mastering his emotions. "I ain't going to be no embalmer, Papa. I want to be a businessman, like you. I'm quitting school and I want to work for you . . ."

Tyree leaped to his feet and crashed his right fist upon his desk.

"Fish, goddammit, this ain't what I *want!*"

"But that's what I'm going to do, Papa," Fishbelly stated his case.

"But your education, boy!"

"Look at how I sold that box, Papa. I don't need no education. I can git on."

"You want to be like all them other ignorant niggers?"

"I know enough now, Papa," he argued. "I'm going to work for you and you don't have to pay me if you think I ain't worth it."

"Fish, I had plans for you. University and all—"

"University don't mean a thing, Papa. What white folks care about a university nigger?"

"It's for the *future,* Fish!"

"I want to make money, Papa. That's what *counts!*"

"Fish, I'll send you to any school that money can git you into—"

"Then I'll work for somebody else," Fishbelly told him.

Tyree stared at his son with a twitching mouth, shocked by

the clear declaration of independence he had heard. He sat at his desk, blinked, then lowered his face into his hands. He straightened and said with a rueful smile:

"If you start working for anybody else, I'll kill you. . . ."

"Don't talk like that, Papa," he begged. "I'll be your right hand. You can trust me."

Tyree sighed. Fishbelly felt that he was on the edge of victory.

"I know I can trust you, Fish."

"Then it's a deal, Papa?"

Tyree heard desperate hope in his son's voice; he was sentimental and did not wish to slay that hope.

"Awright, Fish. If that's the way you want it."

Joy made Fishbelly leap to his feet.

"Thanks, Papa!"

"But, lissen, Fish, it ain't going to be easy."

"I know; I know."

"Sit down, Fish. And lissen to me."

He sat, with excitement coursing through his blood.

"I hoped different for you. But I ain't one to drive folks against their nature, to dog 'em to do what they don't want to do. You can't do things right when you do 'em against your heart. And you know better'n me what you can do. . . . I'm hiring you, see? And you going to work, goddammit, work night and day, till your tail drops. I'm your *boss!* You going to be a *man* now. And if I catch you in that Grove 'fore sundown, I'll break your goddamn neck!"

"Yeah, Papa."

"I'm giving you what I'm giving Jim, fifty dollars a week. But you going to *earn* it. Sometimes you'll work nights—"

"And how about a car for me, Papa?"

"Naw, naw . . . Wait, Fish. Later—"

"A secondhand one? I can keep it up myself and—"

"Well, if you find a bargain . . ."

"Papa, I'm with you till the curtain comes down," he sang out his allegiance.

"Now, Fish, you got to be patient and understand things. I want to break you into a lot of things you don't know. *Important* things. I'm going to break you in slow-like, one thing at a time, see?

"Son, I ain't one to blow off my mouth, but I'm a power amongst niggers, but most of 'em don't know it. And it's better they don't, 'cause they wouldn't let me alone a minute of the day. Now, I got a lot to say in this town about what niggers go to jail and them that don't. In this kind of life you got to know what you doing, putting one foot 'fore the other. White folks *respect* me, Fish. They ask me what they ought to do in Nigger Town. And I tell 'em. And I never go back on my word."

"I git you, Papa."

"Now, your first job's collecting rent. Each Sat'day you go down on Bowman Street and make them no-good niggers pay. If they don't pay, give 'em notice to git out. They'd rather drink up their money than pay rent—"

"I know the kind, Papa."

"I'm going with you the first time.... Now, on every Sat'day night, about two o'clock in the morning, you collect from Maud Williams. I guess you remember her, hunh?"

"Yessir, Papa."

"She's going to give you a hundred and twenty dollars. Twenty dollars of that is her rent. The other hundred is for us and the police. Fifty goes to the chief of police. We keep fifty. Git it? A fifty-fifty split."

"I got it, Papa."

"Say nothing to *nobody* about this. Fish, it's worth my life if this gits out—"

"Sure. I ain't no fool, Papa."

"And don't let Maud Williams stall you. Make her pay on the dot, or we'll have the police close up her dump."

"Yeah, Papa."'

"Watch Maud. She's sly. She'll try to tempt you with meat, sicking gals on you. Don't touch a deal like that. Meat and money don't mix. Pay cold cash for what you want, if you see a good-looking gal. Business is business and meat's meat."

"Right, Papa."

"That's all now." Tyree frowned, then groaned: "Goddamn, I wish you was in school. But if you ain't, you work."

"Right, Papa."

Drunk with freedom, he walked home on air. He was at last on his own, a part of the black community. Tyree was a prince of a father. And he had hinted at secrets, power connections with the white folks. Goddamn! He would soon be in on it all. "There ain't a nigger living in town as lucky as me," he whispered to himself. "I'll have a car. Fifty bucks a week. I'll take Gladys out of that Grove dump and put her in a flat on Bowman Street. . . ." But he would not tell her now; he would tell her only after he had bought the car, some clothes . . ."And I'll keep Gladys like Papa keeps Gloria," he whispered into the warm, velvet darkness.

22

And Tyree had not lied. For one month, from early morning until late at night, Fishbelly worked to the point of dropping, and when he did get home his bones ached, his head felt heavy, and his lower jaw sagged; often he was too exhausted to eat.

"You trying to go too fast," his mother scolded at mealtimes. "You was better off at school. You ain't old enough to play a man's role yit."

The Saturday rent collections were a nightmare. He had to pull up and down rickety tenement stairs, knocking at flimsy doors, wrinkling his nostrils against the stench of frying pork, boiling cabbage, and foul odors; seeing the people of his race in their homes in various stages of nudity; being cursed at and threatened; wanting to plug his ears against browbeating complaints about leaky roofs, broken windows, collapsing outdoor privies, and water faucets that would not open or close.

Friday night would be spent checking the rent file, filling out and signing receipts to be given; then, starting out at six o'clock Saturday morning, he would pause before the Bentley door, hearing loud voices within.

"Rent man!" he would call, rapping.

There would be a quick silence; then a man's voice would boom gruffly:

"Who the hell's that knocking at my door?"

"RENT MAN!" he would call louder.

"It's that damned old rent devil again," Mrs. Bentley's voice would sound sarcastically.

"Don't come in here! We ain't got a damn thing for you!" Bentley would hurl a defiant shout.

And he would struggle vainly for an apt reply.

"I'm leaving a five-day notice," he would warn.

"We don't give a damn what you do!" Mrs. Bentley would scream.

"I'm putting the notice under the door!" he would threaten.

Silence. Then the door would open and Mr. Bentley, a railroad worker, would loom some six feet and four inches, clutching a bottle of beer in his right black fist, nude to the waist, his evil-looking tiny red eyes anchored in fat, and his black, muscle-bound body exuding a pungent musk.

"Tyree got goddamn nerve sending a little Lead-Kindly-Light nigger like you for my rent!" Mr. Bentley would bellow. "Shoo, you little fly-nigger, 'fore I swat you and mash your guts out! I ain't giving you nothing, not a damn cent, not a lousy red copper! Tyree ought to pay me for living in this dumpy, cheap chicken coop. Hell, I ain't paying no rent *this* week or *next* week neither——"

"Here's your notice to move, Mr. Bentley," Fishbelly would say, extending the slip of paper.

"He, he! And what you want me to do with *that?*" Mr. Bentley would ask derisively. "Use it in the toilet or paper my walls?"

And behind Bentley would loom the Bentley family: fat, sloppy Sue and her black offspring rising in height from two feet to five feet ten, clustered about a kitchen stove serving as a makeshift table. Placed around the stove's apron would be plates, and the family would be standing and eating with their fingers. The wooden floor would be bare, dirty; the windows covered with ragged shades; the musty corners stuffed with moldy clothes.

Fishbelly would stand, nervously smoking, listening to that

stupid raillery, forcing a smile, even pretending to laugh, all the while holding the five-day notice to vacate. Finally Bentley would pull on a dirty work shirt, darken his red right eye with a greasy cap's battered visor, and, gaunt and grim-mouthed, glare at Fishbelly. (Once, his foul verbal attempts failing, Bentley had fired his .32 into the ceiling to frighten him!)

"*Ought* I pay you or *oughtn't* I?" Bentley would ask himself, yet speaking so that Fishbelly could overhear. "Hell, naw! I ain't paying!" Bentley would suddenly shove Fishbelly aside and stalk out, slamming the door shut.

And Fishbelly would smile tightly while the Bentley family collapsed in laughter.

"You heard 'im! You ain't gitting a damn dime this week," Mrs. Bentley would howl, munching a pork chop held in greasy black fingers.

The children, black eyes swimming, would be in stitches. The door would open and Bentley would peer hesitantly in, then stare at Fishbelly with mock surprise, exclaiming:

"Nigger, what you doing in my house? Who the hell ask you in here?"

"*I* didn't!" Sue would scream, covering her face with her half-eaten pork chop.

"He just walked in!" the children would chant.

Bentley would enter, scratching his head, eying Fishbelly slyly.

"You slipping in my house to mess with my woman while I'm working, nigger?" he would demand. "I'm going to fill you full of daylight!"

And Sue would lift her hands, right fist clutching the chop, shuffle her feet, twisting her body, her black cheeks puffed tautly, as though trying not to laugh. Then laughter would erupt and she would howl:

"Lawd, this is a *mess!*"

The giggling children would do a St. Vitus dance. Bentley would snatch the five-day notice and ram his hand into his pocket and pull out a crisp ten-dollar bill and clap it into Fishbelly's hand, saying:

"There's your rent, nigger! And it ain't for *you;* it's for your *pa!* And tell that buzzard I don't want to see 'im till the day I die. And then I won't be able to see 'im, but he can have this old body of mine!"

Rocking laughter would sound as Fishbelly would take the money and surrender the receipt.

"Lawd, he sure looked funny! We had 'im in a go-'long!" the family would chorus.

Why did they act like that? Yet he dared not even hint that he thought their behavior stupid, for Tyree had warned him that a critical attitude would shut him off from them forever.

"Fish, don't ask me why our folks act like that," Tyree had said. "For our folks, it's natural. Ain't that good enough answer for you?"

And there was white-haired, seventy-year-old Miss Hanson, a retired schoolteacher living alone in one disinfectant-reeking room on a government pension. She would be waiting for him each Saturday morning, clad in black, her spectacles on the tip of her flattened, brown nose, showing an ivory-colored, false-teeth smile; and the rent, in a bowl and a saucepan, would be ready for him upon the table.

"Good morning, Miss Hanson," he would greet her. "I'll take the rent, if you don't mind."

"I do mind, but there it is," Miss Hanson would cackle.

Every Saturday morning he would witness the same weird ritual. Miss Hanson would take a pair of tweezers and fish coins out of the saucepan holding a solution of disinfectant. Next, she would snare four one-dollar bills from the bowl with tweezers. Fishbelly always watched openmouthed as Miss Hanson dried the money with a towel.

"There you are, Mr. Tucker," she would say, pointing to the coins.

"Thank you, ma'am," he would say, stuffing the money in his pocket. "I owe you fifteen cents."

"That is correct," Miss Hanson would say.

Fishbelly would count out the change and Miss Hanson would watch with horror-struck eyes.

"Lord, how can you *do* that?" Miss Hanson would whisper in terror.

"Why you so scared of money, Miss Hanson?" he would ask her.

"Because it's *dirty!*" Miss Hanson would cry. "That money's been in the hand of every nigger in town! It's full of germs. Keep on handling that money, and you'll catch a disease."

"You just *think* that." Smiling, Fishbelly would give her her receipt.

Miss Hanson would trap the coins with her tweezers and drop them into the disinfectant. "That's one thing I don't understand about people," Miss Hanson would wail. "They bathe, brush their teeth, wear nice clothes, want clean food, and then they touch money all day long, money that's been in the hands of even those nigger whores on Bowman Street, with all their venereal diseases. *Think of it!* Mr. Tucker, money carries *germs!* Doesn't your common sense tell you that?"

"Guess so," he would mumble, a trifle intimidated.

"Look at you, standing there smoking that cigarette. You're putting it in your mouth with the *same* fingers you used to give me my change. Why, you're *eating* germs, Mr. Tucker!"

"They ain't killed me yit," he would say defensively.

"But they *will,* if you're not careful," Miss Hanson would warn.

Funny woman, Fishbelly would tell himself as he went out. But, the moment he was upon the street he would nervously and unconsciously toss away his just-begun cigarette and then elaborately wipe his hands hard upon his handkerchief, murmuring: "Gee, but it's hot today..."

As he pushed on each Saturday hunting for dollars, his horizon broadened and he discovered why his friend Sam was so racially bitter. When he called at Sam's home Sam's father would not surrender the rent until after he had delivered himself of a lecture upon the greatness and superiority of black men in history. Mr. Davis was a skinny, cross-eyed little man with a hypnotic manner of speech.

"Fish, as I live and breathe, you'll see the black man's birthright redeemed in your lifetime when Ethiopia stretches forth her wings.... The hour's done struck. Our time's done come. There was a time for the yellow man, the brown man, the white man; now's the time for the *black* man. Read your Bible, son. Gawd's done wound up the clock of history and our hour's striking....

"Look at the world and you see the *black* man's rising. He's rising everywhere but in America. It makes me sick to see black folks scraping and bowing to this no-good white trash when black folks was once kings of Ghana, the great black kingdom in Africa. . . . Be proud of being black, son. Live black, die black, eat black, sleep black, buy black, sell black, love black. . . . The white man's done conquered us 'cause he's made us 'shamed of our hair, our skin, our noses—'shamed of Africa. There was a time when the black man was high up! Read, Fish. I got a plenty books here you can borrow and they'll tell you things that'll make you proud of your *blackness*. . . . Hold on, Fish! Did you know that the Egyptians was *black?* Did you know that an English king had a *black* wife? Did you know that Beethoven had *black* blood in 'im? Read, Fish."

"Yessir," Fishbelly would mumble. "I'll ask you for one of them books one day. But right now I ain't got no time for reading."

"Baby Jesus," he would grumble as he left. "I don't want to read nothing about Africa. I want to make some goddamn *money.*"

The most distressing home at which Fishbelly called for rent was that of Aggie West, who was now organist in the Mount Olivet Baptist Church. Aggie was rarely in when Fishbelly presented himself for the five dollars due, but Mrs. Sarah West, who washed, cooked, and cared for children in white families, was. A pillar of the church and a choir singer, Mrs. West had regular but vague communications from God, communications which she hoped would become clearer in time. She had petitioned heaven to find Aggie a job and to cure Aggie's younger brother, Bunny, a crippled idiot who sunned himself all day in the front window of the parlor. It was widely assumed that Bunny's walled eyes, drooling mouth, and spastically twisted limbs were the work of God; indeed, Mrs. West took a kind of mute pride in Bunny's state of idiocy, for that was a kind of proof that God had, for reasons unknown, noticed her.

Mrs. West was always ready with her rent and her demands.

"Mr. Tucker," she would begin tearfully, "please help me with Aggie. He needs a job and nobody'll hire him. Why? I don't know. And he's a *good* boy; he sews, cooks, washes, irons, and takes care of the house. I ain't had a minute's trouble with 'im since he was born. He's polite, tidy, and bright as a button. But nobody'll give 'im any work. Now, is that fair, Mr. Tucker?"

"What can Aggie do, Mrs. West?" Fishbelly had asked her once.

"Just about *anything*," she had said fervently.

And Fishbelly had known that that "anything" meant that Aggie could only play the piano. . . .

"I'll ask around," Fishbelly had promised her.

"That'd be wonderful," Mrs. West had sighed.

Fishbelly could not believe that Mrs. West did not know what was "wrong" with Aggie, for that "wrong" was so obvious in Aggie's too-cultivated and swishing behavior. Whenever he was in Aggie's presence he wanted either to hit him or laugh at him. One day he had asked Aggie:

"You find a job yit, Aggie?"

Aggie had rolled his eyes, put his hands on his hips and exclaimed:

"Heavens, no!"

"Can't you-all use Aggie in the undertaking parlor?" Mrs. West had asked. "He ain't scared of no dead folks."

And when Fishbelly had asked Tyree, Tyree had leaped to his feet and exploded:

"Hell naw, Fish! Nothing like that can't *never* happen! What would folks think if we had a 'fruit' working around them stiffs! They'd have cat fits! We need Aggie like we need a hole in the head. Men wouldn't want to come to us to be buried even when they was *dead*. . . . Fish, folks git strange notions about what goes on in undertaking places. I once had a nineteen-year-old gal to fix up. Died of a bad heart. Her ma swore she was a virgin and mebbe she was. I don't know. But you know that that gal's ma wouldn't leave my 'shop' till we buried that gal! Said her gal was a virgin and she wanted to make sure she was *buried* a virgin. . . . Naw, Fish; no Aggie or nothing like 'im can ever come in this 'shop'."

Jake and Guke, the alcoholic twins who handled the hearse-ambulance, were also Tyree's tenants, and Fishbelly had always to listen to their wives' bill of complaints. Guke's wife was a worried, mousy, black little woman with four small children, and she would ask:

"Is Add Guke drinking heavy on the job, Mr. Tucker? Lawd, I don't know what to do with that man! I try to be good wife to 'im, but it don't help. You know, he was once a clerk in the post office, making real good money, but his love for whiskey made Uncle Sam fire 'im. Whiskey sure done made this family suffer. I done begged Add on my knees with tears in my eyes, and still he drinks like a thousand fishes. If I had a dollar for every bottle he's killed, we could retire. . . . Why he drinks like that, Mr. Tucker? Reckon he could be worried about something?

"Mr. Tucker, I want to ask you something real serious, just between you and me, see? Somebody said that us black folks ain't got brains like white folks, that white folks' brains is in the *front* of their heads and that black folks' brains is in *back* of their heads. . . . Now, Mr. Tucker, you reckon that's true? You ought to know. You see folks when they dead. If black folks' brains is in the *back* of their heads, then they couldn't think real straight, could they, Mr. Tucker? Their thoughts'd git kind of lost, wouldn't they, if them thoughts had to travel all the way from the *back* of their heads to the *front* 'fore they could do anything? Mebbe that's why Add Guke forgits when I tell 'im not to drink? Lawd, I wish I could cure that man of drinking. We never have enough to eat. We just manage to pay rent. The kids ain't got enough clothes. And all on account of Add's drinking. . . ."

Fishbelly would leave, promising to watch Add Guke's drinking and to find out if black men's brains were in front or in back of their heads.

Jake Lamb's wife plagued Fishbelly with the issue that weighed heaviest on her heart. Mrs. Lamb, an enterprising woman, used the front room of her house as a hairdressing salon. Amid fumes of burning oil, Mrs. Lamb would pull a sizzling iron comb through kinky, greasy tufts of hair to kill it and make it straight, straight like the hair of white folks.

"Mr. Fish," Mrs. Lamb would begin, "is we 'colored folks,' is we 'Africans,' is we 'Americans,' or is we just plain old 'black folks'? That's what I want to know. We was black when we came from Africa a long time ago, but since then we been all mixed up with red blood, white blood, black blood, and brown blood.... We ain't white, 'cause our skins got color in 'em; and we ain't black no more. Now, white folks call us 'colored'; but ain't that 'cause they don't know *what* to call us? And ain't they got to call us *something?*

"Mr. Fish, I think that we done got to be another race, mebbe something like them Indonesians.... Don't you think we ought to find another name for ourselves? And if we found one, wouldn't it straighten everything out awright, Mr. Fish?" Mrs. Lamb would ask as she thoughtfully pulled her hot comb through a long length of kinky hair, making it straight.

One night, depressed and dog-tired, Fishbelly complained to Tyree:

"Papa, this rent collecting's showing me something.... Our folks is *sick*, Papa. All the black folks I meet's worried to death about white folks—talking about 'em all day and all night. They laugh, sing, and dance, but they *worried*—"

"Fish, forgit that stuff. Your job's collecting rent. Git enough dollars, and you'll never have to worry none. There ain't no problem a dollar can't solve. Just git you a million dollars, and then tell me what you worried about. Till then, stop talking *race*."

Fishbelly's prowling after dollars made him discover his Black-Belt world, made him feel the tissue of its squalor and the texture of its numbed hope unfolding daily before him. His racial universe became vividly concrete, a strange organism living parasitically upon the vast body of a white organism which it could not ever really know.

One morning Professor Butler, the high-school principal, dropped a humorous hint to Fishbelly, a hint that enabled him to grasp the structure of his racial world, the origins of its peculiar strength and the genesis of its fanatic feebleness.

"Well, Fish, my boy. I was sorry to see you leave school," Professor Butler said. "But if you want to go out into the world, then, by all means, do it. I'll give you a little rhyme that'll help you to understand our folks. I didn't invent this ... but listen to it:

Big niggers have little niggers upon their back to bite 'em.
And little niggers have lesser niggers, and so on ad infinitum.

207

And the big niggers themselves, in turn, have bigger niggers
   to go on;
While these again have bigger still, and bigger still, and so
   on.

"Watch that rhyme, Fish, and you'll see that it explains a lot. The white folks are on top of us, and our own folks are on top of our folks, and God help the black man at the bottom."

Fishbelly laughed at that ditty, but, as he dashed down dusty streets hunting defaulting tenants, as he scoured dance halls, bars, restaurants, and dives, he learned that that ditty was truer than funny. What he heard and saw made him tell himself: "These niggers walking around in their sleep." He sensed in them a profound lassitude, a sort of lackadaisical aimlessness, a terribly pathetically narrow range of emotional activity veering from sex to religion, from religion to alcohol. He found them ready to explode over matters devoid of real content and meaning. His Black Belt teemed with crimes against the person: assaults, knifings, shootings stemming from drunken brawls. "We niggers fighting each other and we don't even know it," he told himself with amazement.

As yet incapable of detachment, he never grasped any significant processes in the squalid lives he saw; he knew that something was dead wrong, but he had no notion what it was. A white world beyond his ken had laid its cruelly clumsy hands upon him and had made him self-conscious about his and his people's lives, but he could not comprehend the outlook of that alien world that had spoiled his own world for him. Grudgingly accepting being classed with his people, he was, deep in him, somewhat afraid of them; though he spoke their language, shared their pleasures and sorrows, there was in him some element that stood aside as though in shame.

As he took in dollars and passed out receipts, he could not help but divide the Black-Belt people into two general groups: the "independent niggers" and the "dependent niggers." The "dependents" worked for whites and Fishbelly could feel their timidity and fear; the "independents" farmed, operated their own businesses, and practiced professions, and Fishbelly could sense their greater degree of self-respect and aggressiveness, even if that aggressiveness was more often directed toward their own people than toward whites. Yet he knew that both the "dependent niggers" and "independent niggers" were, in turn, dependent upon a white world for a definition of their lives.

Fishbelly learned that, of the ten thousand Clintonville blacks, some one thousand resided in Addison Addition, where he had his home. Many of those thousand black home-owners had edifices ranging in quality from "shotgun" shacks to ornate bungalows. They were men like Tyree, Dr. Bruce, Mr. Jordan (Zeke's father)—owners of bars, restaurants, grocery stores, drugstores, barbershops, undertaking establishments, etc.; there were also a few schoolteachers, postal clerks, and preachers. Locked in their black ghetto for business as well as pleasure, deprived of ownership of the basic riches of the community in which they lived, shunted by violence and the threat of violence out of participation in the government that governed them, a few of these homeowning blacks, among whom was Tyree, looked with hot greed upon the paltry stream of hard-earned dollars trickling from the white world into the black world—dollars brought in by the sweat of maids, washerwomen, and butlers—and sought ways and means of culling a share of those all-too-few dollars for their own pockets before they flowed out of the Black Belt and back into the pockets of the white man.

The other nine thousand Clintonville blacks lived in and around Ford's Ridge, of which Bowman Street was the main artery. They were illiterates and semi-illiterates: domestics, laborers, car washers, porters, elevator operators, messengers, and night watchmen, and a vast mass existing on the naked margins of hunger. They were quartered in flimsy tenements or shacks resting so casually on the red clay that it seemed that a strong wind could send them tumbling. . . .

"Papa, I swear, I don't see how niggers live," Fishbelly told Tyree.

"Don't worry, Fish. Them niggers just hibernating. Niggers is tough. Even the white man can't kill 'em."

One morning while running an errand for Tyree he passed his high school, where his erstwhile classmates were lined up prior to entering the building to take summer courses. Nostalgia filled him; he had been out of school for only two weeks, but it seemed an eternity. Professor Butler signaled on his bell for the students to sing.

DANG-DANG . . .

Tremulously hopeful voices rose, swelling hauntingly through the sunlit air:

> *Oh, Mary, don't you weep, don't you moan,*
> *Oh, Mary, don't you weep, don't you moan,*
> *'Cause Pharaoh's army got drown-ded.*
> *Oh, Mary, don't you weep.*
>
> *If I could I surely would*
> *Stand on the rock where Moses stood,*
> *'Cause Pharaoh's army got drown-ded.*
> *Oh, Mary, don't you weep.*

The song's strains faded and Fishbelly stood with misty eyes and tight throat. His childhood was gone; he was a man, and that song's innocence clashed in his mind with the scenes he had witnessed in Black-Belt homes and he was dismayed. He watched the students march into the school to the beat of the bell and he shook his head murmuring:

"They better tell Mary to weep for 'em, and to weep for a long, long time, 'cause what they got to face in this world's Gawd-knows hard. . . ."

In rent collecting the women were his worst trial, wanting to pay in dribbles, a dollar now, another Wednesday. Many refused to open their doors until he had slipped the five-day notice under the sill. Others pleaded to be let off, swearing to pay double next week, a contingency against which Tyree had warned him.

"Fish, if they can't pay five dollars *this* Sat'day, how in all hell can they pay ten dollars *next* Sat'day? Be hard on these nigger bitches. They so crooked they could hide behind cork-screws and you couldn't see 'em; they so bad they don't even throw a shadow in the sun; they so evil they could steal the sweetness out of a ginger snap without breaking the crust. . . . Fish, if you let a nigger bitch owe you fifty dollars and give her a five-day notice to git out, she just might have sense enough to go and find another place to stay. Make 'em pay, Fish; that's the rule. Play it safe. Remember, we black and we can't rent to white folks. So we have to be hard on our folks if we want to make money."

There were women who tried to swap their bodies for rent, who waited for him naked upon beds in semidarkened rooms, leaving doors slightly ajar, calling out when he knocked:

"Come in, Mr. Rent Man!"

And he would enter, breathing fetid air, arguing as the woman tried to coax him. To have given her the slightest acknowledgement would have encouraged her aggressiveness. And if he had touched her, he could not have gotten a penny for rent. To every fleshly advance, he had to mutter:

"I'm waiting for that rent, ma'am."

And some would finally say:

"There 'tis, under the dresser scarf."

Or:

"Here. Feel under the pillow for it, if you want it."

And he would grope for the money, avoiding the woman's tempting, searching eyes.

And Maud Williams was true to her hoary profession, never ceasing to bait him with a strange girl in exchange for rent, or half of it, or a quarter of it, or even a tenth of it—always bargaining. She would call into the bedrooms of the rambling wooden flat:

"Bee! Say, there, Bee! Come here!"

And Bee, yellow, shapely, would come strolling, as stripped as Eve, her eyes nonchalantly wide.

"Yessum," Bee would drawl dutifully.

"Fish, ain't she about the prettiest thing you ever laid your eyes on?" Maud would ask.

And Bee or Martha or Clara or Irene would smile sweetly at him.

"She's real cute, Maud, but I want that rent," he would say.

"Lawd, hear that man!" Maud would pretend outrage. "Look what Tyree done made out of 'im! Bee, git back in your room. This nigger don't know what's good even when he's looking dead straight at it."

In the end she would pull up her skirt, roll down a stocking over a thick, black leg, and take out a green wad and count bills as she put them into Fishbelly's hands—bills still warm from body heat.

"Maud, some folks'd be scared to touch this money if they saw you taking it from there," he told her one Saturday night.

"He, he!" Maud had cackled. "Money's always clean, son." She would stare at Fishbelly, mumbling slyly: "Nigger, you sure got a head for business. Don't nothing faze you, do it, son? One day I'm going to have a gal in here that'll make you forgit you ever went to Sunday school. There ain't a man born of woman that can turn down *everything*. He can have seven-'leven wives and be true to 'em all and still fall one day. Just depends on how he's feeling and how she looks. . . . I know; this stuff ain't new to you like it was that first night when Tyree dragged you in here—"

"He didn't *drag* me in here!" Fishbelly had protested.

"You was brought in here by the scruff of your neck, like you was a wet kitten!" Maud had howled with laughter. "I going to make you slip up yit. One night I'm going to have a gal in here and you'll swear that the sun rises and sets in her navel. . . . And when that happens, I'm going to laugh my goddamn head off!"

Fishbelly grew hard behind the façade of a fixed smile, hid cynicism by sympathetic inflections of his voice, developed a pretended indifference to the squalor he saw, and learned to conceal compassionate impulses that would have made it impossible to collect rent. He was able to see Gladys only in fitful snatches. But, as that awful first month drew to a close, Tyree embraced him declaring:

"Fish, goddammit, I'm going to talk to you like a preacher! 'Well done, my son!' You *made* it! I was wondering how you could stand up under it. I throwed you in the water to let you sink or swim. Dammit, you can *swim*. Now, I'm going to take the pressure off you a little. Fourth of July's coming. . . . Take a couple of days off and git the kinks out of your system."

"Papa, I found a jalopy. I want you to see it and—"

"Let Jim look at it. He knows cars. If he says it's a buy, then we'll git it. But that damned jalopy's your expense, not mine."

"Yessir, Papa," he hummed with joy. His goal of freedom was almost within grasp.

23

He bought the jalopy, some new clothes, and, on the afternoon of the Fourth of July, he called for Gladys.

"Baby, we dancing at the Grove tonight," he told her. "Zeke and Tony's joining the Army and we pitching a boogie-woogie."

"Fish, I thought you'd throwed me over," Gladys chided him.

"I been working night and day. I got a lot to tell you," he hinted at disclosures. "I'm making a new deal all around. . . . Let's start with me." He turned as though he were modeling clothes. "You like my new suit?"

"It's a cool killer, Fish." She fingered the cloth's texture. "Real tweed, ain't it?"

"English stuff," he bragged. "No white man in town's got any better. Outside is a jalopy and it's all mine."

"Gee, Fish. Let's take a spin," she suggested eagerly.

"That's just what I was going to say," he told her. "Today we celebrate. I been having it tough—"

"I ain't seen you but four times this month—"

"I'm going to make it up to you, honey," he consoled her, leading her to the jalopy. "It ain't no Rolls-Royce, but it'll take us places and bring us back."

His attention banished the slight roundedness from her shoulders and kindled an elusive sparkle in the depths of her brooding eyes. She climbed into the car and shook her tumbling brown hair out of her face and looked at the world with a new confidence.

"I ain't dressed for no Fourth of July," she said, tugging critically at her skimpy skirt.

"I'm gitting you some new things," he said as they pulled off. "Where to?"

"Straight through the center of town," she called in child-like glee.

"Right," he assented.

Black boys tossed firecrackers into dusty streets and detonations sounded under the car wheels. He loved her tawny skin, the tilt of her head; when she was out of the smoky dimness of the Grove, her body showed lithe and her face had a proud profile. They rolled swiftly through the Black Belt, hearing explosions, and entered the well-swept, tree-shaded streets of the white area.

"It's nice here," Gladys said.

"Yeah. They keep it clean. We got ten thousand folks and the whites got fifteen thousand; we all pay the same taxes, but they don't keep our streets clean like this," he told her. "They got four times as much space to live in as we got. We live in a hole; they live in the open. . . ."

She was silent. He braked the car for a red light in front of a drugstore before which loitered a group of teen-age, blue-jeaned white boys. Fishbelly saw their unsmiling, baffled eyes staring at Gladys, then they nudged one another with their elbows. The traffic eye winked from red to green and he got under way, hearing a derisive shout:

"Nigger lover!"

His hands gripped hard upon the steering wheel as he glanced at Gladys who was looking straight ahead with a serene face. Did not that insult mean anything to her?

"They spoke to *you*," he told her gently.

"I heard 'em," Gladys said, chuckling slightly, her expression unchanging.

Her reply disturbed him. Was she enjoying her role?

"What you think of stuff like that?"

"I don't let it touch me," she said proudly.

Her reaction still failed to please him.

"White folks ever bother you?"

"I wouldn't let 'em," she said defiantly.

He felt slapped. Even Tyree knuckled under to whites, and

here was a slip of a defenseless girl boasting that she would not let them touch her. Was that her sly way of bragging about her white skin? Didn't she care about what other black folks suffered? Or was she pretending she never got angry? Perhaps she did not have enough imagination to grasp what it all really meant?

"I could *kill* them bastards!" he spat.

"Aw, they just crazy, mixed-up kids," she mumbled calmly.

"Crazy, hell," he said. "That craziness gits folks killed!"

"They don't know what they doing." Irritation was in her voice.

"The hell they don't!" he contradicted her.

"Honey, let's don't talk *race,*" Gladys begged. "It's so wonderful out . . ."

Fishbelly's sky darkened. She defended white people! Maybe she thinks she's *white!* Well, she sure *looked* white. Maybe she came often to this part of town? She could walk these streets among white people as much as she liked and nobody in the Black Belt would be the wiser. Hell, maybe she had customers among white men! He had never before considered that possibility and it fanned his rising hate of her color. He loved her because she was whitish, and yet he was now feeling that her whiteness was eluding him even though she sat there in the car beside him, even though she was willing to let him hold her in his arms tonight.

"You ever pass, Gladys?" he asked with soft suddenness. It took her so long to answer that he thought that she had not heard. "Tell me," he urged her; there was an edge in his voice now. "You ever pass?"

"Well," Gladys began, still looking ahead, her silky hair blowing behind her in the hot wind, "not for *real,* anyhow."

He hated her so much at that moment that he could have grabbed a handful of her diaphanous hair and flung her from the car. He saw her delicately tapering white fingers lift wisps of flowing hair and toss them from her eyes. He could almost feel the crown of hair on his head, hair that had been straightened, and he was ashamed of it. Bet she sure loves that damned hair of hers, he growled silently to himself.

"What you mean, 'Not for real'?" he imitated her with a jeer.

"I never pass 'cause I want to," she explained. "When I go to a department store to buy something, they treat me white and I *let* 'em. It's too much trouble to start explaining. . . . You know."

"I don't know," he said.

"Aw, Fish!"

"You don't tell 'em you white, but you don't tell you black either, hunh?" He was trying to hurt her.

"Fish, try to understand. It's just easy for me that way, that's all. If they don't *know* I'm colored, they take me for white," she spoke reluctantly.

"But do you *tell* 'em you colored?" he insisted.

Her cheeks blazed red with anger.

"What you want me to do? Carry a sign saying: I'M COLORED?"

"Skip it," he muttered.

"What's the matter, honey?"

"I said skip it," he snapped.

"Don't be mad at me, Fish."

"I ain't mad." Her pleading tone had mollified him a bit.

"When they know I ain't white they treat me just like they do you," she said.

"Not the *men,*" he could not help but say.

"Naw," she admitted. "The men insult me on the street." She spoke without anger, her eyes pensive.

The traffic thickened and Fishbelly braked and found himself in a double lane surrounded by cars in which white people sat. He was alongside a big black Buick and saw a white family inside staring at him and Gladys.

"Look at me till your eyes rot," he mutterred.

"Aw, Fish, forgit 'em."

The car ahead of him advanced and he rolled forward and stopped alongside a white man in a Ford. The man's head poked inquisitively out of the window and for a split second Fishbelly could see, like an image in a half-forgotten dream, the picture of a white man's blood-streaked face pinned beneath that overturned Oldsmobile in the woods on that far-off summer day and he stared hard and unblinkingly back at the white man in the Ford while the image dissolved.

"Where you-all from?" The white man asked bluntly.

"China!" Fishbelly flung at him contemptuously and pulled swiftly ahead, leaving the man staring.

"Good for you!" Gladys yelled, laughing.

Goddamn . . . What the hell was there to laugh about? Didn't she know that the white man had been trying to find out if he had the right to interfere, to raise a mob against him? Didn't she know that black men were killed for riding in cars, side by side, with women of her color? Or did she regard it all as a child's game? It was plain that he would have to educate her, tell her what the racial score was. They were cruising now on the outskirts of town, driving past wealthy white homes set amid green lawns.

"Let's git a drink at Henry's," he suggested.

"Okay," Gladys said.

Henry's was the main Black-Belt bar, but it was almost empty at that hour of the afternoon. They took a table in a corner. He sat looking at her. He was planning to take over this woman completely, but he would have to get her straightened out about many things; he would have to pry into her and find out how she really felt about black people and white people. Didn't she know how he felt? Couldn't she guess? Or did she know and didn't respect it?

"Gladys, what do you think of white folks?"

"What you mean, Fish?"

"I asked you a question—"

"Fish, they just *white,*" she answered earnestly.

He realized in a flash that, though black of skin, he was really much whiter mentally than she was or ever could be, though she was whiter of skin than he. Gladys did not possess enough imagination to see herself or the life she lived in terms that white people saw black people, terms which he had experienced at their hands, terms which he *knew.* Fishbelly hotly rejected the terms in which white people weighed or saw him, for those terms made him feel agonizingly inferior; then, in his reacting against his sense of inferiority, he had to try to be like them in order to prove to himself and to them that he was not inferior. Yet, in his trying to be like them he was trapping himself; he had to admit his inferiority of situation, accept it before he could rise above it. And he was astounded that Gladys could feel or sense none of this. In a certain way she

217

was mentally much *blacker* than he was, though she looked *white!* He stared dreamily out of the door of the bar, hearing firecrackers popping in the streets, seeing an American flag billowing lazily in the hot breeze.

"Ever had any trouble with white folks?" he asked her.

"Naw," she said. "What you worrying about, Fish?"

He gaped. Her whole life was and had been a big, nasty trouble from white folks and she was calmly denying it. She was a half-white bastard whore who had given birth to a half-white bastard girl child who was most likely destined to grow up and give birth to yet another half-white bastard girl child who would grow up to be a whore, yet she had never had any trouble from white folks. Maybe Gladys did not know what trouble was? Maybe what had happened to her appeared merely normally unfortunate? Suddenly he realized that she had already told him the truth: *she agreed with the whites!* They were right and she was wrong! An accident had anchored her on the wrong side of the racial fence and she had merely sighed and accepted it, as though someday another accident would redress the mishap and make up for all the inconvenience. In her daily life Gladys could, in a limited sense, be either white or black; and, because she could be white sometimes, she felt that it was right for the streets in the white areas to be clean, and, because the streets in the white areas were clean, the whites were, therefore, right. They had money and the say-so and that was proof of their rightness.

"You think they treat us *right?*" he asked, sipping his whiskey.

"Fish, stop worrying about *them,*" she said. "Look, you got a car. You got money. You wear better clothes than them poor white-trash white boys who hollered at me in front of the drugstore—"

"You think it's money and that's *all?*" he asked.

"Money's a lot," she said.

"My papa's got money and he acts and lives like a nigger—"

"Don't talk like that about your papa," she reproved him.

"It's the truth," he insisted. "Do they *treat* us right?"

"In what *way,* Fish?" she asked with pleading eyes.

"Hell, Gladys, can't you *see?* We go to black schools and

their schools are better'n ours—"

"Oh, that?" she asked softly, simply.

"Yeah, *that,*" he said scornfully, realizing that her mind was incapable of comprehending the elementary complexity of it all. "And they *kill* us too," he added bitterly.

"But who's talking about killing anybody?" she asked, offended.

"They killed Chris—"

"Oh!" She stared at him hard. "You talked about him once," she said wonderingly. "Was he kin to you or something?"

Anger rendered him speechless. She was hopeless. Yet he loved her. He wanted to be with her. Was it her racial innocence that made him love her? Was it because she was a shadowy compromise that was white and not white? Was it because she looked white and had to live in the Black Belt with him? He stared deep into the amber fluid in his glass and tried to think of life and race in the terms that Gladys felt them. If the black man that the white people killed was your father or brother, then they were bothering you, but if they killed a black stranger, then it was none of your goddamn business. . . . Yeah, poor little Gladys was just a woman and didn't know. He would take this woman and teach her.

"Gladys," he whispered.

"Yeah, baby. Don't worry—"

"I got something real serious to tell you."

"Hunh huh."

He relished the power he had over her; he could tell from the manner in which she had responded that she had no notion of what he was about to reveal.

"Sweetheart, I'm taking you out of that Grove," he told her.

The idea was so alien, unexpected, that it took time to sink home. Then her head shot up and her petulant lips parted in astonishment.

"What you mean, Fish?"

"I got a three-room flat for you over—"

"Fish!" Her eyes were round, moist circles of brown. "Really?"

"Yeah. It's on Bowman Street."

"Fish, you fooling?" she asked in a tremulous whisper.

"Baby, I mean it."

Her lips moved soundlessly, as though she were afraid to speak.

"Fish, you really want me?" she asked incredulously.

"Goddammit, I do."

Her white hands flew across the table and seized hold of him, tightly, spasmodically.

"And your folks, Fish?"

"Mama won't know. But it's okay with Papa. Anything I do is okay with 'im if I don't make no trouble."

"I won't make no trouble, Fish. I swear. I'll obey you!"

A string of firecrackers popped outside like a machine gun and Gladys flinched and leaned hard against him.

"I want you to stay home and be *true* to me," he warned.

Tears flooded her eyes; she flung herself into his arms.

"I'll do anything you say."

"I won't be able to be there all the time."

"I'll wait for you, Fish," she gasped. "I never thought you wanted me that much. . . . I didn't think this could happen to me. . . ." She stared at him through tears, smiling sadly, reluctantly ."I'll cook for you. I can sew. Git me a sewing machine, hunh?" She did not wait for an answer; she moved nervously in her chair. "Darling, I want to ask you something . . ."

"Sure."

"Can I bring my baby there?"

"Hell, it's your place and—"

"Aw, Fish!" she wailed. She clutched him. "Fish, tell me something," she said in a rush of words. "You—" Her voice choked off in a sob.

"What's the matter, honey?"

She closed her eyes before she spoke.

"You won't never hold what I was against me?"

He pressed her close to him.

"The past is past," he said. "From now on, it's *all* past."

She opened her eyes and stared at him—eyes that were begging redemption, salvation.

"Fish, I'm older'n you. I ain't asking to marry—"

"Papa wouldn't let me marry nohow. And I ain't ready for that," he told her frankly but tenderly.

"Why d-didn't you t-tell me b-before?" she asked in gasps.

"I didn't know if I could work it out," he told her. "Now, Gladys, you free to do what I ask?"

"I'm *free!* I'm yours and nobody else's; I'm yours for as long as you want me," she swore.

"Okay. I'm sending a truck for your things in the morning."

"Yeah. Anything you say, Fish."

She threw back her head and looked off, then swabbed her wet eyes with a balled handkerchief. He had never before seen a woman in the throes of redemption, had never before witnessed the light in the face of a woman whose destiny had been changed in the twinkling of an eye. He saw lines of tension about her mouth already leaving. Then fear showed in her eyes.

"Fish, you wouldn't fool me about something like this?"

"Naw! Naw!"

"If you fooling me, I swear I'll just lay down and die. . . ."

"I'm keeping you. That Grove's finished."

She grabbed him again and wept. Then she asked slyly:

"Take me to the Grove for the last time. I want to dance. Then I'm taking you home with me, for keeps!"

"Sure thing."

He paid and they left. Dusk was falling when they neared the Grove and, as they turned into the dirt road leading to it, they smelled the cloying scent of magnolias and heard hot jazz filling the gloam.

"I want to dance!" Gladys yelled excitedly.

He parked the car and they ran inside and slid rhythmically onto the dance floor, swaying and dipping to the music's beat.

"I'm dreaming," Gladys whispered.

"You a dream," he said. "A dream in the daytime."

"Nobody'll never know how happy I am tonight," she sighed.

They danced a second time. The Grove was hot, like a steam bath. Eyes closed, the black musicians played furiously, shaking their sweaty faces.

"Look at them cats," Gladys said. "They really sent, hunh?"

"They gone," he said.

Outside, detonations blasted the summer night. Fishbelly was tired.

"Say, let's git some air," he said. "I can't breathe in here."

"If you want to," she said.

He felt her vibrant body bouncing alongside his as they went outside where a faint breeze blew. They found a grassy spot beneath an elm tree and sat and looked at a sky burning with huge yellow stars.

"Darling, lissen . . . If I'm moving tomorrow, I ought to tell Fats right now. He's a mean thing and losing me might make 'im mad if I wait till the last minute, see? Fats been in jail a lot and he's got some evil ways about 'im."

"Sure enough? Didn't know Fats was ever a jailbird."

"He's been in four or five times," Gladys said.

"No wonder he can run this outfit," Fishbelly mused. "Okay. Tell 'im. I'll be here, waiting for you."

He rose and pulled her to her feet. She kissed him with a new kiss, a kiss that had no reserves. Then she pulled away.

"Fish, you sweet, I can't *believe* it!"

She ran like a shadow across the darkened fields and vanished into the rear door of the Grove. Fishbelly could see golden lights gleaming through the wooden beams and the thick-hanging moss suspended from the tin roof. Thunderous jazz rocked hypnotically. He sat and lit a cigarette. He was tired, but things were going his way. He had done it; he would be with Gladys. It was not for always, but it was enough; it was what he wanted. And he would talk to Gladys, change her, make her understand what it was like to live day and night under that white shadow.

A month's drudgery had depleted him and his nerves tingled as his fatigue ebbed. He stretched out upon the grass and eddied smoke through his nostrils. Far off, a firecracker exploded. Next came a soft, swishing sound that echoed eerily. "Fourth of July," he muttered. "Somebody shooting off a rocket." Then he was staring at a strange, faint radiance in the sky above him; it was as though a full moon had burst from behind a dark bank of clouds. He looked wonderingly at the sheen while a vague disturbance moved in him. He cocked his head, hearing a confusion of dim, incomprehensible voices. He thought he heard a muffled scream, but he was not sure. He frowned, turned his head, and saw the Grove glowing white inside. The music had stopped at some moment in the immediate past, a moment that he could not remember. The wind wafted him a whiff of smoke. Yes, it was that bright light in the Grove that had cast that funny sheen upon the sky. A medley of slurred speech reached his ears. What's happening? Oh yes; they had turned on those powerful spotlights that they used when some member of the band was playing a wicked solo. But, naw! *There was no music!* He stood abruptly, peering intently at the dance hall. He took an involuntary step forward and stood still. A soft, greenish halo suddenly enveloped the moss-covered building, a halo that turned quickly blue and deepened. He was hearing piercing screams now and the bluish light became a radiant sea of orange-colored flames roiling upward toward the sky.

"Some fool nigger's done started a fire!" he spoke aloud.

He was running wildly toward the Grove before he knew it. A mountain of billowing smoke gushed up and out of the dance hall from all sides, then a sheet of red flame erupted and where the Grove had stood was now an immense column of leaping fire, filling the world, roaring whirlwind-like, casting up surging floods of sparks.

"Gawd, it's on fire!" he panted, galloping forward.

He sprinted to the Grove's back door, through which Gladys had vanished. He stopped, gaping. The door was open, but jammed with human bodies, piled one atop the other. Their faces were distorted and their mouths were open. But they were making no sounds. He felt enclosed in a nightmare. Behind the bodies were solid walls of flying flame.

"Gladys! Gladys!" he screamed.

Hellish heat hit his face. Save for crackling, licking fire, all was profoundly quiet. There had been screams, but now not one voice came from the interior of the raging dance hall. The black faces stuffed in the doorway seemed to be gasping for breath. The heat was increasing so rapidly that he had to back off. He could not react to what he saw; it was not true . . . But it *was* . . . The blinding glare of hurling flames gouged at his eyes.

"Gladys!" he screamed, then waited, his body shaking.

Oh Gawd, she *couldn't* be in there! He grew aware of dark forms of people milling slowly, aimlessly about and he heard a babble of distraught voices. He turned, looking; people walked as though in their sleep, dazed. He spied one of the Grove's bartenders, Clarence; he ran to him and grabbed him, feeling waving flames lashing hotly at his back.

"Clarence, you seen Gladys?" he asked in a tense whisper.

"Hunh?" Clarence grunted. "I just got out myself . . . I feel dizzy. My head. Say, you got a match?"

Clarence's request rattled Fishbelly. Automatically he fumbled in his pockets, found a folder of matches, struck one, and held the flame to Clarence's cigarette and watched the man suck greedily, his black face lit by boiling lava and rolling fire.

"Thanks," Clarence mumbled, moving off unaware, it seemed, that twisting flames were leaping twenty feet from him.

Then, with a sense of shock, Fishbelly realized that the dance hall was burning and that he did not know where Gladys was. He felt snared in a net of shadows. What had happened? He wanted to perform a mental act and annul the fire and live again in a normal world. But, no . . . Again he ran to the doorway; behind the heaped-up bodies was a background of banks of glowing, white fire. Jesus . . . *Naw!*

He dashed madly, circling the blazing, smoking inferno, wondering why no sounds were coming from it, and rushed to within twenty feet of the front door. It, too, was heaped with bodies, some of which had most of their clothes torn from them. It was clear that they had been trying to get out, had grappled and trampled one another. The searing heat would not let him approach the door. He was frantic. Gladys was in there and he had to go in and get her out! But how? The dance hall had two doors and he had been to both of them and they were blocked with inert bodies. He looked about desperately. Yes; high up in the back wall was a small opening for ventilation; he recalled it now. He raced breathlessly to the rear again and stared up; the opening was white hot with seething jets of leaping fire.

He glared about at the survivors. They were whimpering, their stunned, unblinking eyes staring at the flaming building. A crying black girl was threading her way through the crowd, calling:

"Where's Bob? Oh Gawd! Bob! Didn't he git out?"

Fishbelly saw Teddy arrive, stop, stare, then yell:

"Susie's in there!"

Oh Gawd . . . Susie was Teddy's sister. Teddy tried to rush toward the roaring building and several men caught him and held him.

"You can't go in there, you fool! You'll git—"

"I got to git Susie!" Teddy screamed, breaking loose and running toward the back door.

A huge black man stepped in front of the sprinting Teddy and clipped him on the jaw.

"Take that fool away! He'll burn in there. . . ."

Fishbelly watched a group of men drag the hysterical Teddy off, fling him to the ground, and hold him as he screamed and moaned.

A brown girl whom Fishbelly knew as Cecile came limping, her dress half torn off her.

"Cecile!" Fishbelly called to her.

The girl did not answer; she stared at him blankly, then wandered off, dragging her right leg. He followed her, grabbed her and yelled:

"You see Gladys in there?"

"I just got out . . . Oh Gawd, my leg . . ." Cecile looked at Fishbelly and blinked. "Aw, yeah . . . I saw Gladys . . ." Her voice died away.

He moaned, feeling his knees buckling. *Gladys lost?* That could not be. . . . Again he raced around the dance hall, seeing dazed figures wandering about. He began to hear acutely; it was as though until now the shock of the fire had rendered him deaf. The fire was mountainous, circling, spiraling upward in humming whiplashes of flame.

"It's on fire!"

"They all still *in* there!"

"Lawd, somebody *do* something!" an old woman called.

"Git the fire engines!" a man called.

"What happened?" Fishbelly asked the man.

"A fire broke out like *that*," the man answered, clapping his hands. "They *in* there, they *in* there . . ."

Fishbelly groaned, not wanting to believe it. He felt like

screaming. Gladys gone? NAW! A hand came upon his shoulder and he turned. It was Buck, one of the doormen who had been on night duty.

"Fish, my Gawd, they all in there!" Buck wailed. *"All* of 'em!"

"You seen Gladys?" Fishbelly asked him.

"It was that damned moss," Buck keened. "It went up like lightning—"

"You seen Gladys?" Fishbelly screamed at him.

"Hunh? Naw . . . I don't know," Buck mumbled, confused.

For minutes the suddenness of the fire stunned the survivors, but more people were beginning to scream now. Fishbelly stood in a stooped, mute posture before the roaring blaze, feeling lancing waves of heat cutting into his body and forcing him farther and farther back. Entering that furnace was out of the question; one could not advance into it for six feet without being charred. Tall red flames shot up, trembling and shaking against the black sky, blotting out the stars, raining sparks far and wide.

For the second time Fishbelly felt that he was dreaming and would awaken to find the Grove as it had always been. An explosion sounded deep in the heart of the flames; some beams began falling inward and the heat became blistering, driving him farther back. At the very tiptop of the fire a tongue of flame detached itself and floated red and gleaming, a curving roll of sharp fire slicing like a pulsing scythe into the black trees.

Timber cracked and popped. The fire sang, seeming to create a wind of its own that whipped across his tightened, hot face. The night was filled with screams now. A man came running and, in the glare, his face was like a glistening black mask; the man shouted:

"Let's knock a wall down! It ain't too late! Let's git a pole!"

"What pole?" Fishbelly asked, eager but bewildered.

"Did somebody go for the fire engines?" a man asked.

"Look, I got a car. Who'll go?" Fishbelly asked.

"I'll go, Fish," Buck volunteered.

Fishbelly tossed his car keys to Buck and pointed to the jalopy.

"Go, man!"

Buck ran toward the car.

A man heaved in sight, pulling a long, heavy pole, his mouth gaping from effort, his teeth gleaming in the fire's glare.

"Let's try and knock a wall down!" he called.

Fishbelly joined several men who took hold of the pole and, backing off a few feet, ran forward, jamming it ramrodlike into the outer, flimsy beams. Smoke almost blinded them. The second attempt made them choke and bend double, stagger back from blasts of heat, their eyes streaming tears. Fishbelly saw that one man's eyebrows had singed off and he noticed red sparks smoldering in another man's kinky hair. They made a last attempt with the pole, but were driven off by baleful tides of heat, stumbling, coughing. A wind current blew the total heat of the fire into their midst; they froze in their tracks, shivering, gasping, speechless. The men dropped the pole and backed creepingly off. The dance hall spluttered like a giant, glowing torch.

From directly behind Fishbelly came a terrifying scream; he turned and saw an old woman, her hands lifted, her knees bent, screaming without stopping; her eyes, glistening in the glaze of the flames, stared at the fire-ravaged building and the tears on her shriveled cheeks glittered like rubies.

"Some of her folks must be in there," Fishbelly muttered, moved.

"It's that damned moss," a man was whimpering.

"How many folks in there?" Fishbelly asked.

"A heap of 'em. Only some got out. They jammed the doors and blocked the others, trapping 'em," the man explained. "I lost my horn . . ."

He was one of the musicians and he looked with dull, bloodshot eyes at the choiring flames.

"What can we do?" Fishbelly screamed.

Out of the red dark Maybelle loomed, running toward him; she passed him as though she had not seen him. He took out after her, yelling:

"Maybelle! Where Gladys? Maybelle, stop! Where Gladys?"

He caught up with her and spun her around. She stared at him with wide, scared eyes.

"Where Gladys?"

"Hunh?" she answered, blinking.

"Gladys . . . Ain't you *seen* her?" he asked, coughing, feeling strangled by smoke.

Maybelle shook her head, her black skin gleaming like polished metal.

"Naw. I was home—"

"Gladys home?"

"I don't know," Maybelle mumbled, disorientated.

Aw Gawd, maybe Gladys was home! Fishbelly circled the gutting flames to escape the sizzling heat, seeing flowery clusters of red sparks showering in the night, and found the path leading to Gladys's house. He dashed down it, looking disbelievingly back every second at a fire so ferocious that no one could get near it. He followed a curve in the path, leaving the sight of the conflagration, imagining Gladys as he wanted to see her, that is, at home in her bedroom, powdering her face. He came to her front door and rattled the knob violently. It was locked.

"Gladys! Gladys! Gladys!" he screamed and pounded his fists against the door.

There was no response. He gritted his teeth, wondering if he were wasting time. Maybe there was something back there that he could do where the flames were leaping? Then he backed off a few steps and hurled himself against the door. There was a splintering of wood, but the door held. He crashed himself a second time against it and it sagged in and collapsed flat. He entered, fumbling for the light switch.

"Gladys!" his voice echoed through the house.

A repugnant possibility shocked him. What if she had come here to turn a fast trick? As revolting as the idea was, he wished it were true. He lumbered from room to room, clicking on lights; he came to the kitchen and found it empty. Good Gawd! One moment there had been peace and hope, then fire and tragedy. Reeling, he went back through the house and stood upon the front porch and saw rising red flames turning night into day. Screams, honking auto horns, and racing motors sounded far and near. He recalled Gladys's going into the dance hall to talk to Fats. . . . *That's it!* Find Fats! He loped again to the scene of the fire. The crowd had grown vast, but it was an awed, quiet crowd.

He saw Maybelle again; this time she was calm.

"It was that moss, Fish," she said tearfully. "Them fire folks had warned 'em a heap of times—"

"Maybelle, think . . . You seen Gladys?"

"I don't know. Not tonight, Fish," she said. "I took a man to my house and left 'em dancing. I heard Fats say there must've been a hundred in there. Looks like about fifty got out. The rest was trapped. . . ."

"You seen Fats?"

"Last time I saw Fats he was in there," Maybelle told him.

"Oh Gawd! Poor Gladys," he sobbed, squeezing his eyelids shut.

"LOOK!" Maybelle screamed, grabbing him and pointing.

"What?" Fishbelly opened his eyes and followed the line of her arm.

"LOOK AT THEIR HANDS!" she screamed, still pointing.

He saw what she saw. In the upper part of the fire-filled building the moss had burned away and, extending through the wide-spaced two-by-fours, were black hands and legs.

"They *moving;* they ain't *dead,*" Maybelle whispered.

He stared; the shadows cast by the waving flames gave the illusion that the hands and legs were in motion. He edged closer. Naw . . . Those hands and legs had been thrust through the spaces between the beams by those who had tried desperately to get out. . . . Fishbelly clasped his hands before him, feeling that he was looking at Gladys's dead body.

Fire roared, unabated, the throb of its heat beating upon his eardrums, drying the sweat on his face. There sounded a series of dull explosions in the lower portion of the fire and, presently, a strong, suffocating stench of alcoholic steam filled the air.

"That's them beer barrels cracking open!" a man called out.

Fishbelly felt a nervously trembling hand come upon his arm; he looked around; it was a stout black woman who was unaware that she was clutching him. He held still for a moment, then gently disengaged his arm from her hysterical grip and walked off a few feet, leaving the woman with her hand uplifted, the fingers moving imploringly in emptiness, her bulging eyes glassily reflecting the churning flames.

From the distance came the wail of fire-engine sirens, but he knew that the firemen would be too late. What baffled him had been the awful silence of the people in the dance hall; in the beginning there had been a few screams, but they had died away strangely. More cars sped up, their wheels skidding in the dust of the road, their yellow lances of light stabbing the darkness.

"Gladys," Fishbelly wailed for the last time, then was gripped by shivering despair.

The full sense of the tragedy had now sunk home to the people and there was uncontrollable weeping and moaning calls toward the white-hot building. The sirens were closer. Fishbelly wanted to act, to smash something and end this nightmare.

He saw his jalopy roll up and Buck leap out.

"They coming," Buck said. "Any folks git out?"

"Naw . . . Buck, stop and think . . . *Did you see Gladys?*"

"Man, Fats told me to git some ice. I went and got a bucketful and was coming back when I seen the fire and I run like hell—"

"Did you see Gladys come *out?*"

"Fish, I didn't see her."

Though the heat of the flames singed his face, he felt like a lump of ice. He glanced down at himself and saw that his coat was ripped; the backs of his hands were skinned and blistered. Pain throbbed in his left leg.

"It's dying down a little," a man called.

The flames and the smoke were abating, but the tin roof was an incandescent lake shimmering in the night. Fire engines screamed up, their sirens blasting the air, their headlights slicing the dark. Braking wheels lifted clouds of clay dust, palling the trees. White firemen leaped from trucks and Fishbelly saw them working frantically with their hoses.

"Jesus Christ!" one exclaimed.

"It's already *gone!*" another said.

Fishbelly watched the firemen unlimber a hose and a gleaming stream of water shot up, made an arc, and hit the molten tin roof; there was a furious sizzling and hissing as the water bounced from the glowing roof, spraying hot showers of rain into the dazed crowd.

"Git the folks back!" a fireman yelled.

"Anybody in there?" a tall white fireman asked.

"A lot of folks, young folks," a black man breathed.

"Good God!" the fireman said.

Somebody grabbed Fishbelly's arm and spun him around. It was Zeke.

"Zeke!" he screamed.

"Jesus, man!" Zeke said, staring at him. "I was scared for you. You seen Beth?"

"Naw. Ain't she with *you?*"

"Naw. Oh Gawd."

"And Gladys? You seen her?"

"Naw. Was she in there?"

"Zeke, she went in five minutes 'fore it started," Fishbelly moaned. "Goddamn..." He recovered himself. "Tony and Sam?"

"They on their way here. We had to meet our gals here..."

They stared at each other, unable to speak. Zeke turned and walked off, his mouth twisting.

The water of the fire hoses pounded the hot tin roof, hissing, bubbling, sending bright columns of fog high into the night while a scalding drizzle floated down. The dirt road leading to the Grove was choked with whites and Negroes thronging forward. Then came the high-pitched wail of another siren, different from the others.

"That's the fire chief," somebody said.

A small red car skidded, halted, and a big-boned white man with white hair leaped out and stood.

"Hold it!" the fire chief shouted.

The white streams of turgid water slackened, dribbling away.

"How long has it been going?" the fire chief demanded.

"Only a few minutes, Chief. But it's lost," a fireman answered.

"Were there many in there?" the fire chief asked.

"The doors are blocked with 'em. And there's plenty inside."

"What happened?" the fire chief asked.

"That moss blazed up and nobody could get near it," a fireman explained.

"*I warned those niggers about those violations,*" the chief muttered. He lifted his voice. "Okay! Let the water go and get these people back!"

Ten streams of water now thundered against the roof, boilingly jutting upward.

"Whoever's in there is sure gone now," the fire chief said, shaking his head. "If they weren't burned, they're smothered."

A fireman went to the chief and reported:

"Chief, it must've happened *quick*. . . . That moss burned like wildfire. All the air was cut off and the smoke did the rest. The people in there were asphyxiated in two minutes flat."

"What a freak of a fire," the fire chief muttered, taking off his hat.

Fishbelly turned away. Minutes later he found himself wandering along a dirt road, crying: "Gladys . . . Why did I let her go in there?" He tramped doggedly back to the fire, seeing drifting clouds of steam through his tears. The police were arriving now, their sirens filling the night, drowning out the shouts and screams of the firemen and the crowd. More cars came, emptying out men and women, black and white, who rushed to the perimeter of the dance hall that was now one solid mass of baleful heat. Water dripped; steam shrouded the trees; then Fishbelly smelled a curious odor that drowned out the scent of magnolias, that overcame the stench of evaporating beer, and made even the acrid sting of the smoke unimportant.

"Jesus, I know that smell," a firemen said. "They ain't burning, they're *cooking!*"

Fishbelly felt like vomiting; he could no longer stand upon his feet. He got into his jalopy and laid his face flat against the steering wheel and stared at the streams of shooting water. He caught snatches of conversation:

". . . they say most of 'em were smothered . . ."

". . . how many in there? . . ."

". . . somebody said about fifty . . ."

"All niggers?"

". . . all niggers, nothing but niggers . . ."

". . . some Fourth of July . . ."

". . . whoever heard of covering a dance hall with *moss?*"

". . . who owns the place? . . ."

". . . some nigger doctor called Bruce or something . . ."

". . . it's dying down now; the firemen are gitting close to the front door . . ."

Fishbelly went back to the shell of a dance floor, whose interior still seethed with fire. As the heat died down, people edged closer, shielding their faces from the heat with their hands, peering, murmuring, pointing to the tangled and charred bodies cramming the doorway. Firemen were trying to dislodge the bodies while streams of water hurtled above their heads.

"Give us a hand here, will you?" a white fireman called.

Several black men rushed forward and tugged at the bodies, pulling them free and stretching them out upon the grass. Fishbelly saw a woman's arm partially dissolve, the flesh failing to adhere to the bones. He shuddered. Firemen were crowding into the front doorway now, sending streams of water before them. Fishbelly tried to enter to search for Gladys, but a white fireman pushed him back, bawling:

"Keep out, nigger! Too much smoke!"

He gave up. He saw the chief of the fire department and went and stood discreetly near him. A fireman staggered out of the front door, his face red, his eyes streaming tears, coughing.

"What's up, Bob?" the chief demanded.

"There're forty-two bodies in there," the fireman said.

"Naw!" the chief exclaimed.

"Yessir. Most of 'em are asphyxiated . . . Only a few burned. The fire raged all around 'em and above 'em, Chief. Strange thing. It was that damned moss, dry as hell. . . . It cut off all the air."

"By God, somebody's going to pay for this," the chief growled.

Crowds swarmed over the fields amid smoke and steam, looking at the smoldering ruins, walking timidly among bodies sprawled upon the grass. As the flames waned, the firemen mounted spotlights whose beams enabled them to continue working. Then Maybelle was at Fishbelly's side, calling:

"Fish! They just found Fats. He's over in the woods."

"In the woods? He dead?"

"Naw. But he's mighty bad hurt. Come on."

Hope leaped into him. Maybe Gladys was somewhere too, living. . . . He followed Maybelle into a patch of woods to the left of the Grove. A knot of people stood about a prone figure. It was Fats, breathing heavily, writhing in pain.

"Fats," Fishbelly called softly.

"Hi, Fish," Fats breathed.

"How you feeling?"

"Kind of bad."

"You seen Gladys?"

Fats shook his head. Fishbelly knelt beside him.

"Was she *in* there?" he asked Fats.

"S-she said she wanted to s-see me about something . . . Told her to w-wait . . . Heard the phone ringing and w-went to answer it . . . First thing I know the p-place's on fire . . . Fire everywhere . . . Broke a p-plank under the s-steps . . . Crawled through . . . S-started running . . . I fell . . . Too w-weak . . . Passed out . . ." Fats's whispers died away.

He had now spoken to the last person who had seen Gladys alive; there was no hope. He watched them place Fats upon a stretcher and bear him toward an ambulance, then he stumbled along, half-conscious, his lackluster eyes staring vacantly; he was seeing again that dim photo of that smiling white woman that he had choked down his throat that day in the police car. Gladys had been a living white-and-black fantasy and she had gone up in smoke; he had felt that she could have redeemed everything for him and now she had vanished. Yet he was already following her in his future seekings.

Maybelle came running to him, her black face tight with anger.

"Now, this is a bitch!" she cried through her tears. "That white doctor says Fats needs a blood transfusion, and needs it quick! Now, there's a goddamn *white* hospital about half a mile from here, but they got to take Fats *ten* miles to a black hospital! That's a real bitchy thing! Goddamn these white folks!"

Fishbelly was dismayed that Fats could not get prompt medical treatment, but he was too grief-stricken to respond properly. Gladys still haunted him; he walked at random among the crowds, unable to give her up. Aw, maybe she was lying suffering somewhere in the woods like Fats had lain? He re-entered the woods. Then he was still. Ahead of him was a familiar figure. He went toward it.

"Fish!" the figure called.

It was Dr. Bruce.

"Doc!" he exclaimed. "You here?"

"Sh," Dr. Bruce cautioned him.

The doctor's face was ashen, wet, and blotched. Why was he dodging here in the woods when he was needed?

"What the matter, Doc?"

"I don't want anybody to see me here," Dr. Bruce said, his arm shaking. "Fish, how many people died in that fire?"

"Somebody told the fire chief there was forty-two—"

"Naw! Good God!" Dr. Bruce exclaimed and staggered. He caught hold of a tree; his body shook.

The doctor took a bottle out of his pocket and emptied a fistful of white pellets into a trembling palm and lifted that palm toward his mouth. Fishbelly leaped instinctively forward and slapped the doctor's hand, knocking the bottle and scattering its contents to the ground.

"Don't do that, Doc!" Fishbelly cried.

"You don't understand!" Dr. Bruce wailed. "I'm *responsible* for those people, Fish!"

"Wasn't your fault." Fishbelly confronted the doctor by putting his arm about his shoulders. "Don't take it that way, Doc."

The doctor grew gradually calm.

"I d-don't k-know," the doctor said. "Where's Fats?"

"He hurt. They took 'im to the hospital—"

"Have you seen Tyree?" the doctor asked.

"Nawsir . . . Doc, I lost my gal in that fire . . . ," he wept.

"Take it easy, Fish." Fishbelly's state brought the doctor back to his professional attitude. He stopped and retrieved the bottle.

"Naw, Doc!" Fishbelly protested through his tears.

The doctor shook out two pellets and tossed the bottle away.

"Take one; it won't hurt you," the doctor said, handing Fishbelly a pellet. "I'm taking one too."

"W-what they for, Doc?"

"It'll calm you," the doctor said, inserting a pellet into his mouth and swallowing.

Hesitantly, Fishbelly swallowed a pellet.

"Fish, I got to see Tyree. Is he at his office?"

"Don't know. Mebbe Papa's there."

Dr. Bruce left, weaving unsteadily among the dark trees. Fishbelly watched him until he was lost from view.

"Gawd, poor Doc's scared to death about them folks dying in that fire," Fishbelly mumbled to himself.

He returned to the scene of the fire and met Buck.

"Aw, Fish," Buck said, clutching his arm. "They found Gladys."

"Where?"

"She laid out on the grass—"

"Naw! Naw!"

The worst had been confirmed. That sadly smiling white face had been swallowed up in flames. Then he felt suddenly calm; it must have been the pellet that he had taken. He followed Buck, stepping over corpses, and then he was standing above her, looking down into her face. Her posture made her look as though she were sleeping; her lips were slightly parted, with just the ghost of a petulant smile on them. The only disfiguring mark was a tiny cut on the left side of her chin. She seemed about to speak, except that her brown eyes were opened and filmed. "Naw, she'll never speak again . . ."

He whimpered and turned away, stumbling toward the road in the dark. He passed Beth; she was lying on her back, her head swollen to twice its normal size. "Poor Zeke," he whispered. "Good thing he's going to the Army . . ."

He had loved Gladys and in one night he had won her and lost her. The tension in him suddenly gave way; yes, it was that pill that Dr. Bruce had given him, for his mind was as clear as a bell. He gazed calmly over the wide litter of dead bodies and he smelled the odor of death: "cooked niggers . . ." He looked at the staring and murmuring white men and women, his mind now anchored in the logic of the workaday world. These bodies had to be buried and burying people was

236

his father's profession. He saw the chief of police, the man to whom Tyree paid bribes each week. Yeah, that was the man to talk to. He approached the chief of police and confronted him.

"Chief," he addressed him softly.

"Yeah, boy. What do you want?"

"I'm Fish, sir. Tyree's son."

"Fish Tucker, hunh? Well, you look like your father. Where is he?"

"Don't know, sir."

"He'd better look into this mess," the chief of police said.

"Chief, where they taking these bodies?"

"Don't know. Our morgue's not big enough for all these niggers."

"Well, sir, there's our high-school gym—"

"By God, you're right."

"It's got running water and everything—"

"Yeah?"

"And there's them rub-down tables that we can use for embalming. And right above 'em is a lot of pegs for clothes; we can use 'em for hanging gravity bottles. I heard somebody say there was about forty-two bodies. . . . Takes about two hours to fix up a body. That's eighty-four hours of work, if we git at it night and day. . . . In all this heat, we ought to start on 'em tonight, sir."

"That's right," the chief of police muttered, speaking through his teeth and rocking on his heels, looking at Fishbelly with unblinking eyes.

"You know Papa and if you just tell the coroner to give us the death certificates, we'll handle 'em all."

"You would, hunh?"

"Yessir," Fishbelly assured him.

The chief of police turned and yelled:

"Say, Dupree!"

"Yeah!" Dupree said.

Dupree, middle-aged, stocky, wearing eyeglasses, came forward.

"Dupree, you're the coroner and I want you to get a load of this . . . This is Fish Tucker, Tyree's son. Well, he's got it all figured out. He says we can use the gym of the nigger high school for a makeshift morgue. He says that, after the inquest, you can make out all the death certificates and send 'em to Tyree's place—"

"Now I've heard everything," Dupree said, blinking.

"Well, Chief, *somebody's* got to bury these people," Fishbelly argued.

"Did Tyree send you to me?" the chief asked him.

"Nawsir."

"You just thought this up all by yourself?"

"Yessir. Burying folks is our business."

The chief of police chuckled and looked out over the smoking ruins of the Grove.

"Well, goddammit, I'm going to give 'em to you," the chief said grimly. "Is that all right with you, Dupree?"

"Anything you say, Chief," Dupree mumbled with a tight smile.

"Thank you, sir," Fishbelly said.

"Goddammit, you're the biggest, boldest body snatcher that ever hit this part of the country." The chief of police laughed.

"Boy, tell your papa that when he comes to the city hall we're going to give 'im a medal," the coroner said, moving away.

"You and your papa are go-getters, aren't you?" the chief of police said. "You deal in hot meat, cold meat, and houses—"

"Don't mean no harm, Chief," Fishbelly mumbled, confused.

"That's the trouble. You don't mean any harm. All right. They're yours." The chief swept his hand over the sweep of corpses. "I hope you make a million dollars." He laughed and turned away, muttering: "Tyree's going to need it."

Fishbelly was puzzled. What did the chief of police mean? Well, anyway, he'd gotten the business. Tyree would be glad. The flames had now completely died away, leaving only lingering wisps of white smoke floating above the scorched trees. He looked up; dawn showed in the sky. A few remote and pale stars gleamed overhead. It seemed impossible that the night had fled. He ambled down the dusty road, tired, overwrought, gripped by a curious state of unfeeling. He started in surprise as he came upon his jalopy, for Tyree was sitting in it, his head lowered, his eyes hard upon him.

"Papa!" he called.

Tyree leaped from the car and ran to his son and hugged him frantically.

"Goddammit, I thought I'd lost you, son! Nobody'd *seen* you!"

"But I was there all the time, Papa."

"I asked and asked—"

"Why didn't you come and look—?"

"You alive," Tyree whispered hoarsely, ignoring Fishbelly's question. "That's all I care about . . ."

"I lost Gladys, Papa."

He wept now; he felt that he could. Before, amidst all the people, white and black, there on the field near the Grove, he had not felt like weeping; but now here with his father, he could weep.

"Easy, son. It's going to be awright," Tyree said, patting his back.

"She was good to me, Papa."

"I know, son."

"We'd taken a flat—"

"Poor Fish," Tyree sighed.

"And she was so happy. . . ."

"Son, come on," Tyree said with a sudden change of tone. "Get in my car. Quick. Leave your jalopy; Jake'll come for it. . . . I know you all broken up, but we got work to do."

He stared at Tyree's face through his tears, knowing better than to ask questions. He ran alongside Tyree until they came to his car, got in, and a few moments later they were rolling through Black-Belt streets. A red fireball of sun hung on the rim of the east. The excitement caused by the fire had filled the streets with men and women who stood about gossiping.

"Goddamn," Tyree muttered.

"What's the matter, Papa?"

"Nothing, son."

"You can tell *me!*" he urged Tyree.

"You got enough to worry about, Fish. That poor Gladys—"

"Papa, Dr. Bruce's looking for you," Fishbelly told him. "He was hiding in the woods by the Grove. You know, Papa, he tried to kill himself . . ."

Tyree stopped the car by slamming the brake to the floor.

"When?"

"A few minutes ago. He was upset about the fire. Said he had to see you."

"Mebbe he's at my office now," Tyree said.

"And, Papa," Fishbelly blurted, "the bodies, *all* of 'em, are for *us!*"

"What bodies?"

"Them folks that died in the fire, Papa. I got the chief of police to tell the coroner to give us all the death certificates. They going to use the high-school gym for a morgue—"

"How many bodies?" Tyree asked quietly.

"More'n forty, Papa. And that chief of police says he hopes you make a million dollars."

Tyree was staring dead ahead of him and sweat was oozing on his face.

"You asked 'im right *there* at the fire?"

"Sure, Papa. I got to 'im 'fore anybody else did," Fishbelly explained. "He was a little surprised, but he said yes."

"Hunh huh," Tyree grunted.

Something was wrong. Tyree did not seem pleased.

"Didn't I do right, Papa?"

"Sure. It's awright, son," Tyree said in a tone of false approbation.

The car rolled in silence. What was wrong? Didn't you go for business that was lying right under your nose? Tyree's right hand opened the glove compartment and took out his gun. Fishbelly felt goose-pimples breaking out over his skin, for he remembered the last time that he had seen Tyree handle the gun like that.

"What's happening, Papa?"

"There's trouble, Fish," Tyree said heavily.

"*Race* trouble, Papa?"

"Something like that, Fish," Tyree mumbled. "It's all mixed up."

"Any white folks after *us,* Papa?"

"There's more'n forty folks dead, son. And somebody's got to pay—"

"Papa, that's *just* what the fire chief said."

Tyree started, then stared; he lifted his right palm to his

forehead and wiped away sweat. His eyes grew glassily bloodshot.

"The *fire chief* said that?"

"Yessir. But we ain't got *nothing* to do with that fire, Papa."

"Goddamn," Tyree growled, then bit his lips.

"But, Papa, w-we ain't m-mixed up in that *fire . . . ?"*

"Yeah and naw, son," Tyree said in a whisper.

"How? What you mean, Papa?"

"It's a long story, son," Tyree sighed. "Just you stick by me and you'll find out everything. This is going to be awful tough—"

"But I'm tired, Papa. I want to git some sleep—"

"This ain't no time to sleep, Fish," Tyree chastised him. "You said you wanted to be a *man*. Awright, you a man now. You got to be at my side night and day from this minute on, till this business is finished. This is the hardest fight I ever had in all my life. If *I* lose, *you* lose. I'm fighting for you now, son. If they beat me, you got to take over and run things, even though you just a kid." Tyree swallowed and paused. "Mebbe you was right in quitting school, 'cause in the trouble I'm facing I can't trust nobody on this earth but my own flesh and blood, my own son."

Fishbelly felt horribly guilty; he had been thinking of his own comfort when Tyree had dire need of him.

"Sorry, Papa. I'll stay with you, by you. . . . But what's wrong?"

"Stick close to me and look and lissen. You'll see what it is," Tyree said, looking compassionately at his son. "You grieving for Gladys, but you just got to forgit her, son."

Tyree held the gun in his right hand and steered the car with his left, looking around, and peering out of the rear window.

"Papa, is somebody *after* us?" he asked a second time.

"For a fact, I don't know, Fish," Tyree confessed.

"Is it the *white* folks?"

"Mebbe."

"Tell me, Papa!" Fishbelly was boiling with anxiety. "I want a gun too, Papa!"

"Naw!"

"You got a gun! I want to help, Papa!"

"If there's going to be any shooting, I'm doing it, son."

Fishbelly sighed, watching Tyree's washed-out face, a face that looked thinner, older, but, at the same time, more vital than he had ever seen it. He's scared . . . *But about what?* They entered the neighborhood of the undertaking parlor, but kept rolling.

"Where we going, Papa?"

"Keep quiet, Fish."

He settled back and waited. The car stopped in front of Gloria's house. Tyree reached into his pocket and pulled out a flat packet wrapped in brown paper, then peered at Gloria's dark, shut windows.

"Reckon she up yit?"

"Want me to go and see, Papa?"

"Yeah. Ring her bell. When she comes to the door, tell her I want to see her. Quick."

He got out of the car and ran across the walk and up the wooden steps and pushed his thumb against the doorbell. There was no response. He rang again, this time longer.

"Who's there?" came Gloria's voice.

"Me. Fish. Open the door, Gloria."

Gloria's white face showed against the semidark background of the hallway and fear leaped into him for a moment, then it was gone. She was in her bathrobe.

"What's the matter, Fish?"

"Papa's in the car. He wants to see you. Quick!"

"All right," Gloria said after a moment's hesitation.

He accompanied Gloria to the car, the rear door of which was held open by Tyree. She sat huddled on the edge of the back seat, her face thrust anxiously forward.

"What's happened, honey?" she asked.

"Gloria, lissen and do just what I tell you," Tyree began quietly. "I ain't got much time, see? Me and Doc's in trouble. This package's something the chief of police wants to git his hands on. . . . It's the canceled checks I done give 'im for the last five year—"

"Oh God!" Gloria said. "What happened, Tyree?"

"Don't ask no questions, honey," Tyree said. "Just hide these checks, and hide 'em good and don't let nobody see you

242

do it. You know a place for 'em?"

Gloria stared, biting her lips.

"There's an old well in the shed; it's dry. I can put 'em down in it in a bucket. Nobody'll think of looking in there. And the well's top is all covered with firewood—"

"That's the place. That's all, honey."

"But, Tyree, what's *happened?*" Gloria begged.

"Ain't you heard? The Grove burned down last night," Tyree said.

"There's more'n forty dead," Fishbelly told her.

Gloria put her doubled fist against her teeth.

"God in heaven," she moaned. Her round, frightened eyes clung to Tyree's face. "Poor Tyree . . ."

"It's awright," Tyree mumbled. "You go and git them checks hid, *quick*. And if I don't see you for a few days, you'll know why."

Gloria turned beseechingly to Fishbelly.

"Fish, take care of your father—"

"I'm with 'im night and day," he told her.

Gloria thrust the packet into her bosom and got out of the car.

"Darling, keep in touch, won't you?"

"Sure. Git going."

She fled down the walk and vanished through the front door.

"That's done," Tyree sighed.

When Fishbelly realized that Tyree was hiding evidence of the corruption of the chief of police, apprehension filled him. He recalled now that when he had asked the chief of police for the right to bury the forty-two dead, the chief had joked brutally with him.

"Papa, did I do something wrong in gitting that business?"

"Forgit it, son," Tyree mumbled.

They rolled again, this time toward the undertaking parlor. Jim was waiting on the porch. He ran down the steps to the car.

"Tyree, the chief of police has been phoning you for an hour," Jim said.

"I know," Tyree said. He got out of the car and spoke slowly. "Lissen good, Jim. Take Fish's car keys and tell Jake to git his jalopy; it's parked out by the Grove. Then you got to handle something big. We got more'n forty bodies to fix up—"

"Wheew," Jim whistled. "The fire?"

"Yeah. Fish got the business. They giving us the death certificates. Now, Jim, we don't want the other nigger undertakers gitting jealous, see? Phone 'em in all the other towns and ask 'em to meet you at the coroner's office. Then divide up the bodies, but be on the level with 'em. This fire's making a big stink and we don't want 'em saying we hogging the business. Go easy on the dead folks' relatives. Most times the family'll let whoever's got the death certificate handle the body. But this time, Jim, if a family don't want us to handle the body, then give it up. Me and Doc's on the spot and we don't want 'em saying that niggers made money out of the Grove and then made money burying the folks that got killed in the fire . . . It's sticky, Jim. Can you handle it?"

"I'll try, Tyree," Jim mumbled.

"Tell Curley Meeks, Joe Nash, Jim Poplar, and Dick Paley to bring their emergency embalming kits. And no fuss with nobody, see? Anybody ask you anything, tell 'em to see Tyree. Now, Jim, you got to haul all them bodies to the high-school gym for identification. Git the casket companies to lend you some trucks, 'cause nobody in town's got enough hearses to handle that many dead folks. You going to need a lot of extra formaldehyde, plaster of Paris, hardening fluid. . . . Better git your orders in quick.

"Now, Jim, we going to cut funeral costs 10 per cent, 'cause this is kind of wholesale business, see? I reckon you'll have to drape black crepe on some trucks to git them folks to the graveyard. Jim, you got to do all this yourself: gitting gravity bottles, clothes, cosmetics—everything. I'm going to be tied up. There's trouble about that Grove fire. . . ."

"I see," Jim murmured. "You got it tough. Say, Dr. Bruce's waiting for you in the office."

"Yeah? Now, look Jim . . . I ain't in to the chief of police till I done talked to Doc, see?"

"I get you, Tyree," Jim said sadly.

Fishbelly followed Tyree into the office where Dr. Bruce sat huddled and mute. The two men did not speak. Fishbelly sat and stared at them, wondering what was happening. One man was a doctor and the other an undertaker; one was his father and the other his friend; one was ignorant and cunning and the other was educated and frightened. He knew that when they talked he would learn what the fear, the whispers, and the creeping about in the dark had been for.

24

Tyree lowered the window shade against the sun's growing glare, then switched on the desk lamp, whose sheen threw into relief the three black faces in the room. Tyree next lifted the phone's receiver from the hook, brought out a bottle of whiskey and three glasses, and placed them upon the desk. Fishbelly knew that something awful had to be discussed, that something mortally serious had to be decided, and his teeth felt on edge from suspense.

"Take what you want, Doc," Tyree mumbled, pouring himself a third of a glass.

"I need it," Dr. Bruce said. The doctor's fingers trembled as he poured a stiff drink and gulped it, then stared blankly. "We haven't got much time, Tyree."

"I know," Tyree said. "That's why I cut the phone. We ain't talking to nobody till we done settled things, hunh?"

"Tyree, the chief of police and the chief of the fire department were at my house three times this morning," Dr. Bruce began.

"Let's face it, Doc," Tyree said softly. "They going to arrest you. When forty-two folks, black or white, die all at once, folk git *scared*."

"They want a scapegoat," Dr. Bruce said. "And I'm *it*."

"Yeah, but take it easy, Doc, I'm with you all the way," Tyree said. "We hiring the best lawyers in this country and fighting this case all the way to the Supreme Court—"

"Hell, Tyree," Dr. Bruce spoke huskily. "Lawyers can't help me. The evidence is against me—"

"Man, money *talks!*" Tyree said thunderously.

Dr. Bruce leaped to his feet, his face twitching.

"Tyree, don't hand me that bunk! I'm *black!* They're after me! They—!"

"And I'm with you, man!" Tyree shouted his whisper. "I'm behind you."

"You going to hire lawyers while I sit in jail and rot?" Dr. Bruce asked mockingly. "Hell, no!"

"Don't git excited, Doc," Tyree said uneasily. "What you gitting at?"

"Tyree, you're my partner. We're in this Grove business fifty-fifty—"

Aw Gawd! Fishbelly had been hoping against hope that that was not true. He felt his tongue grow dry and hot.

"Sure," Tyree agreed smoothly. "But I'm your *silent* partner. We agreed on that; we said my name wasn't to have *nothing* to do with that Grove!"

"I knew it!" Dr. Bruce hissed, his face livid with fury. "As soon as trouble starts, you *run!* But, goddammit, Tyree, you *can't!* The grand jury's going to indict me for manslaughter and I won't stand trial alone for the death of forty-two people! We split the profits fifty-fifty and we're going to shoulder the responsibilities fifty-fifty! We face this together, both *you* and *me!*"

"Take it easy, Doc" Tyree begged nervously. "Let's think this over. . . ."

Stunned, Fishbelly could scarcely believe what he had heard. Tyree owned half of the Grove! He leaned back in his chair and his breath escaped him in a deep sigh. He understood now why Dr. Bruce had been hiding in those woods, why he had tried to kill himself, why the chief of police had stared at him and had said: "You're the boldest, biggest body snatcher that ever hit this part of the country." Tyree owned a part of the Grove in which forty-two black people had lost their lives and the owner's son was asking for the business of burying those who had perished! *That white man must've thought I was crazy.* Then another realization hit him: he and his family had been living off the immoral earnings of Gladys! The money he had paid her for the right to sleep with her had found its way back into his own pocket! He hung his head in shame. He was a kind of superpimp. . . . And he had condemned Gladys because she had not shared his feelings toward white people. It was only after a few moments that he could lift his head and follow the bitter argument raging between Tyree and the doctor.

"Let's git the record straight!" Tyree thundered. *"You* own that goddamn Grove, *I* don't! I only put up half the operating money—"

"Tyree, you got half of the profits!" Dr. Bruce shouted. "You're my *de facto* partner."

"What that *de facto* mean, Doc?" Tyree asked, blinking, a dangerous glint entering his eyes.

"Papa, it means you a partner in fact and in law," Fishbelly told him.

"And that's correct," Dr. Bruce argued. "The law will hold you to it."

"What good's my going to jail along with you?" Tyree tried another approach. "I can't pull strings if I'm in a cell. Doc, you upset. Calm down. You *scared*—"

"Don't insult me." Dr. Bruce's body quivered. "I'm fifty years old and I could get ten years in prison for the death of those forty-two people—"

"It won't come to that, I tell you," Tyree tried to reassure him.

"Tyree, I don't know the men in the city hall. You do. They're friends of yours. And, so help me God, you're going to stand at my side in this thing." Dr. Bruce was adamant. "I can prove that you were my partner. So admit it!"

Fishbelly was inclined toward Dr. Bruce's logic, but he felt that Tyree was right to insist upon the terms of the original agreement.

"We don't have to make up our minds now." Tyree evaded the issue.

"By God, we do! We'll decide it *now!*" Dr. Bruce screamed. "I'll be arrested any minute . . . AND I WON'T ACCEPT THIS ALONE, TYREE!"

There was silence. Tyree drained his glass and stared at the floor. Fishbelly heard the small clock on the desk ticking as loud as thunder. He looked at it; it was nearly noon. A knock came upon the door and they all started.

"Who's there?" Tyree called.

"Jim!"

Tyree rose and unlocked the door. Jim leaned to him and whispered:

"It's your wife, Tyree. She's upset. She's had no word—"

"Oh Gawd," Tyree moaned. "I clean forgot—"

"Tyree! Tyree!" Emma's hysterical voice filled the hallway. "Where Fish? Oh Lawd, my poor baby. . . . Tell me, Tyree!"

"Come in, Emma," Tyree called. He turned to Fishbelly. "Your mama worried about you."

Emma entered with a fearful, creeping movement, her tear-wet face turning from man to man, then she sank to the floor, sobbing.

"Child, I thought you was dead," she cried. "Nobody told me *nothing!*"

"Fish's awright, Emma," Tyree said soothingly. "Sorry, but I been busy's hell. . . ."

Fishbelly went to his mother and lifted her tenderly.

"I'm awright, see?" he said.

"You ain't hurt none?" Emma asked him. "Your *clothes!* They torn and burned—"

"It ain't nothing, Mama. I was just trying to help the others."

"Git hold of yourself, Emma. You can't stay here. We got serious business. Jim's taking you to the car and Jake'll drive you home."

"Right, Tyree," Jim said.

"Go along with 'im, Mama," Fishbelly said. "We'll be along when we through here . . ."

"My boy . . . I thought you was dead," Emma sobbed as Jim led her away.

Tyree shut the door, frowning.

"Goddammit, I can't think of everything," he moaned.

"Tyree, are you my partner or not?" Dr. Bruce resumed his attack.

A tremor went through Tyree's body and his eyes were

wild, glassy. He took another drink and stared at his son, at Dr. Bruce, then at the floor.

"If that's the way you want it, what the hell can I do?" he consented bitterly.

"Then we fight *together*," Dr. Bruce said, his eyes gushing tears. "That's all I wanted, Tyree. Just be loyal. . . ."

"Have it your way," Tyree mumbled in defeat.

"What's our defense going to be?" the doctor asked logically.

"There's a lot of angles, Doc," Tyree said.

"What, for instance?"

"I got evidence against that chief."

"How can we use it?"

"We can blackmail 'im into making 'im help us."

"What else?"

"We might try to find somebody to take the rap for us."

"Who?"

"Don't know . . . You still want me in that courtroom? I could be more help to you if I was free—"

"You *got* to be with me, Tyree. You just *got* to be."

A loud knock sounded upon the front door. Tyree crept to the window and peered out from behind the edge of the shade.

"It's the chief of police," he whispered.

"What're we going to do?" Dr. Bruce asked in terror.

"'What we going to do?'" Tyree echoed the doctor's words scornfully. "We going to let 'im in. What the hell you think we can do?"

Dr. Bruce half rose, then sat, his eyes crazed with anxiety.

"Goddammit, git yourself together, Doc." Tyree snorted contemptuously. "Mebbe you ought to take a pill or something." He went out of the office.

25

The chief of police entered. Tyree, cringing a bit, followed.
The tall, heavy-set white man stood, his eyes roving. He wore
the blue uniform of his office and his left arm gleamed with
gold braid for long service. His gray eyes finally settled on
Dr. Bruce.

"My men are looking everywhere for you, Doc," the chief
said.

"I'm right here drinking with my friend," Dr. Bruce said.

The chief looked from Dr. Bruce to Tyree, then to Fishbelly.

"Well, you got the business, Tyree," the chief said, lighting
a cigarette. "By God, Fish was there grabbing at those bodies
before they were cold. . . . Ha, ha!"

Embarrassed silence hung in the room and the clock's ticking sounded like the salvos of a cannon. The smile on every
face in the room hid hate, fear, and anxiety. Tyree clapped
Fishbelly on the back and, forcing a hollow laugh, crooned:

"Yessir, Chief. Fish's my right hand. Ain't you, son?"

"Yessir, Papa," Fishbelly replied meekly, his heart thumping.

"And your left hand too," the chief growled out of the
corner of his mouth.

When the chief had entered the room Fishbelly had felt a
sense of dreaminess, of mental confusion. All the bitterly turgid arguments that had raged had had meaning only in terms
of this white ambassador from the white world. His coming
had annulled the reality of their lives, for the black men
present were not their own masters. And Fishbelly knew what
was making Tyree move with stooping shoulders, with a per-
petual grin on his sweaty face, with bloodshot eyes looking

always out of their corners, with knees slightly bent—it was the presence of a white man. Tyree was masking his motives to mislead the white man, to put him at a disadvantage; he was making himself the semblance of compliance, of a castrated shadow man who would always say yes. And Fishbelly knew that Dr. Bruce's saying that Tyree was his friend had had a strong effect upon the chief, for it was clear in his stony look that the chief had not expected to find the two black men forming a common front. That big-boned white man was hatching what tactics? "He's wondering if them two niggers is planning something against 'im," Fishbelly whispered to himself, feeling something within him withdrawing, dwindling in the face of this white enemy who negatively ruled the Black Belt, who sold justice, right, liberty, who said what could or could not be done.

"Drink, Chief?" Tyree asked.

"Don't mind if I do," the chief murmured, pouring a quarter of a glass and downing it. "Good whiskey, Tyree."

"Help yourself, Chief." Tyree forced a grin.

"Thanks, Tyree." The chief cleared his throat and, rising, walked aimlessly about the office, then suddenly pulled off his coat and draped it over the back of his chair. "Tyree?" he called softly.

"Right here, Chief," Tyree sang with make-believe eagerness.

"Who am I dealing with? You *and* Doc, or *just* you?"

"Well . . ." Tyree hedged.

"We're partners, Chief," Dr. Bruce said in a steady voice.

"What does this nigger doctor know, Tyree?" the chief asked in an ice-cold tone, hitching his thumbs into the cartridge belt girting his waist and making the gun butt jiggle.

"What you mean, Chief?" Tyree played ignorant with wide eyes.

"This is damned dangerous business, Tyree," the chief stated. "I know I can depend on you to keep a stiff upper lip. . . . You've been before that grand jury three times and never spilled a thing. But I didn't bargain on this nigger doctor, see? Okay; he's here. What does he know?"

"*Know,* Chief? You know what we know," Tyree cried naïvely.

Fishbelly had bristled when the chief had used the word "nigger"; but his tension ebbed when Tyree failed to react. Then he realized that the chief had been trying to see if the black men before him were subservient.

"Listen, Tyree, I'm giving it to you straight." The chief spoke in exasperation. "You've been paying me by check. I told you not to. But, because I know you, I was a damn fool and took them. Now, your bank sends you the canceled checks at the end of each month. Tyree, where the hell are those canceled checks? I'm asking because this goddamn fire mess has blown the lid off everything. You're going to be put on the witness stand again and that special district attorney's going to want to know how the Grove remained open in face of all the fire-violation notices that were sent out. . . . What're you going to say if they press you about that fire? I know men, Tyree. You're on the spot. But don't get any ideas in your head about swapping some canceled checks to get off about that fire . . ."

Fishbelly sat crushed. The chief's voice had been murderous, cold. He watched Tyree leap to his feet, his eyes popping with that exaggerated fear that black people knew that white people expected from them.

"Chief!" Tyree's voice was shrill. "You done known me for twenty years! You can trust me, Chief! I told you a thousand times I burn them checks!" Tyree lied with all the force of his histrionic art.

"Where do you keep your checkbooks and papers, Tyree?" the chief asked.

"Right here. In this office," Tyree said, as though suspecting nothing. "Why, Chief?"

"Open your safe and let me see what you've got," the chief ordered. "If you're not hiding anything, you'll let me look—"

"Good Gawd, Chief!" Tyree hollered in a high-pitched whisper. "You don't believe me? Well, I do declare! Sure. You can look. . . . I ain't never thought of nothing like hiding your checks, Chief. You my friend. . . . Lawd, Chief, you make me think you don't trust me no more." Tyree's voice sounded full of tears. "You can see anything I got. Fish, open the safe for the chief."

"Sure, Papa." He rose and removed the calendar screening the safe in the wall.

"Chief, have you a warrant for that kind of search?" Dr. Bruce asked, his face twitching.

The chief spun on his heel and faced the doctor.

"Goddammit, I was waiting for that!" the chief snarled. "I know an uppity nigger when I see one! What the hell do I need a warrant for? Nigger, understand one thing: Tyree's my *friend.*" He looked at Tyree. "Ain't you, Tyree?"

"Sure, Chief! You can see *anything* I got!" Tyree pretended breathlessly. He leered at Dr. Bruce with a face twisted with simulated rage. "Doc, you just keep out of this! You talk too goddamn much. This is something between *me* and the *chief!*" He turned to Fishbelly. "Got that safe open, son?"

"Almost, Papa." He trembled as he twirled the dial.

"A nigger talking about warrants," the chief sneered. His voice dropped low, menacing. "Be careful, nigger."

"It's open, Papa," Fishbelly called, stepping aside, feeling secure, knowing that Gloria had hidden the checks. He smiled grimly as he watched the chief rummaging in the safe, tossing bundles of greenbacks upon the desk.

"That's just my money." Tyree cautiously implied ownership.

"I'm not interested in your money, Tyree," the chief said. Then he stiffened, spun, shouting: "By God, *here's one!*" The chief held aloft a canceled check. "Goddamn nigger says he burns 'em! Why the hell didn't you burn *this?*"

Fishbelly blinked, feeling about to drop. What had happened?

"Where?" Tyree demanded in a wail. "Let me see that!"

"Are you lying to me, Tyree?" the chief asked.

"Lawd Gawd in heaven!" Tyree's voice was a pleading chant. "Honest, Chief, that one come in night 'fore last. . . . I ain't had time to burn it yit. 'Fore Jesus, that's the truth! Look for more of 'em, Chief! You'll see there *ain't* no more!" Tyree extended his hand. "Give me that check, Chief. I'll show you what I do with 'em!" He snatched the check and scratched a match and held the check over the flame, and, with hard, fixed eyes, watched the paper blaze up, turning it in his fingers. He dropped the remainder into an ashtray and it turned into a charred, crinkly black wisp. "There, Chief. I was going to burn that last night, so help me Gawd, if it hadn't been for that damned Grove fire." And he gazed at the white man with the eyes of a dog. "Chief, if I'd been a-trying to fool you, I would've took everything out of there. You can trust me, Chief."

The chief sighed, relaxed; his lips twisted in a wry smile.

"All right, Tyree," he said. "If you'd been holding out on me, you sure would've got rid of that." He sat heavily and took another drink. "After this, no more goddamn checks, see?"

"Just as you say, Chief," Tyree sang his agreement.

"Nigger, did I need a warrant for that?" the chief asked Dr. Bruce.

"A warrant?" Tyree went into a gale of counterfeit laughter. "You *know* you don't need no warrant with me, Chief!"

Fishbelly wondered how on earth Tyree had overlooked that check!

"Chief," Tyree called in a small, timid voice.

"Yeah, Tyree," the chief said.

Tyree rose, sat, closed his eyes and rested his head in his palms; then he straightened and stared at the white man. Fishbelly knew that gesture; Tyree was ready to counterattack. The quieter, the more nervous Tyree became, the more dangerous he was.

"Chief, you coming here looking for them checks makes me think you know something's about to happen." Tyree's accusation was impersonal.

"Listen, Tyree, the syndicate can't touch that special district attorney, Lou Bell, that the state legislature's put in there. We got a friend or two around the grand jury, but we can't control that jury. That means that you're going to be *indicted*. And Doc too. It's that goddamned fire; it's an open-and-shut case. You'll get out on bail. When the case comes into court the syndicate'll go into action and make things as easy as it can for you."

Fishbelly felt chilled. He knew that fear had driven the chief to look into Tyree's safe, for he was afraid that Tyree might talk under pressure. Guilt for the Grove fire had trapped the black men and even the chief of police could scarcely help them. But Tyree could turn state's evidence and gain a risky immunity.

"Oh Lawd, Chief," Tyree moaned.

"What's the matter?" the chief asked.

"You know what's bothering me, Chief," Tyree whispered reprovingly. "I know too goddamn much to sit on a witness stand! How can I protect Doc, me, and *you*—"

"What're you scared of, Tyree?"

"Chief, they going to ask me how that Grove managed to run with all them fire violations against it—"

"And what're you going to tell 'em?" the chief asked crisply.

"What *can* I tell 'em?" Tyree countered the chief's question.

Fishbelly listened with clamped teeth. They were at the heart of the problem now. How could Tyree, on the witness stand, explain that the Grove remained open in spite of fire violations, and *not* implicate the chief of police? The white man was asking Tyree to protect him in his testimony before the grand jury, and he was promising to help Tyree when the case came to trial.

"I'm behind you; you'll come out all right," the chief promised.

"Chief, when I'm on that witness stand, if I talk, I'm guilty, and if I don't talk, I'm guilty. What can I *say?*"

"Keep your testimony strictly to that fire," the chief advised coldly. "You don't know *anything* else."

Three pairs of black eyes roved, weighing possibilities. Could the chief bribe the jury when the case came to trial? *Would* he? Could they trust a white man that much? Dare they hint that they had hidden evidence and would blackmail him unless he made a strong effort to help them? Or would the chief want to kill them if he suspected that? The black faces in the room were coated with sweat.

"I agree with the chief," Dr. Bruce said suddenly.

"The nigger doctor's got sense," the chief muttered.

Fishbelly knew that Dr. Bruce was hiding behind Tyree, that he was backing on the chief protecting Tyree in order to protect himself.

"I don't want to git on no witness stand," Tyree murmured with closed eyes, pretending to tremble. "That district attorney might *make* me talk . . ."

Fishbelly saw fright flash in the chief's eyes.

"Testify about the fire and keep your mouth shut about us," the chief insisted. "We'll help you. We always have . . . That fire's got the whole town roused. The fire chief sent *seven* notices of fire violation to Doc—"

"I didn't see 'em!" Dr. Bruce said stoutly.

"Goddammit!" the chief exploded. "Can't you niggers understand? There's a *record* of those violations! People are wanting to know if the fire's the fault of the fire department or your fault." The chief rose and placed his palms against his chest. "Don't blame me for the fire; I didn't start it. Tomorrow the grand jury's indicting the owners of the Grove. That's certain."

Tyree's sigh was like a moan; then he threw himself tentatively upon the mercy of the white man he trusted least on earth.

"What can we do, Chief?" he asked.

The chief screwed up his eyes and pronounced judgment:

"Sell your property and prepare to defend yourselves!"

Fishbelly flinched. What the chief had said could mean anything. Tyree would be indicted and, during the course of the trial, the whites would bleed him of every penny he had ever made. But did not this scheming white man, in order to keep on collecting his weekly bribes, wish hotly to save Tyree from jail? Fishbelly recalled that Gladys had told him that Fats had been in prison four or five times. By Gawd, why could not an old jailbird like Fats be made to take the rap? Should he suggest it?

"Papa," Fishbelly called.

"Yeah, Fish," Tyree encouraged him.

"Gladys told me something about Fats. . . . Seems like he's been in jail four or five times. Let's say that Fats got them notices and didn't know what they was. . . . Fats can't read and he just threw 'em away."

"Fats can't *read?*" Tyree asked with eager indignation.

"That's right," Dr. Bruce said. "Fats wouldn't know his

name if it were painted on the side of a boxcar in letters a yard high."

"There's our man," Tyree said emphatically.

"Goddamn," the chief mused, shifting in his chair. "I remember that Fats. Bad nigger..."

"Bad, bad, *bad*," Tyree cried. "You can have ninety-nine colored folks, and there'll always be *one nigger!* Fats uses guns, knives, and he's been mixed up with dope, Chief." Tyree's eyes reflected a combination of aggressive balefulness and fear. "Let's git that nigger, Chief."

"Yeah, that nigger's been in all kinds of trouble," the chief said slowly.

"What about Fats, Chief?" Tyree asked with an urgent glare in his eyes.

"Could be," the chief said, pulling down a corner of his mouth.

"How much time would he git if he confessed the fire was his fault, Chief?" Tyree prodded the white man to guess.

"Maybe five years, with time off for good behavior," the chief hazarded.

"That's ain't bad," Tyree judged. "Fats is used to jails."

They stared at one another, weighing this probability.

"Fats is plenty wise," the chief warned them. "You'd better make 'im a pretty good offer."

"Two thousand dollars," Dr. Bruce offered.

"Make it four thousand and Fats might bite," the chief suggested.

"Four thousand dollars? I buy that. Okay," Tyree said.

"You want me to talk to him?" Dr. Bruce asked. "I'm a doctor and I can see him—"

"Wait," the chief said. "It'd be better if I saw 'im first and softened 'im up a bit. If I start poking around into Fats's past, he'll get worried and by the time Doc gets to 'im he'll be ripe."

"Check," Dr. Bruce agreed. "Let's phone right now and see if he can receive visitors. He's in the Booker T. Washington Hospital."

"Why not?" the chief said.

"Now we using our heads for something more'n a place to

hang our hats," Tyree crooned, leaping monkeylike across the room and grabbing the phone and stealthily easing the receiver back upon the hook and pushing the phone into the white man's hand. "Here, Chief."

"Sure. I'll help you. I'll throw the book at that nigger," the chief said. He dialed and, while waiting for a response, he spoke gently to Tyree: "Tyree, I'll have to have some cash to work on this."

"Sure, Chief. How much?" Tyree's teeth showed in a false grin.

"Make it fifty for the moment," the chief said.

"Right, Chief," Tyree said, taking out his billfold and extracting a fifty-dollar note and extending it.

"Hold it," the chief said. "Hello," he spoke into the phone.

"(. . .)"

"Don't move, Chief," Tyree whispered gently, tucking the bill into the white man's top shirt pocket.

"Thanks, Tyree," the chief whispered. ". . . Hello. This is Chief of Police Gerald Cantley speaking . . . Yeah, I want to know if you got a nigger there by the name of Fats . . . Hold it a second." He looked at Dr. Bruce. "What's Fats's last name, Doc?"

"Brown," Dr. Bruce said with dry throat.

"Fats Brown," the chief continued into the phone. "Yeah. He was injured last night in the Grove fire. . . . Yeah. Okay." The chief turned to Tyree and Dr. Bruce. "They're checking . . ."

There seemed to be hope. Fishbelly prayed that Fats could be a stand-in for Tyree and Dr. Bruce.

"Yeah?" The chief spoke into the transmitter.

"(. . .)"

"Yeah. That's right?"

"(. . .)"

"Oh! Okay. 'By."

The chief hung up and lifted his glass and drained it.

"No dice," he said. "Fats died about an hour ago."

"Hell," Tyree muttered and sank loosely upon his chair. "We back where we started."

Fishbelly gritted his teeth, staring at Tyree's drawn, sweaty face.

"Anything else, Tyree?" the chief asked, rising and putting on his coat.

Fishbelly stifled a sob. Gawd, this couldn't happen!

"I'm afraid I'll have to send for you two tomorrow," the chief said. "The grand jury meets in the morning. If there's an indictment, I'll have to pick you up about noon." The chief pursed his lips, staring into space. "Naw . . . I don't want your people to see you're being arrested, Tyree. I'll phone you the grand-jury decision and you two come down to the city hall. You're not running away; you've got property. I'm sure you'll be out on bail before sundown."

"Chief," Tyree chanted, high-pitched, desperate.

"Yeah, Tyree," the chief replied, eying Tyree with a certain degree of pity.

"I know what to do, Chief!" Tyree cried in singsong through his nose. "But I'm *scared—!*"

"Scared of what?"

"I'm scared you won't help me."

"I'll help you, Tyree," the chief consoled him.

Tyree and the chief looked at each other. The white man's eyes were blank, free of fear, devoid of emotional commitments; the black man's eyes were evasive, filled with distrust, juggling imponderables. Fishbelly knew that Tyree was trying to decide if he should leave his case in the white man's hands. Instinct said no. Ought they not fight instead with the weapons of the canceled checks? Since they were all, white as well as black, guilty; since the Grove could not have operated in violation of the fire laws without the connivance of the police; why should only the black men alone stand trial? But what would happen if Tyree exposed the partnership he had with the police in order to lessen the pressure upon him and Dr. Bruce? If the chief of police were there in the dock with him, much of the blame could be lifted from his shoulders. But it would be almost worth his life to unmask the men in the city hall. And if he were indicted and free on bail, the chief could come to him repeatedly for money, on this pretext or that, and he would have to give. Since he could not trust the police, and since he could not fight them, could not there be a compromise? Tyree lowered his head, his lips hanging loose and open. He backed slowly to a chair and sat, staring at the floor.

"I want to say something, Chief," he whispered.

"Go ahead, Tyree."

"Now, lissen, Chief, don't go *misunderstanding* me—"

"I'll try to understand. What is it, Tyree?"

Clashing impulses were so powerful in Tyree that he rose and walked nervously to the shaded window, then back again to the chief. His voice came tense, cracked:

"Chief, you done known me for twenty years and I'm straight and solid . . ."

"Yeah," the chief said, blinking slowly, trying to anticipate Tyree.

"Chief, you know I ain't no agitator; don't you?"

"Yeah, Tyree. I know that."

"I ain't no sorehead neither. You know that?"

"You're okay, Tyree," the chief said, nodding.

"I was 'fore that grand jury three times and was loyal to you. That district attorney *begged* me to testify for the state and told me nobody could touch me if I did—"

"I know all that, Tyree."

"Now, you say they going to indict me—"

"That's right, Tyree. But these two things are *different*. Our business is *one* thing; that fire's *another*—"

"That district attorney couldn't tempt me to go against you—"

"Tyree, we're in a syndicate together; that was our *bargain!*"

"Now, you pushing me out there all alone, Chief!"

"Nigger, do you want to change your testimony before the grand jury?" the chief asked him bluntly.

"Oh Lawd Gawd, nawsir, Chief! I'm loyal to you! But, Gawd knows, I need *help* now—"

"But we're going to *help* you, Tyree!"

"I'm a nigger you can trust. . . . Tell me: You believe that, Chief?" His voice terminated somewhere in his head in a squeal.

"I trust you, Tyree."

"Now, look, Chief, you know I ain't no politician." Tyree hummed his case, staring at the white man; he swallowed, groped for words. "I'm just a nigger trying to save his skin— my life's savings for my son sitting there right 'fore your eyes.

He's young and he's got his whole life 'fore 'im. Now, Chief, there ain't but one way to *really save* me. . . . But it's hard for me to say it. I ain't never said nothing like it to no white man. . . ."

"Speak, Tyree. What's on your mind?"

"I ain't never been for no social equality. You know that, don't you, Chief?"

"Yeah," the chief drawled thoughtfully. "But what—?"

"Chief, just let me talk for five minutes and *promise* you won't stop me. Will you?" Tyree begged, his voice running off into little squeaks, his face oozing sweat, his knees bent in unconscious supplication.

"All right. But what are you getting at?" the chief asked, frowning.

"You won't stop me from talking?" Tyree hedged further.

"Why are you asking me that?" The chief was wary now.

"Chief, just *promise* you won't stop me till I done finished," Tyree cried.

"Talk, Tyree. I won't stop you," the chief committed himself with uneasy compassion.

Tyree took his lungs full of air and when he spoke his voice was strained, tremulous, higher-pitched than a woman's.

"Chief, them folks don't know a thing about us," he began. "They—"

"Who?" the chief asked, puzzled.

"The white folks, Chief," Tyree whispered as though communicating a dreadful secret. He swallowed, blinked. "You said you was going to let me talk; you *promised—*"

"I'm not stopping you," the chief's voice was low, guarded.

"Chief, there's something in the law about a jury of your *peers*. . . ." Tyree paused, watching the white man's face for its reaction. "Now, Chief, I know that law ain't meant for us niggers and I ain't saying it is. . . ."

The chief blinked and rubbed his chin reflectively.

". . . and your folks don't know us black folks, how we live, what we feel, what we got to do to git along. . . ." Tyree's eyes weighed the chief. "Chief, only *black* folks can understand *black* folks. Chief, I don't want to be judged by your white law. Now, when time comes for our trial, if only that jury could have just six black folks on it—that jury that's trying me, see?—just *six* niggers, Chief—"

The chief rose and opened his mouth, but Tyree ran forward with uplifted hands, pleading:

"Please, Chief! Don't talk! You done *promised!* Just let me finish? If I'm wrong, then you tell me. You know I'll listen to you, Chief...." Tyree's voice broke from sheer passion; he went to the desk and fortified himself with another drink. "Now, Chief, I know there ain't never been no jury in this town with no niggers on it. *I know that, Chief.* But I ain't preaching no race mixture. I'm just a scared nigger trying to save my skin.... There ain't a nigger in this town, nowhere in this whole county, that would sit on that jury without saving *me* and *you!* Put six niggers on that jury, and to sit on that jury who'd be fool enough to vote me guilty? Now, just think, Chief. You git my meaning?"

The chief sat and sighed.

"Goddamn," he breathed, looking off. "I never thought I'd hear you say anything like that, Tyree." He stared at the black man in amazement, then said flatly: "I know what you mean, Tyree; but, goddammit, it just *can't* be. It can *never* happen. You're talking wild, crazy—"

"It could be just for *once*," Tyree begged in a singsong. "Just for *me*, Chief."

"Hunh," the chief grunted meditatively. "That's Judge Moon's court and he's a Ku-Kluxer. Hell, he doesn't like niggers, Tyree. He's not like me. He even hates that black gown of justice he wears in that courtroom. If I talked to 'im about your wild idea, he'd run me out of town pronto. I see what you're getting at, but it'll never work around here. So forget it, Tyree."

"It could work *once*," Tyree sobbed now. "Then I'd be free, Chief. And you won't have to worry none...." His tear-drenched eyes widened knowingly. "Then that jury could go back being all white, see, Chief? All I'm asking is a favor from my good white friends, a *special* favor. This ain't no social equality...."

"Tyree, don't take me for a fool!" the chief bellowed in sudden anger. "Wouldn't the niggers have to sit in the same jury box with the whites? That's social equality!"

"But, Chief, the judge could say it's a special day, like Easter or Thanksgiving—"

"Nigger, you've gone nuts." The chief spat in disgust.

"Chief, they could put a board in that jury box to separate the white folks from the niggers, like they got on the streetcars and busses," Tyree whimpered out of compromise.

"Aw, Tyree, you talk like a baby—"

"I'm burying niggers every day in *black* graves right alongside *white* graves with a wall between 'em." Tyree tried to make his idea seem normal.

Fishbelly had listened with a deepening sense of despair. He had not been able to disagree when the chief had characterized Tyree's plea as babyish, for he knew that Tyree had appealed as a child appeals to a parent. Even had Tyree won his claim, he would, in winning, have lost.

"Tyree, that's a pipe dream," the chief said. He looked at the impassive face of Dr. Bruce. "Hell, I thought that Doc would've been coming up with a damnfool notion like that, not *you*, Tyree. . . ."

Tyree sat for several seconds, mute, frozen; then he sprang tigerishly forward, sliding to the floor and grabbing hold of the chief's legs.

"I'm lost!" he cried. "I been your friend for twenty years and you done turned your back on me!"

"Let me go, Tyree," the chief said, moved, amazed.

"I been loyal to you, ain't I, Chief? You can't let me go to jail and rot—"

"What the hell can I *do*, Tyree?" the chief yelled at the black man at his feet. "You're getting dangerous to me *and* yourself!"

"Tell 'em to try a mixed jury, Chief. Just for *once*, just for *me*, for poor old *Tyree*. . . ." He lifted his sweaty face and glared at the chief. "You can't let this happen to me," he spoke with almost human dignity. Then, as though afraid, he let out a drawn-out moan of a woman with ten children telling her husband that he could *never* leave her.

"Oh, to hell with you, Tyree!" the chief thundered. "What're you doing to me?" He shook himself loose from Tyree's clinging arms, moved to the center of the room and stood glaring as though snared by invisible coils.

Fishbelly saw Tyree's red-rimmed, tear-brimming eyes watching the bayed white man's face with a coldly calculative stare.

"Goddamn!" the chief shouted and banged his fists upon the desk, rattling the whiskey bottle and glasses.

Fishbelly was transfixed. *Was that his father?* It couldn't be. Yet it was.... There were two Tyrees: one was a Tyree resolved unto death to save himself and yet daring not to act out his resolve; the other was a make-believe Tyree, begging, weeping—a Tyree who was a weapon in the hands of the determined Tyree. The nigger, with moans and wailing, had sunk the harpoon of his emotional claim into the white man's heart. But why was the chief so moved? Why was he reacting to this outlandishly presented claim? Frightened of the elementary emotion before him, Fishbelly swallowed and moved nervously. What kind of compassion had Tyree evoked in the chief and how deep was it? The chief was guilty along with Tyree and Dr. Bruce, guilty of accepting bribes from them. But now all the plotting and counterplotting had been forgotten. With all the strength of his being, the slave was fighting the master. Fishbelly saw that the terrible stare in the chief's eyes was so evenly divided between hate and pity that he did not know what the chief would do; the chief could just have easily drawn his gun and shot Tyree as he could have embraced him.

"You got to do it! You got to save me, Chief!" Tyree sobbed, advancing slowly, nodding his head.

Fishbelly wanted to scream in protest. Yet he realized that Tyree had no other method of fighting, of defending himself.

"Papa," Fishbelly called, weeping for shame.

"GODDAMN YOU, TYREE!" the chief screamed, paradoxically pleading for mercy.

"Have pity on me, Chief!" Tyree begged, pressing home his advantage. "If they going to put me in jail, it's better for you to kill me, Chief! *Shoot me, Chief!*"

The chief's face flushed beet red. He lifted his clenched fists and hammered furiously upon the desk, crying out through shut teeth:

"Oh, goddamn this sonofabitching world! Goddamn everything!"

Tyree began to time his moves; he hung his head, his lowered eyes watching the emotionally wrought-up white man like a cat following the scurryings of a cornered mouse. The chief turned, not looking at anything or anybody. Fishbelly knew that Tyree was weighing whether to act further; then he sniffled and remained silent. The chief lumbered to his chair and sat heavily.

"Goddamn, Tyree," he spoke forlornly. "Maybe I can tell 'em *something*." He straightened warningly: "But they're not going to *do* it; they'll *never* do it!"

"Please, Chief," Tyree purred. "Just for *me.* . . ."

Fishbelly saw Tyree's chest heaving and he felt that he was watching something obscene.

"Tyree, I'm going to tell Judge Moon just what you told me. I'm going to ask 'im if he can make this an exceptional case. I'll ask 'im to do it for you *personally.* . . . Because you're a goddamn good nigger."

"Thanks, Chief," Tyree sighed through his nostrils.

"Tyree, would the niggers on such a jury acquit you?" the chief asked with lifted eyebrows.

"If they didn't, I'd kill 'em," Tyree vowed through tears.

"Okay," the chief sighed. "You'll hear from me."

The chief left, with Tyree showing him out. Returning, Tyree collapsed upon a chair and whispered:

"I did all I could, Doc."

"You did," Dr. Bruce said reverently. "That was why I wanted you with me, Tyree."

"You got to know how to handle these goddamn white folks," Tyree muttered. "But it took everything out of me. I'm *beat* like I was never beat in all my life."

"Tyree, you scared me," the doctor said. "I thought you'd hidden those canceled checks."

Tyree threw a scornful look at the doctor and laughed compassionately.

"Doc, I know the white man inside out. I left that *one* check in that safe on purpose," Tyree explained. "If that chief had found no checks in that safe, he would've been dead sure I was lying. Now he thinks I just forgot that one check. . . . *And he feels safe.*" He hitched up his trousers with an upward-shrugging motion of his arms and elbows and spoke in a growling masculine voice: "Hell, Doc, I done saved up enough evidence against that goddamn chief to send 'im to jail for ten years!"

Minutes later they stood facing one another upon the front porch. The sun's hard glare showed their drawn, pinched faces. From the right came a truck bearing a legend: THE GOLDEN DELL CASKET SERVICE. It rumbled into the driveway and went to the rear of the building.

"Coffins," Dr. Bruce mumbled, wiping sweat from his face.

"Yeah," Tyree said.

"I hope we're not in jail this time tomorrow," the doctor sighed.

"Yeah," Tyree said absent-mindedly. "So long, Doc."

The doctor climbed into his car.

"'By, Tyree. 'By, Fish," he called as he drove off.

"See you," Fishbelly called. "Come on, Papa. You tired. I'll drive you home in my jalopy."

"Naw, son," Tyree rejected the offer. "We going in my car. Your convertible's too goddamn open for me. I want to ride where I can have my gun on my lap."

26

Emma received them tearfully, exhorting them to eat; but they were too emotionally depleted to take more than a mouthful. Spurning Emma's pleas to be told what was wrong, Tyree stretched out upon the sofa in the living room and stared silently at the ceiling. Fishbelly hovered nearby, chain-smoking, brooding upon how he could help. He knew that the chief was certain that Tyree's fears of white reprisal would keep him loyal to his police partners in crime. But why should the chief be carefree and only Tyree bear the burden of fear? The line of race was drawn even among thieves. . . . Each tentative solution that Fishbelly's mind entertained was compulsively formed of whites controlling black destinies. His fantasies had often pictured him as heroically battling in the racial arena, but he had never visualized racial war having this form. His imagination had always pitted him physically against a personal enemy, but this enemy was vague, was part white, part black, was everywhere and nowhere, was within as well as without, and had allies in the shape of tradition, habit, and attitude. The acute compassion that had gripped the chief could have made him kiss Tyree as readily as kill him. Fishbelly now realized that had it not been for that fire he would never have known the real attitude of the chief. White people lived with niggers, shared with them, worked with them, but owed them no human recognition.

"Papa, tell me something," Fishbelly requested.

"What, son?"

"That chief . . . Is he kind? He ever help you?"

"Fish, white folks give us what's left over and call it kindness," Tyree said, looking at his son with a smile so bland that it was bitter.

"Papa, that chief's your friend. Now, if you was white, wouldn't he be trying to keep you out of jail?"

"Hunh," Tyree grunted. "White folks think jails was *built* for folks like us."

Guilt stirred Fishbelly's memory. He had proposed Fats as a sacrificial stand-in for Tyree. He had acted toward his people like the whites acted. What had that chief thought of that?

"Then that chief looks as *us* just like he looks at *low* niggers like Fats?" Fishbelly asked.

"Fish, there ain't no *low* niggers and *high* niggers for white folks," Tyree mumbled tiredly. "We all the same to them, except when they can git something out of us."

He knew that Tyree was telling him the truth now, for he could feel the hard logic of living embedded in it. He yearned to help, and his eagerness made him toy with the notion of acting out something that he did not feel.

"Papa, can't we serve 'em in some way and git 'em to help us?"

"Sure, Fish," Tyree said, lifting his whiskey bottle. "Me and Doc's going to jail. That's serving 'em. They'll feel safe and think no more dance halls'll burn down."

Fishbelly sighed, brooding. He was tired; he dozed in the armchair, his left leg twitching.

Late that afternoon Zeke and Tony came to say good-by; they were leaving that night for Army training. The occasion was awkwardly inarticulate, for all of them had lost loved ones in the fire.

"I wish to Gawd I was going with you-all," Fishbelly told them.

"I'm glad to go," Zeke confessed. "After that fire, I don't want to stay here."

"Me neither," Tony said.

"You niggers going to forgit to write," Fishbelly accused them.

"Hell, naw, man. We going to write," Tony pledged.

"We ain't dropping our old buddies," Zeke swore.

"After you through training, where they sending you?" Fishbelly asked.

"Don't know. Mebbe Germany. Mebbe France," Zeke said.

"We'll git a chance to go to Paris, mebbe," Zeke opined.

"I done heard of that cool town." Fishbelly sighed.

"Man, they say the wine's bitter and the women's sweet in Paris," Zeke smiled.

"They say they don't bother colored folks there," Tony said.

"Damn! Ain't no place like that in this whole world," Fishbelly mumbled, laughing ruefully.

"They say in Paris white folks and black folks walk down the street *together*," Tony sang in a tone of frightened hope.

"I ain't going to believe that till I see it," Zeke said. He rubbed his fingers against the seat of his chair. "I'm touching wood."

Zeke and Tony left to walk to the railroad station, leaving Fishbelly feeling doubly abandoned. He returned to Tyree's side and found him opening another bottle.

"Not too much, Papa," he pleaded.

"I can handle it, son."

Jim phoned from the office to report progress in the high-school gym and to ask advice. Emma moved about ghostily, frequently passing the living-room door to observe the mood of her husband and son, but not daring to ask for details. At seven o'clock she timidly begged to bring them plates of food. Tyree consented. Father and son ate sitting on the sofa, resting their plates on their knees, chewing wordlessly, swallowing mouthfuls that they could not taste. Finished, Tyree took another pull from the bottle.

"Why don't you go to bed, son?"

"I ain't sleepy. I want to stay with you."

"Good boy," Tyree said, patting his son's shoulder. "Don't worry. It'll be awright. I been through things tougher'n this."

At ten o'clock they heard a car stop, start, then enter the driveway.

"See who it is, Fish," Tyree ordered, rousing himself, taking his gun from under a pillow on the sofa and pocketing it.

Fishbelly rushed to the window and peered out.

"A big Buick, Papa," Fishbelly whispered. "White man's in it. He got a nigger chauffeur. Somebody important . . . The white man's coming to the door, Papa."

Tyree rose and put on his coat. The doorbell pealed. Emma went hurrying past in the hallway.

"Emma, let Fish git it," Tyree checked her.

Emma's eyes flashed with apprehension and she vanished into her room. Fishbelly opened the door and confronted a tall, heavy white man dressed in black.

"Is Tyree in?"

"Who calling, sir?"

"I'm Mayor Wakefield," the man said.

"Oh Lawd, it's my old friend, Mr. Mayor!" Tyree called with loud, false glee. "Come in, Mr. Mayor! Ain't seen you in a coon's age, sir!"

"Thanks, Tyree." Mayor Wakefield advanced into the living room, looking about. "Nice place you got, Tyree."

"Oh, Mr. Mayor, it ain't bad. It'll do for a poor man like me." Tyree bared his teeth in a mirthless grin. "You like a little drink, sir?"

269

"No, Tyree. I stopped by to have a word with you," the mayor said, sitting, keeping on his hat, and looking wonderingly at Fishbelly.

"That's my son, my side-kick and partner," Tyree crooned proudly. "Gitting old, Mr. Mayor, and I'm glad to have a boy like that to take over someday."

"I see," the mayor said. He turned sharply to Tyree. "How old are you, Tyree? You're about my age, aren't you?"

"Me, Mr. Mayor? He, he! I was forty-eight last March," he chortled.

"The older a man gets, the more sense he ought to have," the mayor observed.

"That's right, Mr. Mayor." Tyree bubbled with manufactured joy. "Older and wiser." He swallowed, waiting.

Fishbelly was on edge; the highest official of the town had called on his father, but the honor was eclipsed by anxiety.

"Tyree," the mayor began, "I been hearing some strange things about you."

"What you mean, Mr. Mayor?" Tyree asked without moving his lips, his posture suddenly abject, frozen, tense.

"Judge Moon came to me an hour ago," the mayor said. "He was upset. He said that the chief of police reported to him that you're agitating for niggers to sit on juries—"

"Nawsir!" Tyree cried, rising. "Mr. Mayor, I swear 'fore Gawd I ain't done nothing like *that!* I don't mean to dispute you, sir. But that ain't what I meant—"

"Then what in hell did you mean?" the mayor asked brutally.

"Mr. Mayor, this is a great big misunderstanding—"

"Tyree"—the mayor spoke flintily—"are you in touch with Communists?"

Tyree blinked several times to convey the impression that he was stupidly foolish; then he wet his lips with his tongue.

"Gawd, nawsir, Mr. Mayor!" Tyree breathed in meek despair. He advanced, stopped, and stared humbly into the mayor's face. "Mr. Mayor, I don't know no Commonists. Ain't got no use for 'em. If I saw one, I'd kill 'im, so help me Gawd." Tyree felt uncertain of his ground. "That is, if he wasn't *white*.... I ain't killing no *white* folks—"

"Now, you're talking like a good nigger," the mayor said.

"Aw, nawsir, Mr. Mayor," Tyree singsonged to reassure the white man. "I ain't messing in no politics." He began a low whining. "Mr. Mayor, I'm in trouble 'cause of that Fats nigger. He got all them niggers burned up in that Grove fire 'cause he got them notices about fire violations, but he couldn't *read*. He didn't know what them notices was and he threw 'em away 'fore Doc could see 'em."

"So?" the mayor asked coldly.

"Now, that grand jury wants to indict me and Doc for manslaughter—"

"That's *natural!* You were *careless!*" the mayor's words shot neat and clean.

"But I ain't guilty of no manslaughter!" Tyree wailed.

"You owned a part of that dance hall, didn't you?"

"Nawsir, I didn't *own* it. Doc *owned* it—"

"You put up money; you had half interest in the *profits.*"

"But I didn't have no part in *running* it," Tyree cried with tear-filled eyes.

"Didn't you and that nigger doctor give orders to that Fats nigger?" the mayor asked.

Tyree was silent.

"Answer me, Tyree!"

"Yessir," Tyree moaned.

"Then what are you beefing about?" the mayor demanded.

Like a cut shot in a movie, Tyree was transformed. He lifted his head and closed his eyes.

"That grand jury's going to find me guilty of something I ain't guilty of!" Tyree yodeled his misery in a whinnying holler of despair. "That's how this business of us niggers sitting on the jury came up when I was talking to the chief. I ain't no Commonist and I ain't asking for no social equality. Mr. Mayor, you know we niggers is satisfied. . . . And there ain't nothing on this earth I hate more'n them Commonists. I just said to the chief that if, for *once,* just ONCE, six niggers was on that *particular* jury, then I could git me some justice—"

"Nigger, you've gone crazy," the mayor said flatly. The mayor stared at Tyree, then asked with a disdainful smile:

"How could you make six niggers on a jury vote for you?"

"They just wouldn't vote against me, Mr. Mayor," he whimpered.

"You want to pack our juries with niggers who'll vote for niggers?" the mayor asked.

"Niggers voting for me's *justice*," Tyree wept. "Mr. Mayor, don't judge me like you judge your folks. I'm *black!* You know what that means here in the South. I ain't complaining, but I need help . . . Tell me what to do, *please*, sir!"

"Sell your property and prepare to defend yourself. You're in trouble, Tyree," the mayor told him. "And forget this nonsense about niggers sitting on juries; that'll never happen in this state. And tell that nigger doctor the same thing."

Tyree leaned forward and rested his head on the arm of the sofa.

"Moooooooum, mooooooum," he moaned a wordless plea.

"Stop that whining and face up to what you've done," the mayor snapped at him. "The families of those dead people are going to sue you. Do you realize that?"

"They wouldn't sue if I wasn't found guilty," Tyree sobbed. "I ain't got no money—"

"You're the richest nigger in town," the mayor said snortingly. "And God only knows how you made it. How much money have you got, Tyree?"

Without replying, Tyree rocked and moaned with shut eyes. Fishbelly knew that Tyree was acting, but that acting was so real that shame wrenched him.

"Don't carry on like that!" the mayor shouted, moved.

"I done served you faithfully! No matter what you asked me to do, I did it! The Bible says: 'Even if you slay me, yet will I trust you'! Now, I need friends and my white folks turn their backs on me," Tyree keened with shut eyes.

The mayor rose and gazed silently at the sobbing black man; he glanced at the door, as though about to leave, then sat again. He shivered, then sighed.

"I'll see what I can do, Tyree," he said slowly. Then, as though to himself: "What in hell can we do with your niggers . . . ? Now, listen, Tyree. Forget this damned business about niggers on juries!"

"I ain't never said nothing like that, Mr. Mayor," Tyree

rose, sweating through tears. "But you got to *save* me—"

"You'll get out on bail. Come to me and let me know what your resources are. I'll advise you how to clean up this mess," the mayor said with a smile.

"Yessir. Thank you, sir," Tyree mumbled with downcast eyes.

"I'm going now. Get your affairs straightened out."

"Thank you, sir." Tyree sighed dispiritedly. "Fish, see Mr. Mayor out. . . . Good night, Mr. Mayor."

"Good night, Tyree."

Fishbelly let the mayor out of the front door and watched him enter his car, the door of which was held open by a black chauffeur. When the car had driven off, he returned to the living room and was surprised to see Tyree putting on his hat.

"Where you going, Papa?"

"Fish," Tyree growled, his eyes blazing red, "I don't like what that goddamned white man said. I see it *all* now. *They jealous of me*. They done made up their minds to break me. We got to see Doc. These white folks think I won't fight 'em. But I will; I'll fight 'em and ride the black cat off the deep end to hell, so help me Gawd! When a man asks you how much money you got, he's planning to pick you clean, take every cent you got. And I ain't going to let that happen. I'll *die* first."

"Sh, Papa," Fishbelly warned. "Don't let Mama hear you."

"Come on," Tyree said, leading the way to the front door.

"Tyree!" Emma called distressfully. "Tell me what's happening!"

"Go to bed, Emma. See you later," Tyree said, pulling Fishbelly after him.

A moment later they were in the car. The motor roared and Tyree headed into the street, whimpering in despair:

"Gawd, I'll kill 'fore I lose all my money. . . . I'll kill, kill, *kill!*"

27

"What we going to do, Papa?"

"Fish, I'm gitting them canceled checks from Gloria," Tyree muttered firmly. "We got to use 'em. It's now or never. If I'm on trial, that goddamn chief of police's going to be right in that courtroom with me!"

Fishbelly sucked in his breath. Tyree was resolved to strike against the men in the city hall, hoping that such a blow would relieve him of pressure. How would the chief respond? He would most certainly react violently, for his official career and honor were at stake. Fishbelly sighed, realizing how fragile and helpless was the position of his people. The naked fact was that there was nothing left for them but flight. Tyree should stall for time, sell his property, and go away. Where? North? No. He could be extradited. . . . Then maybe go to a foreign country where people spoke another language, ate other foods, had alien habits. But such a world was beyond Fishbelly's imagination.

"Papa, you reckon you ought to do it?"

"Fish, you want to be poor and hungry?" Tyree countered. "That's what it *means*. Either I fight and win, or I do nothing and lose. And *you lose* too. If I do nothing, they'll clean me out. I'm throwing away my life to let 'em take all I ever made. Life comes to just *nothing*. I brought you into this world and I ain't going to leave you here black and naked and scared and hungry and alone. It ain't *right*. You see me crying and begging—well, that's a way of fighting. And when that way don't git me nothing, I have to do something else."

"Yessir, Papa. But don't go too far."

"A man's got to do what he's got to do," Tyree said.

They halted in front of Gloria's house.

"Fish, git that package from Gloria and put it in your pocket and come here to me," Tyree ordered. "If the chief's men come along, I'll drive off and you take the package back and tell Gloria to hide it again. Understand?"

"I got you, Papa."

"And don't let Gloria follow you out here."

"Okay, Papa."

Gloria received him in her bathrobe. But when she heard what he wanted she could scarcely move or speak.

"I want to talk to Tyree," she said.

"He ain't coming in and said for you not to come out."

"But this is *bad!*" she cried.

"Gloria, he's waiting in the car. We in a hurry."

"I must speak to him—"

"Papa ain't going to talk to you, Gloria!"

"Fish, for God's sake, don't let him do anything foolish. He's wanting those checks because he's desperate. I know Tyree. But, God in heaven, he can't fight the police and win! *They'll kill him!*"

"Look, Papa knows what he wants to do," he told her.

Gloria bit her lips and closed her eyes.

"He oughtn't do it; he oughtn't do it," she repeated.

"Papa's waiting, Gloria!" he told her tensely.

"All right," she relented despairingly. "Wait here."

She ran from the room. He stood looking at the bed that still bore the imprint of her body, studying the rouge, powder, lipstick, and perfume arranged neatly upon her dressing table. How calm and ordered was her life compared with the seething fury of Tyree's!

Gloria entered, her eyes circles of fear, hugging the package to her bosom, not wanting to surrender it. She sank upon her bed and stared blankly before her.

"I oughtn't give 'em to you," she whimpered, blinking against tears.

"Naw! Give 'em here, Gloria," he commanded.

She bent over convulsively for a long moment, then straightened and handed him the checks, sobbing.

"Papa's going to be awright," he consoled her.

"What's happening?" she asked in a tiny voice.

"I'm scared Papa's got to go to jail," he told her. "That

grand jury's indicting 'im 'less he can head it off."

"Tell Tyree to do *nothing*," she whispered fiercely. "He can't *win!* He ought to *leave!*"

"But he's got to try to fight—"

"But he can't win against whites!" she sobbed. "They have the law, the guns, the juries—*everything!*"

Her intelligence, her whiteness, her flawless manner of enunciation made him endow her with the magical power and cruel cunning of the white world and he began to believe her. Maybe Tyree ought to give up and flee. . . .

"Fish, tell Tyree *not* to fight," she pleaded.

"They going to put 'im in jail and take all his money—"

"Let them *have* it!" she was emphatic.

"Aw, Gloria . . . Papa's waiting . . ."

He hurried from the house, feeling more depressed than ever. He entered the car and slid in beside Tyree.

"How come you was so long?" Tyree asked.

"She all upset, Papa. She didn't want to give 'em."

"Yeah. I thought that." Tyree sighed and started the motor. "Women can't understand these things."

Tyree drove through dark, quiet streets, handling the car with his left hand, keeping his gun in his right, now and then resting it upon his knees while shifting gears. They parked about a block from where Dr. Bruce lived. Tyree got out and looked left and right.

"Come on, Fish."

They went to the house and around to the back door.

"Don't want them goddamn white folks seeing me meeting Doc," Tyree grumbled. "They'll think we plotting. He rapped upon the windowpane. "Let me in, Doc! Quick! It's Tyree!"

A moment later Dr. Bruce opened the door.

"What's happened, Tyree?"

"I got to talk to you, Doc."

"Come in, Tyree," Dr. Bruce said. "But you've got to meet somebody first. A newspaperman's here—"

"Man, I don't want to meet no reporters," Tyree wailed. "White man or nigger?"

"One of us. . . . From up North," Dr. Bruce explained. "He's already written an article about us."

"What it say?"

"It said we violated the fire laws—"

"Goddamn! There they go trying us 'fore we git into court!" Tyree exploded.

"We've got to straighten this man out," Dr. Bruce said. "He's got his story from the city hall."

"Don't like no newspapers," Tyree grumbled, following Dr. Bruce into the receiving room.

A tall, skinny black man sat with pencil and paper in hand. He rose.

"The name's Simpson," the man said. "You're Mr. Tucker?"

"That's me. Now, what's this you putting in the papers about us? And what paper?" Tyree was aggressive.

"The Chicago *Guardian*," Simpson said. "A purely factual—"

"There ain't no facts about me that you can print without hurting me," Tyree declared. "Print the truth about me, and I'd be dead 'fore sunup."

"Tyree, the story of this fire has gone all over the country," Dr. Bruce said. "Let's face it."

"Goddamn," Tyree scowled. "How come you didn't come to us instead of sucking around them goddam white folks at City Hall? You can't prove that fire's our fault. Can we help it if that Fats nigger couldn't read—?"

"I'm not fighting you, Mr. Tucker," Simpson said. "I want the story."

Fishbelly stared at the black man from Chicago, noticing his ease, detachment, and superior manner.

"You writing fellows do a lot of harm," Tyree growled. "Hell, I'd give you a thousand dollars to keep that story out of the papers—"

"I'm writing another one," Simpson said, laughing. "I'll sell it to you for that thousand dollars, Mr. Tucker."

"Hell," Tyree said, laughing. "I ain't in favor of no kind of writing, especially if it's about *me*. . . . But there's more to this fire mess than you can see—"

"What?" Simpson asked.

"Man, I live in a trap with these goddamn white folks and I can't tell what I know," Tyree sighed.

"Simpson, let me try to explain our position," Dr. Bruce

said. "We're all black in this room, hunh? Let's talk straight."

"I appreciate that," Simpson said.

"I'm a doctor," Dr. Bruce began. "I serve our people. They have little money. I don't make enough out of my practice to live on. I treat most of my patients for almost nothing. That's why so many professional black men operate businesses on the side. Business is a side line that enables me to make both ends meet. The same's true with Tyree. . . . Understand the motive behind our operating a dance hall; it's important—"

"It's a common pattern," Simpson said. He turned to Tyree. "Mr. Tucker, there's a rumor that you're demanding that our folks be put on juries . . ."

"Now, look, Simpson," Tyree drawled. "There ain't going to be no niggers on juries down here. Not now, anyway. I just mentioned that jury business to let the white folks know that we know that they got things stacked against us. Put that in your paper, but don't say I said it. If you do, I'll sue you for lying about me."

Nervous laughter floated through the room.

"Well, that's about all," Simpson said, rising. "I'll do my best."

Dr. Bruce guided Simpson out and Tyree paced, brooding. Each event was lifting him to a higher pitch of nervousness. Fishbelly was afraid that Tyree was verging on violence. When Dr. Bruce returned, Tyree said:

"Doc, the mayor was by to see me tonight."

"Good God! What did he want?"

"I know what the score is now, Doc. They aim to pick us clean; they got us in a crack and they ain't going to let us go till they done squeezed us dry."

"I feared that," Dr. Bruce said heavily.

"The mayor told me to sell everything I got. And he said the same goes for you."

"What can we do, Tyree?" the doctor asked. "I'm pretty old to start all over again."

"I ain't aiming to start all over again," Tyree vowed darkly. "If they pull me down, so help me Gawd, I'll drag 'em down with me."

"How?"

Tyree tossed the batch of canceled checks upon the sofa.

"Doc, I'm going to spill *everything*," Tyree said.

Dr. Bruce swallowed. He walked aimlessly about the room, then sat.

"You think you ought to, Tyree?" he asked quietly.

"Once they indict us, they got us licked." Tyree was logical.

"Yeah," Dr. Bruce sighed his agreement.

"The only way to stop 'em is to blow things sky-high!"

"But how? Who'll take these checks and act on them? If that chief just *thought* you were thinking of doing this, he'd kill you like—"

"That's what I want to talk to you about," Tyree told him.

Dr. Bruce lifted the packet of canceled checks, undid them and sorted through them at random; he repacked them and flung them on the sofa.

"This is a life and death matter, Tyree," he said.

"That chief's got enemies aplenty," Tyree reminded him.

"And all of 'em are scared to death of him," Dr. Bruce pointed out.

"Just tell me the name of *one* white man in this town who ain't scared," Tyree demanded.

"There's McWilliams," Dr. Bruce said. "He ran against the mayor in the last election. He's outspoken and he's a reformer. But would he act on *this?* Hell, he's a Mississippi white man too. Nine times out of ten he feels toward us like that chief does."

"Yeah, but we got to take a chance," Tyree was desperate.

"Then McWilliams is your man," Dr. Bruce said. "He's the only one with guts." The doctor shook his head. "Suppose McWilliams took these checks and made a deal with them? Where would that leave us?"

"You think there ain't no hope, Doc?"

"It's possible."

Tyree rose; his face twitched; his lips quivered.

"Then, by Gawd, I ain't going to let 'em git away with it!" he yelled. "I'll drag 'em down with me! I'll kill a white son-ofabitch 'fore I let 'em break me! I swear!"

Fishbelly knew that Tyree had reached the breaking point.

"Papa," he called reprovingly.

Tyree pulled his gun and waved it wildly in the air.

"I'll kill! I ain't no coward!"

"Tyree!" the doctor shouted at him.

"I ain't going to lose like this, Doc!" Tyree raged. "For twenty years I grinned and slaved and bowed and scraped and took every insult that a man can know to git something, and now they ask me to give it all up! I won't! I'll die first!"

"Tyree, sit down! Calm yourself," Dr. Bruce urged. "Here, take this. . . ." He handed Tyree a pill and a glass of water. "You can't think straight feeling like that, man."

Tyree glared about, then swallowed the pill. He began weeping. The doctor patted his shoulder.

"That's better. Let it come out like that."

Fishbelly sat beside Tyree's racked body, hating the flowing tears, convinced that any reaction was preferable to weeping. Gloria was right: they should all clear out. . . . Oh, Baby Jesus, how poverty-stricken was their outlook, their chances, their hopes! All of their hours were spent frenziedly within the life area mapped out by white men. Suddenly he willed himself as far away from this sodden hopelessness as possible. But the moment his mind tried to embrace the idea of something different, it went blank. He had heard of Jews wandering from nation to nation, of refugees roaming the face of the earth, but black folks remained in the same spot in peace and war, in summer and winter; they either obeyed or dodged the laws of the white man and never moved except from one set of white masters to another. They had grown used to accepting white tormentors as a part of the world, like trees, rivers, mountains—like the sun and the moon and the stars. . . . All right, since they did not know enough to run, it was better to lash out at something, no matter what.

"Let's show these damned checks to that McWilliams," Fishbelly said. "It's better'n *nothing*."

"You right," Tyree said.

"There's nothing else we can do," the doctor said.

Fishbelly now felt afraid; they had agreed with him too quickly. He had made a random suggestion based on despair and they had leaped to embrace it. Well, why not act? Any action was better than this rot of uncertainty.

"If we going to do it, we better do it quick and give 'em to

280

McWilliams tonight so he'll have time to think about it," he told them.

"I'm ready to see 'im now," Tyree said.

Dr. Bruce hesitated.

"You know what this means? We're carrying the fight into the camp of the enemy—"

"But there's nowhere else to fight, man," Tyree declared.

"If we can git them white fighting amongst themselves, mebbe some pressure'll lift off us," Fishbelly put in.

Dr. Bruce picked up the phone book and leafed through it. "Here's his number. Want me to call him?"

"What we going to tell 'im?" Tyree asked.

"He's heard about that fire," Dr. Bruce said. "I'll tell him that we've got something on it that ought to interest him politically."

They were silent. They were playing their last card and they had to be sure that they were playing it right.

"Wonder if that McWilliams hates niggers more'n he hates crooked chiefs of police?" Fishbelly asked slowly.

"Only God knows that," Dr. Bruce said. "That's something we have to find out. You think a man's got cancer, but you never really know until you open him up. I'm all for operating."

Tyree smiled bitterly.

"Awright, Doc. Goddammit to hell. Let's operate!"

28

Dr. Bruce phoned. McWilliams was in and he listened most intently to Dr. Bruce's guarded explanations. Yes, he was definitely interested and wanted to see the canceled checks. When could he visit Dr. Bruce and Tyree? Right now. He would be over in half an hour. And tell no one else. Dr. Bruce hung up.

"He's coming. He sounded interested as hell, but you never know."

"Let's git together," Tyree said determinedly. "McWilliams is white, and he ain't no friend of ours. . . . He's for good government and all that. Awright, we hand 'im this stuff and ask 'im to git it to the grand jury. Now, I'm dead sure that the chief's had to split his take with the higher-ups. So, if they indict us, they got to indict all the rest of 'em, see? *That's the deal.* The burning of the Grove, the women doing their business, all them folks being dead was not 'cause of fire violations. The law was paid to let the Grove run." His voice sank low. "It ain't going to keep us out of jail, but I want them white bastards in that court answering questions right alongside of me. If they git off, I git off. They just as guilty as me."

"It's desperate, but it's our only chance," Dr. Bruce said.

The phone rang. They looked at one another. Dr. Bruce picked up the receiver and spoke into the transmitter.

"Dr. Bruce speaking." He listened, then glanced sharply at Tyree. "I see," he murmured, his eyes roving the room. "We'll discuss it," Dr. Bruce said. "If we come, we'll be there in half an hour. If we don't, then we won't be there. Goodby." He hung up.

"Who was that?" Tyree asked.

"McWilliams. He says he can't come. He says it's better for us to come to his house—"

"I ain't going!" Tyree shouted. "He's acting like all the other goddamn white men. He done thought it over and got scared."

"He swears he's interested," Dr. Bruce said, scratching his head. "I don't get it." Baffled, he shut his eyes. "He wants those checks. Why won't he come for 'em?"

"You reckon it's a trap?" Fishbelly asked.

"Could be," Tyree said. "White men don't invite niggers to their *houses*. When visiting's done, white folks come to *us*. I ain't never been in the mayor's house, but he's been in mine."

"Well, we can drop it. Or go and take our chances," Dr. Bruce summed it up. He looked at his watch. "Thank God, it's night. That's a swanky neighborhood McWilliams lives in. Even the chief of police lives out there somewhere." He bared his teeth in a grimace. "Maybe we ought to sell our property, burn those damned checks, and get the hell out—"

"They can git us anywheres, Doc," Tyree said. "There ain't no place to run to."

The stillness was so profound that they could hear one another's breathing. Occasionally their feet moved nervously on the carpet. The sudden sound of sharp rain dashing against the shingled roof made them lift their heads. Dr. Bruce shut the windows as lightning zipped across the sky and thunder pealed from east to west, dying rumblingly away. The phone's ringing made them start. Dr. Bruce lifted the receiver.

"Dr. Bruce speaking."

"(. . .)"

"Just a moment, Mr. McWilliams." Dr. Bruce covered the transmitter with his palm. "He wants to talk to you, Tyree."

"Give me that phone," Tyree said. He put the receiver to his ear. "Good evening, Mr. McWilliams."

"I'm waiting for you and those documents," McWilliams said.

"Well, Mr. McWilliams . . . He, he! You know we's black folks." Tyree spoke with informative humbleness. "It's best you come to see us."

"Why?"

"You want a pack of niggers tramping through your house this time of night?" Tyree asked him brutally.

"What're you afraid of?" McWilliams asked. "I'm not afraid. Come along."

Tyree's lips parted. No white man had ever spoken to him like that before."

"You reckon it's awright, Mr. McWilliams?"

"Come ahead, Tyree," McWilliams said in a flowing voice. "But let me be honest with you. I'm not fighting *for* you, Tyree. I know you by reputation. I'm fighting for justice in this town. On the basis of that, do you want to trust me?"

Tyree blinked.

"*Who* you say you fighting for, sir?"

"Justice. Justice in this town," McWilliams said.

Tyree pondered. The white man was fighting for justice, but would not fight for him. Tyree was not "legal," was outside of the law. But he was black and justice was after him, trying to send him to jail. Maybe he could sick that same justice on the police chief?

"We better go see 'im," Tyree whispered to Dr. Bruce.

"Just as you say, Tyree," Dr. Bruce sighed.

"We coming right over, Mr. McWilliams," Tyree spoke into the phone. "Good-by."

He stood and patted the gun in his pocket.

"You want to come, Fish?"

"Papa, I'm with you all the way," Fishbelly said.

"Take your car, Doc," Tyree suggested. "The police know mine."

Soon they were seated in Dr. Bruce's car, rolling through rainy night streets. Fishbelly tried to think. Were they doing right or wrong? Then he realized that there was no right or wrong in their lives. Life was a fight to keep from being killed, to keep out of jail, to avoid situations that induced too much shame. Tyree and the doctor were doing what they had to do. It was that or they fled.

"There's the house," the doctor said, pointing.

"Leave your car here. We'll walk," Tyree advised. He hesitated. "Reckon we ought to go in the back way?"

"Let's go in the front," Dr. Bruce said.

They approached the house and mounted the stone steps.

"Once we're in there, we can't back out," the doctor warned.

"We here to do what we got to do," Tyree said. "Fish, push the bell."

Fishbelly lifted his finger to jam it against the white button, and, before he could do it, the door swung open.

29

It was McWilliams, and Fishbelly was disturbed by the man's geniality and directness. McWilliams was in his shirt sleeves; he was tall, fortyish, spectacled.

"Come into the office," McWilliams invited them, leading the way.

Fishbelly had never before entered a white home and he was ill at ease. He followed Tyree, who trailed after Dr. Bruce. McWilliams sat behind his desk.

"Please sit down," McWilliams said.

"Thank you," Dr. Bruce said, sitting.

Fishbelly and Tyree found seats on a small sofa flanking the desk.

"Mr. McWilliams, this is my son, Fish."

McWilliams nodded toward Fishbelly, then came forward, frowning.

"I think I know what you want," McWilliams began. "But I'm not sure. I'm primarily a lawyer. Do you want to hire me to defend you or what?"

Dr. Bruce and Tyree looked at each other.

"Well, sir, I don't know," Tyree mumbled.

"If you don't know, who does?" McWilliams asked.

"Guess I just got to be honest with you, sir," Tyree said, unaware of his purring cynicism. "You heard about that Grove fire?"

"The press reported that forty-two people were asphyxiated. Seems there were some important fire violations," McWilliams said.

"Well, sir, here's the setup. Me and Doc operated the Grove," Tyree recited. "You a lawyer and I can tell you everything went on there. We made some pretty good money. The chief of police let us run—"

"Can you *prove* that, Tyree?" McWilliams shot at him.

"The proof's right here, sir," Tyree said, indicating the packet.

"Checks you gave to the chief of police?"

"Yessir."

"For what?"

"For letting us do what we wanted," Tyree said.

"And what were you doing?" McWilliams asked. "Listen, I'm not prosecuting you. You don't have to answer."

"There ain't no sense in holding back nothing now," Tyree mumbled, loath to go into details. "The only way to help ourselves is to tell the Gawd's honest truth. . . . The chief let us run, didn't bother us, see?"

"He knew what you were doing, didn't he?" McWilliams asked.

"Yessir. He knew."

"Well, what were you doing?"

"We let gals operate twenty-four hours a day there," Tyree mumbled. "Satisfying men, you know. . . . That Fats nigger handled that, collecting money from the gals. Then the chief held off the fire folks when they got rough about violations."

"And the chief's price for these services?" McWilliams asked.

"A hundred dollars a week, sir."

"Wheeeew," McWilliams whistled. "And for what else did he collect from you?" He took off his eyeglasses in a gesture of surprise.

"Well, there's a woman called Maud Williams, sir. She runs a flat, you know. She got gals there. . . . Well, I paid the chief fifty dollars a week from that—"

"What else?"

"Well, I collect ten dollars a week from four other houses for 'im. Now and then I'd kick in when a big poker or crap game got going. Stuff like that, you know."

"Give me those checks," McWilliams said.

Tyree handed over the packet and McWilliams put on his eyeglasses and examined the oblong slips of paper.

"They're made out to *him?*" McWilliams asked.

"Yessir. It was his split."

"Why was he dumb enough to accept checks?"

"Well, I been his friend for twenty years, you see. He trusted me, sir." Tyree smiled shyly.

McWilliams looked at the backs of the checks.

"He endorsed them in his own handwriting," McWilliams breathed in amazement.

"He couldn't cash 'em 'less he signed 'em," Tyree explained.

McWilliams pored over the checks, one after another.

"Five years of payments, hunh?"

"Yessir. But it's been going on for ten years, sir."

McWilliams amassed the checks and sat looking from Tyree to Dr. Bruce. His eyes finally rested upon Fishbelly.

"Is your son involved in this?"

"Nawsir. He's just sixteen. He works for me," Tyree said.

"I'm surprised that what goes on in the colored area pays off so well," McWilliams said.

"Oh, we niggers out there got money, sir." Tyree assured him.

"Why do you say 'niggers'?" McWilliams asked.

"Er . . . He, he!" Tyree stammered, laughing sheepishly. "Just a way of speaking, sir."

"These girls you were letting operate, as you call it—did any of them die in that fire?" McWilliams asked.

"Yessir. About ten of 'em."

"What kind of girls were they?"

"Just poor gals, sir. That's all."

McWilliams rubbed his hand over his face and shook his head.

"How much money did you get from the girls?"

"What they got from the men, they split fifty-fifty with us," Tyree explained.

"And what was that for?"

"That was 'cause we managed 'em, sir. That Fats nigger did it."

"What do you mean by 'managing' them?"

"We took care of 'em, protected 'em. If they got arrested, we got 'em out of jail. The chief helped us there. . . ."

"Could these girls leave if they wanted to?"

"Oh, yessir. Sure. But they never wanted to leave us."

"Personally," McWilliams said slowly, "I detest the idea of buying and selling women, no matter what race or—"

"Well, it was us or somebody else," Tyree explained. "It's business, just like any other. You can't stop that stuff, sir. It goes on. So we just kind of organized it, sir, made it safe and regular-like, you know. . . ." Tyree felt that his ground was weak and he added quickly: "No drunk ever got rolled in the Grove, sir. And Doc took care of the gals—"

"They were *clean,*" Dr. Bruce said, not looking up.

"What do you want me to do?" McWilliams asked with a sigh.

"We want you to git these checks to that grand jury, sir. It's going to git me in trouble, but I'm awreddy in trouble. I lied three times to that grand jury and this is going to make me guilty of what they call perjury. But it's that or being indicted for manslaughter. . . . That chief told me to sell all I got and give 'im the money and he'd help git me off. And I just don't believe 'im, Mr. McWilliams. There ain't no reason for 'im to help me after he gits his hands on my money. Ain't natural . . ."

"You want to turn state's evidence?" McWilliams asked.

"That's right, sir," Tyree said.

"The chief of police accepted bribes from you and here is proof," McWilliams said softly. "Now, who did the bribing?"

"Me. I did," Tyree stated frankly. "You can't operate houses like the Grove and Maud Williams's place without bribes. . . ."

"It's illegal to bribe the law," McWilliams said.

Tyree blinked.

"But the *white man* is the law," Tyree pointed out.

"It's still illegal," McWilliams maintained.

"But the white man took the bribes," Tyree argued. "There ain't no law but *white* law. . . . You say it's against the law to take bribes, but the white man takes 'em."

"And now you don't want the white man to squeeze your money out of you?" McWilliams asked.

"Why should only we suffer and go to jail?" Dr. Bruce asked.

"That's a fair question," McWilliams said, nodding. "But

don't you realize that you were wrong in what you did?"

"There was nothing else to do," Tyree spoke testily.

"That's no defense in a court of law," McWilliams told him.

Tyree rose and stared.

"White men make the law and they let us break it when we pay 'em," he said.

"You still broke the law," McWilliams said.

Fishbelly saw Tyree's swelling, hot bitterness reaching the boiling point. Tyree's hands trembled. What kind of a man was this McWilliams? Was he for him or against him? Why was he harping about the law? The law was the chief of police; the law could talk, could act, could accept bribes. When you wanted something, you asked a white man and he said yes or no and told you how much it would cost.

"But they *white* men!" Tyree insisted, amazed.

"That makes no difference" McWilliams maintained. "It's corrupt to *take* bribes and it's corrupt to *give* them—"

"I ain't *corrupt!*" Tyree was defiant.

"Then what are you?" McWilliams asked. "You just admitted—"

Tyree doubled his fists; he stood in the center of the room and words in wild profusion poured out of him like a torrent of water tumbling over rocks:

"Mr. McWilliams, I ain't corrupt. I'm a *nigger*. Niggers ain't corrupt. Niggers ain't got no rights but them they *buy*. You say I'm wrong to buy me some rights? How you think we niggers live? I want a wife. A car. A house to live in. The white man's got 'em. Then how come I can't have 'em? And when I git 'em the only way I can, you say I'm corrupt. Mr. McWilliams, if we niggers didn't buy justice from the white man, we'd never git any. I ain't got no rights; my papa never had any, and my papa's papa never had any; and my son sitting there ain't got none but what he can buy. Look, Mr. McWilliams, for years I done bought me rights from the white man and I done built a business. I got a home. A car. Now the same men who sold me my rights ask me to give 'em all my money. . . ." Tyree choked at the injustice of it; rage held him speechless. "They got me in a godamn trap! Yessir, they got me!" He began to shout. "But they going to come into this trap with me! They ain't going to milk me dry! I'll die first, you hear? Mr. McWilliams, I can't vote. There ain't no black men in office in this town. We black folks is helpless and all we can do is buy a little protection. If I'm corrupt, who made me corrupt? Who took the bribes? The law, and the law's white. I live in what the white man calls Nigger Town. . . . Mr. McWilliams, I didn't make Nigger Town. White men made it. Awright. I say, 'Okay.' But, goddammit, let me *live* in Nigger Town! And don't call me corrupt when I live the only way I can live. Sure, I did wrong. But my kind of wrong is right; when you have to do wrong to live, wrong is right. . . . But I ain't never had no trouble in this town. Ask them white men in the city hall. They'll tell you Tyree's *straight*. I keep my word. When I told that goddamn chief of police I'd pay 'im a hundred and ninety dollars every Sat'day night, I *did* it. I got it out of the whores and gamblers and gave it to 'im. And he said: 'Thank you, Tyree.' Now, 'cause the fire's done made me look guilty, he wants to take all my money. I say, hell, naw! I swear 'fore Gawd he won't git it! I'll kill first. That's where I stand. I ain't mad at you, Mr. McWilliams. But you got to know straight just what this is. Ain't no use in you talking to me about law and justice. That ain't got nothing to do with me. If the law was fair, I wouldn't be in your house talking like this to you. . . . Mr. McWilliams, can't you see what I mean? This is the life I live. I live it 'cause I got to. And I don't complain. I took the white man's law and lived under it. It was *bad* law, but I made it work for me and my family, for my son there. . . . Now, just don't tell me to go and give it all up. I won't! I'll never give up what I made out of my blood!"

Tyree finished with a dry sob and sat down. For the first time Fishbelly had heard Tyree speak out the shame and the glory that was theirs, the humiliation and the pride, the desperation and the hope. Oh, why had not Tyree said all of this to him before? Why had he to wait until this moment of danger to know how it really was with his father? He saw McWilliams staring at Tyree with an open mouth. Dr. Bruce gaped at Tyree as though he had never seen him before.

"My God," McWilliams sighed, pulled off his eyeglasses. "I never saw it that way."

"It's the way we live every day," Tyree said.

"Do you agree with Tyree?" McWilliams asked Dr. Bruce.

"I'm a doctor, sir," Dr. Bruce said. "But I don't think I could have said it any better."

"Tyree, I don't want to hurt you. You must believe that," McWilliams said.

"Mr. McWilliams, I was hurt when I was born black with an empty gut in Mississippi," Tyree told him bitterly.

"I can do what you want," McWilliams said. "But I cannot guarantee that you won't be hurt more than you are already hurt. That's the problem. The law holds you guilty along with the others. Since you spoke, I know why you did it. But the law does not recognize that excuse. I admit that your people have been terribly provoked. There was slavery, and then there was hate on the part of the white man for the freed slave. Then your people began to *adjust* to an *unjust* situation. And that is what we are dealing with. But only a Solomon could untangle that knot. Your excuse is valid. But what can I do about it? I'll break this foul mess open. I'll chase that chief of police out of office. *But you're in danger!*"

"We awready in danger, Mr. McWilliams," Tyree mumbled.

"Let them indict *all* the guilty, not just the *black* ones," Dr. Bruce said.

"I agree," McWilliams said. "But it's a strange way to get at justice. . . ." He stared long and hard at Tyree. "I'm sorry I asked you why you called your people 'niggers.' I think I know now."

"We niggers 'cause we can't do nothing that's free," Tyree said.

"There are rumors that that city-hall mob has been trying to tamper with that grand jury," McWilliams said. "And that police chief is a dangerous man. He'll stop at nothing," McWilliams said and rose.

Tyree, Fishbelly, and Dr. Bruce rose.

"Thank you for coming," McWilliams said.

They went out; it was still raining. They drove silently to the Black Belt.

"What do you think of McWilliams, Tyree?" Dr. Bruce asked.

"He, he! Funny kind of white man," Tyree said.

291

"He doesn't want to hurt us, but can he help us?" Fishbelly said.

"That's just it." Tyree sighed.

Fishbelly and Tyree got out of the doctor's car and stood in the rain.

"Well, we done hit back," Tyree said.

"Yes," the doctor mumbled. "But be careful."

"Right. Good night, Doc," Tyree said.

"Good night," Fishbelly called.

When they reached home, Tyree said tenderly:

"Son, let's git some sleep. I think we going to need it."

30

As the night sounded with raging rain, Fishbelly entered his room and sank limply upon his bed. So numb was he with fatigue that he was tempted to sleep fully clad. He roused himself, undressed, and slid beneath the covers. The excitement of striking at the police chief had temporarily washed the terrible death of Gladys from his memory and had fogged his realization that Tyree could, barring a miracle from McWilliams, still be jailed, or even slain. Their disclosing the canceled checks now compelled him to consider the possibility that he might have to face the future alone. And then the awful futility of what they had done at McWilliams's stunned him; they had mobilized all of their courage to deal a blow that had not really solved anything. Their running forward with the canceled checks had been more balm for their injured vanity than a guarantee of their safety, more bitter defiance than studied wisdom.

He had constantly hankered to be on his own; yet, when faced with the awful freedom posed by the absence of Tyree, he shrank and sought means of staving it off. He wanted freedom, but with the sanction of a living, indulgent father. If Tyree were jailed, he would have to carry on with Jim's help, but he was young for that, *too* young. And if Tyree were gone, how would he face the whites? He recalled with dismay that, other than those past, bruising brushes with the police, he had no practical knowledge of whites. What would be his attitude when he met them? The mere thought made him wince. Could he imitate Tyree's tactics and make them sorry, sad—make them laugh and feel safe? *"Naw!"* he spoke aloud. Then sighed in the humid darkness, hearing rainy wind lashing the windowpanes. He could not whine, grin, plead; he would die first. . . .

And he saw himself so clearly as the whites saw him that he was certain that the whites could easily detect his adoring hatred of them; they would feel it and kill him. . . . But why was he so firmly sure about the feelings of whites toward black people? He was sure, because, deep in his heart, he felt that the whites were right, but he didn't agree to belonging to that part of mankind that the whites despised! He felt rather than thought this; it came to him in flashes of intuition. On this he and Tyree agreed; the difference between them was that Tyree had automatically accepted the situation and worked willingly within it. Fishbelly also accepted the definition, but he did so consciously and therefore could never work within it. If his town had been an all-black town, he would have gone on and built up Tyree's business with no anxieties. Had his town been an all-white one (in that case, he, too, would have been white!), he could have gone on and built up Tyree's business in a normal manner. But he lived in a black-white town and he had to try to sustain Tyree's business under conditions that the whites had created but despised—and if he accepted those debased conditions and tried to fit his personality into their requirements, the whites would regard him with disdain and hatred, a disdain and hatred with which he, deep in his heart, agreed! Yet he hated himself for agreeing with them, *for he was black.*

Suddenly he half sat up in bed, leaning against his pillow, hearing the storm pounding the house, glimpsing lightning flickering blue past the edges of the shaded window. "What can I *do?"* he whispered wailingly into the dark. If he attempted to grope his way through such dense shadows, he would be killed as surely as Chris had been. Better to flee to some other spot on the earth's surface than let that overtake him. But where? He grew confused, trying to solve a problem about which he could scarcely think.

Yet, maybe, goddammit, there was an out. He would be reserved with the whites, act as sedately as they, stand aloof; then they would know that he had dignity, pride, that he was not the cringing type. But would they really believe that he had such dignity, pride? *Naw!* He honestly did not think so. Why? *He was black.*

The money he had had been made by a black buzzard of a Tyree, a crawling scavenger battening upon only the black side of human life, burying only the black dead, selling only the living black female bodies to the white or black world, buying justice, protection, comfort from those sordid dealings and calling it business. His manhood cringed as he realized once more that the money he had been spending had come partly from poor Gladys's earnings. He leaped from bed, haunted by her reluctant smile, and stood with his hot cheek resting against the wall of the room. "Creeping Jesus," he moaned. He sank back upon his bed, feeling his home and all the Black Belt about him tainted, useless, repugnant.

He shut his eyes tightly, trying to cling to a world ruled by the father he had always known, but wishing that that father could have been another and different kind of man. Then he was dreaming out his problem. . . .

. . . he was sitting at the office desk making out rent receipts behind him the office door opened and he turned and saw Gladys and Gloria entering smiling sweetly and they came to him and kissed him and both of them opened their handbags and began pulling out bundles of green paper money and piling them upon the desk and he said: "But this ain't my money" and Gloria and Gladys smiled and said: "Don't be stupid; it's all yours" and he asked: "But where you git this money?" and they looked like two smiling white women and whispered: "We stole it for you from white men" and he said: "Naw" and they said: "Don't be silly; take the money and hide it" and he stuffed the bundles of money into his pockets and said: "Gawd, I'm rich!" then there was a loud knock at

the door and he was terrified and whisperingly asked Gloria and Gladys: "Who's that?" and they laughingly said: "Don't be scared! It's a friend of ours" and he opened the door and the chief of police stood and said: "All right, nigger. You stole forty-two bundles of money!" and he said: "Nawsir!" and Gloria and Gladys shouted: "He's got 'em in his pockets!" and the chief said: "Empty your pockets, nigger!" and he emptied his pockets of the green bills and the chief asked: "Now, just where'd you get this money?" and he said: "I worked for it" and the chief said: "We'll see about that" and he picked up a bill and said: "This money is marked . . . See? Fish, you bit the bait!" and he looked and on each bill was the smiling face of a white woman and he whirled to Gloria and Gladys and cried: "You bitches! You tricked me!" and the laughter of Gladys and Gloria echoed throughout the under-taking parlor and they said: "You're black and we're white and you'll believe anything we say!" and he turned to the chief yelling: "They're the guilty ones! Arrest them!" and the chief snorted and said: "Listen to a nigger talking about jus-tice!" and the chief pulled out a pair of handcuffs and he ducked under the chief's arm and dashed out of the office into a rear room filled with coffins and he saw his mother beckon-ing to him and calling whisperingly: "Fish, hide in a coffin—quick!" and he climbed into an empty coffin and stretched out and closed his eyes as though dead and he heard the chief running into the room and he felt him standing over him and looking down into his face and he fought against a desire to open his eyes to see if the chief suspected his being alive and then he could resist no longer and he opened his eyes and saw the chief and Gladys and Gloria looking down at him and laughing and the chief said: "All right, nigger. Either you're dead and we'll bury you, or you come out of there and go to jail!"

He awakened in the dark, swallowing as though to keep something down, trying to blink away unwelcome images. Free of dread, he slept again, but fitfully, grinding his teeth in slumber.

31

He opened his eyes and saw a gray, sunless morning seeping in at the edges of the window shades. He put on the light and looked at his watch; it was ten o'clock. He bounded from bed, flung on his robe, and ran into the living room. Tyree, haggard-faced, was sitting on the sofa, fully dressed, fumbling with the morning's paper.

"Why didn't somebody wake me up?" Fishbelly demanded. "Say, anything new, Papa?"

"You needed sleep," Tyree said, extending the paper. "There's something in there about McWilliams and that grand jury. What it say?"

Fishbelly read aloud:

MCWILLIAMS CHARGES FRAUD IN HIGH PLACES
COURT CLERK ASSUALTED THIS MORNING IN PUBLIC
GRAND JURY MEET POSTPONED

Attorney Harvey McWilliams, who ran against Mayor Wakefield during the last city election, said this morning that vital evidence which he had promised to submit to the grand jury had been seized by force and violence by unknown parties.

Mr. McWilliams stated that late last night he had phoned Grand Jury Foreman Samuel Bright and had informed him that he had in his possession evidence regarding police corruption in the city. At an early hour this morning Foreman Bright dispatched Court Clerk Albert Davis to the home of McWilliams where he received a sealed envelope addressed to the grand-jury foreman.

Within a block of the McWilliams home, Albert Davis was set upon by three men who forcibly deprived him of the envelope.

"The criminal attack upon Court Clerk Davis is proof of flagrant corruption in high places," McWilliams said.

McWilliams charged that only parties who feared exposure could have engineered the deed.

Mr. Davis described his assailants as men who knew exactly what they were looking for.

"Five minutes after I left Mr. McWilliams's home, a black sedan stopped beside me and three men leaped out. Two of them held me while the third opened my brief case and extracted the envelope that McWilliams had just entrusted to me. The whole episode took place in full view of passers-by who did not realize what was happening until too late. The men got back in the car and sped off before anyone could take the license number."

Mayor Wakefield said that he was stunned that any man or group of men could have the audacity to attack court personnel in such an open and criminal manner. He pledged a quick and thorough investigation.

Grand Jury Foreman Samuel Bright disclosed that the scheduled session of the grand jury that was to meet in the chambers of Augustus Moon this morning would be postponed. The grand jury had been probing into alleged connections between police officials and vice and gambling interests. . . .

"Good Gawd, Papa!" Fishbelly cried, his hands shaking.

Tyree stared stonily before him and said nothing.

"You think them checks got into the wrong hands, Papa?"

"I don't know, son," Tyree said heavily. "Something's gone wrong. . . . But it's out of our hands." Tyree stood with a hard, bleak face. "Now, now, keep calm, Fish. Finish dressing and git some coffee and come here and sit down. I got to talk to you."

"Papa, that stuff in that paper's about *us*. *I know it*. What can we do?"

Tyree's face was ashy but firm.

"Go do what I told you, Fish," Tyree said. "And not a word to your mama about this. All we need is for her to start blubbering."

"Okay, Papa," he said, feeling the horrible fear that Tyree was mastering. *The checks were lost!* And who could want them but the chief of police? If the chief had got hold of the checks, then Tyree was doomed. And he knew that Tyree knew it. Had they been spied upon? He dressed with shaking hands, then took the cup of coffee offered by Emma.

"How you sleep, son?" she asked him.

"Oh, awright," he mumbled.

"I'm worried. What Tyree doing, Fish?" she asked, fear and tears twisting her mouth.

"Nothing, Mama. How come you crying?"

"Son, don't let Tyree do nothing foolish," she whispered.

"What you talking about, Mama?" He wanted to scream.

"I'm scared for 'im," she whimpered, clutching his arm.

"Aw, Mama, stop!" he chided her, his nerves on edge.

"You and Tyree be careful," she sobbed. "Don't go riling them white folks. They got all the power and—"

"Mama, what you keeping on talking like that for?" He gritted his teeth.

She hugged him and he felt her hot tears on his cheeks.

"When that funeral for the folks that died in the fire, son?"

"Next Friday," he told her.

"Son, if you got any problems, take 'em to Gawd."

"Mama, ain't nothing's going to happen," he muttered. He drained his coffee cup and rose, keeping his face averted. "I got to talk to Papa." He left her abruptly.

He sat beside Tyree in the living room and looked compassionately at him.

"Papa, don't let a white face git *near* you today."

"Take it easy, Fish," Tyree said calmly. "Now, lissen . . . I told Emma I might have to go to jail for a bit. Don't tell her nothing else. Now, if anything happens, I want you to take over. Handle the office. Jim'll help you. You know what to do."

"Oh, Papa," he wailed tensely.

"And Fish, go kind of easy on your mama," Tyree advised. "She don't understand these things."

"Sure, Papa."

The phone rang and Fishbelly picked it up. Jim's voice came over the wire.

"There's a telegram here for Tyree."

"Read it, Jim, and I'll tell Papa what it says."

"Right," Jim said. "You listening?"

"Yeah."

"YOUR PRESENCE NOT NEEDED AT CITY
HALL TODAY
                                        CANTLEY"

"That all, Jim?"

"That's it."

Fishbelly hung up and turned to Tyree.

"The chief wired that you don't have to show up today, Papa."

Father and son stared at each other.

"That chief *knows*," Tyree said softly.

"But how'd he find out, Papa?" Fishbelly asked with tortured eyes. "He don't want to arrest you now. He knows you going to talk."

"That's it, son."

"What we going to do, Papa?"

"We just got to wait, son. That's all we can do."

Again the phone pealed. It was McWilliams. Fishbelly handed the phone to Tyree.

"Tyree, do you know what's in the morning papers?" McWilliams asked.

"Yessir. I know."

"You know what it means."

"I guess that chief's got hold of them checks. That right, Mr. McWilliams?"

"Right. But we can't prove a thing."

"But how'd he know you had 'em, Mr. McWilliams?"

"Tyree, three things could've happened. There could have been a leak from around the grand jury. Cantley could have spied on you and the doctor. Or your phone was tapped. . . . Now, Tyree, it seems that I've failed you. I'm not through with this case. I'll never rest till I get to the bottom of this foul mess. Tyree, I'm phoning you to warn you. You're in danger. *Be careful.*"

"Yessir. I understand."

"Don't you think you ought to have some police protection?"

"Police protection? Nawsir! I don't want no white men near me."

"I see. . . . But maybe you ought to get out of town until this is settled."

"I ain't running, Mr. McWilliams. Running says I'm guilty. And I ain't guilty."

"Well, take care, Tyree. The attack on Albert Davis was the most dastardly thing I've ever heard of. I'm going to fight this thing till I drop."

"Yessir. Good-by, sir."

"I'll see you as soon as I have something definite. Good-by."

Tyree recounted what McWilliams had said.

"They was watching us," Fishbelly mumbled despairingly.

The phone rang for the third time. It was Dr. Bruce, who, too, had received a telegram from the chief of police informing him that he need not appear at City Hall. Dr. Bruce had also talked with McWilliams over the phone.

"How come they ain't arresting us, Doc?" Tyree asked.

"If the chief's got hold of those checks, he doesn't want to see us except to kill us," Dr. Bruce said. "Tyree, for God's sake, keep out of sight until this blows over. The whites are fighting among themselves and that might give us a breathing spell. Keep your gun handy and don't leave the Black Belt."

"Right, Doc. Keep in touch, hunh? I got my gun. I ain't going nowhere but to the office."

Tyree hung up.

"Papa, that chief's plotting something. I know it," Fishbelly warned nervously.

"Son, no matter what happens," Tyree said. "We done won something. They can't git no money from me. Let's git to the office."

As they drove through sunless Black-Belt streets, Tyree reached inside his coat pocket and pulled out a long white envelope.

"Put this in your pocket, son. And hang onto it," Tyree spoke in a faraway voice. "If anything happens to me, then you read it. That lawyer Heith's got one."

"Okay, Papa."

Tyree had given him his last will and testament and he felt crushed.

"Papa, let's go away—"

"Naw. We stay here. And we got to be ready for anything."

"Naw, naw, naw, Papa." Fishbelly was growing hysterical, was beginning to weep.

Tyree stopped the car and turned to him.

"Stop that goddamn crying, Fish!" he growled.

"But, Papa, you—"

"FISH, STOP THAT CRYING!"

"Yessir," he gulped.

"It's awright to cry when it can git you something," Tyree said, driving again. "But crying now ain't no good."

Tyree, while saying a tentative good-by, was handing him the fruits of a lifetime struggle. And what could he say? Nothing. There were no words for such an act, such an occasion. But Tyree could not leave him, not yet. . . . "That can't be!" he cried inwardly. His father had draped about his shoulders an invisible cloak of authority, had made toward him a gesture of faith that went beyond the sights and sounds of the world. He was swamped by a feeling akin to religious emotion, for Tyree had performed toward him an act that linked the living with the dead. He stared out of the car window at the familiar streets that now seemed somehow strange. And his sense of awe deepened when he heard Tyree softly whistling a popular tune, as though he had unburdened himself of an awful load.

"Papa, let's *do* something," he pleaded in a whisper.

"Everything's going to be awright, son," Tyree said.

Entering the office, Tyree greeted Jim heartily.

"Hi, Jim! Everything okay at the morgue?"

"We're all set, Tyree," Jim said.

"Jim, I ain't in to nobody. Git it?"

"Right, Tyree. How're you making out with the chief?" Jim asked.

"I done straightened up and I'm flying right," Tyree sang. "You'll read about it in the papers."

Fishbelly was at Tyree's elbow all that apprehensive morning. He was amazed at how Tyree forgot his anxieties and squelched his sense of guilt for the fire victims and absorbed himself with forging a memorable event out of the mass interment. He phoned and pleaded with all the local black preachers and gained their reluctant consent to hold a collective funeral in the largest Black-Belt church, of which Reverend Amos Jutland Ragland was pastor. In defiance of suspicion pointing toward him, he organized the creation of a gigantic floral wreath "for all them poor folks who died in that terrible fire." Fishbelly scoured the white and black floral shops of the entire town for hundreds of gross of tuberoses, gladioli, lilies, carnations, peonies, dahlias, etc.

"Cover the whole goddamn front wall of that church with flowers," Tyree decreed with grim exultation. "Make it the biggest floral wreath this town ever saw.... To show you where my heart is, I'm donating fifty dollars out of my own pocket."

To the bereaved who called to ask timid worried questions about the origin and responsibility of the fire, Tyree did not bite his tongue as he declared, lifting a black forefinger heavenward:

"Let me tell you the Gawd's truth. Any crooked-brained sonofabitch who gives you a bum steer and tells you I had anything to do with that fire's lying! My own son, my own flesh and blood, missed going up in them flames by just five goddamn minutes. Fish could've been stretched out cold and dead and full of formaldehyde just like all the rest of 'em. You think I'd let a fire start that could burn up my own son? Don't be a fool! And don't let nobody make you believe that Doc had anything to do with it neither. That's just jealous gossip spread by them no-good white folks downtown. We told Fats to take care of things and that nigger didn't. Drinking too much, mebbe. And to show you folks that I'm on the dead level, I'm giving, without nobody asking me, 10 per cent off on every funeral. Tyree's straight and everybody knows it."

His stunned and bewildered clients accepted his explanations and, toward eleven o'clock, the office was free of weeping customers. The most stupendous funeral that Clintonville had ever seen was under way.

"Jesus," Fishbelly marveled, "when Papa's handling dead folks, there ain't a smarter nigger living."

The hours dragged calmly, *too* calmly. Other than keep track of the embalming and creating emergency viewing rooms, the day proceeded in a casual, normal manner.

"It's *too* goddamn quiet," Tyree fretted. "I don't like it."

Fishbelly watched the Black-Belt streets, but not a white face showed, not a single police car could be seen cruising.

"Papa, I want to say something," Fishbelly said.

"Yeah, son. What is it?"

"Let's go away for a few days."

"That's saying we guilty. And we ain't no more guilty than they is," Tyree said.

"We could stay three-four days in Memphis and when we got back things'd be sort of clear," Fishbelly argued.

"Fish, I ain't running. All I got's here. And here I stay."

A few minutes before noon, Jim, wearing his white embalming jacket, came to Fishbelly and whispered:

"Fish, most of the folks are being laid out in the school gym, but Tyree told me to put Gladys in our viewing room. You want to see her?"

Fishbelly closed his eyes and was as still as stone, then he rose and followed Jim meekly back into the viewing room. Gladys lay in a plain white dress in a plain gray coffin that stood in a row of others. He stared at her pale, waxy face holding that hint of a sad smile and he recalled that she had not understood what it meant to be black, and now she was gone. His eyes clouded and he remembered Tyree's impassioned outburst last night in McWilliams's home and he wondered if he and Tyree were guilty of having killed Gladys. . . . "I took the white man's law and lived under it. It was bad law, but I made it work for me and my family. . . ." As always, every time he tried to think about his life, he found himself mulling over the strange reality of the white man. He returned to the office and put his hand on Tyree's shoulder.

"I want Gladys to have another box, Papa. A better one," he whimpered.

"Sure, Fish," Tyree said. "She can have what you want." He laid aside his cigar and called: "Jim!" He pushed Fishbelly gently toward a chair. "Sit down, son."

Jim appeared in the doorway.

"Put Gladys in one of the de-luxe boxes. . . . Wait." Tyree rose and went to the door. "I'll show you." He led Jim out of the office.

Fishbelly leaned his head upon the desk and wept. A few moments later he felt Tyree's hand take hold of his shoulder.

"Son, life's hard, but there's some sweet things in it. Don't go letting this spoil everything, see?"

"I'll try, Papa," he mumbled with trembling lips.

When they went home for lunch, Tyree drove with his gun on his lap, looking left and right. Emma served them with averted face. She refused to eat, pleading a headache. Back at the office, Dr. Bruce phoned and said that nothing had happened.

"I don't like this," Tyree grumbled. "It's *too* quiet."

"Papa, let's leave; let's git in the car and leave *now*—"

"Naw! Running won't help none," Tyree vetoed the idea for the third time.

A little after six o'clock Dr. Bruce was again on the phone. His voice sounded nervous and excited.

"Tyree, Maud's sick," Dr. Bruce explained. "Vera just called me. She's had some kind of an attack. I'm getting over there to see what's wrong. Just want to let you know where I am, see?"

"Okay, Doc," Tyree said. "What's the matter with Maud?"

"I don't know yet; I haven't seen her."

"Keep in touch," Tyree said. He turned to Fishbelly. "Maud's sick. Doc's gitting over there. Bet she's worried about this mess. If that grand jury cracks down, her flat'll have to close."

The hours dragged. At the final moment of daylight the sun burst through for a few moments and drenched the damp streets in gold. Jim announced that the embalming of the forty-two bodies had been completed.

"Tyree, the coroner's verdict was that they died from accidental causes, the nature of which has to be determined," Jim told him.

"That means they ain't made up their minds, hunh?" Tyree asked, staring stonily.

"That's right."

"Well, what's got to be is got to be," Tyree said. "Jim, I know you tired. You'll git a bonus for this. You been on your feet for two days and nights running—"

"I did my best for you, Tyree," Jim said modestly.

"Let's blow for home, Fish," Tyree suggested.

"Okay, Papa."

Just as they were about to leave, the phone rang and Fishbelly answered.

"Fish?" Dr. Bruce's voice hummed over the wire.

"Yeah, Doc."

"Let me talk to Tyree."

"Just a sec, Doc." Fishbelly called Tyree. "Papa, it's Doc."

As Fishbelly handed the phone to Tyree, he was vaguely aware that some cog had slipped in the turning routine of time, but he could not put his finger upon it. He listened while Tyree talked over the phone.

"Yeah, Doc."

"(. . .)"

"What?" Tyree exclaimed.

"(. . .)"

"*Dead?* When, man?"

"(. . .)"

"Good Lawd! About a hour ago? What was wrong?"

"(. . .)"

"Her heart, hunh?"

"(. . .)"

"Was she living when you got there?"

"(. . .)"

"Papa, what's happened?" Fishbelly asked.

"Just a minute, Doc." Tyree turned to Fishbelly. "Maud Williams is dead—dropped dead about a hour ago. It was her heart."

"Maud Williams dead?" Fishbelly exclaimed.

"You there now, Doc?" Tyree spoke into the phone.

"(. . .)"

"Yeah, I git you. Papers, hunh? You stick there till I git over. If Maud asked me to take care of her papers, there must be something in 'em she didn't want nobody to see. Git the

point? What with this trouble, I better git them papers . . .
Where Vera?"

"(. . .)"

There was a pause. Tyree looked distractedly about.
"Damn . . . That nigger bitch was strong's a horse. Didn't
think she'd kick the bucket like that." He spoke again into the
phone. "Yeah. That you, Vera?"

"(. . .)"

"Vera, honey, I'm so sorry . . . Sure. I'll be right over. Lissen, Vera, don't let nobody touch a thing belonging to Maud,
see?"

"(. . .)"

"Okay. See you."

Tyree hung up and rubbed his right hand over his eyes, then
walked across the office.

"You wait for one thing and something else pops up. How
in hell Maud went and died like that?" He stared glumly out
the window. "That makes a problem. Vera's too young to handle the business. . . . Needs a tough woman to do a job like
that." Tyree went to the door. "Jim!" he called.

"Jim, old Maud Williams died about a hour ago," Tyree
announced.

"Good God!" Jim said. "What happened?"

"It was her heart, Doc says."

"Well, Tyree, you have to expect things like that." Jim
spoke philosophically. "We're sending for her? Dr. Bruce
make out the death certificate?"

"Doc's there now. Been knowing Maud for thirty years. I
better git over." Tyree put on his hat. "Fish, stick here till I git
back. Won't be long."

"I want to go with you, Papa," he begged.

"Naw. It ain't far. It's in the Black Belt. Doc's there,"
Tyree told him. "Don't want nobody poking around Maud's
things with all this Who-Shot-John going on."

"For Gawd's sake, be *careful*, Papa!"

"Sure . . . Jim, tell Jake and Guke to bring the hearse to
Maud's in about half an hour, hunh?"

"Right, Tyree," Jim said in a worried tone.

Tyree lingered in the doorway, inserted a fresh cigar into his
mouth and held a match flame to its end.

306

"I'm tired," he mumbled.

"Let me 'tend to it for you, Papa," Fishbelly begged.

"Naw, Fish. Got to do this myself," Tyree said.

"Okay, Papa."

"See you, Fish."

Dreamily, he watched Tyree drive off and he knew that his gun was on his lap as he shifted gears. You ate, slept, breathed, and lived fear. Somewhere out there in the gray void was the ever-lurking enemy who shaped your destiny, who curbed your ends, who determined your aims, and who stamped your every action with alien meanings. You existed in the bosom of the enemy, shared his ideals, spoke his tongue, fought with his weapons, and died a death usually of his choosing. Fishbelly wondered if it would always be like that. Black people paid a greater tribute to the white enemy than they did to God, whom they could sometimes forget; but the white enemy could never be forgotten. God meted out rewards and punishments only after death; you felt the white man's judgment every hour.

He slumped in a chair, sick of this season of death. Maud Williams dead? Didn't seem possible. His lips smiled dryly as he remembered the night that Tyree had taken him up on the hill and had shown him Nigger Town, and then had led him to Vera's arms; and he recalled the sly light in Maud's eye when she had asked him if he had had a good time. . . . There were people whose personalities seemed to exempt them from death, and Maud Williams, with her cackling laughter, her brutally lewd jokes, her amorality, and her business cunning had been one of those.

He heard the evening paper hit the front porch and got it. He saw:

POLICE HEADS DENY LINK WITH VICE RACKETS

Today the city hall was in an uproar following this morning's hijacking of Court Clerk Albert Davis by persons unknown. Accusations and counteraccusations have come from most city government department heads.

Mayor Wakefield called publicly upon Harvey

McWilliams to disclose, in the public interest, the identities of the parties that figured in the evidence which he had promised to submit to the grand jury. This evidence was presumably contained in the sealed envelope of which Court Clerk Albert Davis was robbed in the streets this morning.

Mr. McWilliams countercharged that he could not disclose such information without endangering the lives of his informants.

Chief of Police Gerald Cantley said that McWilliams was libeling the integrity of the police department when he inferred that any citizen went in fear of his life by co-operating with the grand jury. . . .

Fishbelly knew that that story meant that the police chief was daring McWilliams to identify Tyree directly, hinting that there would be no Tyree if it were known that Tyree had betrayed him. The white folks were fighting among themselves. . . . Tyree had been gone for more than an hour when the phone rang. Fishbelly lifted the receiver and spoke into the transmitter:

"Tyree Tucker's Funeral Home."

"Fish? That you?" came a familiar woman's voice that made the hair bristle on Fishbelly's head.

"Who this?" he asked, feeling engulfed in a dream.

"Fish, this is Maud—"

"What?" he asked in a shout, his skin prickling. Though he was unaware of it, he rose, gripping the phone, his eyes dancing.

"This is Maud!" the voice wailed. "You got to come *quick!"*

"But who is this?" he demanded slowly, his mind whirling.

"THIS IS MAUD SPEAKING!" Maud yelled at him over the wire. "Something awful's happened! Come right away!"

"B-but . . . Lissen . . . D-doc phoned . . . And Vera said you were *d-dead* . . . Is this a joke?" he asked, sensing catastrophe crawling somewhere near him.

"Fish, I can't explain everything now," Maud told him with panting breath. "But, man, come! Tyree's been shot! It was a *trap*, Fish!"

Fishbelly's eyes bulged in his head.

"W-where's Papa?" he asked stammeringly, trying to understand.

"Fish, come quick! The police done shot Tyree!"

The room reeled. His brain tied itself into a knot as he tried to think. MAUD WAS ALIVE! The afternoon flashed before his eyes: Doc had called Tyree from Maud's saying that Maud was dead; and Tyree had rushed to Maud's . . .

"W-where Papa? I want to talk to Papa—"

"Fish, for Gawd's sake, can't you *understand?*" Maud screamed. "It was a trick! Tyree's been shot! He's in my flat! Oh Lawd, it wasn't our fault . . . Tyree wants to talk to you. He don't know how long he can last, how long he can hold out—"

Fishbelly dropped the phone as the truth exploded in his tight skull. The muscles of his body jerked taut. Doc had phoned that Maud was dead and Tyree rushed over and the police had shot him! If, at that moment, he could have lifted his hand and smashed the earth upon which he stood, he would have done it. *The white folks had struck!* He doubled his fists and bellowed a harsh moan.

"Gawd, if they killed my papa, I'll kill *everybody!* I'll spread blood, goddammit! Oh, Crawling Jesus, I'll spread blood everywhere!" He snatched up the phone and yelled into it: "Hello! Hello!" But the line was dead. He hurled the phone from him. "Jim! Jim!" he screamed, running into the rear of the "shop," stumbling past coffins filled with the dead. "Jim! Jim!"

"Yes, Fish," Jim came running. "What's the matter?"

"Papa! Papa's been *shot!*"

"What?" Jim blinked.

"Maud told me—"

"Maud?" Jim asked, staring at Fishbelly with glistening eyes.

"She just phoned—"

"But Tyree said Maud Williams was *dead!*"

"I know . . . It was a trick, Jim," he sobbed. "Aw, to hell with this goddamn world! I told Papa to *leave!* We should've been watching for this!"

"But Dr. Bruce—"

"That damned doctor baited Papa for the police and I'll kill 'im!" He ran to a wall and began to beat his fists against it. "Lawd Gawd in heaven, I'll kill every chink-chink goddamn Chinaman white man on this sonofabitching bastard earth!" In frenzied madness he seized a hammer lying upon a box and began pounding walls, coffins, tables, and chairs. "I want to kill, *kill!*"

"Fish!" Jim shouted at him. "Get hold of yourself, boy!"

"Give me a gun, Jim!"

"Stop screaming, Fish," Jim said, grabbing him.

"Turn me loose!" Fishbelly shrieked.

Jim pinned the struggling boy against a wall.

"Leave me alone!" Fishbelly yelled. "I'm going to kill that lousy, stinking, bitchy Maud!"

"Fish, I won't let you run in the streets waving a hammer," Jim told him, shaking him.

Suddenly Fishbelly wilted and began to sob.

"Try to think," Jim advised him. "What did Maud say?"

"She said they baited Papa into a trap. . . . Oh, what dumb suckers we was. . . ."

"Then, Fish, let's get to Tyree," Jim said.

"Yeah. Come with me, Jim!"

They dashed out of the shop and jumped into the jalopy and tore off toward Bowman Street. Fishbelly wept as he drove. "I'll kill that chief . . . I'll kill that doctor . . ."

"You're sure that Maud phoned you?" Jim asked.

"Hell, yes. I know her voice in a million," he whimpered.

"Where's Dr. Bruce?"

"I don't know. . . . I let Papa go off like that," he sobbed in a rage of self-accusation. "White folks got next to them niggers and made 'em trick us! I could kill 'em all!"

"Let's see what happened first," Jim advised, touching Fishbelly to calm him. "Did Maud say Tyree was shot badly?"

"She said she didn't know how long he could last. . . ."

Breathing through open lips, Fishbelly roared through streets whose outlines were blurred by his tears. He swung the car into Bowman Street and saw a small knot of people grouped before Maud's house.

"It's true; it's true," he singsonged.

He braked to a halt and leaped from the car; Jim followed.

A white policeman blocked their path.

"Where you niggers going?"

"I'm Tyree's son. He's in there. He's been hurt—"

"And who are you?" the policeman asked Jim.

"He's Papa's embalmer," Fishbelly identified Jim.

"Captain Hunt!" the policeman called.

A thin, blond, red-faced policeman came forward.

"What's up? Who're these niggers?"

"Tyree's son and a nigger who works for 'em. They want to go in," the policeman explained.

Captain Hunt quickly patted Fishbelly's and Jim's pockets to see if they were armed.

"It's better for 'em to be inside than out here," the captain muttered, waving them toward the house.

Fishbelly glanced about and saw the hearse that Tyree had ordered for Maud and he burst into tears anew. He bounded up the steps. The door opened and big, black Maud confronted him, her face wet from weeping.

"Lawd have mercy on you, son!" she screamed and folded him in her arms.

32

With Maud clinging weepingly to him, Fishbelly was scarcely inside the dim hallway when Vera, her eyes swollen from crying, ran to him.

"Fish," she pleaded, "it wasn't our fault! Don't be mad at us!"

"Where Papa?" he asked apprehensively.

"You don't know what we been through today," Maud moaned.

"I want to see Papa," he begged.

"He here," Maud said absent-mindedly, caressing him

clumsily. "Fish, you got to believe us . . . 'Fore Gawd, they put guns on us and *made* us do it."

"*Who?*" he asked puzzled.

"Them *police*," Maud whispered. "They been here all day."

"You know we wouldn't hurt a hair of Tyree's head," Vera babbled through tears.

They moved awkwardly down the dark hallway and he tried to grasp their ravings.

"And don't go blaming Doc," Maud said. "They made 'im do that phoning—"

"Where Doc?" he asked, feeling hot hate.

"They took 'im," Maud whispered. "Gawd knows where . . ."

He understood now that Tyree had been lured, and that Dr. Bruce had not been a part of the plot. Maud paused, pointing to a spot on the wall.

"Look," she said.

"What?" he asked.

"That's where one of the bullets went," Maud said.

"Where Papa?" he wailed, frustrated.

"They shot 'im in my living room," Maud whimpered.

The hysterical women seemed incapable of answering him; he grabbed Maud's shoulders and shook her.

"I want to see Papa!" he shouted.

"He here," Maud said. "Come on."

Her matter-of-fact tone made hope leap into him, but sober sense told him that Maud was more concerned with proving her innocence than with Tyree's condition. A chill settled in his blood as he realized that she had been speaking of Tyree as though he were already dead! He pushed through the door of Maud's bedroom and halted in consternation. Tyree lay wounded in a whore house! He stepped into the dim room, blinking. The shades had been drawn and for a moment he saw nothing. Then he made out Tyree's form upon the bed. He ran forward and fell upon his knees.

"Papa!" he wept, grabbing Tyree's limp, moist hand.

Tyree did not move or answer. Maud switched on a feeble bedside lamp and Fishbelly saw Tyree's tired, sweaty face, which held a cast of green pallor.

"You hurt, Papa? This is Fish . . . Oh Gawd!"

"That you, Fish?" Tyree whispered with sticky throat.

"I'm here, Papa. How you feeling?" he asked, squeezing Tyree's hand as though to impart strength to it.

"They got me," Tyree sighed.

Maud and Vera began a violent weeping.

"Sh," he signaled them. "I want to talk to 'im. . . ." He bent toward Tyree's ear and tried to speak, but his lips would make no sound. Finally he asked: "A doctor see you yit?"

Tyree shook his head and his glazed eyes closed.

"I'll git a doctor," he said, rising with sudden determination.

"Fish, them police won't let nobody in," Maud warned him.

"But he needs a doctor!" Fishbelly railed.

"Aw, Fish, you don't understand nothing!" Maud yelled at him.

"But he's hurt! He's bleeding!" he shouted back.

"Fish, we phoned the hospital and they sent a doctor, but the police wouldn't let 'im in. They say Tyree's armed and dangerous and—"

"This is a plot to let 'im bleed to death!" he screamed. "I want to git a doctor!"

"Naw! You don't understand nothing," Vera wailed. "Them police down there'll shoot you!"

Fishbelly stared. Every move he made to help Tyree was blocked by some dire warning. And he knew that Tyree's bleeding had been arranged by the chief of police.

"BUT PAPA NEEDS A DOCTOR!" he shouted in a frenzy.

As though to shield him from danger, Maud flung herself upon him, sobbing, and he knew that Maud and Vera were taking it for granted that Tyree would die without medical aid, die in accordance to the dictates of white "law"; they were obeying that white "law," though they grieved for those whom that "law" punished. Despair unhinged his joints and he sank upon his knees at the bedside, seizing Tyree's hand.

"Son," Tyree whispered.

"Yeah, Papa."

"They got me . . . I done lost a lot of blood . . . I'm weak . . . I ain't going to git up from this bed . . . So don't make no trouble . . . It won't do no good . . ."

"Did Doc trick you, Papa?"

Tyree closed his eyes as though wordlessly telling him that the manner of his betrayal did not matter. Fishbelly twisted about and stared up into the stricken faces of the two women.

"What happened?" he asked humbly, coherently now.

"Fish, them police marched Doc in here at the point of a gun right after lunch," Maud recited. "They made 'im phone Tyree twice. . . . And they put a gun at Vera's head and told her what to say over the phone. Poor thing passed out when they let her go—"

"Aw, Fish, you don't know," Vera lamented.

The doorbell pealed. Maud looked at Fishbelly and then at Jim. Tyree roused himself, then sank back to the bed.

"Bet that's the chief," Maud murmured. "Mebbe he'll let us git a doctor now. I'll see . . ."

Maud ran out of the room. Fishbelly saw Tyree's parched lips quiver, as though about to speak; the eyelids fluttered and Tyree's head rolled limply to one side.

"What happened?" Fishbelly asked again with blinking eyes.

"They brought Doc in here crying," Vera whispered rapidly, staring, reseeing the scene. "He was sure they was going to kill 'im. They put a gun at his head and made 'im phone Tyree and say Mama was sick and then phone and say Mama was dead and that Tyree had to come and see about Mama's papers. If Doc hadn't done it, they would've shot 'im."

Aw, yes . . . He had wondered at the time about the strange tone of Dr. Bruce's voice! He rubbed his eyes; he and Tyree had expected trouble from one direction and it had come from another.

"They made me do the same," Vera recited. "I was crying and I said I couldn't say it right, but they said me crying made it sound natural. . . . Fish, I was *sick*, I tell you. I passed out and Mama put water on me. . . . Them police kept talking about some checks. . . . A little later Tyree came. They hand-cuffed the doctor and locked him in the kitchen and they made me go to the door. I tried to whisper to Tyree, but he didn't hear me. . . . He asked me: 'Where Maud?' and I said: 'There in the living room. . . .' I didn't say she was dead and I hoped he'd catch on; but he didn't. . . . He opened the living-room door and they shot 'im. They was waiting for 'im in there. Then they left. They waited in the street and said nobody could come into the house till the chief came." Vera finished and bent to Tyree. "Tyree, tell Fish that that's right. . . ."

Tyree's hand moved upon the bedcover and was still.

"How long ago was that?" Jim asked from the doorway.

"More'n a hour ago," Vera mumbled.

"He been bleeding all this time," Fishbelly moaned. He turned to Jim. "If that's the chief, see if he'll let us call a doctor."

"Git Doc Adams," Vera suggested. "He's close by."

"Okay," Jim said and left.

Fishbelly placed his palm upon Tyree's cold and wet forehead, then buried his face in the bedcovers.

"Son, there ain't nothing to be done," Tyree murmured.

A loud, masculine voice sounded in the hallway. Fishbelly rose and ran to the door. Chief of Police Cantley stood grim and rigid before him.

"Well, Fish is here," the chief said.

"Please, sir. Git a doctor for Papa," Fishbelly begged him.

"Now, Fish, calm down and take it easy," the chief warned coldly. "Don't get worked up. That's what happened to Tyree. . . . He wouldn't't've been shot if he hadn't lost his head and threatened to shoot my men, see? Now, cool off. That nigger Jim's gone for a doctor."

Fishbelly wished hotly to dispute the chief; instead he whispered accusingly:

"He's been bleeding for more'n a hour."

"That's his own goddamn fault," the chief charged. "He rushed my men with a gun and they let him have it. We're taking no chances with a wild nigger."

Fishbelly swallowed, knowing that that had not happened. But Tyree had warned him that nothing could be done. Fishbelly sighed, turned, and went back into the room and saw that Tyree had pulled himself up upon an elbow and was staring with red, sunken, and glazed eyes. He knew that Tyree had overheard what the chief had said.

"Son," Tyree whispered thickly. "Come here, close . . ." He fell limply back upon the pillow. "I got to talk to you. . . ."

"Papa," Fishbelly wept.

"Son, don't stir 'em up.... They'll kill you if they think you going to make trouble. Don't accuse 'em of what they done to me."

"Aw, Papa. Don't talk none. A doctor's coming..."

"We won, son!" Tyree whispered fiercely. "I won my fight! They didn't git my money and that chief's done for.... You'll see. I'll be fighting that sonofabitch from my grave! You got to go it alone. They done me in, but forget it. We won! Look at it that way...."

Tyree's panting words had frightened Fishbelly so much that he glanced over his shoulder to see if the chief was near. But only Vera, her eyes tortured and fear-struck, stood in the room. Fishbelly clung to Tyree's hand and became aware of a pool of warm blood in which he was lying. He wept afresh through clenched teeth.

"They letting you bleed on purpose," he sobbed.

"Sh," Tyree cautioned; his strength was ebbing. "I'm trying to save you, son. *Do what they say!* They ain't got no claims against you, 'less you make 'em scared.... You won't ever want for anything.... Look at that letter.... It's my will. Make like you believe what they say. Let this blow over...."

"Yes, Papa."

"The doctor's here," Maud said, entering and leading an old brown man carrying a black bag.

"Who's that there? Old Tyree?" the doctor asked.

"Yeah," Tyree breathed.

"By Gawd, this ain't no place for you," the doctor said, dropping his bag and perching himself upon the edge of the bed. He lifted Tyree's wrist, felt for the pulse; he gazed at his watch, counting heartbeats. He laid the limp arm thoughtfully aside, then unbuttoned Tyree's shirt and peered at the bloody chest. He looked up.

"Call the hospital to come and give a blood transfusion," the doctor ordered.

"I'll phone," Jim said and left the room.

Fishbelly saw the chief looming in the doorway; he knew that the white man was waiting for Tyree to die. A living Tyree was more dangerous than ever, for he could tell how he had been shot. Oh Gawd, how cool, insolent was the man who had ambushed his father! He sighed, wondering why neither he nor Tyree had suspected a trap when Dr. Bruce had phoned. "We was just to tired to think," he told himself.

"Maud, let's git his shirt off," the doctor called.

They cut away Tyree's shirt and Fishbelly saw two gaping chest wounds from which blood seeped with each heartbeat.

"Two bullets hit the lungs," the doctor murmured, swabbing the wounds with gauze to staunch the blood flow. He covered the chest, rose, took Fishbelly gently by the arm and led him from the room.

They met Jim in the hallway.

"They're sending an ambulance," Jim said.

"Okay," Fishbelly breathed.

"Your mama know about this, son?" the doctor asked.

"Nawsir. I just got here."

"Then you better git her here . . ."

"But can't we take Papa to the hospital?" Fishbelly asked. "I don't want Mama coming *here*."

The doctor pursed his lips and stared.

"It's a question of time, son," the doctor said.

Fishbelly lifted his hand to his mouth; he heard Tyree's death sentence. Jim came forward.

"Jim, take my car and git Mama." Fishbelly paused, uncertain, then added, "And git her quick."

"Right," Jim said and left.

Fishbelly re-entered the room behind the doctor and stood beside the bed. He could hear heavy breath coming and going in Tyree's chest now; the eyes were slightly open, but seemingly without sight.

"Fish," Tyree called weakly.

"Yeah, Papa. Right here," he replied, kneeling, bending close.

"I'm tired, son."

Tyree's head moved from left to right, then was still.

"Fish," Tyree whispered again.

"Yeah, Papa," he answered and waited.

Tyree's chest labored. His body seemed to slump. A tremor went over his lips and he gave a slight cough.

"Papa," Fishbelly called softly.

The doctor lifted Tyree's wrist and felt for the pulse. Tyree's eyes fluttered slowly and his lips parted.

"Papa!" Fishbelly called.

The doctor placed Tyree's arm upon the bed, rose, and took the eyeglasses from his nostrils.

"Papa!" Fishbelly wailed.

"He can't hear you now, son," the doctor said gently. "He's gone. . . ."

"Gawd, naw, naw!" Fishbelly screamed.

He stood and looked about wildly. The chief was just inside the doorway.

"Take it easy, Fish," the chief warned. "Control yourself!"

Maud rushed to him and held him in a tight grip.

"You poor child!" she cried.

"You folks ought to git out of here now," the doctor said, extinguishing the dim bedside lamp.

"Come on, Fish," Maud said, trying to lead him forward.

"Leave me alone!" he shouted, struggling to break loose.

"Nigger, get hold of yourself! Don't make trouble!" the chief warned sternly.

Fishbelly looked lingeringly at Tyree's still, black face and let Maud lead him from the room and into the kitchen. He was too stunned to notice much; but when he saw three white policemen standing about, his grief became tinged by wariness. The chief entered.

"Sit 'im down at the table, Maud," the chief ordered.

"Yessir," Maud said.

Fishbelly sat and stared at the roomful of faces.

"Give 'im a cup of coffee," the chief ordered.

"Sure, Chief," Maud said. "Vera, heat some coffee."

"Yessum," Vera hummed, moving to obey.

"Don't want no coffee," Fishbelly muttered.

"Yeah, you do," Maud said heartily, caressing his shoulder.

"Take a cup," the chief said. "Do you good."

He stared sightlessly, feeling that speech was useless. Then, though choked with sorrow, he became aware of Vera's, Maud's, the three policemen's, and the chief's eyes regarding him, not sadly, not angrily, but just coolly, calmly. He bent forward in another fit of weeping; when he lifted his head he saw that Vera had placed the cup of coffee before him.

"Drink it," the chief said gruffly. "I want to talk to you."

Feeling almost hypnotized, he reached his trembling black

318

fingers and lifted the cup to his wet lips and took a sip, then another. The hot fluid steadied him a bit.

"Fish," the chief lectured warningly, "I want you to listen if you ever listened in your life."

"Yessir," he answered automatically.

"What's happened has *nothing* to do with *you*," the chief said. "Understand that and it can mean a lot to you. Your father was a good man. He was my friend. But he lost his head. And when men lose their heads, they pay for it. . . . Fish, take this the *wrong* way and you'll get fouled up for the rest of your life. Take it the *right* way and settle down and you can take up where Tyree left off. . . . Hear me?"

"Yessir," he replied by reflex, understanding nothing.

"Fish, he's talking to you like a father," Maud announced, nodding sagely. "Lissen to 'im."

"Sure," he agreed without meaning to.

"Greenhouse," the chief called.

"Here, sir," a stout policeman answered.

"Tell Fish what happened," the chief ordered.

"Sure, Chief," the policeman said, looking off. "We were here talking to this nigger woman, Maud, when the doorbell rang. That nigger gal, Vera, answered it. That nigger Tyree rushed in with a drawn gun and Gus let him have it, three times. If he hadn't, that nigger would've killed us for sure. . . . We ran out; we didn't know how badly we'd wounded him. He had a gun and we weren't taking any chances, see? And we didn't go back into the house and didn't let anybody else go in till we knew for sure that he was harmless. That's all, Chief."

A block of ice choked Fishbelly; he wanted to rise and scream: "You lying!" But he could hear Tyree's dying admonition: *Make like you believe what they say. . . . You can't do nothing. . . .*

"Did you hear that, Fish?" the chief asked.

"Yessir," he breathed. What was the use? He sighed and pushed the coffee cup away and rested his hot head on the table, unable to stem the spasmodic heaving in his chest. He was not aware when the three policemen had left. He finally looked up and saw the chief still there.

"You'll be all right, Fish," the chief said and left with a

hard smile hovering about his lips.

Maud stood over him compassionately. Vera sat on the opposite side of the table, looking at the floor, her face washed of expression.

"Fish, honey, everything's going to be awright," Maud sang with sad sweetness.

The back door opened and two brown-skinned girls whom Fishbelly knew by sight entered.

"There ain't going to be no business *today* or *tomorrow*," Maud informed them. "Tyree's dead. He was my friend and his body's in the house."

"Yeah. We know," one girl said, slowly masticating a cud of gum by moving a loose lower jaw.

"Tyree was a goddamn good man," the other girl said.

"Now, just watch that lousy, bitchy mouth of yours, you black slut!" Maud chastised the girl with violent moral fervor. *"Death's* in this house!"

"Sorry," the girl mumbled and hung her head.

"Yeah, Tyree was good and straight and you could trust 'im," Maud went on, as though somebody had disputed her. "Fish, be proud of Tyree. Don't never let nobody talk against 'im to you. You take up where he left off. You hear?"

He sighed, sensing meaning in what they were saying. It was more than compassion that they were conveying: it was business! They were declaring him their new boss, pledging allegiance, signaling their willingness to obey. He knew now the purpose of the chief's lecture; it had been telling him to step into Tyree's shoes; it had hinted that if he could blot out of his mind what had happened to Tyree, things could go on as they had before. In honor of Tyree, the renting of bodies had been banned for one night and one day, but the day after tomorrow would be a day of normal trade.

"You know, Fish," Maud said with a twisted, wistful smile, "life's got to go on. Tyree wouldn't want you just to stop like that. He'd be happy if he thought you was carrying on his—"

A soft knock sounded upon the kitchen door.

"Yeah?" Maud called, irritated at the interruption.

The door opened and Jim poked his head through.

"Excuse me," he said, "Fish, your mama's outside."

"Tell her to come in," Fishbelly said.

320

"Well . . . Er . . . Y-you better talk to h-her," Jim said. "You know. . ."

He followed Jim down the crowded hallway in which young black whores, the doctor, the two white-coated interns milled about. There was a drone of low-voiced conversation; the atmosphere was charged with respect for Tyree, but there was no sorrow.

Jim opened the front door and Fishbelly saw, amid a small knot of people gathered at the bottom of the steps, Emma standing beside the two workmen who handled Tyree's hearse.

"Mama!" Fishbelly rushed to her and attempted to embrace her.

"Don't do that, Fish!" Emma checked him curtly, stepping back.

"What's the matter?" he asked, shocked.

"Why Tyree do this to me?" she asked in helpless despair.

"Mama," he chided her, reaching to touch her.

"Naw, Fish!" She stood with more wounded dignity than grief showing in her dry, hot eyes. That her husband had been slain in a whore house was an unforgivable affront.

"Mama, Papa's dead," he said.

"Did that Gloria whore have anything to do with this?" she asked coldly.

He was stupefied. So she knew about Gloria. . . . This was a new Emma, an Emma who had at long last emerged when the shadow of Tyree had gone from her life. Could this defiant woman be the meek creature who had had the habit of effacing herself at the merest inflection of Tyree's strident voice? She had hidden her hate of Tyree so well that he had never suspected it! He might now come under her authority and he was not used to obeying a woman. Fishbelly grew wary; he was young, but he was also very old.

"Don't you want to see Papa 'fore they take 'im away?" he asked, feeling guilty in spite of himself.

Emma shook her head, her wide, sad eyes holding a stony stare.

"Naw. Not in there," she spoke emphatically.

The black onlookers pushed closer, trying to listen. Then Fishbelly saw the towering, pole-like form of Reverend Ragland coming forward and he noticed that Emma allowed him the privilege that she had denied him; she let him slip his arm about her shoulders.

"Gawd be with you, Sister Tucker," Reverend Ragland said.

"Lawd have mercy," Emma whimpered for the first time.

Somebody in the crowd snickered and Fishbelly knew that they were laughing because Tyree had died in a whore house; he stiffened, ready to lash out at anybody daring to belittle his father.

"Son, I'll never set foot in that foul den as long's breath's in my body," Emma declared firmly, clearly. "I married Tyree for better or worse, to stick by 'im in sickness or death; but going amongst whores was no part of the bargain."

"Papa wouldn't've thought you felt like that," he reproved her.

"Son, don't force your mama," Reverend Ragland advised him.

"I ain't *forcing* nobody," he said peevishly.

"What was Tyree doing in there?" Emma asked.

Fishbelly caught a wry smile on the face of a white policeman lurking near. He leaned to Emma and whispered fiercely:

"They trapped 'im in there, Mama. It was the *white* folks."

"What he do?" Emma asked coldly.

He checked an impulse to slap her and turned his head.

"Son, Tyree couldn't hide what he was doing from Gawd," Emma declared. "Gawd brought it all to the light of day."

"Amen," Reverend Ragland intoned.

"Mama, hush! You don't know what you saying!" He defended his father. "It wasn't Papa's fault if—"

"I know right from wrong," Emma said stoutly, disdainful of being overheard. "I'll never go amongst whores, and, if I have anything to say about it, you won't neither no more. I'll see Tyree when they bring 'im to the church."

Dr. Adams came down the steps and doffed his hat to Emma.

"I'm sorry, Mrs. Tucker," he said. "It shouldn't've been like this. . . ." He turned to Fishbelly. "They taking Tyree to the morgue for the inquest. They'll be giving 'im to you sometime tomorrow, mebbe."

The doctor moved away. Fishbelly glanced appealingly at Jim, who stood discreetly apart.

"You coming home now, Fish?" Emma asked him.

"Naw," he said sullenly, perversely, burning with unspeakable resentment. "Got to git to the office and 'tend to things for Papa."

"I'll see Sister Tucker home," Reverend Ragland offered.

"Thank you, Reverend," Jim said.

Fishbelly watched the preacher lead Emma to his car and drive off. He caught Jim staring at him and he gritted his teeth.

"Where's that hearse?" he asked indignantly; he knew where the hearse was, but felt that he had to say something.

"It's here," Jake, the driver, said. "Been here for three hours."

"Don't you go gitting sassy," Fishbelly growled. "I just asked you where it was—"

"It's here and I ain't sassy," Jake muttered defiantly.

"Stop arguing with Fish and do what you're supposed to do," Jim spoke to Jake with kind but firm authority.

Jake shuffled off and Fishbelly seethed with anger.

"Goddamn," he muttered to himself. The white world and the black world had turned suddenly hostile, menacing; Tyree had gone, leaving a vast displacement that he feared that he could never fill. He felt achingly inadequate, and he knew that his mother, Jim, Maud, Reverend Ragland, and the city police were weighing and measuring him, readying themselves for the attack, each from his own angle of selfishness. He made for his car. "I'm off to the office, Jim!"

A white policeman sauntered toward him.

"Don't let 'em break you down, Fish," the policeman said.

"You go to hell," Fishbelly said under his breath and jammed the accelerator to the floor and shot down the street. Tears burned his eyes and he spoke bitterly, forlornly: "If they think they going to push me around, they crazy." His right hand felt inside his coat pocket and touched the thick, white envelope that Tyree had given him that morning. "Papa left me in charge, and, goddammit, I'm going to take charge and all hell ain't going to stop me!"

Part Three

Waking Dream...

The dream's here still: even when I wake it is
Without me, as within me: not imagined . . .

SHAKESPEARE'S *Cymbeline*

33

Bereft of Tyree, hammered at by exhortation, clamored at by counsel from whites and blacks, Fishbelly, captured by nervous anxiety, clung to Tyree's office for shelter. He respected none of the blacks around him and felt that his ideas about what he should or should not do were as good as or better than theirs. Tense and dry-eyed, he sat at Tyree's desk thumbing the parchment pages of the will, finding the provisions somewhat as Tyree had led him to expect. Had he been of age, there would have been no restrictions upon his share of half of the estate; but, since he was a minor, the will gave temporary psychological advantage to Emma who, until the chancery court could remove the disabilities of his minority, was his guardian. Well, he would find a way of handling his mother. In his apparently pliable but hiddenly obstinate manner, he had always had his way with Tyree and he was certain that he could dominate Emma.

Pending probation of the will and under the guidance of Lawyer Heith, Emma would have use of the house and the right to support herself "in a manner consistent with her past needs from the proceeds of the undertaking establishment." And Rex (Fishbelly) Tucker had the right to make all "collections of 'fees,' bills [levies upon whore houses, etc.]." Then: "In matters pertaining to public relations involving both the business establishment and personal affairs [dealings with the police, etc.] Rex (Fishbelly) Tucker would be the sole agent." Further: "The payment of all private debts [bribes] would be handled exclusively by Rex (Fishbelly) Tucker." James Bowers, the embalmer, was recommended as "acting manager in active collaboration with my one and only son, Rex (Fishbelly) Tucker." The sundry blacks inhabiting Tyree's rickety wooden warrens could be "evicted only with the sanction and approval of Rex (Fishbelly) Tucker." (Hence no one but Fishbelly could really evict Maud!) The title of Tyree's car was to be transferred to Rex (Fishbelly) Tucker; and "the white envelope, reposing in my office safe to which Rex (Fishbelly) Tucker alone has the combination, sealed and marked 'Mrs. Gloria Mason,' is to be delivered as soon as possible after my death to the said Mrs. Gloria Mason by my son, Rex (Fishbelly) Tucker, and the said Mrs. Gloria Mason is under no obligation whatsoever to account for its contents to anyone save those whom she deems worthy."

Huh, bet Gloria's gitting a big slice. . . . Fishbelly now knew that Tyree had, long ago, warned Chief Cantley that, in event of his death, his son would be in charge. Yeah, but there was Mama . . . She was sure to evoke an atmosphere of moral prohibition, using God and the guardianship invested in her by the will. But, no matter what Mama did, he had an area of freedom that she could not touch; what he collected from Maud and others like her, after he had split with the police, was his to do with as he liked.

He folded the will, rose, opened the safe, and found that there was three thousand dollars in cash on hand. The bankbook showed a five-thousand-dollar checking account which he could not touch and which he would ask Lawyer Heith to invest immediately. But the three thousand dollars represented the "take" from the Grove, Maud's and others' flats—"fees" that could not be banked without awkwardly disclosing a higher income than he should have had. And Tyree had decreed: "Fish, that's blood money and it comes too goddamn hard to pay tax on. . . . " Thus Fishbelly had access to it for travel, gifts, perishables, clothes, jewelry, etc., in short, on items that would not ostensibly show as wealth.

He took ten fifty-dollar bills and inserted them into his billfold; he was going to outfit himself with a new wardrobe, trade in Tyree's car for a new model, and take his meals at Franklin's Chicken Shack where other Black-Belt businessmen ate. And, by Gawd, he'd be on the lookout for a new girl friend. What the hell . . . Gladys's being dead in the back room did not mean that he had to be alone, and he was certain that Tyree would have approved.

He pocketed the envelope mentioned in the will, put on his coat, got into his car, and rolled to Gloria's house. A faint light glowed at the edges of the living-room window shades and he wondered if she had heard of Tyree's death. He pressed the bell, then thought or imagined that he heard a faint movement within, and, in the same instant, the soft glow of light at the window edge winked out. He waited, certain that he had seen light, had heard sound. Again he pushed the button, but the house remained dark, silent. "Hell, *somebody's* in there...." He rang once more, sending tinny shrills echoing. No response. Worried, he peered around the edge of the porch; the passage leading to the back yard was empty. Returning to the door, he rang again.

"Gloria!" he called.

He heard a slight creak. Was she afraid? He held his thumb against the button; if she were in, he was determined to get her to the door. "Aw hell," he cursed and turned to leave. Then he saw the window shade flutter. "Goddammit, she's *in* there!" He put his mouth to the door panel. "GLORIA! It's Fish!" Footsteps sounded; the door cracked open; he glimpsed Gloria's face.

"Come in, quick," she said, widening the door and bolting it behind him.

"Why you acting so scared?" he asked her.

She did not answer as she passed him in the darkness.

"Who is it?" a husky masculine voice asked.

"It's Fish," Gloria whispered. "Light the candle."

A second later a dim illumination defined a man's blurred silhouette framed in the hallway's back door.

"Hi, Fish," the man called in a friendly whisper.

Fishbelly stepped into the kitchen and saw Dr. Bruce standing in the flickering candlelight.

"Good Gawd, Doc! What happened to you?"

"Fish, I'm damned glad you came," Dr. Bruce said. "I was afraid to phone you. Look, I'm sorry as hell about Tyree."

Fishbelly stared at the doctor, who looked ten years older. His left cheek was disfigured by a huge, dark lump. His eyes were puffed, bloodshot; he was in his shirt sleeves and the handle of an automatic stuck out of his belt. Two suitcases stood in the center of the floor.

"Papa's dead," Fishbelly mumbled, looking off. "They shot 'im."

"Fish, I want you to know what happened. . . . I don't know what you've heard, but they made me do it. It's hard for a man to confess that he was a dirty rag in other people's hands. . . . The police picked me up at my office after lunch and took me to Maud's. They put a gun at my temple and made me phone Tyree twice. If I hadn't done it, they'd have shot me. Then they handcuffed me and dragged me to the woods to kill me. . . ." Dr. Bruce's voice broke and his body shook. "Fish, I'm just flesh and blood; I'm not brave. I was scared. I swallowed my pride and got down on my knees and cried like a baby. I offered them five thousand dollars and swore I'd leave and never come back if they'd let me go. They were greedy; they told me to get the money and bring it to them at Maud's tonight. I cleaned out my bank account and came here to hide. My car's hidden in Gloria's back yard. I'm driving to Memphis—" The doctor clapped his hand over his mouth and stared at Fishbelly, then wailed: "You want to kill me? Then kill me. I won't resist . . . You feel I killed your Papa—"

"Naw, Doc," Fishbelly whimpered.

"We're leaving *together*, Fish," Gloria said meekly.

Fishbelly shut his eyes. Tyree was dead. Gladys was dead. And now Gloria and Dr. Bruce were leaving.

"Fish, you're young," Dr. Bruce said. "Your life's before you. *Boy, leave! You're doomed here.*"

"Fish, for God's sake, believe what he says," Gloria begged. "Go while you can! Go back to school and give yourself a chance. Fish, don't let them make you follow in Tyree's footsteps. . . . *Don't do it!* You can't win! You'll live in a trap they can close on you any time!"

"Where you-all going?" he asked them.

"Up North," Dr. Bruce said.

He liked these two and their pending flight saddened him. Gloria and the doctor were teaming up; he was alone. . . . Yes; he would leave; but not right now. He needed more money for that.

"I see what you mean," he said soberly. "But I got a lot of things to do first." He slumped into a chair. "But how you going to git away, Doc? They must be watching for you."

"Yes; the police know my car," Dr. Bruce said. "But we have to take a chance."

Fishbelly brooded. Yeah; they'd be caught as sure as hell. . . .

"Look, I'll put you-all in a hearse and git you safe to Memphis," he offered.

"Oh, Fish." Gloria moaned her gratitude.

"I wish you would," Dr. Bruce said.

"What you taking with you?" he asked them.

"Two suitcases and our lives," Gloria said, blinking back tears. "Fish, don't think hard of me for leaving. But Tyree's dead and I'm all alone."

Fishbelly extended the thick envelope to her.

"Papa left this for you."

She sat, opened the envelope, and extracted a batch of paper and a sheaf of bills. She turned her back, bent forward, and wept. She straightened, nervously balling the envelope and cramming it clumsily into her bosom.

"He shouldn't've done it," she sobbed. "I told him—"

"Papa did what he had to do, Gloria," he said.

"Poor Tyree," she whimpered. "He had a bitter pride. I know he died feeling that he'd done right."

"That's just what he said," Fishbelly told her.

"Where's that hearse, Fish?" Dr. Bruce asked nervously. "If the police catch me, they'll kill me."

"I'll phone," Fishbelly said, rising.

"Fish," Gloria said, turning tear-drenched eyes upon him, "why did this have to happen?"

"Gloria, Papa went like a man," Fishbelly told her. "He told me to carry on. And I'm doing that—"

"No!" Gloria wailed, rising, embracing him. "Fish, you don't understand! Listen, the police know that I knew Tyree —all about his business. They'll think that I could be made to give evidence against them. That's why I'm leaving. . . . *I'm scared, Fish!* AND YOU OUGHT TO BE SCARED TOO!"

"I can't run away and leave everything like that," he said.

"But, Fish, you're in *danger!*" Gloria's eyes were wide.

"Aw, naw," he sang softly. "That chief of police told me—"

"You *talked* to him?" Dr. Bruce asked, amazed.

"Sure. I just left 'im," Fishbelly told them.

Gloria and Dr. Bruce stared at each other.

"Sit down, Fish," Gloria said, pushing him into a chair. "Fish, that Cantley *killed* your father."

"Yeah. I know," he mumbled.

"Then how on earth can you work for him?" she asked.

"Ain't nothing else to do," he drawled. "It ain't for always, Gloria."

Gloria stared at him as tears rolled down her cheeks.

"Fish, why do you talk like that?" she asked in the sudden, cool tone of a scolding schoolteacher.

"Like what?" he demanded, blinking.

" 'Ain't nothing else to do,' " she mimicked Fishbelly's flat drawl. " 'It ain't for always, Gloria.' "

Fishbelly was thunderstruck; anger rose in his throat. This goddamn woman was making fun of him!

"I don't care," Fishbelly growled, feeling friendless, abandoned.

"Weren't you in second-year high school when you left?" she asked.

"Yeah. Sure," he muttered.

"Then you can speak correctly, can't you?"

"Sure. I studied English," he said, wanting to slap her.

"Fish, do me a favor."

"Sure. What, Gloria?" He could not look at her.

"Repeat what you said a moment ago in a correct manner."

"Oh," he breathed, looking at the floor, feeling insulted to his depths. "I done forgot."

"You said: 'Ain't nothing else to do. It ain't for always, Gloria. . . .' "

"There is nothing else to do. It's not for always, Gloria," Fishbelly said slowly, clearly, his eyes averted.

"There! You can talk correctly!" Gloria exclaimed with a sweet smile and patted his hand.

"Sure I can," he said stoutly, his teeth on edge.

"Then why *don't* you?" she asked harshly.

"Hell, I just want to talk like everybody else," he argued, slipping back into his flat drawl. "I'm in business, Gloria. If I put on airs, talking like school, folks wouldn't want to trust me no more."

"I understand." Gloria sighed. "You're not angry with me, are you, Fish? Oh, I've never had a chance to talk to you. . . . Fish, don't work in this awful mess. *Go away!* I say this because I care."

"I see what you mean," he said grudgingly.

"Make something out of yourself," Gloria pleaded. "I'm talking like this because I may never have another chance to talk to you. Don't, *don't* be foolishly proud and fight against odds. Tyree was fitted for this racial war, but you are *not.* Dr. Bruce is going. I'm going. We *know.*"

"I'm gitting out," he promised.

"Make it *soon,*" Dr. Bruce said, nodding gravely. "Now, what about that hearse? It'd save us."

"I'll phone," Fishbelly said.

An hour later he helped Gloria and Dr. Bruce into the rear of the hearse that stood in the passage by the side of the house. A silver curl of ghostly moon arched over chimney tops, shedding a dim blue radiance through warm rainy air.

"Lay flat on the floor till you git out of town," he advised them.

"Fish," Dr. Bruce said, extending his hand, "I'm a man. I'm a doctor. But I'm ashamed."

"I know, Doc," Fishbelly said, gripping the palm.

"Fish," Gloria called him.

She bent forward and crushed him to her. He smelled her hair and felt the bundle of papers that she had stuffed into her bosom.

"Leave," she whispered with despairing passion.

"She's right, Fish," Dr. Bruce said.

"Good-by," Fishbelly said.

"So long, Fish," Dr. Bruce said.

"Good-by, darling." Gloria's voice choked. "Think of yourself."

He shut the rear door of the hearse and felt that he was cutting off a part of his life. He walked to the driver who sat up front.

"Jake, don't stop till you git to Memphis," he ordered.

"Right," Jake grunted.

He watched the hearse back out and he followed it to the street and saw it roll off and turn a distant corner under the

sheen of a gaslight and vanish. "She's gone," he told himself.
He got into his jalopy and leaned his head against the steering
wheel and stared with tired eyes into the night. "One of these
days I'll be running too," he mumbled and turned the key in
the ignition.

34

Arriving home, he was surprised to find lights blazing in the
living room and Jim and Emma waiting for him.

"Son, you must be tired," Emma murmured consolingly.

"Fish, Mrs. Tucker asked me over to talk to you," Jim
began awkwardly but affably.

Fishbelly was on guard; their attitude was too friendly to
bode him any good. He sat and cocked his head.

"What's on your mind, Jim?" he asked tersely.

"Fish, we want you to do something for us," Jim said.

"What's that?"

"Go back to school," Emma cried. "Son, you gitting *lost!* I
know. . . . You got money. You want to run around. . . . But
wait a little."

Emma's enlisting Jim as an ally irked him and he scowled.
He had abandoned school with Tyree's consent and he was
resolved not to fuss again with books. The prime sense he had
of himself resided in his compulsion to keep a rendezvous
with a beckoning fantasy whose origin he did not know, but
whose content formed the secret basis of his motives. Though
steeped in vague terror, he felt fated to grapple with that white
world that had slain Tyree and he intuitively regarded as his
enemy anything that stayed him from that encounter.

"Jim," he said quietly, "Papa told me what to do."

"Do you want to end up like your papa?" Jim asked softly.

"Papa gave you your daily bread and you low-rating 'im

'fore he's cold!" Fishbelly accused.

"Fish," Emma appealed, "don't deal with white folks like Tyree did."

"Mama, I know what I'm doing!"

"Did Tyree know what he was doing?" Jim asked sarcastically.

"Don't talk about Papa like that," Fishbelly snarled.

"I'm talking for your own good," Jim said. "Fish, times are changing. I'll handle the 'shop' for you, like I did for Tyree. Go to school and learn how the world's run. Then you're your own man, free, independent—"

"That's Gawd's way, son," Emma put in.

"Lissen . . ." Fishbelly pulled out Tyree's will and waved it. "Papa's will told me what to do."

"May I see it, Fish?" Jim asked.

"Sure."

Jim took the will and thrust it under a cone of light falling from a floor lamp and read it. Emma peered at the pages over Jim's shoulder. Fishbelly waited, smoking nervously.

"The court's putting Fish in full charge," Jim said with a sigh.

"But he's only a child!" Emma exclaimed.

"Mrs. Tucker, you're Fish's guardian, but the chancery court will back Fish's say-so in everyday business matters. I daresay Lawyer Heith is filing the papers right off. And that gives Fish the right to deal with Maud Williams," Jim explained.

"Tyree was a fool to do that," Emma declared.

"Papa ain't buried yit and you calling him a fool!" Fishbelly tried to shame her.

"I'm going to git that will changed," Emma vowed grimly.

"Ha, ha!" Fishbelly laughed jeeringly. "Mama, this ain't your business. If I don't collect, that chief's going to want to know who's stopping me."

"It's dangerous for you to meddle in *that*," Jim told Emma.

"But what can I do?" Emma asked.

"Fish, you're going to collect from Maud?" Jim asked.

"Jim, that's my business," Fishbelly snapped.

"You going to finish up like Tyree," Emma predicted, "lying dead with bullets in you! Lissen, son. We know more'n you; we older'n you. White folks'll let you be a cat's-paw only when they can crush you."

He resented their trying to make him identify himself with them.

"Ain't nobody going to crush me," he stated sullenly.

"Do you trust those white policemen?" Jim asked.

"I don't trust nobody," Fishbelly said.

Emma rose, her eyes blazing anger.

"Gawd's done made up my mind," she announced. "I'm your mama. I gave life to you. I nursed you, fed you, tried to teach you right from wrong. As long's you under this roof, you ain't having no truck with that Maud Williams!"

He was fighting the black world for his right to deal with the white world because of what that white world had done to him. Jim and Emma were demanding that he merge his hopes with their lives, lives which he despised because they were couched in fear and shame. He was with the enemy against his own people, yet he hated that enemy because he saw himself and his people as that enemy saw them.

"Mama, don't talk like that!" he cried.

"I do talk like that. I don't care what's in Tyree's will!"

"Papa told me to collect! I ain't responsible to you!" he shouted. "You want me to go?"

"If you don't obey, then go!" Emma yelled.

"Okay. I'll go! I'll show you!" He moved defiantly into the hallway.

"Fish!" Jim called, rising and following him.

"Keep the hell out of this, Jim!" he screamed. "Your job's in the 'shop'!"

"I know, Fish," Jim said. "You're boss. But I'm older than—"

"Let 'im go!" Emma cried. "You can't teach a fool nothing. He saw how Tyree died, but it don't mean a thing to 'im!"

"I'm gitting out *now, tonight!*" he announced, resolving to break clean. "We got a flat on Bowman Street and I'm moving into it!"

"Suit yourself!" Emma returned. "You ain't going to make my home no headquarters for no whore houses!"

"I'm gitting my clothes," Fishbelly growled.

"Don't touch a thing in this house 'less I say so," Emma

raged with irrational moral fervor.

"You mean I can't git my clothes?" he asked, astounded.

"I run my house like I want to." Emma was adamant.

"See you at the office in the morning, Jim," Fishbelly said.

"Wait, Fish," Jim called. "I'm coming with you."

"I said I'd see you at the office in the morning!" Fishbelly screamed and went through the front door and slammed it so hard that the upper pane shattered. He was trembling with rage, yet there was a quiet elation in him. He had made the first step toward meeting a future that lured him as much as it frightened.

35

In the usual sense of mourning, Fishbelly could not grieve for Tyree, nor could he wholeheartedly hate the men who had slain him. His apprehension of Tyree's life had been predicated too much upon reflections of white attitudes and hence had been too objective to have been based upon love alone. He had felt toward Tyree a most profound compassion, for he knew at first hand how hopeless Tyree's life had been in comparison with the white lives above him. He could no more forget Tyree than he could forget himself, for, in a sense, Tyree was that shadow of himself cast by a white world he loved because of its power and hated because of its condemnation of him. Thus, though he could not grieve for Tyree, his living had to become a kind of grieving monument to his memory and a reluctant tribute to his slayers.

Fishbelly felt each nuanced ripple in the currents of Black-Belt life with his blood. Racial conditioning told him when to act and when to play possum. He made no effort to see Chief of Police Cantley; he knew that when the white man was ready, he would come to him. The grand jury still had not met and he could only guess that Cantley had somehow seized those ill-fated canceled checks. He often thought of McWilliams, but had heard nothing from him. And since McWilliams had failed Tyree, he thought it best not to try to see him. Diligently, he collected the police tributes and divided the loot into scrupulously equal portions: white Caesar's and his own. Maud was overjoyed.

"Fish, since Tyree's gone, I been worried about being raided," she declared. "But now you taking the money and I know I'm safe. The best way to do things is the right way. Ain't nothing better'n cash on the line."

"Don't you worry none," he told her.

"Fish?" she called him gently.

"What, Maud?"

"You ain't mad at me and Vera, is you? You know in your heart we didn't have nothing to do with what happened to Tyree, don't you?"

"Yeah. I know," he mumbled shamefacedly.

"Fish, we black. We ain't got no rights."

"I understand, Maud," he told her with a sigh.

He understood, but he did not respect her. He understood, but he did not respect himself.

"It's always the *man*, hunh?" Maud asked him, laughing dolefully.

"Yeah."

"What *man*?" Maud asked teasingly.

"The *white* man," Fishbelly mumbled, grinning ruefully.

They were silent, seeing themselves as they imagined the white world saw them, their humble hearts touched with shame.

After consulting Lawyer Heith regarding the probation of the will and other current matters, Fishbelly made his first important decision: he ordered Tyree's funeral to be held in common with that of the victims of the Grove fire, a gesture that mollified the reactions of the Black Belt toward the Tucker family. Emma learned of the funeral arrangements too late to make any effective protest. Fishbelly told her coldly:

"That's the way Papa would've wanted it."

Black-Belt gossip made Fishbelly feel that he had been right:

338

"Tyree didn't run off like that doctor; he was sorry for what happened. He just made a mistake and anybody can do that. . . ."

"And them goddamn white folks killed 'im; if they killed 'im, it was 'cause they was scared of 'im. . . ."

"Lawd," a fat black woman exclaimed one morning as Fishbelly collected her rent, "that Tyree was a dog! He was more'n a dog; he was a tiger! He turned these white folks upside down!"

In a Black-Belt bar a drunken Negro crooned:

"That city-hall gang's a bitch! Look what happened to Tyree, the biggest nigger around here. . . . Look what happened to Dr. Bruce. . . . Go against that city hall and you either *dead* or *missing!*"

Fats Brown, whom Fishbelly, Dr. Bruce, and Tyree had wanted to make a scapegoat, was dead and his body unclaimed in the town morgue. Race-conscious Maybelle, shocked and sobered by the loss of so many of her whoring cronies, cut short the renting of her body, joined a store-front church, and planned to become a female evangelist to warn the world of evil. Having fled and his whereabouts unknown, Dr. Bruce had been indicted in absentia by the grand jury for "criminal negligence and multiple manslaughter"; in fact, all the blame had been heaped upon him. Gloria was missing and no one, not even the police, had asked about her; Fishbelly had driven slowly past her house twice, noticing milk bottles and newspapers collecting upon her porch.

Because of the sensational highjacking of Court Clerk Albert Davis and the furious uproar that followed in the press, the mayor had to resign "in interests of public order." The town council had elected, upon the mayor's secret instructions, one of his personal friends to serve as his temporary successor until elections could be held. Police Chief Cantley, whom everybody suspected but against whom nothing could be proved, also resigned, declaring: "Though there is not one iota of evidence against me, I gladly relinquish my office in view of the perturbed state of the public mind. Police work is not basically my line. I'd like to run for governor." A personal friend of Cantley had been appointed in his place.

All all-white coroner's jury found that Tyree's death had

been caused by his "threatening police officers with a gun." Some guessed that Tyree had been killed to keep him from "appearing before the grand jury." Others hinted that he had suddenly gone "Communist and had begun to demand social equality." Whispers said the Tyree had been caught "sleeping with the nigger mistress of the police chief and had been shot to death in a nigger whore house." Cynics said that Tyree had been holding out on police graft and that the police had "rubbed 'im out." Only among the bitter, closemouthed prostitutes and gamblers of the Black-Belt underworld was it known that Tyree had been ambushed; but nowhere was it known that the real motive for his slaying had been the damning canceled checks that Tyree had given to McWilliams that frantic night. Only Fishbelly knew that and his lips, on the dying advice of Tyree, were sealed in self-defense.

Fishbelly took over Tyree's car and then, prompted by a vague but potent instinct, amassed a varied wardrobe: ten tweed suits, five pairs of shoes, twenty shirts, ties, socks— enough clothes, as Jim put it, "to last you five years."

"And whose money is this?" Fishbelly demanded.

"It's yours," Jim admitted.

"Awright, then. Let me alone," Fishbelly requested.

On the thundery, rainy afternoon of the mass funeral, black families came into town not only in cars, but even in buggies and wagons from the surrounding countryside. On Black-Belt streets crepe-wearing men, women, and children were conspicuous. The Grove fire and the personalities connected with it were a topic for all tongues. And the Grove, its burned-out hulk, blackened beams and rafters, its buckled tin roof glaring a rusty red in the hot sun, became a local curiosity about which people clustered and spoke in awed tones. Old folks swore that they could hear, late at night, the screams and moans of the dying; wide-eyed black children told tall tales of seeing ghosts waltzing together after sundown. So many memento hunters probed about the Grove's gutted premises that the police erected signs proclaiming: KEEP OUT.

Though the victims of the fire had been of many religious denominations, Clintonville's black pastors had agreed that Reverend Ragland would deliver the funeral oration—most of the fire victims having been working-class members of his church. For three days before the funeral Reverend Ragland secluded himself to compose his collective sermon, and, when he did deliver it with stomping feet, gasps, hymns, tears, and heart-rending gestures over the forty-two fire dead and over Tyree's body, which reposed in an ornate, bronze coffin, it was declared the most memorable peroration ever heard in Black-Belt memory.

Fishbelly, garbed in black, sat beside crepe-veiled Emma in the first row of the church, his lackluster eyes gazing alternately at Tyree's ebony profile and the whitish, shy features of Gladys, whose coffin, at Fishbelly's request, stood beside that of Tyree's.

"Who that white-looking gal in that coffin by Tyree?" Emma asked.

"Friend of mine," he said.

"What become of that Gloria hussy?" Emma asked.

"Don't know," he mumbled a sullen lie.

And Emma did not mention Tyree again during the ceremony. The gray summer afternoon was stiflingly hot and the myriad banks of floral wreaths, covering the front wall of the church as Tyree had wanted, emitted odors of such cloying sweetness that Fishbelly felt that he would suffocate. The white-robed, fifty-member choir was arranged just beneath the brass pipes of the church organ. Five thousand or more black brothers and sisters and their children jammed the edifice. They were silent, sad, nervous; now and then quiet weeping could be heard. The public stood in the rear of the church, in the aisles, on the steps, outside upon the sidewalk, and even in the middle of the street, necessitating the erection of road barriers to divert traffic. Policemen strolled casually, their white skins showing distinctly amidst the sea of black faces.

Maud, Vera, and the twenty-odd black girls who did their days' work at night in the Bowman Street flat were present. Sam was there. Fishbelly had no chance to say more than a hurried hello to him, for he had been swamped helping Jim with a multitude of details. Gladys's mother, a bent, tan-colored woman holding a two-year-old girl in her arms, came to Fishbelly and introduced herself, pointed to Gladys, then stooped and kissed his hands as she shed hot tears. Fishbelly stared at the infant's pale, yellow face and round, fixed eyes,

eyes that seemed to have never held even a hint of joy. Gladys's mother backed away, weeping.

"Who was that?" Jim asked.

"Gladys's mother and Gladys's little girl," Fishbelly said.

"Good Lord," Jim said. "What'll happen to that little tot?"

The forty-three coffins were lined, oblong box beside oblong box, from one end of a row of stained-glass windows to another, right across the entire width of the church, ranging in horseshoe shape just below and in front of the pulpit, the heads of the coffins pointing toward the pulpit and their ends facing the audience. The pulpit was as yet empty. Fishbelly knew from long observance that Reverend Ragland would enter at any moment from a small door on the left. From the ceiling's vault six huge electric fans hung, their wooden blades spinning slowly in the moist hot air.

Aggie West, church organist, walked with a too-careful manner upon the platform, seated himself at the organ keys, and rubbed his black fingers together. Suddenly Aggie wet his lips with his tongue, bent forward, touched the organ keys, and there rolled forth a deep-voweled hymn of melancholy sound in which the audience and choir joined:

> "Sunset and evening star,
>   And one clear call for me!
> And may there be no moaning of the bar
>   When I put out to sea.
> But such a tide as moving seems asleep,
>   Too full for sound and foam,
> When that which drew forth out the boundless deep
>   Turns again home."

Amid the singing and the organ's roll a few black women gave forth crying sobs.

> "Twilight and evening bell,
>   And after that the dark!
> And may there be no sadness of farewell
>   When I embark;
> For though from out our bourne of time and place
>   The flood may bear me far,

> *I hope to see my Pilot face to face*
> *When I have crossed the bar. . . ."*

Deep-bassed "Amens!" rose and mingled with screams; several black women were escorted by ushers out of the church. Fishbelly saw Aggie dab his balled handkerchief delicately to his damp brow, close his eyes, and bend again to the organ keys:

> *"One sweetly solemn thought*
> *Comes to me o'er and o'er:*
> *I'm nearer my home today*
> *Then I have ever been before. . . ."*

Captured by liquid sorrow and dying organ peals, Fishbelly stared sightlessly, then started nervously: there was Reverend Ragland, tall, black, gaunt of face, red of eye, his expression seemingly furiously belligerent. He lifted his two long arms into the air and stretched them dramatically wide. Silence gripped the black brothers and sisters. Reverend opened his mouth and emitted a rich, carrying baritone:

"Death!"

He moved agilely to the left of the pulpit and bellowed:

"Death!"

He glided to the right of the pulpit and leaned over the upturned faces in the coffins and screamed:

"DEATH!"

Reverend now strode briskly to the pulpit and lifted his eyes to the soaring ceiling and announced in slow, ringing tones of sad amazement.

"Death's been a-riding through this land! I say Death's been a-riding through this old world! Lawd Gawd Awmighty, Death's been a-riding through our hearts! And now you just look, *look,* LOOK—!" His long, skinny, moving finger pointed to the cold, still black faces in the curving array of coffins. "LOOK, I say, at what Death's done done! Death's been a-riding and He done left His calling cards! Death's been a-riding and He done left His fingerprints! Lawd Gawd Awmighty, I can hear old Death's rustling black robe stealing softly away!"

"Gloooory!" an old black woman screamed.

"Yes, yes, yes," a man agreed with trembling joy.

The electrified, sorrow-gripped audience leaned forward, holding its breath. Reverend turned and looked at the solemn-faced choir, nodded, and launched into a song in which the choir joined:

> *"God moves in a mysterious way*
> *His wonders to perform!*
> *He plants His footsteps in the sea*
> *And rides upon the storm.*
>
> *"Ye fearful saints, fresh courage take!*
> *The clouds ye so much dread*
> *Are big with mercy, and shall break*
> *In blessings on your head."*

Reverend signaled for the end of the song as cries swept the church:

"Tell it! Tell it!"

"Look down on us, Lawd!"

"Mercy, mercy, have mercy, Jesus!"

"Who dares," the reverend asked in a wild cry, "say 'No!' when the old Angel of Death calls? You can be in your grocery store ringing up a hundred-dollar sale on the cash register and Death'll call and you'll have to drop the sale and go! You can be a-riding around in your Buick and Death'll call and you have to go! You about to git out of your bed to go to your job and old Death'll call and you'll have to go! Mebbe you building a house and done called in the mason and the carpenter and then old Death calls and you have to go! 'Cause Death's asking you to come into your *last* home! Mebbe you planning on gitting married and your wonderful bride's a-waiting on the altar and you on your way and old Death calls: 'Young man, I got another bride for you! Your *last* bride!'"

"Lawd, it's true!"

"Gawd's Master!"

"Be with us, Lawd!"

"Don't matter if you white, black, rich, poor, man, woman, or child, Death can knock on your door," the reverend whispered hoarsely. Then he crooned sadistically: "You dancing to sweet music, cheek to cheek with your sweetheart on the dance floor, and Death'll call you in a low voice: 'Come and waltz with me!'"

"Susie! My poor little Susie!" Teddy's mother wailed.

A rhythmic swaying of bodies and a nodding of heads filled the church. Fishbelly sat stolid; he had heard funeral sermons all his life and he could, if pushed, have preached one himself; but this sermon was different. Tyree lay before him, forever gone, and now there was no one between him and that hostile world of whites.

"Now, don't be a fool and go blaming Death!" Reverend warmed up to his theme. "Death ain't nothing but Gawd's *special* messenger! His Pullman car is the cyclone! His airplane is the wind! His streetcar is the thunderbolt! There ain't but one thing you can say when Death taps on your door: May the Good Lawd have mercy on my soul!"

"Be with us, Lawd!"

"It's Gawd's business!"

Reverend signaled for a song and lifted his voice with that of the choir and the organ's booming peals:

> *"We give Thee but Thine own,*
> *Whate'er the gift may be:*
> *All that we have is Thine alone,*
> *A trust, O Lord; from Thee. . . ."*

Reverend waved for silence, advanced to the edge of the platform, stared down at the coffins filled with mute black faces, and spoke in quiet, matter-of-fact tones:

"Some folks in this town's talking about trying to find out who's guilty of causing these folks to die. They even talking about sending folks to jail." Looking out over the sea of black faces, he gave forth an ironic, hollow laugh. "Ha, ha! Don't them fools know that no man can kill 'less Gawd wants it done? Not a sparrow flies 'less Gawd lets it fly. Not a raindrop falls 'less Gawd says: 'Yes, rain, you can fall!' You think you so powerful that you can kill another man? You a fool! You kill and call it killing, but you only putting a name on something that Gawd's done done! When Gawd's a-working, you shut your big mouth and keep still! When Gawd calls you, it's for your own good! Oh, if we could, just for one second, see through Gawd's eyes, how foolish and ignorant we would know we is!"

Agitation swept the audience. Reverend stared down into the cold, dead, black faces while voices chanted dolefully:

"It's the truth!"

"Lawd, save us!"

"Right there 'fore my eyes is one of the men who owned the Grove dance hall!" Reverend pointed to Tyree, then to another coffin. "And there's a man who worked for 'im! Death trapped the boss and the worker!" Reverend pointed to yet another black face. "There's a man who blew a horn for the girls and boys to dance!" He turned, pointing to a batch of rather plain coffins. "There's the boys and girls who did the dancing!" Reverend walked to his pulpit and banged his fist down upon the open leaves of the Bible and demanded: "Now, who figgered all that out? Who understands the Divine Plan of Justice? On the Fourth of July, Gawd reared back and said:

"'Death, come here!'"

"Wonderful Jesus!"

"'Death, go down to that place called *America!*'"

"Lissen to the Lawd!"

"'Death, find that state they call *Mississippi!*'"

"Gawd's a-talking!"

"'Death, go to a town called *Clintonville!*'"

"Lawd, Lawd, Lawd!"

"'Death, find me a man called *Tyree Tucker!*'"

"Gawd's King!"

"'Death, I want you to tell Tyree Tucker that I want to see 'im!'"

"Have mercy, Jesus!"

A black woman gave a prolonged scream and began leaping about; ushers rushed to her and led her bounding body out of the church.

"'Death, tell Tyree that I don't care *what* he's doing, he's got to come home!'"

Fishbelly felt an involuntary chill go over him. Emma clutched his arm and bent forward and sobbed. Reverend stepped back as he impersonated God; his face registered

346

shock, surprise. Still speaking for God, he said:

"'What you saying to me, Death? You say Tyree's busy? You say he's got some mighty important men to see? Death, lissen to me. This is Gawd Awmighty talking! Now, you just go right back down to America, to Mississippi, to Clintonville, and tell that Tyree Tucker to stop being sassy! Tell 'im to drop everything this *minute!* 'Cause His Maker wants to see 'im!'"

"Just lissen to Gawd!"

Reverend walked angrily from one end of the pulpit to the other, speaking in a low, intimate, furious tone:

"Imagine telling Gawd that Tyree's busy!" He paused, stooped, pointed his right hand to the vault of the church and screamed: "When Gawd calls you, you have to answer whether you want to or *not!*"

"Amen!"

"Glory, glory, glory!"

Reverend walked back to his pulpit, took off his eyeglasses, stared down into the cold black faces and spoke to them tenderly:

"And you-all answered 'Im, didn't you? You obeyed 'Im, didn't you?" Reverend glared balefully at his audience and asked tersely: "Who out there'll dare say that these folks standing this minute 'fore Gawd's throne's sorry? What you know about Gawd's business? *Nothing!* When Gawd speaks, lift your eyes and sing:

> "*When I survey that wondrous cross*
> *On which the Prince of Glory died,*
> *My richest gain I count but loss*
> *And pour contempt on all my pride....*"

"Hallelujah!"

"Holy, holy, holy!"

He returned to the edge of the platform, mopped his dripping brow with a white handkerchief, and spoke scoldingly to his hearers:

"You can have your say.... Gawd'll let you.... He's patient, all-knowing...." Then, thunderously: "You can talk your old big black mouth off, He don't care none! Huh!

There's folks who think they tough . . . they hard . . . they done killed and cheated and lied and ain't scared of nothing. . . ." Reverend advanced to the extreme tip of the platform and looked down into the thin black face of a young man in a plain coffin and said: "Charlie Moore, they tell me you done been in a lot of jails. They say you done faced a lot of judges in the courtrooms. . . . Well, Charlie, you in your *last* courtroom now!" His voice grew lyrically sadistic: "You now facing the Most Powerful Judge of 'em *all!* Tell me, Charlie, who's going to be your lawyer now?"

"Tell 'im, Preacher!"

Reverend bent forward and whispered hoarsely:

"Lissen, Charlie, I'm going to sing you a song:

> *"There's a land that is fairer than day*
> *And by faith we can see it afar;*
> *For the Father waits over the way,*
> *To prepare us a dwelling place there.*
>
> *"In the sweet by and by*
> *We shall meet on that beautiful shore. . . ."*

"Gawd's done said it!"

"He's preparing a place for us!"

Reverend flicked sweat from his brow and returned to the attack:

"Who would've said a month ago that I'd be standing here saying the last words over forty-three of Gawd's children? Who dares say how many of us'll be here a year from now? Your future's in the hollow of Gawd's hands! Now, there's men in this town who say that they run it!" Reverend's voice became scathing: "Let 'em go on thinking they run it! The men who run this town can be white as snow, but *we* know who's boss! GAWD'S THE BOSS! And He's more powerful than the president, the governor, the mayor, the chief of police . . ."

Fishbelly felt a gentle tug upon his sleeve. He glanced around. Jim bent to him with a letter and whispered:

"Jake brought this. It's special delivery, registered."

"Thanks, Jim." Fishbelly took the thick envelope and pocketed it. He looked at Reverend Ragland, but his attention was centered upon the letter. He stole a glance at the envelope and saw his name written in bold, feminine characters. The return address read: Lucy Crane. But he knew no Lucy Crane. It was postmarked Detroit. And he knew no one in Detroit. . . . Distracted, he rose, tiptoed down the aisle, and went out of a side door and into the men's washroom. It was empty. He ripped an edge from the envelope and drew forth a thick batch of paper. There was a letter which began:

Darling Fish:

I know that you will be surprised to hear from me. I had thought of writing you for a long time; finally I made up my mind to tell you something that might be of use to you. I've kept the enclosed canceled checks until now, for I was unable to decide what to do with them. Tyree sent them to me and asked me to do with them what I thought best. I'm now no longer in Clintonville and I cannot talk with you. So you must use your own best judgment as to what to do with these. These were the checks (I don't think you knew it!) that were in the letter you brought to my house the night that the doctor and I left for Memphis. . . .

He paused, frowning; he turned the page and saw "GLORIA." Good Gawd! What checks was Gloria talking about? He read on:

Tyree pretended to you, to Dr. Bruce, and to the chief of police that he had destroyed these checks; he also told McWilliams that he had burned them. But Tyree trusted nobody, as you can see. So, Fish, if the checks that Tyree gave McWilliams have not done what Tyree wanted, then here is further proof. Need I say more?

But, Fish, for God's sake, be careful. If you feel in any way uneasy about using these checks, then burn them. Remember that Tyree lost his life because of them.

349

I've not put my correct return address upon this envelope, for the doctor has to be careful. He has found a job, but it is far below his capacity. You know that there's an indictment hanging over his head and he dares not practice medicine. And, Fish, tell no one where we are or that you've heard from us.

I think of you often. I feel guilty for having left, but if I had remained, there was nothing that I could have done. Try and go back to school. Don't play the game that Tyree was playing; it's too dangerous. All my love.

Fishbelly peered over his shoulder as his throat tightened with fear. He turned over a check and saw "GERALD CANTLEY." Oh Gawd! Tyree lay dead for having given checks like these to McWilliams, and now he held them in his hands! He could be killed if Cantley merely suspected that he had these checks. . . . He had to hide them *now!* No; his leaving the church would excite comment. He'd hide them right after the service.

He stood staring, feeling that Tyree was still alive and extending out of the void a hand of protection over him. *Protection?* These checks could be his death warrant. And how Tyree had fooled them all! Gloria was right; Tyree had never trusted anybody. Even when dying, he had been "acting," playing a game of duplicity. Tyree had said that he had burned the canceled checks dealing with the *first* five years of his bribing the chief of police, but he had hidden that batch and had given McWilliams the batch of checks dealing with the *last* five years of bribery! Fishbelly now recalled how strangely Gloria had acted with the letter he had taken to her that night; she had turned her back to read it, then had hurriedly crammed it into her bosom and had begged him to flee! Ah, now he understood what Tyree had meant when, dying, he had said that he would fight them even from his grave.

He pocketed the letter and went upon the front steps of the church; four white policemen stood casually at the edge of the dense crowd. Jesus . . . His knees shook. No; he had to be calm, had to control himself. He went back into the church and sat beside Emma and tried to listen to the torrid words leaping about him. Reverend was giving vent to a singsong shout punctuated by deep explosions of breath and a stomping of his right foot upon the floor.

". . . there ain't no death *hunh bomp* we all a part of the Living Gawd *hunh bomp* and Gawd said: 'I go to prepare a place for you! *hunh bomp* 'If it wasn't so I wouldn't've told you!' *hunh bomp* we all go to sleep in Gawd, but we all rise again *hunh bomp* and no man can kill you . . ."

Fishbelly shuddered. Yes, the police could kill him if they knew he had those checks.

". . . Gawd sees all things *hunh bomp* His Eyes are every-where *hunh bomp* His Eyes spy out your smallest secret thought *hunh bomp* . . ."

It was not from God, but from the spying eyes of white men that he was trying to hide his thoughts. His prayers were not asking to go to heaven, but to escape the white man. He sweated fear as the church rocked to the reverend's words. Tyree had used those checks as a weapon against the chief of police and had lost. He stared at Tyree's still, black profile and bent forward and wept. Emma's arm settled about his shoulders.

"You feel Gawd, don't you, son?" she asked in a whisper.

He tensed, wanting to scream: "Naw, it ain't Gawd I feel; it's the white man!" But he held himself in.

He could take no more of it; he rose, tiptoed again to the men's room, struck a match and held Gloria's letter and enve-lope over the flame and watched the paper burn, turn black, crisp, and fall into a urinal. Where could he hide the checks? An impulse cried: Burn them! Naw! Tyree's dying wish had been that these checks should protect him. But how? He slipped the shoe off his right foot and inserted the checks flat under his sole, just as Zeke had hidden the photos of the naked white people that day. When he got home he would hide them. His hands trembled; it seemed that he could taste death on his tongue, feel it in the pores of his skin. The choir was singing and he knew that the sermon was over. He would leave Jim to look after Emma and take care of things at the graveyard and he would go straight home.

He remained in the men's room until he heard the benedic-tion being said, then went to the back of the church and saw the congregation filing slowly past the coffins to take a last look at the departed. When he reached the vestibule and people were beginning to leave, a hand grabbed his arm. He whirled. It was Maud.

"Fish, I got to talk to you," Maud whispered tensely.

"Hi, Maud. What's the matter?"

"I got something to tell you, *quick*," she said.

"Sure. In the morning at the office—"

"Naw, Fish. It's got to be *now*."

"I'm going home. You want to come along?"

"Yeah, Fish," Maud said eagerly.

He felt uncomfortable having Maud with him while those checks were in his shoe. He led her to his car, then instructed Jim to take over. He drove away with Maud, looking wonderingly at the faces of the white police.

"What's up, Maud?" They were out of sight of the church now.

"Let's git to your place first," she said distrustfully.

"Okay," he mumbled, worried.

Did she know? Naw; impossible. . . . He sped to his flat and ushered her into his rooms, rooms that he had planned for Gladys. Maud plumped her vast body into an armchair.

"Fish," she said, getting at once to the point, "there's something *wrong!*"

"What you mean?"

"Last night Cantley was by my flat."

"What he want?"

"He asked me about *you*, Fish," Maud explained. "He wanted to know if you was fighting 'im. He asked about some checks that Tyree left—"

"What?" Fishbelly backed away from her and settled upon the edge of his bed. *"What* checks?"

"Lawd, I don't know," Maud said.

That almost forgotten curtain of billowing blackness swooped toward his eyes: he was losing the sense of his legs, his arms, his head. . . . *Naw!* He could not pass out now, not with those checks in his shoe. The checks had come into his possession barely an hour ago, and Cantley was asking about them. And Cantley had had Tyree killed because of them. . . . *How in hell had he found out?*

"Maud, I don't know nothing about no checks," he lied.

"Fish, that white man's scared to death of you," Maud warned.

"But why?" he demanded, "acting" now, trying to make Maud believe him, for he knew that Cantley would surely talk to her.

"Don't know," she said. "But he's scared and I'm scared of scared white folks."

"Maud, just what Cantley ask you?" Fishbelly asked.

"Cantley said Tyree double-crossed 'im by giving some checks to McWilliams. And he asked if you was going to do the same."

"But I don't know nothing about no checks!" Fishbelly cried. "I thought the chief wanted me to work with 'im." He swallowed. "There ain't no checks."

"If what you say is true, then you better see that white man and git 'im straightened out," Maud urged him.

Yes; Cantley had sent her to sound him out. He was in danger!

"Maud, I'm doing what Papa said," Fishbelly told her. "Don't the chief want to do business?"

"I'll tell Cantley." Maud's tone was neutral.

She did not believe him and he knew that if Maud had to choose between him and Cantley, she would choose the white man.

"Maud, tell the chief I'm with 'im," he spoke fervently. "I'll do what he says, so help me Gawd!"

"I'll tell 'im." Maud sounded a little more believing. She sighed, rose. "I'll try to calm Cantley down..." She stood admiring his little flat. "Nice place you got here, Fish."

"I planned it for Gladys," he told her.

"Poor boy," Maud murmured. "You lonely, hunh?" She was suddenly all business. "Want me to send you a nice gal? I got a new one in from Jackson, sleek as a cat—"

"Naw, Maud. I ain't in the mood."

"I know. You grieving... I'm for you, Fish," she said. "'By now."

"See you, Maud."

Maud left. He stood in the middle of the room, brooding. He had to hide those checks before the ceremonies at the graveyard were over. He looked about. Yeah, he could slip them in between the wood and the glass of the mirror. Naw, Cantley would find them. It'd be better to dig a hole and bury 'em. Naw; it was daylight and he would have to wait until dark to do that. Ah yes; slit a hole in the mattress and push them inside it. Aw hell; he had heard of that too often. Goddamn, he had to burn these checks; there was nothing else to do. He was not tenaciously tricky like Tyree. He locked the door, took the checks from his shoe, and went to the fireplace. He heard somebody running up the stairs. He froze, his heart thumping. The footsteps continued on up to the third floor and he sighed, scratched a match to flame and was about to hold the checks over it when his eyes caught sight of a brick—one end of which was loose—embedded in the chimney's left wall. Aw, pry out that brick, cement the checks *behind* it and blacken the cement with soot! *Gawd, yes; that was it!* He needed some cement and a trowel. There was a hardware store downstairs.

He pushed the checks into his pocket and ran from the room. Five minutes later, he was buying cement, a trowel, a putty knife, oilcloth and asbestos. Back in his room, he spread an old newspaper over the chimney hearth and hacked the cement from around the brick and pried it out. He then wrapped the checks in oilcloth and asbestos and stuffed the packet into the hole. Using the trowel, he broke off a part of the brick so that it would fit smoothly, be in line with the chimney wall. He filled a basin with cement and poured in water and worked it into a soft mass. Scooping up palmfuls of cement, he plugged the crevices, plying the putty knife. He paused, staring down at the spread newspaper, his lips hanging open. The photo of a smiling white woman looked up at him and he recalled the awful day of terror when he had swallowed a white woman's face. . . . All of his life he had been hiding something from white people! And now he was concealing evidence of the guilt of whites; the whites were guilty and he was guilty because he knew that they were guilty, and he had to hide his knowledge of their guilt, or they would detect what he knew and kill him. Sweat fell like tears from his face upon the image of the smiling white woman. . . . After he had cemented the brick, he blackened the wet cement with soot. There it was; no one could tell that the brick had been disturbed. He rolled up the newspaper, blotting out the white woman's hauntingly seductive face, took the bundle to a garbage can in the hallway and pushed it far down, under reeking refuse. Then he washed and dried his hands.

He was as damp as though he had been out in a rain. He changed his clothes, then, for the first time since Tyree's death, took a stiff drink to steady his nerves. He remembered Gloria's telling him: "Go away, Fish. Leave before it's too late. . . ." Yeah, I'll leave as soon's I git enough money. . . .

A soft knock came upon the door. Was that Cantley? He glanced at the fireplace; the bricks looked natural. Yes, it was no doubt Cantley, for only the police, Emma, and Maud knew where he lived.

"Who there?" he called.

"McWilliams," came the reply.

Fishbelly stared, hesitating, then opened the door. Tall, lean, McWilliams loomed before him.

"Hello, Fish," McWilliams said.

"Hi, Mr. McWilliams," Fishbelly hummed.

"May I come in?" McWilliams asked. "I must talk to you."

"Oh," Fishbelly mumbled. "Yessir. Come on in."

McWilliams entered slowly, looking around, then sat in the armchair. Fishbelly had never before received a white visitor and he did not know how to act.

"Smoke, Fish?"

"Er . . . Yessir," he mumbled.

McWilliams poked his pack at Fishbelly, then held a match flame for his and Fishbelly's cigarettes.

"I've been wanting to talk to you for some time," McWilliams began. "Then something came up this morning that made it necessary for me to see you at once."

"Yessir," Fishbelly said, glancing at the soot-blackened brick in the chimney. No expression showed on his face; his deadpan was reflex when he was facing a white man.

"Fish, I failed Tyree," McWilliams spoke huskily.

"Papa was expecting what happened," Fishbelly said flatly.

McWilliams stared at him for a long moment.

"Life's not entirely hopeless," McWilliams said softly.

"Don't know," Fishbelly breathed.

"Have the police been in touch with you?"

"Yessir . . . Nawsir . . . Just Maud—that woman who has a flat."

"What did she want?"

"She worried," Fishbelly explained. "Seems the police been asking questions about me. . . ."

"Fish, I got your address from your mother," McWilliams explained. "Now, Fish, Tyree's dead and the doctor's gone. So it's only you who are left. I owe you an explanation. I gave those canceled checks to Albert Davis, a trusted man, to take to the foreman of the grand jury. You heard what happened. We are certain that the chief of police's men waylaid Davis and got those checks, but we can't prove a thing. And we are certain that Tyree's being killed was because Cantley saw those checks. Now, maybe you think I'm pretty dumb. But no one counted on anybody's being so criminally bold as to go to such lengths. . . . I've known the foreman of that grand jury since childhood and he's an honest man. But the evidence never got to him. I know that no excuse can bring Tyree back. I can't say that I agreed with Tyree; he had a rather strange outlook. But he was fighting in his way. . . . I tried to fight Tyree's enemies and I lost. But there's one thing you must know. The men who killed Tyree are *my* enemies too. You understand?"

Fishbelly blinked. It was a new thought and he did not know what to think. White men fought white men for black people's sake?

"I-I g-guess I see what you mean," he stammered.

"Let's be honest, Fish. You don't quite get me, do you?"

"Don't know, sir."

"Fish, one thing only stands Cantley off me . . . There are people who will fight for me. Cantley may kill me too; I don't know. But I'm going to keep fighting for decency in this town as long as I live. Now, Fish, I want to warn you. Cantley got hold of a copy of Tyree's will. Do you know that?"

"Nawsir."

"Wasn't there something in that will about a letter that you were to take to a woman named Gloria Mason?"

"Yessir. I took it."

"Do you know what was in that letter? Where's Mrs. Mason?"

"Don't know, sir. Don't think she's in town, sir."

"Cantley thinks that the Mason woman has those checks, that they were in that letter—"

"Papa's dead . . . The doctor's gone . . . Why folks want to know about them checks now?" Fishbelly asked.

"Fish, under the statute of limitations, you cannot prosecute a man for a crime like bribery after five years have passed," McWilliams explained. "Now, Cantley swore to the grand jury that he'd never accepted any money from Tyree. Now, if it can be proved that he did accept money, then he can be indicted for *perjury*. . . . The grand jury asked him if he had accepted money from Tyree during 1942, 1943, 1944, 1945, and 1946. Those canceled checks prove that he *did* accept money during the years that he swore that he *didn't*. Cantley can get two years in jail for each time he lied. He can go to jail for ten years if—"

"It's just like it was before?" Fishbelly asked tensely.

"Yes. The canceled checks are still good."

Ought he dig those checks out of that chimney and give them to McWilliams? Naw. Tyree had done that and now Tyree was dead. If he gave up those checks, he, too, had a good chance to be killed.

"Can you get in touch with the Mason woman?" McWilliams asked.

"I don't know nothing," Fishbelly mumbled nervously.

"Fish, I want to ask you a question," McWilliams said, frowning, staring at the floor.

"Yessir," he said uneasily.

"Are you still collecting for the police?"

Fishbelly's teeth clamped tight. Would McWilliams make trouble for him? If he did, then Cantley would protect him. . . .

"I'm doing what Papa told me to do." He found a compromise.

"They killed Tyree and you still work for them?"

Why lie? McWilliams knew what he was doing. . . .

"Yessir," he confessed finally, realizing for the first time that he did not know whose side he was on. He was on nobody's side. He was for himself because he felt he had to be. He was black.

"Don't do it, Fish," McWilliams begged him. "It's no good for *you,* for *your people,* for the *town*—"

"The police run it," Fishbelly said.

"And the police are *wrong.* Is it only money you want?"

"Nawsir."

"Then *stop!* You're not going to starve. You're too young to be in that foul business."

"I'm planning to leave later when—"

"There may be no 'later' for you. The police have you in their power and they can do with you what they want.... Well, I guess this is too big for you," McWilliams said and sighed.

"Can I stop?" Fishbelly asked suddenly, his eyes wide with fear.

"That's a good question," McWilliams said. "If you really want to stop, perhaps we can find a way. We'll talk about this later.... Fish, I came to tell you that the police are watching you—"

"But there *ain't* no checks!" he wailed, his eyes hot with the threat of tears.

"I'll keep you informed about what I know," McWilliams said, rising. "Good-by, Fish."

"Good-by, sir."

McWilliams left. Fishbelly was torn by conflicting feelings. He was convinced that McWilliams was honest, or he would not have come to see him. An impulse made him run to the door and open it.

McWilliams was halfway down the stairs. He paused and looked up.

"I want to speak to you, sir," Fishbelly said.

McWilliams returned, entered the room, and shut the door. "Yes?"

"You see ... I don't know how to say it ... B-but ... Look, suppose there's a hundred white men lined up there on the sidewalk—"

"You'd want to shoot them all, wouldn't you?" McWilliams asked, smiling wryly.

Fishbelly's eyes stared, glassy from shock.

"Nawsir! That ain't what I meant."

"You hate white people, don't you, Fish?"

"Nawsir. I don't hate 'em. Just scared of 'em, sir."

"That's a way of hating, Fish."

"But I can't *help* it. You'd be scared too, if you was in my place."

"Maybe I would," McWilliams said slowly.

"There's *ten* of 'em for every *one* of us. They armed and every word they say makes you know they hate you. . . . But I didn't start out hating 'em. Honest."

"When do you hate them, then?"

"When they try to kill me, I can't help but hate 'em." He avoided looking at the white man.

"You called me to tell me something," McWilliams said.

"Well, I was saying that if there was one hundred white men lined up out there on the sidewalk, there ain't no way in the world for me to know which one's honest and which one's crooked. They ain't got signs on 'em and they all look alike, see?"

"I got your point," McWilliams said.

"But I believe you honest," Fishbelly told him at last.

"It's not until *now* that you believe that I'm honest?" McWilliams asked, amazement showing in his eyes.

"Well, if you want me to be honest with you, yessir."

"Well, Fish, I'm kind of glad to know that, at least."

"How can I tell if a white man hates niggers or is willing to treat 'em fair?"

McWilliams gazed at Fishbelly for a long time.

"Fish, did Tyree trust me?"

"Nawsir," Fishbelly told him frankly.

"Why?"

"He didn't know you, sir."

"Then why did he bring me those checks?"

"Papa was gambling," Fishbelly explained softly, swallowing. "He wouldn't't've been surprised if you'd turned 'em in."

"Do you trust me, Fish?"

"I think you honest," Fishbelly said.

"Why do you say it that way?"

"All you can git out of coming to me is trouble; and, if you willing to risk that, then you honest."

"But do you *trust* me?"

Fishbelly did not answer; he looked toward the fireplace.

"Maybe you can't trust honesty if it's white?"

"We black folks live like we have to." Fishbelly still evaded.

"All right, Fish. I'm going. Thank you for being honest with me. Here. Let me shake your hand—"

"Sir?"

"I want to shake hands with you."

"With me?"

"Yes." McWilliams extended his hand.

"But how come?"

"Because you told me the truth."

Fishbelly stared at the white man, then slowly extended his hand.

"Good-by, Fish."

"Good-by, sir."

When the door was shut Fishbelly stood and stared in agony. Ought he call that white man back and give him those checks? No; he could not do that, not yet; he did not have that much trust in anybody in the world, not yet. He lay on his bed and an impulse made him bury his face in his pillow and sob.

36

Next morning he feared what the day would bring. As he dressed, he debated: Ought he flee? Or ought he stay and try to fit in? When he reached the "shop," Jim met him at the door.

"Cantley's in there," Jim whispered.

"Yeah?"

He steeled himself and pushed into the office. Cantley, dressed in civilian clothes, sat resting the weight of his body on a chair's hind legs, his hatbrim snapped over his right eye, a cigarette slanting from his lips. He was whittling a match-stick with a pocketknife blade; when he saw Fishbelly, he clicked the knife shut and lifted his huge body to a standing position, his gray eyes searching Fishbelly's face.

Fishbelly felt a sense of defenselessness enter him; he could not determine what kind of reality he reflected in the white man's mind.

"Good morning, Chief," he hummed.

"You're late." Cantley spoke without smiling and pocketed the knife.

"Yessir. That funeral kind of took it out of me." He exhibited a placating smile.

"Fish, I want to talk to you," Cantley said.

"Yessir."

Realizing that the very images of his mind, if known, could merit the penalty of death, he fought off the feeling that the white man could read his thoughts.

"You saw McWilliams last night, didn't you?" Cantley asked.

"Oh, yessir." He tried to disclaim responsibility for the white man's visit. "Last night there was a knock on my door —and there he was.... Chief, that Mr. McWilliams got a crazy idea that Papa left some canceled checks around. But he wrong, Chief. I told 'im so. The only checks was them that Papa gave to 'im. There *ain't* no more."

Cantley licked his lips and came close to Fishbelly.

"Are you sure of that, Fish?"

"Yessir. Papa said so."

"That doesn't mean a goddman thing!" Cantley spat. "Tyree was a much sharper nigger than I thought. He lied to me with tears in his eyes. He fooled me once, but I'll be goddamned if he'll fool me again—even if he's dead. Damn nigger should've known I was watching 'im.... He swore he'd burned all of those checks except the one I found in his safe, then he handed 'em over to that damned McWilliams. Now, Fish, if there are any more checks around, I want 'em, and I want 'em goddamned quick!"

Instinctively he knew that a mere denial was not enough; it was only by lying convincingly about those checks that he could save his life. Those checks were a weapon, but a weapon that he was afraid to use, yet he did not want to surrender them.

"There ain't no more checks, Chief!" His voice quivered. "I swear there ain't! I'm working for you. I don't want no trouble. I'll do what you tell me!" Shame made him bend forward and sob.

"Awright," Cantley drawled. "That rain in your goddamned face ain't helping me any."

The note of relaxation in the white man's voice eased his tension. Yes, in spite of himself, he was "acting" as Tyree had "acted," and he hated it, and he hated the man who was making him do it.

"Fish, didn't you take a letter to that Gloria Mason woman?"

"Yessir."

"What was in it?"

"Don't know, sir."

"You broke your goddamn neck getting that letter to her the very night Tyree died. Why?"

"I read the will and did what Papa said."

"Was it a *thick* letter?"

"Don't know, sir." Fishbelly blinked, simulating simple-mindedness.

"Hell, Fish, didn't you have that letter in your hand? *Think!*"

"Yessir. I had the letter, but—"

"Was it *thick* or *thin?*"

"There was something in it, yessir. But it wasn't *so* thick—"

"*That* thick?" Cantley asked, measuring distance on his finger.

"N-nawsir, not *t-that* thick. . . ."

"Then *how thick?*" Cantley demanded, his gray eyes unblinkingly on Fishbelly's face.

"Don't know, sir. Some money was in it—"

"How many pages did that letter have?"

"Lot of pages . . . Chief, that letter *wasn't* thick like them checks Papa gave Mr. McWilliams—"

"Don't get smart, nigger. You're lying to me!"

362

"Nawsir! I *ain't* lying!"

"Where's that Gloria woman?"

"Don't know, Chief. Mr. McWilliams said she was gone."

"Didn't you know that doctor's car's standing in her back yard?"

"Nawsir. I ain't been by there," he lied.

"Did McWilliams say where she was?"

"Nawsir. He asked *me* where she went. I told 'im I didn't know, Chief. Just like I'm telling you."

"When you took that letter to Gloria, you saw her read it?"

"Yessir. She was in the kitchen, fixing coffee."

"What did she take out of it?"

"Some money, bills . . . Then the letter."

"Where was she when she did that?"

"On the other side of the kitchen, sir. I think . . ."

"Just you two were there?"

"Yessir," he lied, seeing the doctor and Gloria and realizing that there had been no coffee.

"What were you doing when she read the letter?"

"Drinking coffee—"

"So you didn't see her all the time, hunh?"

"N-nawsir," he said haltingly. "I wasn't watching her, see?"

"Did you see her hide anything?"

"Nawsir, I wasn't thinking of that—"

"I know you weren't. But *think,* Fish."

"She was crying, sir. Kind of bent over, like—"

"Did she have her purse in her lap?"

"Don't know, sir. Her back was turned, see? And she put the letter and the money in her bosom and—"

"Aw, in her bosom . . . Then it could've been the checks, hunh?" Cantley asked him eagerly.

"Yessir," he drawled, simulating confusion. "But I didn't see 'em."

"Hmmnn." Cantley was silent, thoughtful. "You haven't heard from her?"

"Nawsir," he said with dry throat.

"How long did Tyree know that woman?"

"Don't know, Chief."

"You're Tyree's son and you expect me to believe that?"

"Chief"—Fishbelly begged to be believed—"I was in

363

school till just a few months ago." His tears began to flow again.

"Dry up that goddamn water," Cantley ordered.

During the silence Fishbelly sensed that it was time to go on the offensive.

"Chief, if I knew where there was any checks, I swear to Gawd, I'd tell you. I don't want no trouble."

"Tyree said the same goddamn thing!"

"But *I* mean it, Chief! Tell me what to do!"

"Get me those goddamn checks!" Cantley shouted in a frenzy.

"But I don't know nothing about 'em!"

"Fish," Cantley's voice dropped low, "do you know how Tyree was killed?"

Fishbelly blinked. He knew, but he knew that he was not supposed to know.

"Resisting arrest," he mumbled, looking off.

"Do you *believe* that?"

"That's what you told me, Chief."

"I asked you do you *believe* it?"

"Yessir," he breathed; the lid on his right eye throbbed.

"Fish, I'm going to give it to you cold and straight. You're working for a syndicate. Tyree was killed because he broke his word. Luckily, no real harm's been done. Tyree's giving those checks to McWilliams didn't mean a damn thing. But Tyree was a smart nigger. He left something with Gloria and we don't know what it was. Then Gloria left *suddenly*—for some reason. I figure it this way. Either she ran off because she had those checks and was scared, or maybe that grand jury's got her hidden somewhere, pumping her, see? If that's true, then we're in the soup. Now, Fish, you're mad about what happened to Tyree—"

"Nawsir!" he shouted, his lower lip quivering.

"It'd be natural. Niggers can get mad—"

"I ain't mad at nobody, Chief!" he screamed, seeking refuge in the folds of prejudice in the white man's mind.

"Take it easy, boy," Cantley mumbled. "Fish?"

"Yessir?"

"I don't know you like I knew Tyree," Cantley said.

A wave of fear rolled through him. The white man was now

trying to peer into his secret heart.

"You *know* me, Chief," he sobbed a passionate lie.

"No, I *don't*," Cantley was emphatic. "You're one of these new kind of niggers. I don't understand you."

"You *know* me! You *know* me!" he panted.

"Then what kind of nigger are you? You say you're loyal, but maybe you're aching to kill me right now, hunh?"

"Nawsir!" He rose and ran to Cantley and Cantley grabbed him in his collar.

"If you hated me, could you tell me to my face, nigger?" Cantley hissed through clenched teeth.

Fishbelly's eyes were some two inches from the white man's, staring unblinkingly. Had he spoken, he would have told the truth and he would have been killed. He swallowed and stared. Cantley flung him to the floor and stood staring at the shaking body.

"I don't know what the hell to do with you," Cantley muttered, turning toward the door. He paused, spun, and glared at the boy.

"I want to work, Chief," Fishbelly sobbed, not looking up.

"I don't *trust* you!"

"You *can* trust me, Chief!"

"Then tell me about those checks!"

"I don't know! I don't know!" he screamed, seeing the fireplace in which he had cemented the checks.

Cantley stared silently. Fishbelly sensed that the white man was about to come to a decision, a decision that he feared. He had to distract the white man.

"Chief?"

"Yeah?"

"I got your money here."

"Oh yeah. I forgot . . ."

Fishbelly rose, opened the safe, and took out a packet of green bills.

"There, Chief. Fifty-fifty, like Papa said."

Cantley jammed the packet into his pocket. A void hung between them. Fishbelly could think of nothing to say and he feared Cantley would speak again. He studied the white man, then said softly:

"You can look in the safe, if you want to, Chief."

"Goddamn you, you black sonafabitch! I wish to hell I could *believe* you!" Cantley screamed. "But you *can't* tell me the truth!" Cantley gasped for breath, then screamed again. "Hell, no! You can't speak what you feel!" Cantley's anger turned against himself. "I swear to God, I don't know what we can do with you niggers.... We make you scared of us, and then we ask you to tell us the truth. And you *can't!* Goddammit, you *can't!*" Cantley whirled and went through the door, slamming it shut so violently that a deafening bang filled the room.

Fishbelly's lips moved soundlessly, then he blinked and slumped into a chair and stared sightlessly into space.

37

All that afternoon he sat in the office, brooding. There was but one solution: he had to flee before Cantley killed him. Go North and go to school? Naw; the idea of school filled him with distaste; he had grown far beyond the attitude needed to study and he no longer possessed that stance of emotional dependence that would have made of him a good student.

Go North and open a business? But, not being of age, he would have to have an adult partner; and he needed capital. Or, if only he knew where Gloria and Dr. Bruce were! But they were lost in the darkness of a great and distant city.

Well, he would leave, but he would first amass a sum of money from the "fees." Meanwhile, he would try to allay Cantley's fears by placing himself in Cantley's hands. Could he calm Cantley by surrendering, say, half of the checks and keeping the other half as a defensive weapon? No! To tell Cantley now that he had sobbed out a lie would make Cantley kill him on the spot.

Six o'clock found him still anchored in indecision. He had

had no appetite for lunch and the muscles of his stomach fluttered as though a flock of sparrows were beating their wings against his insides. He took a long drink of whiskey; it helped. . . . A knock upon the door made him start.

"Yeah?" he called.

The door opened and Emma, tight-lipped and dour, advanced upon him. Jim followed.

"Fish, I want to talk to you," Emma said.

"Sit down, Mama," he said, looking inquiringly at Jim.

"If you don't mind, Fish . . . Mrs. Tucker asked me to be here."

"Sure," Fishbelly mumbled irritably.

Emma sat while Jim perched himself upon an edge of the desk. Fishbelly was nettled. Yeah, they going to hammer at me. . . .

"Fish," Jim began softly. "I couldn't help overhearing what you and Cantley said this morning—"

"So what?" Fishbelly snapped, enraged that Jim had heard his pleading.

"Well, something's happened that ties in with it," Jim said. "The police searched your mother's house from top to bottom today."

"Really, Mama?" Fishbelly asked; he was shaken.

"Yeah, son. They was looking for some checks, they said."

Fishbelly hid his face in his hands. First, Maud had warned him. Then McWilliams. Then Cantley. And now Emma and Jim were offering him proof. He was sorry for what had happened to Emma and, because he was helpless to do anything about it, he grew angry and ashamed. For a moment his confidence fled him.

"What you want me to do?" he asked Emma quietly.

"Son, don't *provoke* these white folks," she begged.

"I ain't provoking nobody!" he yelled at her. "I'm *black!* That's all the provoking I'm doing!"

"Give them white folks what they looking for," Emma pleaded. "Cut loose from what Tyree was doing. It ain't for me I'm asking. It's for *you,* your *life!*"

"She's right, Fish," Jim concurred emphatically.

"But I ain't got what they looking for!" he cried.

"Then leave," Jim advised. "They're after you and they're

not going to stop until they *kill* you."

"Nobody's going to kill me," he stated with assumed bravado.

"You don't know what these white folks'll do," Emma said.

"Mama, I ain't the cause of this!" he shouted. His nerves gave way and he slapped the top of the desk with his open palm. "You living on what Papa slaved for, and you telling me to run and leave it! I *won't!*"

"We know, we know, Fish," Jim said soothingly. "But the white folks think you're after them and they're scared. Look, you're not like Tyree. You say the right words, but they don't believe you."

Fishbelly stared about distractedly, feeling that Emma and Jim were siding with the whites against him, wanting him to extol the omnipotence of the white world. And he was certain that if Emma knew that he had those checks, she would demand more adamantly than even Cantley that he give them up.

"Son, save yourself 'fore it's too late," Emma whined.

He studied her, weighing his chances in terms of cold cash.

"If I go, how much income from the 'shop' will you give me?" he asked her.

Emma glanced at Jim and Jim was embarrassed.

"Thirty dollars a week," Emma mumbled.

"Naw!" Fishbelly snorted.

"Forty." Jim bargained for his absence.

"Naw!" Fishbelly was scornful.

"Well, fifty dollars then," Emma conceded in a tone of finality.

"Hell, naw! I stay *here!* I can't live on that!"

He had three thousand dollars in cash and they were offering him fifty dollars a week! He could pick up that much money from the whores on a Saturday night without half trying.

"If you went to school, I'd make it more," Emma hinted.

"I ain't going to school," he said flatly.

"You are *spoiled!*" Jim exploded.

"You can't say that to me," Fishbelly rasped at Jim.

"*I* say it!" Emma shouted. "Tyree *spoiled* you—"

"Then I'll *stay* spoiled," Fishbelly retorted. "Now, leave me alone!"

"Awright, son," Emma sighed. "Have it your way. Gawd knows, I done my part." She rose, her eyes wet and red. "Lawd have mercy on you. . . ." She turned to Jim. "Take me home, Jim."

"All right, Mrs. Tucker," Jim said.

Fishbelly watched them leave with a cold face; then he banged his fists upon the desk in a frenzy of rage and despair. "What they think I am?" He reached for the bottle and took a pull, then pushed it into his pocket. He locked the "shop" and drove to his flat. He fell upon his bed and stared vacantly at the ceiling. There was no way out. "Okay. I'm licked," he said aloud. "I'll take the cash in the safe, take the fifty dollars a week Mama wants to give me, and leave—leave in the morning. I can't stay here with every hand against me." He closed his eyes and whimpered: "Papa, there ain't nothing else for me to do! You left something that's *marked* me! It's like it's in my *blood!* I can't live with it here!" He opened his eyes, but he did not see the room; he shouted: "My papa, my papa's papa, and my papa's papa's papa, look what you done to me!"

His resolution to flee lifted some of his tension. For the first time since Tyree's death, he thought of the girls at Maud's. Maybe he ought to go to Maud's and drench his senses in forgetfulness, drown out this damned panic. . . . No. He did not want to go; dread had washed him clean of sensuality.

38

He drifted to sleep. How long he slept, he never knew. He was awakened by a timid knocking upon his door. He opened his eyes and stared. His light was still burning. Had there been a knock? Then the knock came again, this time louder.

"Yeah?" he mumbled and rolled from bed and stood on sleep-numbed slightly drunken legs. He ambled to the door and opened it; he felt that he was still asleep. A young blond white girl stood looking at him, her lips parted.

"Are you Fish?" she asked in a whisper.

He did not answer. In fact, he had not really heard her; he did not really believe that he saw her. He was staring at an image in a waking dream. A sensation of fear flashed warningly through him, but he resisted the signal, for he was convinced that the girl he saw was not real, that her white face, her blond hair, and her slightly parted red lips were delusions.

"Aren't you Fish?" the girl demanded again, a little louder this time.

"Hunh?" he grunted, taking a backward step.

The girl advanced into his room and closed the door, not shutting it completely, leaving it a bit ajar.

"You are Fish, aren't you?" she insisted. "Maud told me to come here—"

"Maud?" he echoed her stupidly.

"Yes. Listen...I'm in trouble...You must hide me." She spoke rapidly now. She shut the door completely, making the lock click. "The police—"

"Naw!" The word burst out of him before he knew it. The clicking of that door had awakened him fully. *This was no dream!* Fear seethed in him. The white girl's face floating before his eyes was a dream image that had concerned him almost all of his life, something that he feared so deeply that he had had to choke it down in him, out of sight, out of his mind, something toward which he had always been drawn with a sense of dread. He opened his lips to speak, but could make no sound.

"What're you afraid of?" the girl asked him and smiled.

It was her smile that did it. Had she not smiled, he would have stood there talking to her with icy throat; but her smile unhinged him. He swept her aside and stood with his back to the door, looking at her, not breathing.

"You oughtn't be here," he panted.

"What's wrong with you?" she asked, smiling broadly now. "Maud told me—"

"Naw!" he exploded and opened the door and went through it sideways, as though the woman were contaminated.

"Listen, I want to talk to you—"

"Naw!"

He tumbled down the narrow stairs, taking them four and five at a time, his breath whistling in his throat. A thousand thoughts thronged his mind, all boiling down to one imperative: Find Cantley! Something was happening and he dared not think of its meaning. Instinct declared in him that he had been snared by the white world. Yes; he'd phone Cantley. He was absolutely certain that the girl was white; she was whiter than Gloria, whiter than Gladys had been . . . He reached the bottom of the stairs and swung wildly through the door and went down the steps to the sidewalk. He dashed in the direction of the corner drugstore, then halted. A dark car stood about ten feet from him and the door opened and Cantley stepped out and ran toward him.

"Chief!" Fishbelly called.

Then he was aware of policemen running toward him, closing in from all sides.

"Chief!" he wailed, his eyes dazed. "I was looking for you. . . . There's a gal upstairs who says Maud sent her. . . . She *white*. . . . Go and see—"

"Take it easy, Fish. What you upset about?" Cantley asked.

Fishbelly spun about. From the window of his room had come a scream. His window was wide open and the white girl's head, her blond hair streaming wildly from her face, was thrust out; she was looking down at the policemen and screaming. A crowd of black people began to collect upon the sidewalk and look upward in amazement. Policemen were now running into the door of the tenement. Fishbelly looked from the screaming girl to the policemen who surrounded him, then he whirled to Cantley.

"Chief, what's happening?" he wailed.

"We're asking you what's happening, Fish?" Cantley said quietly.

"Don't know, sir. I was going to phone you—"

"What for?"

"About that gal who came to my room—"

"What're you talking about, Fish?" Cantley asked, eying him fixedly.

"That nigger's in some kind of trouble," a policeman said.

"There's a white gal up there," Fishbelly muttered. "I didn't ask her to come in. She said Maud sent her—"

"Look, you boys better get up there and see what this nigger's raving about," Cantley said. "Come along. And bring that nigger. . . ."

"But I—"

"Shut up, Fish, and come along!" Cantley ordered.

Cantley led the way up the stairs and the other policemen followed. Fishbelly could hear the girl sobbing now. He was enclosed in a hot dream. The girl had been "planted" on him! He was being framed for rape! Naw . . . No horrible thing like that could happen. But he felt that what was happening had to happen; he had been waiting for something like this to happen to him all of his life.

A red-faced policeman came running down the steps.

"It's a white lady!" the policeman was yelling. "She says she's been attacked! Says a nigger tried to rape her—!"

Fishbelly stopped, his tongue paralyzed and cleaving to the roof of his mouth.

"Naw!" he yelled. "Naw!"

"Get on up those steps, nigger!" a policeman behind him said.

"But it wasn't *me!*" Fishbelly screamed. "There ain't been no rape!"

A blow landed between his shoulder blades.

"Get up the steps, nigger!"

"I ain't done nothing!" he screamed.

"GET UP THOSE STEPS."

"Yessir," he breathed, mounting the stairs behind Cantley.

As he neared his room he could hear the woman crying and talking incoherently. Yes; they had framed him! His stomach muscles knotted tightly and for a moment his sight dimmed. Oh, if he could only find a window, he'd leap out! He stumbled and a policeman gave him a kick.

"Get up those steps and no goddamn tricks, nigger!"

"But I ain't done nothing," he sobbed.

"Shut up, Fish!" Cantley hollered.

The door of his room was open. Cantley entered and he followed, strangely anxious to look at the woman who had dropped out of the sky into the dark night of his fear. He stood frozen; the girl was now in her panties and brassière and most of her clothing law strewn about the floor. She was glaring at him, pointing, sobbing:

"There's the nigger. . . . H-he tried to r-rape me—"

"But—"

"Nigger, don't open your mouth while a white woman's talking!"

"But, mister—!"

A blow came between his eyes and he reeled. He found himself resting on his knees, near one of the girl's discarded stockings.

"Fish, goddamn," Cantley was saying to him. "Whoever thought you'd get into this kind of mess."

"But, Chief—"

"Did that nigger hurt you, miss?" Cantley asked the girl.

"You just came in time," the girl sobbed.

"Are you sure that that's the nigger?" a policeman asked her.

"He's the one! I'm sure! I'd know 'im in a million!"

"But how'd he get you up there?"

"I was looking for a nigger woman to do some washing," the girl recited, with her round, blue eyes wide with make-believe fear. "This nigger said he knew a woman, said he'd take me to her. . . . I followed 'im to this room and he locked the door and wouldn't let me go. . . . I started screaming. . . . He tore off my clothes. . . . I kept screaming and he ran away—"

"Naw!" Fishbelly yelled. "Naw! Naw!"

"Shut your damned mouth, nigger!"

He knew that protest was useless. Yes; it was Cantley putting him on the spot. He looked at the girl. How on earth could such a dainty, pretty girl lie like that? He knew now why Cantley and the policeman had been lurking down there in the street; they had been waiting to hear the scream of the girl.

"I saw that lady less'n a minute and I run—"

"Shut up, Fish. You're in goddamned serious trouble," Cantley said.

Fishbelly sighed, then bit his lips. Oh Gawd, was it to end like this?

"Get this nigger out of here before there's trouble," a policeman said. "Take the lady down first."

"Yessir," a policeman answered.

"Where do you live?" Cantley asked the girl.

"I-I live. . . . Oh God, my husband . . ." The girl fell across the bed and sobbed.

Fishbelly sank to the floor and stared listlessly. He had never seen the girl before, yet he had lived with an image and a sense of her almost all the days he had been alive. *Oh Gawd, why hadn't he fled?*

"Take the lady into the back and give her her clothes," Cantley suggested.

"Right," a policeman said, picking up the stray garments that lay about the floor.

Fishbelly did not realize that he had fallen upon one of the girl's shoes and the policeman kicked his back.

"Git to hell off the lady's clothes, you black bastard!"

He hugged the wall, hearing them leading the weeping girl out of the room. He turned and stared at Cantley.

"Chief," he whimpered. "For Gawd's sake, don't let this happen to me; they killed Papa, but I ain't done nothing! I ain't seen that lady 'fore tonight. . . . She just come to the door—"

"Just keep saying a white woman come to see you, and I'll kill you right now, nigger!" a policeman threatened him.

Crouching against a wall, he remained in a kind of stupor until the moment came for them to take him down to the police car. He saw Cantley watching him. Had Cantley given the word for them to kill him? *But Cantley wanted those checks; if he were killed, how could Cantley get hold of them?* If they were going to kill him because they thought he had the checks, why had they bothered sending the white girl to his room? He stared dully at the fireplace; the checks Cantley so badly wanted were *three feet* from him! Could he stop the frame-up by giving Cantley the checks? No. Cantley would take the checks and tell the policemen to shoot him. He prayed that they would not kill him because they were hoping that he could reveal the whereabouts of the checks. A policeman snatched him to his feet and clamped a pair of handcuffs upon his wrists.

"Nigger, go quietly down those steps," the policeman said.

"One false move and I shoot!"

"Fish, do what they tell you," Cantley warned him.

"Yessir," he breathed.

Then panic seized him; they were going to lynch him; he knew it,; they were going to loop a rope about his throat and tie that rope to the back of an automobile and drag him through the streets of the town, like they had done to Chris.

"Chief!" he cried. "Don't' let 'em kill me!"

"Stop yelling, Fish," Cantley told him.

"Don't let 'em kill me! I'll tell you—"

"FISH, DON'T GET EXCITED!" Cantley shouted.

He had been about to tell where the checks were, but Cantley's voice brought him to his senses.

"Chief, I'm loyal to you," he sobbed.

"Remember what happened to Tyree, Fish." Cantley's voice was deadly cold. "Don't lose your head. Do what they tell you. . . ."

A policeman pushed him and he walked dreamily out of the door and began to descend the steps, seeing black faces ducking from sight and hearing doors slamming shut. Those black men and women did not want the police to know that they knew him! He was alone, disowned by his own. And those were the people from whom he collected rent each Saturday morning, with whom he joked and told stories. . . . He reached the landing, then went down the steps to the sidewalk. Terror gripped him; he looked around for Cantley, but Cantley had gone.

"Chief! Chief!" he screamed, tears streaking down his black cheeks.

A crowd of black people blocked the sidewalk.

"Git back! Break it up! Go home!" the policeman shouted.

"Chief! Chief!" Fishbelly moaned.

He was pushed into a police car and he gazed about vainly for Cantley. And neither could he see the white girl who had accused him.

"I didn't do it! I didn't do it!" he hollered.

"Shut up, nigger!"

Two policemen were in the front seat and one sat to either side of him. They were moving toward the center of town. He dared not hope for life, yet he knew that if they were going to lynch him, they would have headed toward the woods on the outskirts of town.

They stopped in front of the tall, white building in which the town jail was housed. Fishbelly remembered that far-off day when he had been marched through that huge door on a charge of trespassing. The police pushed him out of the car.

"Walk ahead, nigger!"

He went stumbling toward the big door. Five minutes later he was standing before a police captain who sat behind a high desk.

"Is this the nigger?"

"That's him, Captain!"

"I thought Tyree taught you better sense than this," the captain snorted. "Didn't you know that touching a white woman is the worst thing on earth for you to do?"

"I didn't—"

"Where's the lady?" the captain asked.

"The matron's bringing her in, Captain."

"I want to see Mr. Cantley," Fishbelly whimpered.

"Mr. Cantley's not the chief of police now," the captain said. "The new chief of police is Mr. Murphy."

"Here's the chief now!" a policeman called out.

Fishbelly watched a wiry, rawboned white man dressed in blue enter.

"You all in one piece, nigger?" Chief Murphy asked.

"I want to see Mr. Cantley," Fishbelly begged.

"I'm the chief of police," Murphy said.

"I ain't done nothing," Fishbelly whimpered.

"We'll see about that," Murphy said.

"Let the lady through!" a policeman called out.

Fishbelly saw the white girl being led in by a police matron.

"You want to make a statement, miss?" Murphy asked her.

"Yes, I'm Mrs. Carlson," the girl said.

"Are you ready to take down Mrs. Carlson's statement?" Murphy asked a man sitting at a table.

"Yes, sir."

"Just tell us slowly what happened, Mrs. Carlson," Murphy said.

Mrs. Carlson repeated, more coherently this time, the story that she had told the policemen in Fishbelly's room.

"Naw, it ain't true!" Fishbelly screamed while she spoke.

"Interrupt her again and you won't have a trial," Murphy warned. "Is there anything else, Mrs. Carlson?"

"I was still in the room when the police came," she said in conclusion. "I was afraid to leave. . . . I thought maybe he was waiting in the hall and would kill me."

Silence. Fishbelly saw white faces staring at him.

"I didn't do that," Fishbelly mumbled hopelessly.

"Was this lady in your room, nigger?" Murphy asked him.

"Yessir, but I didn't *take* her there—"

"Just answer my question, nigger!"

"She knocked at my door—"

"You're lying, you dirty nigger!" Mrs. Carlson screamed.

The police matron calmed Mrs. Carlson, patting her arm.

"Don't excite yourself, dear," the matron said.

"Did that nigger violate Mrs. Carlson?" Murphy asked the matron.

"I found no evidence of such and she says that he didn't. Luckily, that beast didn't get that far," the matron said.

"You may go after you've signed your statement, Mrs. Carlson," the captain said.

Fishbelly watched Mrs. Carlson sign the statement and leave the room on the arm of the matron.

"Nigger, you'll be held for trial," Murphy said. "You can be hanged for this."

He knew that words were useless, yet he was detached enough to look at himself through the eyes of his captors and he was amazed that so many white faces could conspire against one frightened, lonely black boy. . . . Their finding the girl in his room was the hardest part of the accusation to refute. He could not say that she had come into his room without uttering a dire insult against the purity of white womanhood. Indeed, the anger that such a statement was capable of rousing could cause his death before he ever entered a court. And Cantley had so rigged the trap that had snared him that he could never convince them that he had not lured her there. Was Cantley trying to get him hanged? Or was he being railroaded to jail so that information could be squeezed out of him?

He was led down a corridor to a cell and locked in. He

stood, dazed. *It was not true!* But there were steel bars all around him. What he had dreaded most on earth had come upon him. One night long ago Tyree had dragged him into Maud's whore house to keep precisely this from happening. He was in the kind of trouble for which there was no help within the scope of his people. He stood until exhaustion made him sink upon the hard bunk.

A compulsive tremor ran periodically down his legs. Where was his car? Could he get word to McWilliams? Did his mother know? Did Jim know? Would the police find those canceled checks cemented into that chimney? He had not eaten since morning, yet he could not have eaten had he tried, for the muscles of his stomach were strung too taut. Weariness pushed his back against the wall; he must have dozed, for, the next thing he knew, Cantley was standing in the open cell door. He rose and ran to him.

"Chief!" he cried.

"Sit down, Fish!" Cantley's voice hissed with icy hate.

Fishbelly backed to the bunk and sat, staring wonderingly at Cantley.

"I didn't do it," he mumbled. "You *know* that, Chief?"

"What the hell are you talking about?" Cantley asked.

Fishbelly blinked. What was Cantley saying? He had been there when they had arrested him.

"But you was—"

"Don't talk about that *girl,*" Cantley said meaningfully.

"But, Chief, I was—"

"Where are those checks, Fish? *I want 'em!*"

Fishbelly swallowed. *So that was it!* He had been arrested for rape because it was feared that either he had the checks or knew where they were. He was being subjected to the fourth degree, not the third. . . . He had either to give up the checks or lie in jail and rot. He shut his eyes, thinking. If that was the game, then he would rather rot in jail than give up the checks.

"Didn't you hear me, Fish?"

"Yessir," he breathed.

"Where are they?"

He opened his eyes and when he spoke, it was about the checks, but the meaning of his words dealt with himself, with his sense of being a humiliated human being.

"Chief, there ain't no checks! Papa would've told me. . . . If I had any checks, I'd give 'em to you," he lied with a new, strong passion.

"I see. We'll have to sweat 'em out of you, hunh?"

"Chief, git me out of this," Fishbelly urged. "And I'll do anything you say," His aim now was to get his freedom and not give the white man what he wanted.

"Goddammit, you can beg like Tyree," Cantley muttered.

"But I didn't *touch* that lady—"

"Stop talking about that rape charge," Cantley drawled, looking off. "Where's that Gloria?"

"Lawd, I don't know, Chief. I swear."

"Do you realize how important those checks are, Fish?"

"Yessir."

"If you knew where they were, would you tell me?"

"I'd tell you anything, Chief."

Chief of Police Murphy came to the cell door.

"How's it going?" Murphy asked.

"He won't give," Cantley said.

"Well, keep 'im on ice," Murphy said and left.

Cantley sat beside Fishbelly on the narrow bunk.

"Fish, I'm having Maud do your collecting," Cantley said. "Your share'll be ready for you when you leave this jail."

"But that lady says I raped her—"

"Forget that," Cantley said. "Murphy's my pal. We'll help you if you help us."

"But *how,* Chief? I don't know nothing about no checks!"

"You know anybody who knows Gloria?"

"Nawsir."

"Fish, this is a life and death matter. *We've got to get hold of those checks!*" Cantley insisted. "Play ball with me. . . . I'll enlarge your beat. You'll collect from every cathouse in Nigger Town and be king among your people. . . . Let's clean up this thing."

"Reckon you going to kill me," he whispered in despair. "There ain't nothing I can do. . . . That lady says I took her to my room. You know I ain't that crazy, Chief."

"The girl has nothing to do with this," Cantley told him. "Satisfy me about those checks, and you walk out of here in the morning."

"But, Chief, I run straight to *you!*" Fishbelly argued. "You know I wouldn't run to the police if I was *guilty.*"

"You didn't run to *me,*" Cantley said coolly.

"You was gitting out of your car—"

"I wasn't there, Fish. I'm no witness for you," Cantley said.

"You was in my room—"

"Are you calling me a liar, nigger?" Cantley asked brutally.

"Nawsir, nawsir..."

Fishbelly's muscles were as stiff as steel. If he gave up the checks now, they'd kill him. But what if they found them in his room? They could kill him and say that he had been lynched for rape.... Well, goddammit, he had to gamble.

"Awright, kill me," he breathed hopelessly.

He felt himself sinking into a cold numbness into which human voices could not penetrate. He did not wish to speak ever again, to look with his eyes again, to listen again. The world had rejected him and he would reject that world. Tyree had been ambushed and slain; he was alone and he had failed. All right; he would *go. But he would not tell what he knew!*

He partially blacked out; then he felt Cantley shaking him.

"Think it over, Fish. I'll see you again," Cantley said and left.

Well, it was a matter of time now. They would have to kill him, for he would not talk. He stretched out upon his bunk and his eyes closed in a stupor of sleep.

39

He awakened next morning with limbs of lead. Already he had forgotten the rain and the wind, the night skies and the day skies. Yes, he should have fled, but that opportunity was forever gone. Sitting hunched in his drab cell, he began to realize dimly that there was something missing in him, and it was not a capacity for feeling or thought. There was some quality of character that the conditions under which he had lived had failed to give him. Just beyond the tip of his grasp was the realization that he had somehow collaborated with those who had brought this disaster upon him.

His people possessed no memory of a heritage of a glorious past to which he could cling to buttress his personal pride, and there was no clearly defined, redeeming future toward which he could now look with longing. He had only the flat and pallid present. He was unencumbered with emotional luggage, but there was no adventurous journey he wanted to make, no goal toward which he sought to strive. Other than a self-justifying yen for imitating the outward standards of the white world above him, there had not come within the range of his experience any ideal that could have captured his imagination. Other than a defensive callousness toward his own people which he practiced to be free to act out his own limited daily aims, other than the masked behavior he adopted toward the whites, other than the secret fantasy which he sought to realize while denying it, he had no traditions, no mores to sustain him.

Toward noon he was led into a small room with a high, barred window. Jim was there. Fishbelly sat and a dim smile flashed on his face, an automatic smile that was a part of him, a smile that would perhaps be on him when he died.

"Okay, Jim. Go on. Say it," Fishbelly mumbled.

"Say what?" Jim asked, baffled.

"Say, 'I told you so.' Say, 'You had it coming.'" Fishbelly tried feebly to fend off attack while concealing his trembling hands.

"No, Fish," Jim said compassionately. "I'm here to help you, if I can."

"I didn't touch that goddamn white gal," Fishbelly declared.

"I know you didn't," Jim said.

"How's Mama?"

"She's taking it hard, Fish. She can't understand it," Jim said. "Fish . . . Remember: they're making you suffer for what Tyree did."

"Papa did what he could," Fishbelly sighed.

"But this is serious, Fish," Jim said. "They're charging you with trying to rape a white girl—"

"It ain't that gal, Jim. It's the white folks trying to make me say something I don't know. What can *I do*, Jim?"

"You need a lawyer," Jim said. "What about Heith?"

"Naw. Heith ain't no good for this sort of thing. I want somebody who can stand up to these white folks, somebody who ain't scared. I need McWilliams—"

"Aw, he loused up things for Tyree," Jim warned. "You think he can help you?"

"If *anybody* can, he can."

"Then write him and ask him to represent you," Jim advised, proffering pencil and paper.

"Write it for me, Jim," Fishbelly mumbled. "I ain't got hold of myself. . . ."

Jim scribbled the letter to McWilliams and Fishbelly signed it. He knew that Cantley would not like his summoning McWilliams, but he knew that if anybody could make Cantley pause, it was McWilliams.

But McWilliams did not come the next day, nor the next; in fact, not a single person spoke to him for almost a week. Upon the ninth day of his confinement he was told that he had another visitor. It was McWilliams.

"Thought you wasn't coming," Fishbelly told him.

"I had to fight to get in to see you," McWilliams said. "Now, Fish, start from the beginning, no matter how unimportant it may seem to you."

He related what had passed, but omitted all reference to Gloria's sending him the canceled checks and his cementing them into the chimney.

"I'm sure that that girl was a 'plant,'" McWilliams said. "She was the excuse to get you behind bars and scare you into telling all you know about those checks."

"But I don't know nothing about them checks!" Fishbelly lied.

"Fish," McWilliams said, "My guess is that that woman won't show up to press the charge against you. Stick it out. When they take you into court, I'll be there. Do nothing; say nothing."

382

"That's all I can do," Fishbelly mumbled.

Back in his cell he realized that he would be waiting a long, long time. He was timidly sure now that they were not going to kill him. Once Cantley's fears were allayed, he would be let out. But he had no control over Cantley's fears.

He was not called into court until three weeks later. Mrs. Carlson was not there.

"Your Honor, the plaintiff is confined to a nursing home due to emotional shock sustained from the defendant's attack," the state's attorney declared.

"Your Honor, this is most unusual," McWilliams said. "It is quite simple to take a deposition of Mrs. Carlson's testimony—"

"The plaintiff is suffering from nervous distress and is incapable of making a coherent deposition," the state's attorney contended.

Fishbelly listened while McWilliams argued for his release on bail, but the judge ruled that this "was a capital offense and it does not serve the public interest to grant bail."

McWilliams leaned toward Fishbelly and whispered:

"Fish, I'm afraid you'll have to sit it out. I'm surer now than ever that the woman won't show up. I've investigated her; she's a common sort. . . . You know. Like the kind who works for Maud. Cantley doesn't want her to take the witness stand. I'd tear her to bits."

"It's long," Fishbelly complained.

"It could be *worse,*" McWilliams reminded him.

A week later the turnkey brought him a letter that had been opened. He stared wonderingly at the foreign stamps on the envelope. Had Gloria written him? He studied the stamps, reading *"République Française."* He pulled out sheets of paper and looked for the signature; it was signed "Zeke." Good Gawd . . . Zeke was in France! He read:

Dear Fish:

Hi, old Fishy-O! You still swimming in the great big sea? Well, just don't you go biting on any old hook with a worm on it, boy. Having a good time? Hope so. Man, we are stationed at Orleans, not far from Paris. It rains here most of the time, but we got good old cognac to keep us warm. I see old Tony about once every weekend and we talk a lot about you and Sam. By the way, how's old Sam? Is that nigger still raving about Africa? Fish, I do think that black nigger's crazy.

Man, Gay Paree is some burg. Both me and Tony's learning a little French and we get to Paris almost every weekend. Man, Paris is cool. Paris is crazy. These frogs over here even know about rock and roll. And what they don't know about jazz you can put in a thimble. Man, you ought to see these French cats go. These frenchies can jitterbug from away back.

Say, man, Mama wrote me that you was in some kind of trouble. It ain't true, is it? If it is, I sure hope it ain't bad. Man, I don't have to tell you to be careful with them old Mississippi crackers. They done drunk so much rotgut and slept with their own mamas so much they can't see straight no more. You know how they are. They ain't at all like these French frogs who don't care none.

Fish-O, you still a big shot? Making plenty of easy money? Mama said you was riding around in your papa's car. . . . Say, I sure was sorry to hear about Tyree being killed. Man, what won't them old white folks do? If I know old Tyree, he must have given them white folks a fit before they killed him.

Man, you must be a killer-diller! Why don't you come to Paris and spend some of your money? Living's cheap over here and you sure would like these crazy broads. Man, these blond chicks will go to bed with a guy who's black as the ace of spades and laugh and call it Black Market. Man, it's mad. You know what I mean.

Give my love to your mama. Man, I still think about that Grove fire and all the good friends I lost in it. Is that Grove going again? I only hope that whoever takes it over this time will have sense enough not to cover it with *moss!*

I'll be glad when I get out of the Army, cause I'm thinking of settling down for a spell in good old Paris. Man, it's good to live in this grayness where folks don't look mad at you just cause you are black.

Tony says hello and keep your shirt on. He says don't
do nothing he wouldn't do. Let us hear from you, old
Fishy-O.   Your pal,
                                            ZEKE.

Fishbelly folded the letter and stared. What he had read was
like a voice from another world. And Zeke thought that he
was having a good time. Goddamn . . . Zeke did not know the
half of it. Oh, if only he could get out of this jail and go to
Paris! Zeke's letter made him restless, bitter. Ought he to give
up those checks? No. It was too late now. Goddammit, if he
could get out, he would go, go, go!

40

Weeks dragged. Winter came and Fishbelly was still in his
cell, isolated from other black prisoners. Once a week an old
trusty took him for a walk in the jail yard for a few moments
of air.

"I don't understand it," the old trusty grumbled. "They
treating you with kid gloves. You a real pet nigger. You got no
complaints."

Though Cantley had not been to see him, McWilliams visited him almost every week and urged him to patience.

"Fish, Cantley's mob controls the jails, the courts, the
judges," McWilliams explained. "I'm not scolding you, Fish,
but you and Tyree helped to make them strong."

"Mr. McWilliams, I ain't *never* going to do that again,"
Fishbelly swore contritely.

"When you help an illegal gang, you build up something
that can crush you," McWilliams said.

"How long they going to keep me?" Fishbelly asked forlornly.

"When they realize there's nothing to be gained by keeping you, they'll let you go. It's not right, but what can I do?"

McWilliams made two determined efforts, both futile, to obtain Fishbelly's release on writs of habeas corpus; but each time he succeeded in getting Fishbelly into a court, the judge refused to grant bail.

"I'm tired of this," Fishbelly complained. "Let 'em try me or kill me!"

"No, no, Fish," McWilliams reasoned with him. "The last thing they want to do now is try you. The longer they stall, the better are your chances of going free. That woman is not coming into court."

He had been in jail so long that he felt that he had been born there. Almost every waking hour he saw that fireplace where he had entombed those checks. Someday he would dig them out and fling them at Cantley, some way, somehow. . . . They allowed him cigarettes and an occasional magazine, but no newspapers. Through Jim he learned that the "shop" had been prospering. Tyree's will had been probated, his minority disability had been removed, and Maud was collecting his "fees" and turning them over to Cantley, who was keeping his share. One development surprised and baffled him. Jim told him that Emma was now working in the office. Mama a businesswoman? He was certain that Tyree would never have permitted it. Well, when he got out, he'd take over. Naw! He was going away. . . . .

It was upon Tyree's life that he now brooded most. How had Tyree gotten along with whites for so many years while he, who had faced them for but a few days, was in jail? Until the terror of the week of Tyree's death, he could recall only one other time when Tyree had been frightened or angry, and that had been when Chris had been killed. Had Tyree feared the whites and hidden it? Yet he knew that pride would have kept Tyree from revealing his fear to him. Maybe Tyree had lived with fear so long that he had gotten used to it, could not call it by its right name? Tyree's instinctive wisdom, a wisdom that could not be found in books, had held the hostile whites at bay. He had inherited Tyree's position with no way to cope with it and he was filled with dread. He was a prisoner without having committed any overt act of wrong except that

386

he did not know how to act in a reassuring manner toward the white enemy.

His trial was listed for December and, again, when he went into court, Mrs. Carlson was not there. The attorney for the state informed the court that Mrs. Carlson was in a "distraught and highly incoherent condition and could not appear or make a deposition." McWilliams demanded that the case be dismissed for lack of evidence, and, again, his arguments were rejected.

"But, Your Honor, we are dealing with a boy nearly seventeen years of age," McWilliams protested. "He has already spent more than six months in jail. He is growing up in custody. This boy should be in school, not behind bars!"

"He should not have gotten into this trouble," the judge said coolly. "The charge against the prisoner is a grave one. The case will continue."

McWilliams accompanied Fishbelly to his cell.

"I'm sorry, Fish," he said. "But hold on. It won't be long now. Cantley was not even in court. I'm positive he has no intention of letting that woman appear."

"Yessir," Fishbelly sighed.

Spring found him still confined. He brooded listlessly, feeling his body shorn of emotion. Why, of all things, had Cantley chosen to bait him with a white girl? He stared through shuttered lids, recalling that moment when, half asleep, he had opened the door of his room and had seen the white girl's unreally beautiful face. He had never before been alone with a white girl and he now tried to recapture the sensation of unreality that had filled him. Had he run the very moment he had opened the door and had seen her, it would not have been possible for her to have said that he had been with her for more than thirty seconds. But, no; he had stood there, stupefied, dumbfounded, unable to believe that she was real.

White men made such a brutal point of warning black men that they would be killed if they merely touched their women that the white men kept alive a sense of their women in the black men's hearts. As long as he could remember he had mulled over the balefully seductive mystery of white women, whose reality threatened his life, declared him less than a man. In the presence of a white woman there were impulses that he must not allow to come into action; he was supposed to be merely a face, a voice, a sexless animal. And the white man's sheer prohibitions served to anchor the sense of his women in the consciousnesses of black men in a bizarre and distorted manner that could rarely ever be eradicated—a manner that placed the white female beyond the pitch of reality. Fishbelly had never known a single white woman, had never met one. And now a sharp pathos filled him as he understood anew the anxiety that had made Tyree drag him into Maud's whore house. . . .

"Poor Papa," he spoke aloud in a voice of amazement. "I never touched a white woman in all my life, not even her *hand!*"

41

Just before daybreak next morning Fishbelly was roused from sleep by clanking keys and the metallic thud of the bolt in the lock of the cell door. He lifted his head and squinted through the dull corridor light. Two dim shadows loomed beyond his cell door.

"Git in there, nigger!" a guard rasped as a black man was shoved into Fishbelly's cell.

Fishbelly sat up, staring; until that moment he had been alone; now it seemed that he was to have a cell mate.

"Don't push me," the black man mumbled, stumbling toward the bunk that stood opposite Fishbelly's.

"Shut up or I'll split your goddamn skull," the guard said, shutting and locking the cell door.

"Sonofabitch," the black man muttered under his breath.

The guard left and Fishbelly examined the newcomer, who had sunk upon his bunk and was holding his head in his hands. The man's clothing was dusty and torn, his hair disheveled, his eyes bloodshot, and his right arm was trembling as though in the grip of nervous ague.

"You hurt, buddy?" Fishbelly asked him softly.

"Hunh? Who there?" the man asked.

"Me," Fishbelly said. "Name's Tucker. They call me Fish."

"You scared me," the man mumbled. "Didn't see you. Thought you was white. . . ."

"Naw, I ain't white," Fishbelly drawled. "What they got you for?"

The man crept to the door, stared through the bars, then turned.

"It was that goddamned Cantley," the man hissed. "Said I stuck up a bar. If it hadn't been for him, I wouldn't be here. Oh, I could kill that goddamn sonofabitch!"

"Mebbe my lawyer can help you," Fishbelly told him. "What's your name?"

"Bert. Bert Anderson . . . Naw; I ain't got no money for no lawyer. Say, you know, I ought to spill what I know about that Cantley," Bert whispered. "I could blackmail him. I know a cathouse just out of town he collects from . . ."

"Don't know about that," Fishbelly drawled cautiously. "Cantley's dangerous—"

"Not if you really got the lowdown on 'im," Bert said. "And I got it. . . . Say, what you in for?"

"Hunh," Fishbelly snorted. "Man, they saying I tried to rape a white girl."

"Naw! Jesus Christ!" Bert exclaimed, sitting beside Fishbelly. "Man, they could've *lynched* you—!"

"Right! But I didn't touch that white bitch," Fishbelly said.

"These white folks'll do anything," Bert breathed. "Framed you, I bet."

"That's it. But my lawyer says I'll git out soon."

"Say, you know that old Cantley?" Bert asked.

"A little bit and that's too much," Fishbelly sighed.

"Gee, I wish I had a partner like you to help me when I git out; I want to get that Cantley. . . ." Bert's voice growled: "I hate that sonofabitch's guts! I could kill 'im!" Bert grew confidential: "He rich, you know. Made a pile of dough out of grafting us niggers. Lissen, they tell me he killed a nigger who crossed 'im about some graft—"

389

"What nigger?" Fishbelly asked, his interest quickening.

"Don't know his name. A *big* nigger. A undertaker..."

Fishbelly stared with parted lips. Good Gawd! Bert was talking of Tyree and did not know that he was Tyree's son!

"... they tricked 'im into a whore house and shot 'im to hell," Bert's voice held a note of sympathetic awe.

Fishbelly was on the verge of identifying himself when the trusty called:

"Fish Tucker!"

"Yeah!"

Fishbelly went to the cell door.

"Come on, nigger. Time for the yard," the trusty said.

"Let's skip it today," Fishbelly said, not wishing to leave this dynamic Bert who had the kind of attitude toward whites that he liked. He had been alone much too long and Bert's presence was causing a warm glow of comradeliness to burn in him. "I'll walk tomorrow."

"You take your walk now or wait till next week," the black trusty said.

"Better go with 'im, Fish," Bert counseled.

"Aw, awright," Fishbelly said, sighing.

He followed the trusty through the corridor, down iron steps, and along another corridor toward the big door giving onto the jail yard. He noticed that the old trusty loitered absent-mindedly; indeed, so slowly did the trusty shuffle along that Fishbelly's gait, even though he was barely moving, made him crowd the trusty's back. Then suddenly the trusty was at his side, mumbling under his breath.

"How's that weather outside?" Fishbelly asked.

"*Bad,*" the trusty said, pulling down his lips.

"Raining?"

"Yeah. But you can't *see* it," the trusty muttered.

"What you talking about?" Fishbelly asked.

"How you like your new side-kick?" the trusty asked suddenly.

"Hunh? Oh, he awright. Ha, ha! Kind of hard on white folks—"

"He really hard, or he *playing?*" the trusty asked.

"He sure *acts* hard," Fishbelly said.

"Man, go it by yourself," the trusty said in a faraway voice.

"Hunh?" Fishbelly asked, blinking.

"Son, the white man's got many ways to send news," the trusty drawled, caressing his words, eyeing Fishbelly as he unlocked the door leading to the sun-drenched yard. "They got *tele*vision, *tele*phone, *tele*gram, *tell-a*-woman, *and tell-a-friend*—"

"What the hell you talking about?" Fishbelly demanded, stepping into the yard. "Say, you said it was raining. . . ."

"It *is*, but you can't see it," the trusty said.

"What's eating you?" Fishbelly asked, wondering what the trusty was obliquely hinting at.

"Let's walk," the trusty said.

Bothered, Fishbelly followed him, not caring to look at the sun or the sky. What was the matter with the old man? Twice he attempted to draw the trusty out, but could get nothing from him.

"Time's up," the trusty growled abruptly. "Can't stay out a minute overtime, 'cause niggers tell tales."

"Okay," Fishbelly mumbled, baffled still more.

The trusty unlocked the door to let him into the jail and whispered fiercely:

"The best thing to do with a stool is *set* on it!"

"What you mean, man?"

"Skip it, if you don't git it."

Back in his cell, Fishbelly was distracted, thoughtful. Bert sat on the edge of his bunk, watching him. That damned trusty had acted mighty strange. Was he angry with him? But Jim had tipped him often and generously.

"What's on your mind, pal?" Bert asked.

"Nothing, man," Fishbelly said, forcing a smile.

"You got a funny look in your eyes," Bert said slowly.

"Aw, just wondering how long I'm going to be in this jail."

"Yeah. Seeing that sun gits you down, hunh?"

"Damn right."

"Say, Fish, let's me and you team up when we git out of here. We could work out something to git us some big dough."

"How?" Fishbelly stared at Bert's tense black face.

"I want to git something on that Cantley—"

"Like what?" Fishbelly asked, seeing the fireplace in which

he had cemented those canceled checks behind the brick.

"What you know about Cantley?" Bert asked.

"Don't know much," Fishbelly said preoccupiedly, wondering if he could blackmail Cantley with those canceled checks. It was a new and exciting thought.

"You got anything we can use against him?" Bert asked in a confidential whisper.

Fishbelly held still as something dark and horrible worked deep in him, stirring powerfully, trying to come to the surface. He saw that fireplace and, at the same time, heard the old trusty's cryptic growl: *The best thing to do with a stool is set on it!* Fishbelly's eyes grew round, fixed, and he looked at Bert as though he had never seen him before. His muscles flexed, his head and chest grew hot. He sprang up, the crooked fingers of his hands reaching for Bert's throat. He was upon the man before the man could rise from the bunk and the weight of his lunge carried Bert backward violently, ramming his head against the stone wall with cracking impact.

"Goddamn sonofabitching *stool!*" Fishbelly screamed, raining blows upon Bert's head. "I'LL KILL YOU!"

"Stop!" Bert screamed.

With ferocity born of rage, Fishbelly lashed his fists piston-like into Bert's face.

"Want to stool on me, you bastard?" Fishbelly hissed.

Bert screamed incessantly, thrusting elbows, knees, and legs to ward off Fishbelly's ravaging attack. A loud gong began to clang throughout the jail and Fishbelly was dimly aware of figures at the cell door.

"Break it up, niggers!" a guard called.

Fishbelly had the fingers of his right hand about the lower part of Bert's throat and he could feel the nails sinking into flesh as Bert heaved and flayed his fists, clawing, trying to break Fishbelly's grip. Fishbelly hung on, his life itself centered in those fingers gouging Bert's throat. He clung to Bert even when he felt the white guards tugging at him.

"Turn 'im loose, nigger!" the guards shouted.

They finally pulled Fishbelly away. Bert collapsed upon the floor, gasping for breath. Fishbelly swung a vicious kick into Bert's ribs.

"I'LL KILL A STOOL!"

"Stop, nigger, or I'll conk you!" a guard threatened.

Fishbelly backed off, looking with lowered eyes at the white guard towering over him with a truncheon.

"Take 'im out or I kill 'im," Fishbelly growled.

A clamor of voices rose from the other prisoners.

"You trying to start a jail break, nigger?" a guard asked.

"Nawsir," Fishbelly panted. "But I don't like no stools! Take 'im out or I kill 'im!"

"Git out, nigger," a guard said, giving Bert a kick.

Bert pulled to his feet; the guards grabbed him and shoved him out of the cell. Fishbelly sat, his chest heaving, his eyes blinded with tears of rage. Then he glared sullenly about, unable to believe that Bert had gone. The prisoners' clamor died gradually as Bert, bleeding and staggering, was led away. The cell door was locked.

"You gone crazy, nigger?" a guard asked Fishbelly.

"I ain't crazy," Fishbelly muttered.

"Why you fighting that nigger?" a guard asked.

"*You* know," Fishbelly said.

The guard left, shaking his head. A little later the old black trusty shuffled past Fishbelly's cell, looked in, winked, then passed on, singing:

> *I'll be glad when you're dead,*
> *You rascal you . . .*

Chastened, Fishbelly sat. Gawd, what a fool he had been about to be! He had been on the verge of taking a spy into his confidence and revealing the whereabouts of the checks! He lay on his bunk and bit his lips.

Footsteps sounded. Fishbelly looked up. Chief Murphy stood at his door.

"Well, Fish, looks like you don't like Bert," Murphy said.

"I kill a stool," Fishbelly hummed.

"You know you're going into court in the morning for this, don't you?" Murphy asked. "You'll be charged with first-degree assault."

"I don't care," Fishbelly mumbled, nursing his bruised knuckles. "But I kill a stool!"

"How'd you know he was a stool?" Murphy asked with a light smile.

"I could *smell* it," Fishbelly growled.

Murphy left.

So wrought up was he that he refused to eat at noon. Two hours later Cantley stood at his cell door.

"Goddamn, Fish, what's got into you?" Cantley asked. "They say you went wild this morning. . . ."

"Chief," Fishbelly said, not even rising from his bunk, "don't send no niggers to spy on me. I *kill* 'em!"

"Goddamn, nigger, you're much smarter than I thought," Cantley said with a wry smile. "But you're going to stay in jail a lot longer."

"I don't care none," Fishbelly said forlornly.

He heard Cantley walk away. All right, let 'em kill 'im. . . . He could kill too. They thought he was a dumb nigger, but he'd show 'em. Night fell, but he could not sleep. He lay staring in the darkness, prey to a fever of despair.

At ten o'clock next morning they took him to court and in fifteen minutes he was sentenced to two years in jail, the sentence providing a deduction of the six months he had already served.

"Why did you do it, Fish?" McWilliams asked him that afternoon.

"Mr. McWilliams, that nigger was spying on me," Fishbelly argued. "I went for 'im. Goddammit, I'd do it again."

"I'm sorry, Fish. I could've gotten you out at the next court hearing, but now you've got to serve a year and a half. You mustn't let these people provoke you."

"I don't care," Fishbelly repeated. "It ain't your fault."

Alone again, he bowed his head and brooded. He felt hopeless, at the mercy of white men. They knew how and when to make him fight against himself. They were punishing him and they had made him heap more punishment upon himself. He stood, trembling; then shut his eyes and screamed into the darkness:

"I DON'T CARE!"

42

A few mornings later the turnkey took him into the visitors' room and he was surprised to see Jim and his mother. He felt guilty as he faced them, for their predictions had come true.

"Hi, Mama. Hi, Jim," he mumbled.

"Awright, son," Emma said. "How you?"

"Oh, okay," he said with false heartiness.

Emma gazed at him wistfully, then suddenly began to weep.

"What's the matter, Mama?" Fishbelly asked her.

"Fish, what happened?" Emma asked in a whisper. "That Mr. McWilliams said you had a fight and you got to serve eighteen months—"

"Mama, I couldn't help it," he said. "They put a bad nigger in my cell. Had to git 'im out."

"What was wrong?" Jim asked.

"Nigger was a *stool*, Jim."

"Fish, take it easy," Jim begged.

"I *am*, Jim!" Fishbelly cried. "But that nigger was talking about getting me to help blackmail Cantley. . . . What was I going to do? It was his life or mine. I tried to *kill* 'im!"

"Pray, son," Emma whispered. "Gawd'll deliver you."

"Fish, do you really know anything about those checks?" Jim asked.

"I don't know *nothing!*" Fishbelly swore feverishly. "They can kill me, but they can't git nothing out of me!"

"Ues you head, boy," Jim pleaded. "That's all I can say. Look, you need anything?"

"Naw," Fishbelly drawled. "The 'shop' okay?"

Jim leaned back in his chair and spoke with a new, strange note of confidence.

"Everything's shipshape, Fish."

"That Mr. McWilliams is a nice man," Emma said. "He said he was still going to try to git you out."

"But it's long," Fishbelly sighed.

"What're you planning to do when you come out, Fish?" Jim asked.

"Don't know," he lied.

He planned to leave but he did not want to tell them, for fear that they would want to dictate his actions. Never had he missed Tyree as much as now; never before had he felt so inadequate; and never had he dreamed so ardently of new places, new faces.

"Fish," Jim began with a slight smile, "Emma and I want to tell you something very important—important to *you* and to *us*."

"Yeah," Fishbelly said, and waited.

"Emma and I are going to get married fairly soon," Jim announced.

Fishbelly started, looked at his mother, and a soundless protest leaped up in him. He felt deceived, excluded. . . . Naw . . . Tyree was being betrayed. He kept his eyes on the floor, not wanting Jim to see the hot displeasure in them.

"We love each other, son," Emma told him beggingly. "I don't want to be alone. Me and Jim git along together."

Fishbelly looked at Emma with fresh eyes; she was not at all old-looking.

"Emma's life has been kind of hard," Jim said. "I want to give her a break. I'm planning to go into business on my own soon."

"I see," Fishbelly said.

He resented Jim's hinting that Tyree had not been kind to his mother. But what could he do? He was in jail. He sighed. Yes; when he got out he would go. That was sure now. If he stayed, Jim and Emma would hammer at him, try to rule him.

"Ain't you going to say nothing, son?" Emma asked with a pathetic smile.

He could have slapped her.

"I hope you-all'll be happy," he mumbled.

"Fish, I don't know how you were brought up," Jim said. "But we'll get along. I think I understand you. I want to be a good stepfather to you."

"Okay," Fishbelly mumbled, disguising his rejection.

Jim was not going to be any kind of a father to him, and, by Gawd, they could not get their hands on his money or property. He sat in his cell with a new sense of bleakness. Jim and Emma marrying . . . Awright. The hell with it. Jim's being a good man did not make him like him. Jim had another outlook upon life, an outlook that differed from his and Tyree's. Oh God, if only Cantley would be honest with him and give him his share of the "fees"; he would take what was in the safe and go without telling a soul. The hell with it all. . . .

43

Orleans

Dear Fishy-O:

Man, I can't tell you how sorry I was to hear about your trouble. Mama wrote me all about it. What a mess. Man, be careful with that mess of crackers they got there in that Mississippi mud. What Mama told me made me never want to come back. Them white folks is just jealous of us as all hell. Man, be mum and play dumb and get the hell out of that mess. Tony almost cried when I told him you was in jail for rape. He couldn't take it for a minute; he just looked at me like I done told him that Jesus Christ was dead. Man, we all know you didn't do anything like rape. After all, you get enough gals not to go raping anybody. Have you got you a good lawyer? You better get you a Jew lawyer. They real smart and can out-talk them slow crackers down South. And, man, don't talk back to them crazy white folks; you know how they are. Just say yes, yes, yes; and then get out of jail and leave. Man, shake the dust off your feet and go and don't look back once. It ain't worth nothing to talk back to white folks and then lose your life. You remember that night when we went to that fair and we saw that crazy white woman showing us her tits? That's the way they do and they say we rape them. Damn. Man, white folks is mean. If somebody would prove to me that God's white, I don't think I would ever go to church no more. God just can't be like these goddamned white folks. Fish, I told you in my last letter you ought to come to France. Man, you got some money and that is all it takes over here. Get out of jail and come over here and take a long rest from all of that white folks mess. France ain't no heaven, but folks don't kill you for crazy things. These white folks just more like real human beings than them crackers back there in Mississippi. Let us hear from you, man. We think about you a lot. If we was there, we sure would be fighting for you. 'By now.

> Your pal,
> ZEKE.

That letter made up his mind. It was to France he would go, to Paris. The moment he was free, he would be off. He hungered for freedom so badly that he trembled when he thought of it.

44

One month before the end of Fishbelly's second year in jail, when he was just one week shy of his eighteenth birthday, Cantley and Chief Murphy came to the door of his cell. It was nearly midnight. What was happening? Fishbelly had been sleeping and now he sat up, filled with anxiety, his heart beating so violently that he felt he could not breathe. He was certain that something was up, that Cantley had not come for nothing.

"Hi, Fish!" Cantley greeted him jovially.

"Good evening, Chief," Fishbelly said, rising.

"My, my, that boy sure looks well," the chief said.

"How're you feeling, Fish?" Cantley asked.

"Okay," he mumbled.

"Just 'okay'?" Cantley asked with chiding echoes.

"I'm fine!" Fishbelly mustered a false glee.

"That's better," Cantley drawled.

The turnkey unlocked the cell door and Cantley and the chief entered. Fishbelly was grateful that they had spoken so cordially. Official judgment in courtrooms was not important; the decisive decisions of the white world came through personal contact, personal decrees made on the whim of the moment by men who held godlike power. Cantley sat beside him upon the bunk.

"Mad at me, Fish?" Cantley asked with a twisted smile.

"I ain't mad at *nobody,*" Fishbelly lied with a tinge of hysteria.

"That's the way I like to hear a nigger talk," the chief said. The chief placed his hand on Cantley's shoulder. "Gerald, I think we ought to *help* this nigger. He hasn't been any trouble."

"I've been kind of thinking about that myself," Cantley said.

Fishbelly waited. His throat felt so tight it burned.

"Goddammit, Fish," Cantley said. "I'm a monkey's uncle, but you've put on weight here in jail! And you've gotten *taller!*"

"Yessir," he mumbled. "Think so." He kept his eyes averted.

Cantley frowned and wagged his head negatively.

"You know, Fish," Cantley said, "that woman never showed up."

He knew that Cantley was referring to Mrs. Carlson.

"What woman, Chief?" he pretended ignorance.

"You see!" the chief exclaimed. "The nigger's forgotten all about it!"

"I'm talking about the bitch who claimed you tried to rape her," Cantley said.

"Oh," Fishbelly said softly.

"Have you heard from Gloria?" Cantley asked.

"Nawsir."

"What about that doctor?" the chief asked.

"Nobody's heard of him," Fishbelly said.

"Who's this writing you from France, Fish?" Cantley asked.

"Oh, just some friends of mine in the Army," Fishbelly said offhandedly.

"Sounds like they don't like our Mississippi," Chief Murphy said.

"Oh, they just talk like that," Fishbelly said vaguely.

"Planning on going to France or something, Fish?" Cantley asked.

Fishbelly let his eyes grow round and he turned to Cantley.

"Oh, nawsir!" he exclaimed. "I ain't lost nothing over there."

"Those French are dirty," Cantley said emphatically. "You're better off here, Fish."

"Yessir. I think so too, sir," he lied with as much conviction as he could muster.

Cantley rose and, with a sudden, playful movement, slapped Fishbelly on the shoulder. Fishbelly had ducked his head when he had seen Cantley's hand coming toward him, but now registered a smile, hoping desperately that all was well.

"Goddammit, nigger, you're *all right!*" Cantley said, grinning.

"Yessir," Fishbelly hummed.

Cantley reached into his pocket and drew forth a packet. Fishbelly was frozen with anxiety. Had they found the checks he had cemented into the chimney? He held his breath. Cantley unwrapped the packet and tossed a batch of green bills upon the bunk.

"That's your cut until now, Fish," Cantley said. "Fifty-fifty. Count 'em."

Fishbelly relaxed, breathing again. He searched the white

man's face, suspecting a trick.

"Take your word for it, Chief," Fishbelly sang in a muted tone. He looked at Cantley with pleading eyes. "But I can't spend this in *here*."

"And who the hell said you're staying here?" Chief Murphy asked. He turned toward the cell door. "Pat, come here. You got that writ?"

"Sure. It's right here," the turnkey said, coming forward and extending a slip of paper.

"Fish," Cantley said, taking the paper, "here's something you've been looking for for two years."

"Yessir. What it mean?" Fishbelly asked.

"Hell, it means you're *free!*" Cantley said. *"We* did it! That McWilliams bastard didn't have a goddamn thing to do with it. Your *friends* did it. Get me?"

"Yessir."

"Are you happy?"

"Oh, yessir."

"Well, what you standing there like that for? Get the hell *dressed—*"

"Now?" Fishbelly asked.

"Hell, yes!" the chief of police sang roughly.

"I'm taking you out of here tonight," Cantley said.

"Pat!" Chief Murphy called. "Bring this nigger his clothes!"

"Yessir," a voice answered.

Fishbelly waited, not knowing what reaction he should give. He did not want to appear too glad, for fear that would make them suspect that he was calculating; but neither did he wish to look too morose, for that would hint that he was perhaps harboring notions of revenge. For a second he was wary, then instinct prompted a compromise. He bent his face to the bunk and wept.

"What's the nigger blubbering about?" Chief Murphy asked, grinning.

"Aw, leave 'im alone," Cantley said in drawl. "Let him get dressed."

They left and his tears ceased at once. He counted the money. It was almost three thousand dollars. That meant that Cantley had enlarged his "beat" among the black prostitutes; it also meant that Cantley needed him to collect "fees." Dressed, he lingered in the cell. The turnkey came and unlocked the door.

"Straight ahead, nigger. They waiting for you."

He felt that he was moving in a dream as he walked down the corridor. Cantley and Chief Murphy met him.

"Come on, Fish. Get in my car. Now, where do you want to go? To Maud's for something hot? A bar? Or to your mama's?" Cantley asked.

"To my flat, sir," he mumbled.

"You don't want to wrassle a gal tonight?"

"Nawsir."

"Have it your way," Cantley said, leaving.

The night air smelled sweet. He sat beside Cantley in the car and stared at the high, blue stars glazing a black velvet sky. Hot tears coursed over his cheeks.

"What in hell you crying for? It's all over. You're *free*."

"Can't help it, Chief," Fishbelly gasped.

The car stopped in front of the Bowman Street tenement where he had his flat.

"Everything all right, Fish?"

"Yessir. You want me to collect Saturday?"

"Sure. Just like always. I'll be at the office in the morning and give you the other addresses."

"Yessir."

"And have some *fun*, Fish."

"Oh, yessir."

"Good night."

"Good night, sir."

He stood upon the deserted sidewalk and watched the red taillight of Cantley's car vanish into darkness and his black face grimaced into an expression of hard hate. He took out his keys and mounted the steps, glancing apprehensively over his shoulder. He unlocked the door of his room, paused, seeing the image of that white girl's face that had confronted him two years before. He went inside, switching on the light. Cobwebs covered the furniture. He examined the fireplace; the brick hiding the checks was intact. He circled the room, then went to the wardrobe and pulled out his suits; dust and moths had ruined them.

"Hell," he breathed.

He would buy new clothes in New York. He bolted the door, found a screw driver, stooped to the fireplace, and began hacking softly at the cement, prying it away from the edges of the brick. He eased the brick from its hole and saw the asbestos-wrapped packet; he peeled off the oilcloth. Aw yes; here they were.... He stuffed them into his pocket, turned out the light, locked the door, and went down the steps. Upon the sidewalk he came face to face with Maud.

"Fish!" she cried and hugged him to her bosom.

"Hi, Maud," he said, patting her shoulder.

"You done grown!" she said, looking him up and down.

"A little," he said.

"Mr. Cantley told me you was free!"

"Yeah. Just got out."

"And I'm sure glad, Fish," she ran on, smiling. "I *told* that Cantley you was innocent. It wasn't that white gal. They was scared of them damned checks."

"Yeah. I know."

"You going to collect?" she asked him.

He liked Maud, but thought it best not to trust her.

"Sure. Yeah," he lied.

"Fish?"

"What?"

"You want a gal? I got a pretty one.... Let's celebrate. Everything's on *me* tonight—"

"Thanks just the same, Maud. But I got to git to the office. Business."

"Then tomorrow night?"

"You bet. Sure thing."

"Promise?"

"It's a deal."

"I'm so happy for you I could cry," Maud sighed. "Got to git back and look after them bitches. Got to keep your eyes on 'em. Good night, Fish."

"Night," he said, walking rapidly away.

Damn Maud. Goddamn 'em all to hell. He was leaving. Half an hour later he let himself into the office and opened the safe. He took out the packet of bills and stuffed them into his pocket. He was ready. He trembled. Suddenly he wept, bending over the desk. He straightened, dried his eyes, mumbling: "Papa, I'm leaving. . . . I can't make it here."

Ought he to call home and speak to his mother? Naw . . . He would not say good-by to anyone. He would not tell Jim. He would say nothing to McWilliams. He would just leave. Take a train. . . . That was it. Right now.

He walked through the silent night streets to the railroad station, watching for white policemen. He saw none. He entered a door marked "FOR COLORED." He went to a ticket window marked "FOR COLORED." He waited until the white clerk inside the booth had finished selling tickets to white men and women at another window.

"What you want, boy?" the clerk asked absent-mindedly.

"Ticket to Memphis, sir. When's a train leaving?"

"In about two hours."

He paid for his ticket and went into the waiting room marked "FOR COLORED." He sat; he was sleepy, but he dared not close his eyes. If he saw Cantley, he'd say that he was going to Memphis for just two days. . . . But he saw no one. Three hours later he sat on a hard seat in the Jim Crow section of a coach. He had almost six thousand dollars on him. He looked at Zeke's letters. He would cable Zeke from New York to meet him at the air terminal in Paris.

Next afternoon at two o'clock a blond young white woman leaned over Fishbelly and murmured:

"Don't you know how to fasten your seat belt? Like this . . ."

He let her strap him to the seat of the plane, holding his breath as he watched her head of golden hair, her white skin. The plane's motors roared and the craft taxied out upon the runway and then, minutes later, he felt giant wings lifting him high into the air and he was zooming through sunny skies, traveling eastward on the first lap of a journey that would take him far, far away.

Two weeks later Fishbelly reclined in the seat of another plane; he was nervous and his palms were sweaty. The roar of four mighty engines filled his ears with thunder; from his seat by the window he watched two of the plane's four propellers boring through resisting air. It was afternoon and the sky was boundlessly high and blue. He pressed his cheek against the window glass and stared downward; far below, a vast sweep of fluffy white clouds stretched away like a field of ripe cotton.

The flight bulletin at which the air hostess had let him glance had told him that he was some twenty thousand feet over the Atlantic. It was the first time in his life that he had sat surrounded by white men, women, and children with no degrading, visible line marking him off. His knees were held stiffly together, as though he expected his presence to be challenged. For more than two hours he had avoided looking in front of him, had always kept his eyes to left or right. Finally he stared directly at the object that rested under the dreadful taboo; the young woman ahead of him had a head of luxuriant, dark brown hair, the wispy curls of which nestled clingingly at the nape of her white, well-modeled neck. His Bowman Street experiences made the rounded firmness of the woman's throat a symbolic stand-in for the exciting, hidden geography of her body and he grew tense, for that simple image, just two feet from him, was the charming trap that could trigger his deepest fears of death. His heart pounded as he stared at close range upon the alluring but awful image and, while looking at it, its aspect of sentient, human life evaporated and was replaced by a dubious, disturbing reality that resided more in the balked impulses of his heart than in the woman's existence. The woman was as unreal and remote as had been that bleeding white man he had left to die under that overturned Oldsmobile on that far-off summer day when fear had robbed the world of its human meaning.

"Hunh?" Fishbelly grunted, coming out of his brooding.

"Have you a light?" the young man to his left was asking him.

"Sure," Fishbelly said.

He held the flame of his lighter to the young man's cigarette.

"Thanks," the young man said.

"That's awright," Fishbelly mumbled.

"It's a long flight, hunh?" the young man asked.

"Sure is," Fishbelly agreed.

"Going to Paris?"

"That's right. You?"

"No. I'm heading for Italy. I'm going to look at the village in which my father was born."

"Oh. Your father living there now?"

"Oh no. My father's dead. He died in America. He left Italy when he was a young man and went to America. He made me promise him that I'd go and see his village. You see, my father was in love with America. When I was a kid my father used to talk to me about America like a man describing a beautiful woman. He called America 'My Wonderful Romance'... Isn't that something?"

Fishbelly looked at the man out of the corners of his eyes. Was the man trying to make fun of him? Naw... He seemed perfectly serious.

"Yeah. Guess that's nice," Fishbelly said. "Why he asked you to see his village?"

"He wanted me to see the poverty and ignorance of the village in which he'd been born. He told me that that was the only way that I could really appreciate what America had done for him and for me."

"Oh," Fishbelly breathed. He was silent a moment, then he said softly. "Some people got all the luck."

"You're from New York?" the young man asked.

"Naw... From down South."

"Oh! What state?"

"Mississippi," Fishbelly mumbled uneasily.

"Wheew," the young man whistled. "Boy, say, that's really the South.... Tell me, how is it down there?"

Fishbelly grew uncomfortable. What did the man mean?

"It's awright," he said with a slight edge in his voice.

"That's not what I heard," the young man said. "I was told that the whites down there are pretty hard on your people."

Fishbelly flinched inwardly and some part of him withdrew. Why was this man probing into him, invading the dark, shameful areas of his heart—areas that he felt he had to hide from the gaze of strangers? He was not yet emotionally strong enough to admit what he had lived.

"That ain't true," he told the young man with quiet heat.

"No?" the young man asked, lifting his eyebrows.

"We live just like anybody else," Fishbelly maintained, feeling a hot flush spread over his body.

"But I was through the South once when I was in the Army," the young man went on, "and I saw those damned signs: 'FOR WHITE' and 'FOR COLORED.'"

"We don't think about that," Fishbelly declared, his teeth on edge.

"God, *I* would if *I* lived there and was *colored*," the young man said.

"Shucks, we forgot that stuff," Fishbelly lied with a forced and nervous laugh.

The young man leaned back and smoked, then smothered his cigarette and slept. Fishbelly brooded. Would he ever find a place that he could call "My Wonderful Romance"? That man's father had come to America and had found a dream; he had been born in America and had found a nightmare. Out of the corners of his eyes Fishbelly compared the young man's suit with his own and found that his was by far the superior in style, cut, and texture of cloth. As though hypnotized, he stared at the back of the man's hairy, white hand that lay but four inches from his own left hand. Suddenly that white hand, like the image of the woman sitting in front of him, began to alter its reality. It became more than just a human hand. Unconsciously, stealthily, Fishbelly drew his hand in, covering his right black hand with his left black hand, trying vainly to blot out the shameful blackness on him.

45

Hours later he stood and took down his traveling kit and extracted from it a thick envelope. Sitting, he drew forth the letter that he had written to McWilliams and reread it:

Dear Mr. McWilliams:
    I don't know what you are going to say or think of me when you get this letter and the canceled checks. I

lied to you about these checks. Papa left them and I was just too scared to give them to you. You are going to say that I did not trust you and that I lied to you and you are going to be right. I did tell you a lot of lies. These checks was in the letter that I took to Gloria Mason that last night I saw her. But I didn't know that she had these checks until she sent them to me; I didn't know what was in the letter I took to her. Well, I hid these checks. I was scared, that was why I hid them and said nothing about them. Mr. Cantley could have killed me, but I wasn't going to say one word. I knew where the checks was hid all the two years I was in jail, but I knew that if I gave them to you Mr. Cantley would know who gave them and he would have had his men kill me just like he had his men kill Papa and he would say that I was resisting arrest or trying to run away. And I knew if I had told Mr. Cantley that I had lied to him and where he could get hold of the checks, I was finished. I was finished no matter what I did. So I waited and sweated it out. Mr. Cantley can't get hold of me now so I'm sending you these checks for you to use any way you want. I hope to God that you put that Mr. Cantley in jail for a good long time. I don't care none no more. I don't know how long I'm going to be in France and I don't know if I'm going to like living in France, but I know that I don't ever mean to go back to Clintonville, Miss., to live any more. For all the many lies I told you I can only say I'm sorry, very sorry, but I told you them lies cause I was scared, more scared than you will ever think. Now maybe you are going to say that I didn't trust you, but it was not only that. I just didn't want another murder to happen, cause I was dead sure that it would have happened to me. Thank you for all the help you gave me and if I owe you a fee for your help while I was in jail, then you write me in care of my mama and I will send you the money. I know what you want to do with these checks and they are yours, but I think you ought to say to folks that you just found them. Mr. McWilliams you are the only honest white man I ever met. You are more honest than I am. I was not honest with you cause I was scared, so don't think too hard of me for all the lies I told. I don't know what kind of work I'm going to do, but I'm not ever going to collect any more fees. I'm through with that kind of stuff. It killed my papa and it almost killed me. I hope that Mr. Cantley won't try to hurt my mama or Jim (he's going to be her husband now) cause she didn't know nothing about these checks. I am the only one who is guilty. Thank you.

Yours sincerely,
REX (FISH) TUCKER

Well, he would mail that letter and the checks as soon as he got to Paris and all of his bridges to the past would be destroyed.

46

Later the air hostess paused and looked at him with a shy smile.

"You're not sleeping?" she asked him.

"No'm," he mumbled.

"With your dinner, do you wish tea or coffee?" she asked.

Fishbelly blinked and a cornered look came into his eyes.

"No, no; I don't want to eat," he said tensely.

"But you can't go without food—"

"I'm not hungry," he said.

"You're not ill?" she asked.

"Not at all," he said stoutly.

The woman's face showed concern, then she moved on, glancing at other passengers stretched out in sleep, their relaxed faces reflecting the curtain of dreams shielding their hearts from the claims of waking hours. But Fishbelly sat looking at the dream images of his life with wide-open eyes. He had answered the hostess hesitantly, for it had been difficult for him to know that he had no need now to hang his head and drawl a "no'm" or a "yessum" or a "yessir" or a "nawsir." His muscles had tautened when he had omitted from his speech the intonations of "nigger" obsequiousness.

From the plane's window he saw night swoop down and swallow up his world and the world of the whites who sat about him. He shared their daily world, but his past made his world different from theirs. He had fled a world that he had known and that had emotionally crucified him, but what was he here in this world whose impact loosed storms in his blood? Could he ever make the white faces around him understand how they had charged his world with images of beckoning desire and dread? Naw, naw . . . No one could believe the kind of life he had lived and was living. Was it not better to deny his world and accept the world that the others saw and lived in? Was it not better to lie, as he had lied to the sleeping white man at his left elbow, and declare that his world did not exist? Above all, he was ashamed of his world, for the world about him had branded his world as bad, inferior. Moreover, he felt no moral strength or compulsion to defend his world. That in him which had always made him self-conscious was now the bud of a new possible life that was pressing ardently but timidly against the shell of the old to shatter it and be free.

This resolution of denial and acceptance that he was now making was not born of a will toward deception; he was not "acting" now; it was a free gesture of faith welling up out of a yearning to be at last somewhere at home; it was his abject offer of a truce. Knowing that he was relatively free from fear and pressure, he was now more willingly anxious than ever to confess that he was maybe wrong and that others might be right. He was now voluntarily longing to pledge allegiance to a world whose brutal might could never compel him to love it with threats of death.

Nervous fatigue made him sigh as the waves of his emotions washed between shores of dread and desire, straining like the heaving, trapped sea in the darkness far below. All that night he did not close his eyes and now and then his restless body gave a slight shudder as the images of his waking dream whirled tensely in their too-tight orbits. He peered out of his window and saw vast, wheeling populations of ruled stars swarming in the convened congresses of the skies anchored amidst nations of space and he prayed wordlessly that a bright, bursting tyrant of living sun would soon lay down its golden laws to loosen the locked legions of his heart and cast the shadow of his dream athwart the stretches of time.

By the year 2000, 2 out of 3 Americans could be illiterate.

It's true.

Today, 75 million adults...about one American in three, can't read adequately. And by the year 2000, U.S. News & World Report envisions an America with a literacy rate of only 30%.

Before that America comes to be, you can stop it...by joining the fight against illiteracy today.

Call the Coalition for Literacy at toll-free **1-800-228-8813** and volunteer.

**Volunteer
Against Illiteracy.
The only degree you need
is a degree of caring.**

Ad Council   Coalition for Literacy